A Century of Detection

A Century of Detection

Twenty Great Mystery Stories, 1841–1940

Edited by
John Cullen Gruesser

McFarland & Company, Inc., Publishers
Jefferson, North Carolina, and London

LIBRARY OF CONGRESS CATALOGUING-IN-PUBLICATION DATA

A century of detection : twenty great mystery stories, 1841–1940 / edited by John Cullen Gruesser.
p. cm.
Includes bibliographical references.

ISBN 978-0-7864-4650-6
softcover : 50# alkaline paper ♾

1. Detective and mystery stories, American.
2. Detective and mystery stories, English.
3. I. Gruesser, John Cullen, 1959–
PS648.D4C42 2010 823'.087208 — dc22 2010028931

British Library cataloguing data are available

Front cover: 1904 illustration for Edgar Allan Poe's "The Murders in the Rue Morgue" by Charles Raymond Macauley

Manufactured in the United States of America

McFarland & Company, Inc., Publishers
Box 611, Jefferson, North Carolina 28640
www.mcfarlandpub.com

To my mother, whose copy of *The Complete Tales and Poems of Edgar Allan Poe*, now much battered but still extant, introduced me to detection nearly forty years ago: Thanks for nurturing my love for the written word.

To my old friends Mike the California anesthesiologist, Phil the campus cop extraordinaire, Tim the Kentucky farmer, and Joe the Wall Street exec: We've passed the half-century mark but we're still hanging in there (Crisis, what midlife crisis?)

To my wife Susan: There is no mystery as to why I love you.

Contents

Preface

This anthology of mystery stories published between 1841 and 1940 has been conceived with two audiences in mind: general readers who enjoy detective fiction and instructors of and students in undergraduate courses devoted to the genre. The book fills the pressing need for a wide-ranging anthology of early detective stories. The concise introduction provides an overview of the literary form and, along with the author headnotes, information about each of the stories. *A Century of Detection* offers fans of detection and students of the form: (1) classic texts by Edgar Allan Poe, Sir Arthur Conan Doyle, G. K. Chesterton, and Susan Glaspell; (2) largely unknown gems by such famous authors as Wilkie Collins, Mark Twain, Bret Harte, Baroness Orczy, Dashiell Hammett, Chester Himes, and Ralph Ellison; and (3) innovative and historically significant stories by the lesser-known writers Mary Wilkins Freeman, Anna Katharine Green, Pauline Hopkins, Carroll John Daly, and Cornell Woolrich. The book's selections have been grouped into six roughly chronological, thematic categories intended to showcase the fluidity of the genre: The Invention of Modern Detection; Variations on Poe, Expansions of the Form; The World's Most Celebrated Detective; Gender, Sexuality, and Detection; Tough Guys; and Race and Detection.

This book would not exist without the sage advice, generous assistance, and emotional support provided to me by a large number of people. My thanks to Beth Sweeney, the late Tom Cook, Whitney Hao, Chip Hughes, Lewis Moore, Nancy Grayson, Ed Shannon, Marilyn Rye, Jonathan Eburne, Alisha Knight, Tish Crawford, Lois Brown, Lee Horsley, Cindy Hamilton, Vince Emery, Lawrence Jackson, Valerie Wilson Wesley, Claude Julien, Hanna Wallinger, Malin Pereira, Eric Sundquist, Elizabeth Ammons, Carole Shaffer-Koros, Alan Robbins, Robert Fyne, Linda Best, Bob Hunt, Scott Peeples, Richard Kopley, Jana Argersinger, Jeffrey Savoye, John Bird, Rachel Adams, Charles Nelson, Richard Katz, Bert Wailoo, Roslyn Targ, Lesley Himes, Allan Nevins, Anthony Mattero, John Callahan, Donn Zartesky, Keith Alan Deutsch, Marianne Hardart, Frances Spilman, and librarians at Kean University, the Library of Congress, the New York Public Library, the Museum of the City of New York, and the Delaware Art Museum. I must give special thanks to my students at Kean University, both those who have taken my English 3221 Detective Fiction course since 1998, and, in particular, my research assistants, the members of my fall 2009

English 4812 class, who helped me prepare the texts of and annotate the stories, investigate the lives of the authors, and compile the list of suggested readings: Stephanie Bowles, Jessica Corsaro, Eric Cortes, Cassandra McLean, Bijal Pandya, Anna Petrosky, Adriana Ramirez, and Joseph Tingle.

Introduction

Providing a chronological and thematic survey of the first century of modern detection, *A Century of Detection* has been conceived to appeal to the general reader as well as to be used in combination with other texts in undergraduate classes devoted to the study of the genre. Detective fiction has significance not simply on account of its popularity but also because it has evolved as modern society has evolved. Despite its association in many people's minds with British authors, manners, and settings, writers from the United States pioneered its two major varieties — the classic or analytical story, invented by Edgar Allan Poe in the 1840s, and hard-boiled fiction, which began to appear in the early 1920s. The range of directions in which authors have taken detection serves to substantiate Raymond Chandler's contention that it is a "fluid" form that defies "easy classification." No doubt Poe, who craved but never achieved sustained popular success as a fiction writer, would have been surprised to discover that in the second half of the 1800s the genre he launched would reappear in action-packed dime novels featuring protagonists such as the Old Sleuth, New York Detective, and Nick Carter, as well as in several books about the exploits of America's most famous detective agency (well known for its trademark open eye, the eye that never sleeps), supposedly written by Allan Pinkerton himself. He would certainly be shocked to learn that two generations after his death white women and African Americans would embrace detection as a means of addressing social and political issues of particular concern to themselves. Moreover, he would likely be amazed to find that over the last 160 years the descendants of his aristocratic French detective have come in an array of shapes, sizes, nationalities, genders, socioeconomic classes, sexual orientations, political points of view, and ethnic and racial backgrounds.

The Invention of Modern Detection

Tales of detection have been around almost as long as literature itself, with stories from the Bible, *Oedipus the King*, "The Three Princes of Serendip," *Hamlet*, Voltaire's *Zadig*, and William Godwin's *Caleb Williams* standing out as some of the most notable examples. Critics generally agree, however, that Poe founded modern detection in the 1840s. This was an era known for its hoaxes, including P. T. Barnum's notorious Feejee Mermaid, concocted by sewing a monkey's upper body to the lower half of a fish. Poe debunked but also perpetrated such frauds, which, despite being rigged in the house's favor, appealed to audiences because they offered diversions from the daily grind and an opportunity to match wits with the hoaxer. In three tales featuring C. Auguste Dupin, Poe conceives of detection as competition between himself and his readers, whom he challenges to arrive at the solution to the mystery while stacking the deck in his favor by using stratagems designed to throw them off the trail. He also stages a series of contests between characters and makes reference to games of skill and games of chance to underscore the competitive nature of detection and explain the analytical ability that enables the protagonist to come out on top. Moreover, after creating the first story, "The Murders in the Rue Morgue" (1841), he essentially competes with himself in its two sequels. In "The Mystery of Marie Rogêt" (1842–43), based upon a real case, Poe pioneers armchair (i.e., purely textual) detection, and in "The Purloined Letter" (1844), he produces his most concise and, in the opinion of many, his most successful detective story, which concerns the location of a pilfered document. By striving to rework and outdo what he has already done, Poe weaves authorial competition into the fabric of detection, inspiring a diverse range of writers to vie with him — and each other — to bring innovations to the form. Apart from the sensation created by "The Raven," Poe perhaps achieved the most notoriety with "The Gold-Bug." This tale of buried pirate treasure, which hinges upon a secret code and introduces the theme of race into detection through the relationship between the ex-slave Jupiter and his eccentric master William Legrand, won the first prize of $100 in a contest sponsored by the *Dollar Newspaper* of Philadelphia in 1843.

Variations on Poe, Expansions of the Form

Elusive and illusive on account of its baffling mysteries, hidden clues, and tantalizing red herrings, detection frequently contains explicit or sly references to earlier stories, making it highly allusive as well. Appearing fourteen years after "The Purloined Letter," Wilkie Collins's "Who Is the Thief?" (1858) evinces the genre's self-reflexive and competitive nature. In this epistolary tale, a conceited and inexperienced sleuth completely misinterprets the facts he has gathered and reaches comically inaccurate conclusions. The rivalry between the detective and the police, a key element of Poe's Dupin tales, still obtains, but Collins inverts things by having a pair of seasoned London policemen show up an incompetent amateur, Matthew Sharpin, whose name — but not his reasoning ability — resembles Dupin's. Today, comic detectives in fiction and especially film are almost as popular as their serious counterparts. By twisting the conventions of detection for the sake of humor, Collins emulates and extends a process initiated by Poe himself in "Thou Art the Man" (1844) and anticipates such classic parodies as Mark Twain's "The Stolen White Elephant" (1882). Surprisingly, critics have failed to recognize the ways that Twain in this story sends up the man who invented detection. Although most observers acknowledge that parody plays a significant role, they have asserted either that the author is having fun at the expense of a contemporary target or that the white elephant has some kind of hidden meaning that is the key to the tale or the writer's fiction generally. However, Twain, who was attracted to the form (as the relatively large number of texts he wrote that are wholly or partially devoted to detection indicates) but clearly found it problematic, makes specific references to Poe's fiction — and even alludes to his mysterious demise — producing a brilliant comic conflation of the missing animal and pilfered article plotlines of "The Murders in the Rue Morgue" and "The Purloined Letter." In "The Blue Cross" (1910), which evokes "The Purloined Letter" in several ways, G. K. Chesterton draws attention to the metafictional thread Poe sews into the fabric of detection; how, in other words, detective stories can be read as texts about how to write detection. The renowned sleuth Valentin, reflecting on his missed opportunities to capture the criminal mastermind Flambeau, remarks, "The criminal is the creative artist; the detective only the critic." However, by luring Flambeau into a clever trap and thereby accomplishing what the celebrated detective could not, the unassuming and underestimated Father Brown, whose concerns are spiritual rather than legal, disproves Valentin's statement, suggesting that the writer of detection, similar to the truly analytical detective, must be both creative and resolvent.

The World's Most Celebrated Detective

In *A Study in Scarlet* (1887), Sherlock Holmes dismisses Poe's detective as "a very inferior fellow." However, Sir Arthur Conan Doyle, who drew on his medical school teacher Joseph Bell to create the unforgettable Holmes (whose idiosyncrasies he highlighted through his sturdy chronicler Dr. John Watson), openly acknowledged how much he owed to Poe. Ample evidence of this debt appears in two stories from *The Adventures of Sherlock Holmes* (1892) and a third from *The Memoirs of Sherlock Holmes* (1893). "A Scandal in Bohemia," a variation on the stolen article mystery first seen in "The Purloined Letter," memorably depicts Holmes being beaten at his own game and having to reassess his assumptions. In "The Adventure of the Speckled Band," as in "The Murders in the Rue Morgue," a dangerous beast figures prominently in a locked-room mystery; however, in contrast to Poe's tale, which eventually turns out to be a missing animal mystery (or a whatwuzit) rather than a whodunit, Doyle has his detective go head to head with and mete out his own brand of justice upon the evil person behind the murderous plot. Just as Poe uses the criminal genius D_____ to highlight the abilities of his detective in the final Dupin story, Conan Doyle creates a foil worthy of Sherlock Holmes in Professor Moriarty, "the Napoleon of crime." In

"The Adventure of the Final Problem," the intellectual contest between Holmes and his archrival leads to a dramatic physical struggle above the raging waters of the Reichenbach Falls. Given their immense popularity, it is no surprise that Conan Doyle's stories have been parodied by Twain and many others. Perhaps the most famous send-up of Sherlock Holmes is Bret Harte's "The Stolen Cigar Case," which, as its title suggests, also takes a jab or two at Poe's "The Purloined Letter."

Gender, Sexuality, and Detection

Anna Katharine Green, whose bestselling courtroom drama *The Leavenworth Case* (1878) contributed to the development of detection, stands at the head of a group of women authors in the late 1800s and early 1900s that expanded the form by creating female detectives and addressing women's issues. In three novels published at the turn of the century, Green teams Ebenezer Gryce, the aging protagonist of several earlier novels, with the amateur sleuth Amelia Butterworth, a confident and outspoken spinster who gradually wins the respect of the skeptical policeman. During her long and successful career, Mary Roberts Rinehart created several women detectives, including Rachel Innes, the unmarried forty-something heroine of the melodramatic novel *The Circular Staircase* (1908). Mary Wilkins Freeman's "The Long Arm" (1895) not only teams an inexperienced, small-town amateur female detective with a seasoned, male, big-city professional but also contains a daring subtext that adumbrates later detective fiction featuring gay and lesbian characters by writers such as Joseph Hansen, Katherine Forrest, and Michael Nava. In a 1910 collection of stories about Lady Molly, Baroness Emmuska Orczy uses a Watson-like narrator, Mary Granard, to chronicle the exploits of the head of the Female Department of Scotland Yard. "The Ninescore Mystery" establishes the pattern for the series: Lady Molly uses her intuition and insight to solve a case that baffles her male counterparts. Green's "Missing: Page Thirteen" (1915) and Susan Glaspell's "A Jury of Her Peers" (1917) illustrate the adaptability of detection to political and social commentary. In addition to containing female detectives, these stories depict women who commit transgressive acts, including homicide. Equating the justice system with a criminal patriarchy and thereby undermining the very foundation upon which detection putatively depends, Glaspell's justly famous story is the more explicitly feminist; meanwhile, "Missing: Page Thirteen," whose diminutive young socialite heroine secretly works for a detective agency, metamorphoses from a stolen article mystery into a gothic tale that is part whodunit and part missing person case. These and other early female sleuths, including Agatha Christie's Miss Marple, serve as forerunners for contemporary women private detectives created by writers such as Marcia Muller, Sara Paretsky, Sue Grafton, and Linda Barnes, who have wrought a remarkable transformation in hard-boiled fiction. Incurably sexist — if not downright misogynist — and unabashedly homophobic by today's standards, tough guy writing has been revised in the last three decades by female (and male) and gay (and straight) writers who have used detection to make keen observations about gender and sexuality.

Tough Guys

The contrast between the ideology and ethos of a story such as "A Jury of Her Peers" and the hard-boiled fiction that began to appear five years later could hardly be more striking. By the 1920s detection had become characterized by elaborate puzzles, effete detectives, and countrified settings. In stark contrast, tough guy writing typically concerns a white male private eye operating in a corrupt and violent urban environment who has a lower-middle-class worldview, a disdain for effeminacy and homosexuality, and a colorful, demotic way of expressing himself. Less concerned with who did what than "what the hell went on," as Chandler put it in a 1949 letter, hard-boiled writers often construct their stories in a manner that harkens back to Poe, changing the game on readers so that they are deceived into solving the wrong problem. Although critics agree that the hard-boiled dick first appeared in the United States in the early 1920s, they disagree as to where this figure came from or why he appeared at that moment. Some regard him as the stoic, self-sufficient frontier hero or Western lawman relocated to a violent urban environment. Some view hard-boiled fiction as a reaction to the devastation of World War I and the randomness of modern life. Others point to the classic detective story, the dime novel, the modernist novel, and the urban and/or proletarian novel as influences. Going against the grain, the recent *Hard-Boiled Sentimentality: The Secret History of American Crime Fiction* by Leonard Cassuto traces the connection between tough-guy fiction and nineteenth-century sentimental novels. However, scholars have overlooked a compelling link between the origins of hard-boiled fiction and late nineteenth- and early twentieth-century United States expansionism. In Carroll John Daly's "The False Burton Combs" (1922), considered by many to be the first hard-boiled story, the protagonist-narrator refers to himself as a "soldier of fortune," aligning himself with Robert Clay, the main character of Richard Harding Davis's popular 1897 novel *Soldiers of Fortune*. There are also unmistakable connections to imperialism in Dashiell Hammett's first true piece of hard-boiled fiction, the brief, Conradian story "The Road Home" (1922), in which the detective figure pursues a man wanted for crimes in the United States all the way to Asia. Even more intriguing is the extent to which the independent and manly qualities stressed in Elbert Hubbard's widely disseminated short story/pamphlet "A Message for Garcia" (1899), about a soldier who delivers a letter from President William McKinley to the leader of the Cuban rebellion during the Spanish-American War, are reflected in Daly's, Hammett's, and especially Raymond Chandler's protagonists. Critics sometimes identify Terry Mack or Race Williams, later creations by

Daly, as the prototype for the hard-boiled persona; however, the false Burton Combs, the protagonist of his earlier *Black Mask* story, possesses the hallmarks of this figure—independence, masculine sang-froid, cynicism about how Prohibition-era society works, a personal code of behavior, street smarts, and a language all his own. Arguably the most important author of detection after Poe, Hammett drew on his own experiences as a Pinkerton detective in "The Road Home" and the subsequent Continental Op stories. He also created Sam Spade, the main character of what is perhaps the best-known hard-boiled novel, *The Maltese Falcon* (1929), as well as Nick and Nora Charles, who appear in *The Thin Man* (1934). Similar to Daly's adventurers and private eyes, Hammett's many detectives, and Chandler's Philip Marlowe, the policeman protagonist of Cornell Woolrich's "Murder at the Automat" (1937) subscribes to his own code. Unlike his captain, who tries to beat a confession out of the most likely suspect, Officer Nelson is determined to get to the bottom of the killing that has taken place in the most anonymous of urban settings, the self-service restaurant. Moreover, he does not hesitate to confront the murderer in the story's deadly endgame.

Race and Detection

Whether they are detached, eccentric amateur sleuths or cynical, self-sufficient private eyes, fictional crime solvers have always been outsiders, and this alienation only increases if they belong to a group that has been relegated to the margins of society. For the African American writer of any era, detection presents significant challenges. As an enormously popular form with well-established conventions, detection would seem a restrictive vehicle for a black author aspiring to do more than entertain readers. Moreover, because it typically requires that the crime or crimes be solved and the established order restored, the genre tends (or at least appears) to be conservative. Thus, in order to preserve the integrity of their plots and characters, African Americans who write detection must strike a difficult balance between genre conformity and genre subversion. In "Talma Gordon" (1900), Pauline Hopkins deftly combines a locked-room murder mystery with one concerning racial identity, as well as addressing the connection between the empire abroad (United States expansionism) and the empire at home (Jim Crow). The *Colored American Magazine* also published her serial *Hagar's Daughter* (1901–02), the first novel by a black writer to include an African American crime solver. It was followed a half dozen years later by John Edward Bruce's *The Black Sleuth* (1907–09), a serial about a West African detective. In 1932, Rudolph Fisher published *Conjure Man Dies: A Mystery of Dark Harlem* (1932), featuring policeman Perry Dart and physician John Archer, the first African American novel with a black detective to appear in book form. Chester Himes (1909–1984) occupies a pivotal position in history of African American detective and mystery writing. "Talma Gordon" preceded Himes's birth by less than a decade; moreover, within five years of his death, the new wave of African American detective fiction had begun. This remarkable literary phenomenon, which led to President Bill Clinton identifying Walter Mosley as his favorite writer, was initiated by the 1988 publication of Dolores Komo's *Clio Browne, Private Investigator* and Gar Anthony Haywood's *Fear of the Dark* and also includes popular mystery series by Eleanor Taylor Bland, Valerie Wilson Wesley, Gary Philips, and Paula Woods. In 1933 while serving seven and half years in the Ohio State Penitentiary, Himes published his first work of detective fiction, "He Knew," in a Chicago African American newspaper, *Abbott's Weekly and Illustrative News*. Henry Walls and John Jones, the black cops in this story, are forerunners of the police detectives Grave Digger Jones and Coffin Ed Johnson, who appear in Himes's long-running series of Harlem domestic novels, beginning with *For Love of Imabelle* (also known as *A Rage in Harlem*) in 1957. This anthology concludes with another virtually unknown gem by the author of one of the greatest novels of the twentieth century, *Invisible Man*. Published almost exactly a century after "The Murders in the Rue Morgue" and Nathaniel Hawthorne's story of the same name, Ralph Ellison's "The Birthmark" appeared in the pages of the leftist journal *New Masses* in 1940 and, like Himes's "He Knew," has never been reprinted until now. With powerful concision the story depicts two black siblings uncovering the awful truth about the death of their brother.

Comprising twenty stories, *A Century of Detection* by no means aspires to be a definitive collection of detective fiction published between 1841 and 1940. Rather, it has been designed to provide some sense of the early history and suggest the remarkable malleability of a genre that has evolved as modern literature and modern society have evolved. A consistently fluid form with an uncanny ability to attract readers, detection has been and continues to be amenable to a diverse range of artistic, personal, ideological, and political programs.

Now, if I could have done this without the knowledge of Professor Moriarty, all would have been well. But he was too wily for that. He saw every step which I took to draw my toils round him. Again and again he strove to break away, but I as often headed him off. I tell you, my friend, that if a detailed account of that silent contest could be written, it would take its place as the most brilliant bit of thrust-and-parry work in the history of detection.

Arthur Conan Doyle, "The Final Problem"

The Invention of Modern Detection

Edgar Allan Poe (1809–1849)

Following a life of tragedy and unrealized dreams, Edgar Allan Poe achieved a posthumous celebrity experienced by only a handful of writers. Born in Boston to parents who were actors, he became an orphan before his second birthday. Poe enjoyed a stable early childhood and received a good education, part of it in England, after being taken in by John Allan, a wealthy Richmond planter. Antagonism between Poe and Allan reached a peak when Poe amassed gambling debts while attending the University of Virginia in 1826, and he inherited nothing when Allan died. Poe's first book, Tamerlane and Other Poems, appeared the following year and, after joining the Army, he was stationed at Fort Moultrie on Sullivan's Island in South Carolina. He attended West Point in 1830 but was dismissed the next year. While living in Baltimore with his aunt Maria Clemm and her daughter Virginia, he began publishing stories.

Beginning in 1835, he worked for a series of magazines but never made much money. He became the editor of the *Southern Literary Messenger* and in 1836 married his thirteen-year-old cousin Virginia. Two years later, accompanied by Maria Clemm, the couple moved to Philadelphia, where Poe worked for *Burton's Gentleman's Magazine* and *Graham's Magazine*. In 1843 his prizewinning story "The Gold-Bug" was widely reprinted. Poe and his family moved to New York in 1844, where he eventually found a job with the *Evening Mirror*. The following year he had his biggest brush with fame with the publication of "The Raven"; he also edited and then became the owner of the *Broadway Journal*, only to see it fold a few months later. Virginia, who first showed symptoms of tuberculosis five years earlier, succumbed to the disease in 1847. Two and a half years later, at the age of forty, Poe himself would die under mysterious circumstances in Baltimore after being found unconscious near a polling place on election day. The malicious and fraudulent actions of his literary executor Rufus Griswold severely damaged Poe's reputation immediately following his death. However, first abroad and later in the United States, his stature increased exponentially, such that by the final decades of the twentieth century, Poe had become a pop cultural icon with filmmakers, musicians (including the Beatles), television programs (especially *The Simpsons*), and even a National Football League team paying homage to him.

Today he is recognized for his poetry, his criticism, and his contributions to science fiction, horror literature, and especially detection. In an 1846 letter to Phillip Pendleton Cooke, Poe explained his method of constructing detective stories: "These tales of ratiocination owe most of their popularity to being something in a new key. I do not mean to say that they are not ingenious — but people think them more ingenious than they are — on account of their method and *air* of method. In 'Murders in the Rue Morgue,' for instance, where is the ingenuity in unravelling a web which you yourself (the author) have woven for the express purpose of unravelling? The reader is made to confound the ingenuity of the supposititious Dupin with that of the writer of the story." As this passage suggests, the main character is only one means Poe uses to deceive. He also creates the illusion of fair play through the device of a seemingly reliable first-person narrator, who stands in awe of and never questions the detective. Moreover, in "Murders" (1841), Poe tricks readers into solving the wrong mystery by seducing them into regarding the story as a whodunit. In his next two tales, "The Mystery of Marie Rogêt" (1842–43), which brings back Dupin, and "The Gold-Bug," a tale of buried pirate treasure, Poe invents armchair detection and creates the first cryptographic mystery respectively. In the final Dupin story, "The Purloined Letter" (1844), the protagonist faces an opponent whose logical reasoning, imaginative thinking, powers of observation, and relish for competition bear a remarkable resemblance to his own. Finally facing off against a worthy adversary, Dupin savors his greatest victory, and thus his creator produces the most satisfying of the series. Conceiving of detection as competition between characters, between himself and his readers, and between the first Dupin story and its two sequels, Poe playfully incorporates character rivalry, authorial sleight of hand, and generic malleability into the form — key elements that largely have accounted for the longevity, popularity, and significance of classic and hard-boiled detective fiction. Moreover, by having the narrator refer to Dupin's previous success at the start of "Marie Rogêt" and "Purloined," he initiates the practice of implicitly or explicitly acknowledging earlier detective texts. Although Poe would no doubt be astounded to learn what has happened to detection since 1849, he would likely take satisfaction in the fact that the way he launched the form has made it necessary for subsequent authors not only to emulate but also to compete with him. Whether they be conventionally conservative in the manner of Agatha Christie or radically experimental on the order of Ishmael Reed, authors have followed in Poe's footsteps by depicting struggles between characters and making references to games while vying with him and other writers of detection to find new ways to outwit, enlighten, entertain, educate, and politicize readers.

The Murders in the Rue Morgue

by Edgar Allan Poe

(1841)[1]

It is not improbable that a few farther steps in phrenological science[2] will lead to a belief in the existence, if not to the actual discovery and location, of an organ of *analysis*. If this power (which may be described, although not defined, as the capacity for resolving thought into its elements) is not, in fact, an essential portion of what late philosophers term ideality, then there are indeed many good reasons for supposing it a primitive faculty. That it may be a constituent of ideality is here suggested in opposition to the vulgar dictum (founded, however, upon the assumptions of grave authority,) that the calculating and discriminating powers (causality and comparison) are at variance with the imaginative — that the three, in short, can hardly co-exist.

[1] *In later versions of the story, Poe included the epigraph "What song the Syrens sang, or what name Achilles assumed when he hid himself among women, although puzzling questions, are not beyond all conjecture," from Sir Thomas Browne's* Hydriotaphia, or Urn-Burial.

[2] *The belief, popular during the nineteenth century, that mental capacity and character traits are indicated by the configuration of the skull.*

But, although thus opposed to received opinion, the idea will not appear ill-founded when we observe that the processes of invention or creation are strictly akin with the processes of resolution — the former being nearly, if not absolutely, the latter conversed.

It cannot be doubted that the mental features discoursed of as the analytical, are, in themselves, but little susceptible of analysis. We appreciate them only in their effects. We know of them, among other things, that they are always to their possessor, when inordinately possessed, a source of the liveliest enjoyment. As the strong man exults in his physical ability, delighting in such exercises as call his muscles into action, so glories the analyst in that moral activity which *disentangles.* He derives pleasure from even the most trivial occupations bringing his talent into play. He is fond of enigmas, of conundrums, of hieroglyphics — exhibiting in his solutions of each and all a degree of acumen which appears to the ordinary apprehension præternatural. His results, brought about by the very soul and essence of method, have, in truth, the whole air of intuition.

The faculty in question is possibly much invigorated by mathematical study, and especially by that highest branch of it which, unjustly, and merely on account of its retrograde operations, has been called, as if *par excellence*, analysis. Yet to calculate is not in itself to analyze. A chess-player, for example, does the one without effort at the other. It follows that the game of chess, in its effects upon mental character, is greatly misunderstood. I am not now writing a treatise, but simply prefacing a somewhat peculiar narrative by observations very much at random — I will, therefore, take occasion to assert that the higher powers of the reflective intellect are more decidedly and more usefully tasked by the unostentatious game of draughts[3] than by all the elaborate frivolity of chess. In this latter, where the pieces have different and bizarre motions, with various and variable values, that which is only complex is mistaken (a not unusual error) for that which is profound. The *attention* is here called powerfully into play. If it flag for an instant, an oversight is committed, resulting in injury or defeat. The possible moves being not only manifold but involute, the chances of such oversights are multiplied; and in nine cases out of ten it is the more concentrative rather than the more acute player who conquers. In draughts, on the contrary, where the moves are unique and have but little variation, the probabilities of inadvertence are diminished, and the mere attention being left comparatively unemployed, what advantages are obtained by either party are obtained by superior acumen. To be less abstract — Let us suppose a game of draughts, where the pieces are reduced to four kings, and where, of course, no oversight is to be expected. It is obvious that here the victory can be decided (the players being at all equal) only by some recherché[4] movement, the result of some strong exertion of the intellect. Deprived of ordinary resources, the analyst throws himself into the spirit of his opponent, identifies himself

[3]*A game like checkers.* [4]*Strange, unusual.*

therewith, and not infrequently sees thus, at a glance, the sole methods (sometimes indeed absurdly simple ones) by which he may seduce into miscalculation or hurry into error.

Whist[5] has long been noted for its influence upon what is termed the calculating power; and men of the highest order of intellect have been known to take an apparently unaccountable delight in it, while eschewing chess as frivolous. Beyond doubt there is nothing of a similar nature so greatly tasking the faculty of analysis. The best chess-player in Christendom *may* be little more than the best player of chess — but proficiency in whist implies capacity for success in all those more important undertakings where mind struggles with mind. When I say proficiency, I mean that perfection in the game which includes a comprehension of all the sources (whatever be their character) from which legitimate advantage may be derived. These are not only manifold but multiform, and lie frequently among recesses of thought alto-

Dupin, right, and the narrator stroll through Paris (Charles Raymond Macauley, 1904).

[5]*A game like bridge.*

gether inaccessible to the ordinary understanding. To observe attentively is to remember distinctly; and so far the concentrative chess-player will do very well at whist; while the rules of Hoyle[6] (themselves based upon the mere mechanism of the game) are sufficiently and generally comprehensible. Thus to have a retentive memory, and to proceed by "the book," are points commonly regarded as the sum total of good playing. But it is in matters beyond the limits of mere rule where the skill of the analyst is evinced. He makes, in silence, a host of observations and inferences. So perhaps do his companions; and the difference in the extent of the information obtained lies not so much in the falsity of the inference as in the quality of the observation. The necessary knowledge is that of *what* to observe. Our player confines himself not at all; nor, because the game is the object, does he reject deductions from things external to the game. He examines the countenance of his partner, comparing it carefully with that of each of his opponents. He considers the mode of assorting the cards in each hand; often counting trump by trump, and honor by honor, through the glances bestowed by their holders upon each. He notes every variation of face as the play progresses, gathering a fund of thought from the differences in the expression of certainty, of surprise, of triumph or of chagrin. From the manner of gathering up a trick he judges whether the person taking it can make another in the suit. He recognizes what is played through feint, by the air with which it is thrown upon the table. A casual or inadvertent word; the accidental dropping or turning of a card, with the accompanying anxiety or carelessness in regard to its concealment; the counting of the tricks, with the order of their arrangement; embarrassment, hesitation, eagerness or trepidation — all afford, to his apparently intuitive perception, indications of the true state of affairs. The first two or three rounds having been played, he is in full possession of the contents of each hand, and thenceforward puts down his cards with as absolute a precision of purpose as if the rest of the party had turned outward the faces of their own.

The analytical power should not be confounded with simple ingenuity; for while the analyst is necessarily ingenious, the ingenious man is often remarkably incapable of analysis. I have spoken of this latter faculty as that of resolving thought into its elements, and it is only necessary to glance upon this idea to perceive the necessity of the distinction just mentioned. The constructive or combining power, by which ingenuity is usually manifested, and to which the phrenologists (I believe erroneously) have assigned a separate organ, supposing it a primitive faculty, has been so frequently seen in those whose intellect bordered otherwise upon idiocy as to have attracted general observation among writers on morals. Between ingenuity and the analytic ability there exists a difference far greater indeed than that between the fancy and the imagination, but of a character very strictly analogous. It will be found, in fact, that the ingenious are always fanciful, and the *truly* imaginative never otherwise than profoundly analytic.

[6] *Authority on games and their rules.*

The narrative which follows will appear to the reader somewhat in the light of a commentary upon the propositions just advanced.

Residing in Paris during the spring and part of the summer of 18 —, I there contracted an intimacy with a Monsieur C. Auguste Dupin. This young gentleman was of an excellent, indeed of an illustrious family, but, by a variety of untoward events, had been reduced to such poverty that the quondam[7] energy of his character succumbed beneath it, and he ceased to bestir himself in the world, or to care for the retrieval of his fortunes. By courtesy of his creditors, there still remained in his possession a small remnant of his patrimony; and, upon the income arising from this, he managed, by means of a rigorous economy, to procure the necessaries of life, without troubling himself about its superfluities. Books, indeed, were his sole luxuries, and in Paris these are easily obtained.

Our first meeting was at an obscure library in the Rue Montmartre, where the accident of our both being in search of the same very rare and very remarkable volume, brought us into closer communion. We saw each other again and again. I was deeply interested in the little family history which he detailed to me with all that candor which a Frenchman indulges only when self is his theme. I was astonished, too, at the vast extent of his reading — and above all I felt my soul enkindled within me by the wild fervor, and what I could only term the vivid freshness, of his imagination. Seeking in Paris the objects I then sought, I felt that the society of such a man would be to me a treasure beyond price; and this feeling I frankly confided to him. It was at length arranged that we should live together during my stay in the city; and, as my worldly circumstances were somewhat less embarrassed than his own, I was permitted to be at the expense of renting, and furnishing in a style which suited the rather fantastic gloom of our common temper, a time-eaten and grotesque mansion, long deserted through superstitions into which we did not inquire, and tottering to its fall, in a retired and desolate portion of the Faubourg St. Germain.

Had the routine of our life at this place been known to the world, we should have been regarded as madmen — although, perhaps, as madmen of a harmless nature. Our seclusion was perfect. We admitted no visiters whomsoever. Indeed the locality of our retirement had been carefully kept a secret from my own former associates; and it had been many years since Dupin had ceased to know or be known in Paris. We existed within ourselves alone.

It was a freak of fancy in my friend (for what else shall I call it?) to be enamored of the Night for her own sake; and into this *bizarrerie*, as into all his others, I quietly fell; giving myself up to his wild whims with a perfect *abandon*. The sable divinity would not herself dwell with us always; but we could counterfeit her presence. At the first dawn of the morning we closed all the massy shutters of our old building;

[7]*One-time, former.*

lighting a couple of tapers which, strongly perfumed, threw out only the ghastliest and feeblest of rays. By the aid of these we then busied our souls in dreams — reading, writing, or conversing, until warned by the clock of the advent of the true Darkness. Then we sallied forth into the streets, arm in arm, continuing the topics of the day, or roaming far and wide until a late hour, seeking, amid the wild lights and shadows of the populous city, that infinity of mental excitement which quiet observation can afford.

At such times I could not help remarking and admiring (although from his rich ideality I had been prepared to expect) a peculiar analytic ability in Dupin. He seemed, too, to take an eager delight in its exercise, if not exactly in its display; and did not hesitate to confess the pleasure thus derived. He boasted to me, with a low chuckling laugh, that most men, in respect to himself, wore windows in their bosoms, and was wont to follow up such assertions by direct and very startling proofs of his intimate knowledge of my own. His manner at these moments was frigid and abstract; his eyes were vacant in expression; while his voice, usually a rich tenor, rose into a treble which would have sounded petulantly but for the deliberateness and entire distinctness of the enunciation. Observing him in these moods, I often dwelt meditatively upon the old philosophy of the Bi-Part Soul, and amused myself with the fancy of a double Dupin — the creative and the resolvent.

Let it not be supposed, from what I have just said, that I am detailing any mystery, or penning any romance. What I have described in the Frenchman was but the result of an excited, or perhaps of a diseased intelligence. But of the character of his remarks at the periods in question an example will best convey the idea.

We were strolling one night down a long dirty street, in the vicinity of the Palais Royal. Being both, apparently, occupied with thought, neither of us had spoken a syllable for fifteen minutes at least. All at once Dupin broke forth with these words:—

"He is a very little fellow, that's true, and would do better for the *Théâtre des Variétés*."

"There can be no doubt of that," I replied unwittingly, and not at first observing (so much had I been absorbed in reflection) the extraordinary manner in which the speaker had chimed in with my meditations. In an instant afterward I recollected myself, and my astonishment was profound.

"Dupin," said I, gravely, "this is beyond my comprehension. I do not hesitate to say that I am amazed, and can scarcely credit my senses. How was it possible you should know I was thinking of_____?" Here I paused, to ascertain beyond a doubt whether he really knew of whom I thought.

_____"of Chantilly," said he, "why do you pause? You were remarking to yourself that his diminutive figure unfitted him for tragedy."

This was precisely what had formed the subject of my reflections. Chantilly was a quondam cobbler of the Rue St. Denis, who, becoming stage-mad, had attempted the role of Xerxes, in Crébillon's[8] tragedy so called, and been notoriously pasquinaded[9] for his pains.

"Tell me, for God's sake," I exclaimed, "the method — if method there be — by which you have been enabled to fathom my soul in this matter." In fact I was even more startled than I would have been willing to express.

"It was the fruiterer," replied my friend, "who brought you to the conclusion that the mender of soles was not of sufficient height for Xerxes *et id genus omne*."[10]

"The fruiterer! — you astonish me — I know no fruiterer whomsoever."

"The man who ran up against you as we entered the street — it may have been fifteen minutes ago."

I now remembered that in fact a fruiterer, carrying upon his head a large basket of apples, had nearly thrown me down, by accident, as we passed from the Rue C_____ into the thoroughfare where we stood; but what this had to do with Chantilly I could not possibly understand.

There was not a particle of *charlatânerie* about Dupin. "I will explain," he said, "and that you may comprehend all clearly, we will first retrace the course of your meditations, from the moment in which I spoke to you until that of the rencontre[11] with the fruiterer in question. The larger links of the chain run thus — Chantilly, Orion, Dr. Nichols, Epicurus, Stereotomy, the street stones, the fruiterer."

There are few persons who have not, at some period of their lives, amused themselves in retracing the steps by which particular conclusions of their own minds have been attained. The occupation is often full of interest; and he who attempts it for the first time is astonished by the apparently illimitable distance and incoherence between the starting-point and the goal. What, then, must have been my amazement when I heard the Frenchman speak what he had just spoken, and when I could not help acknowledging that he had spoken the truth. He continued —

"We had been talking of horses, if I remember aright, just before leaving the Rue C_____. This was the last subject we discussed. As we crossed into this street, a fruiterer, with a large basket upon his head, brushing quickly past us, thrust you upon a pile of paving stones collected at a spot where the causeway is undergoing repair. You stepped upon one of the loose fragments, slipped, slightly strained your ankle, appeared vexed or sulky, muttered a few words, turned to look at the pile, and then proceeded in silence. I was not particularly attentive to what you did — but observation has become with me of late a species of necessity.

"You kept your eyes upon the ground — glancing, with a petulant expression, at the holes and ruts in the pavement (so that I saw you were still thinking of the stones,) until we reached the little alley called Lamartine, which has been paved, by way of experiment, with the overlapping and riveted blocks. Here your countenance bright-

[8]*Prosper Jolyot de Crébillon, French playwright and poet.* [9]*Publicly lampooned.* [10]*And all of that sort.* [11]*Encounter, meeting.*

ened up, and, perceiving your lips move, I could not doubt that you murmured to yourself the word 'stereotomic.' You continued the same inaudible murmur, with a knit brow, as is the custom of a man tasking his memory, until I considered that you sought the Greek derivation of the work 'stereotomy.' I knew that you could not find this without being brought to think of atomies, and thus of the theories of Epicurus; and since, when we discussed this subject not very long ago, I mentioned to you how singularly, yet with how little notice, the vague guesses of that noble Greek had met with confirmation in the late nebular cosmogony, I felt that you could not avoid casting your eyes upward to the great nebula in Orion, and I certainly expected that you would do so. You did look up; and I now was assured that I had correctly followed your steps. But in that bitter *tirade* upon Chantilly, which appeared in yesterday's '*Musée*,' the satirist, making some disgraceful allusions to the cobbler's change of name upon assuming the buskin,[12] quoted a very peculiar Latin line upon the meaning of which we have often conversed. I mean the line

Perdidit antiquum litera prima sonum.[13]

I had told you that this was in reference to Orion, formerly written Urion; and, from certain pungencies connected with this explanation, I was aware that you could not have forgotten it. It was clear, therefore, that you would not fail to combine the two ideas of Orion and Chantilly. That you did combine them I saw by the character of the smile which passed over your lips. You thought of the poor cobbler's immolation. So far, you had been stooping in your gait; but now I saw you draw yourself up to your full height. I was then sure that you reflected upon the diminutive figure of Chantilly. At this point I interrupted your meditations to remark that as, in fact, he *was* a very little fellow — that Chantilly — he would do better at the *Théâtre des Variétés.*"

Not long after this, we were looking over an evening edition of the "Le Tribunal," when the following paragraphs arrested our attention.

"EXTRAORDINARY MURDERS.— This morning, about three o'clock, the inhabitants of the Quartier St. Roch were aroused from sleep by a succession of terrific shrieks, issuing, apparently, from the fourth story of a house in the Rue Morgue, known to be in the sole occupancy of one Madame L'Espanaye, and her daughter, Mademoiselle Camille L'Espanaye. After some delay, occasioned by a fruitless attempt to procure admission in the usual manner, the gateway was broken in with a crowbar, and eight or ten of the neighbors entered, accompanied by two *gendarmes.*[14] By this time the cries had ceased; but, as the party rushed up the first flight of stairs, two or more rough voices, in angry contention, were distinguished, and seemed to proceed from the upper part of the house. As the second landing was reached, these sounds,

[12]*Becoming an actor — buskins: thick-soled boots worn by actors in Greek and Roman tragedies.*
[13]*The first letter has lost its original sound.*
[14]*French policemen.*

also, had ceased, and everything remained perfectly quiet. The party spread themselves, and hurried from room to room. Upon arriving at a large back chamber in the fourth story (the door of which, being found locked, with the key inside, was forced open), a spectacle presented itself which struck every one present not less with horror than with astonishment.

The apartment was in the wildest disorder — the furniture broken and thrown about in all directions. There was only one bedstead; and from this the bed had been removed, and thrown into the middle of the floor. On a chair lay a razor, besmeared with blood. On the hearth were two or three long and thick tresses of grey human hair, also dabbled in blood, and seeming to have been pulled out by the roots. Upon the floor were found four Napoleons,[15] an ear-ring of topaz, three large silver spoons, three smaller of *métal d'Alger*,[16] and two bags, containing nearly four thousand francs in gold. The drawers of a *bureau*, which stood in one corner, were open, and had been, apparently, rifled, although many articles still remained in them. A small iron safe was discovered under the *bed* (not under the bedstead). It was open, with the key still in the door. It had no contents beyond a few old letters, and other papers of little consequence.

Of Madame L'Espanaye no traces were here seen; but an unusual quantity of soot being observed in the fire-place, a search was made in the chimney, and (horrible to relate!) the corpse of the daughter, head downward, was dragged therefrom; it having been thus forced up the narrow aperture for a considerable distance. The body was quite warm. Upon examining it, many excoriations were perceived, no doubt occasioned by the violence with which it had been thrust up and disengaged. Upon the face were many severe scratches, and upon the throat dark bruises, and deep indentations of finger nails, as if the deceased had been throttled to death.

After a thorough investigation of every portion of the house, without farther discovery, the party made its way into a small paved yard in the rear of the building, where lay the corpse of the old lady, with her throat so entirely cut that, upon an attempt to raise her, the head fell off, and rolled to some distance. The body, as well as the head, was fearfully mutilated — the former so much so as scarcely to retain any semblance of humanity.

To this horrible mystery there is not as yet, we believe, the slightest clew."

The next day's paper had these additional particulars.

"*The Tragedy in the Rue Morgue.* Many individuals have been examined in relation to this most extraordinary and frightful affair." [The word '*affaire*' has not yet, in France, that levity of import which it conveys with us,] "but nothing whatever has transpired to throw light upon it. We give below all the material testimony elicited.

Pauline Dubourg, laundress, deposes that she has known both the deceased for three years, having washed for them during that period. The old lady and her daughter

[15] *Twenty franc gold coins.* [16] *A combination of pewter, lead, and antimony.*

seemed on good terms — very affectionate toward each other. They were excellent pay. Could not speak in regard to their mode or means of living. Believed that Madame L. told fortunes for a living. Was reputed to have money put by. Never met any persons in the house when she called for the clothes or took them home. Was sure that they had no servant in employ. There appeared to be no furniture in any part of the building except in the fourth story.

Pierre Moreau, tobacconist, deposes that he has been in the habit of selling small quantities of tobacco and snuff to Madame L'Espanaye for nearly four years. Was born in the neighborhood, and has always resided there. The deceased and her daughter had occupied the house in which the corpses were found for more than six years. It was formerly occupied by a jeweller, who under-let the upper rooms to various persons. The house was the property of Madame L. She became dissatisfied with the abuse of the premises by her tenant, and moved into them herself, refusing to let any portion. The old lady was childish. Witness had seen the daughter some five or six times during the six years. The two lived an exceedingly retired life — were reputed to have money. Had heard it said among the neighbors that Madame L. told fortunes — did not believe it. Had never seen any person enter the door except the old lady and her daughter, a porter once or twice, and a physician some eight or ten times.

Many other persons, neighbors, gave evidence to the same effect. No one was spoken of as frequenting the house. It was not known whether there were any living connexions of Madame L. and her daughter. The shutters of the front windows were seldom opened. Those in the rear were always closed, with the exception of the large back room, fourth story. The house was a good house — not very old.

Isidore Musèt, gendarme, deposes that he was called to the house about three o'clock in the morning, and found some twenty or thirty persons at the gateway, endeavoring to gain admittance. Forced it open, at length, with a bayonet — not with a crowbar. Had but little difficulty in getting it open, on account of its being a double or folding gate, and bolted neither at bottom nor top. The shrieks were continued until the gate was forced — and then suddenly ceased. They seemed to be screams of some person (or persons) in great agony — were loud and drawn out, not short and quick. Witness led the way up stairs. Upon reaching the first landing heard two voices in loud and angry contention — the one a gruff voice, the other much shriller — a very strange voice. Could distinguish some words of the former, which was that of a Frenchman. Was positive that it was not a woman's voice. Could distinguish the words '*sacré*' and '*diable*.'[17] The shrill voice was that of a foreigner. Could not be sure whether it was the voice of a man or of a woman. Could not make out what was said, but believed the language to be Spanish. The state of the room and of the bodies was described by this witness as we described them yesterday.

Henri Duval, a neighbor, and by trade a silver-smith, deposes that he was one

[17] *Sacred; devil.*

of the party who first entered the house. Corroborates the testimony of Musèt in general. As soon as they forced an entrance, they reclosed the door, to keep out the crowd, which collected very fast, notwithstanding the lateness of the hour. The shrill voice, this witness thinks, was that of an Italian. Was certain it was not French. Could not be sure that it was a man's voice. It might have been a woman's. Was not acquainted with the Italian language. Could not distinguish the words, but was convinced by the intonation that the speaker was an Italian. Knew Madame L. and her daughter. Had conversed with both frequently. Was sure that the shrill voice was not that of either of the deceased.

_____*Odenheimer,* restaurateur. This witness volunteered his testimony. Not speaking French was examined through an interpreter. Is a native of Amsterdam. Was passing the house at the time of the shrieks. They lasted for several minutes — probably ten. They were long and loud — very awful and distressing. Was one of those who entered the building. Corroborated the previous evidence in every respect but one. Was sure that the shrill voice was that of a man — of a Frenchman. Could not distinguish the words uttered. They were loud and quick — unequal — sometimes quick, sometimes deliberate — spoken apparently in fear as well as in anger. The voice was harsh — not so much shrill as harsh. Could not call it a shrill voice. The gruff voice said repeatedly "*sacré*," "*diable*," and once "*mon dieu*."[18]

Jules Mignaud, banker, of the firm of Mignaud et Fils, Rue Deloraine. Is the elder Mignaud. Madame L'Espanaye had some property. Had opened an account with his banking house in the spring of the year — (eight years previously). Made frequent deposits in small sums. Had checked for nothing until the third day before her death, when she took out in person, the sum of 4000 francs. This sum was paid in gold, and a clerk sent home with the money.

Adolphe Le Bon, clerk to Mignaud et Fils, deposes that on the day in question, about noon, he accompanied Madame L'Espanaye to her residence with the 4000 francs, put up in two bags. Upon the door being opened, Mademoiselle L. appeared and took from his hands one of the bags, while the old lady relieved him of the other. He then bowed and departed. Did not see any person in the street at the time. It is a bye street — very lonely.

William Bird, tailor, deposes that he was one of the party who entered the house. Is an Englishman. Has lived in Paris two years. Was one of the first to ascend the stairs. Heard the voices in contention. The gruff voice was that of a Frenchman. Could make out several words, but cannot now remember all. Heard distinctly '*sacré*' and '*mon dieu*.' There was a sound at the moment as if of several persons struggling — a scraping and scuffling sound. The shrill voice was very loud — louder than the gruff one. Is sure that it was not the voice of an Englishman. Appeared to be that of a German. Might have been a woman's voice. Does not understand German.

[18]*My God.*

Four of the above-named witnesses, being recalled, deposed that the door of the chamber in which was found the body of Mademoiselle L. was locked on the inside when the party reached it. Every thing was perfectly silent — no groans or noises of any kind. Upon forcing the door no person was seen. The windows, both of the back and front room, were down and firmly fastened from within. A door between the two rooms was closed, but not locked. The door leading from the front room into the passage was locked with the key on the inside. A small room in the front of the house, on the fourth story, at the head of the passage, was open, the door being ajar. This room was crowded with old beds, boxes, and so forth. These were carefully removed and searched. There was not an inch of any portion of the house which was not carefully searched. Sweeps were sent up and down the chimneys. The house was a four story one, with garrets (*mansardes*). A trap-door on the roof was nailed down very securely — did not appear to have been opened for years. The time elapsing between the hearing of the voices in contention and the breaking open of the room door was variously stated by the witnesses. Some made it as short as three minutes — some as long as five. The door was opened with difficulty.

Alfonzo Garcio, undertaker, deposes that he resides in the Rue Morgue. Is a native of Spain. Was one of the party who entered the house. Did not proceed up stairs. Is nervous, and was apprehensive of the consequences of agitation. Heard the voices in contention. The gruff voice was that of a Frenchman. Could not distinguish what was said. The shrill voice was that of an Englishman — is sure of this. Does not understand the English language, but judges by the intonation.

Alberto Montani, confectioner, deposes that he was among the first to ascend the stairs. Heard the voices in question. The gruff voice was that of a Frenchman. Distinguished several words. The speaker appeared to be expostulating. Could not make out the words of the shrill voice. Spoke quick and unevenly. Thinks it the voice of a Russian. Corroborates the general testimony. Is an Italian. Never conversed with a native of Russia.

Several witnesses, recalled, here testified that the chimneys of all the rooms on the fourth story were too narrow to admit the passage of a human being. By 'sweeps' were meant cylindrical sweeping-brushes, such as are employed by those who clean chimneys. These brushes were passed up and down every flue in the house. There is no back passage by which any one could have descended while the party proceeded up stairs. The body of Mademoiselle L'Espanaye was so firmly wedged in the chimney that it could not be got down until four or five of the party united their strength.

Paul Dumas, physician, deposes that he was called to view the bodies about daybreak. They were both then lying on the sacking of the bedstead in the chamber where Mademoiselle L. was found. The corpse of the young lady was much bruised and excoriated. The fact that it had been thrust up the chimney would sufficiently account for these appearances. The throat was greatly chafed. There were several deep scratches just below the chin, together with a series of livid spots which were evidently the impression of fingers. The face was fearfully discolored, and the eye-balls protruded. The tongue had been partially bitten through. A large bruise was discovered upon the pit of the stomach, produced apparently by the pressure of a knee. In the opinion of M. Dumas, Mademoiselle L'Espanaye had been throttled to death by some person or persons unknown. The corpse of the mother was horribly mutilated. All the bones of the right leg and arm were more or less shattered. The left tibia much splintered, as well as all the ribs of the left side. Whole body dreadfully bruised and discolored. It was not possible to say how the injuries had been inflicted. A heavy club of wood, or a broad bar of iron, a chair, any large, heavy, and obtuse weapon would have produced such results, if wielded by the hands of a very powerful man. No woman could have inflicted the blows with any weapon. The head of the deceased, when seen by witness, was entirely separated from the body, and was also greatly shattered. The throat had evidently been cut with some very sharp instrument—probably with a razor.

Alexandre Etienne, surgeon, was called with M. Dumas to view the bodies. Corroborated the testimony, and the opinions, of M. Dumas.

Nothing farther of importance was elicited, although several other persons were examined. A murder so mysterious, and so perplexing in all its particulars, was never before committed in Paris—if indeed a murder has been committed at all. The police are entirely at fault—an unusual occurrence in affairs of this nature. There is not, however, the shadow of a clew apparent."

The evening edition of the paper stated that the greatest excitement still continued in the Quartier St. Roch—that the premises in question had been carefully re-searched, and fresh examinations of witnesses instituted, but all to no purpose. A postscript, however, mentioned that Adolphe Le Bon had been arrested and imprisoned—although nothing appeared to criminate him, beyond the facts already detailed.

Dupin seemed singularly interested in the progress of this affair—at least so I judged from his manner, for he made no comments. It was only after the announcement that Le Bon had been imprisoned, that he asked me my opinion respecting it.

I could merely agree with all Paris in considering it an insoluble mystery. I saw no means by which it would be possible to trace the murderer.

"We must not judge of the means," said Dupin, "by this shell of an examination. The Parisian police, so much extolled for acumen, are cunning, but no more. There is no method in their proceedings, beyond the method of the moment. They make a vast parade of measures; but, not unfrequently, these are so illy adapted to the objects proposed, as to put us in mind of Monsieur Jourdain's calling for his *robe-de-chambre—pour mieux entendre la musique.*[19] The results attained by them are not unfrequently surprising, but, for the most part, are brought about by simple diligence and activity. When these qualities are unavailing their schemes fail. Vidocq,[20] for

[19]*Calling for his dressing gown to hear the [chamber] music better—in Molière's* The Bourgeois Gentleman.
[20]*François Eugene Vidocq, who organized the French national police force, published his* Memoirs *in 1828.*

example, was a good guesser, and a persevering man. But, without educated thought, he erred continually by the very intensity of his investigations. He impaired his vision by holding the object too close. He might see, perhaps, one or two points with unusual clearness, but in so doing he necessarily lost sight of the matter as a whole. Thus there is such a thing as being too profound. Truth is not always in a well. In fact as regards the more important knowledge I do believe that she is invariably superficial. The depth lies in the valleys where we seek her, and not upon the mountain-tops where she is found. The modes and sources of this kind of error are well typified in the contemplation of the heavenly bodies. To look at a star by glances — to view it in a side-long way, by turning toward it the exterior portions of the retina (more susceptible of feeble impressions of light than the interior) is to behold the star distinctly — is to have the best appreciation of its lustre — a lustre which grows dim just in proportion as we turn our vision *fully* upon it. A greater number of rays actually fall upon the eye in the latter case, but in the former there is the more refined capacity for comprehension. By undue profundity we perplex and enfeeble thought — and it is possible to make even Venus herself vanish from the firmament by a scrutiny too sustained, too concentrated, or too direct.

"As for these murders, let us enter into some examinations for ourselves, before we make up an opinion respecting them. An inquiry will afford us amusement," [I thought this an odd term, so applied, but said nothing] "and, besides, Le Bon once rendered me a service for which I am not ungrateful. We will go and see the premises with our own eyes. I know G_____, the *Préfet de Police*, and shall have no difficulty in obtaining the necessary permission."

The permission was obtained, and we proceeded at once to the Rue Morgue. This is one of those miserable thoroughfares which intervene between the Rue Richelieu and the Rue St. Roch. It was late in the afternoon when we reached it, for this quarter is at a great distance from that in which we resided. The house was readily found; for there were still many persons gazing up at the closed shutters, with an objectless curiosity, from the opposite side of the way. It was an ordinary Parisian house, with a gateway, on one side of which was a glazed watch-box, with a sliding panel in the window, indicating a *loge de concierge*.[21] Before going in we walked up the street, turned down an alley, and then, again turning, passed in the rear of the building — Dupin, meanwhile, examining the whole neighborhood, as well as the house, with a minuteness of attention for which I could see no possible object.

Retracing our steps we came again to the front of the dwelling, rang, and, having shown our credentials, were admitted by the agents in charge. We went up stairs — into the chamber where the body of Mademoiselle L'Espanaye had been found, and where both the deceased still lay. The disorders of the room had as usual been suffered to exist. I saw nothing beyond what had been stated in the "Tribunal." Dupin scru-

[21] *Porter's lodge.*

tinized every thing, not excepting the bodies of the victims. We then went into the other rooms, and into the yard; a *gendarme* accompanying us throughout. Our examination occupied us until dark, when we took our departure. On our way home my companion stepped in for a moment at the office of one of the daily papers.

I have said that the whims of my friend were manifold, and that—*Je les ménageais:*[22]—for this phrase there is no English equivalent. It was his humor now to decline all conversation on the subject of the murder, until after we had taken a bottle of wine together about noon the next day. He then asked me, suddenly, if I had observed any thing *peculiar* at the scene of the atrocity.

There was something in his manner of emphasizing the word "peculiar," which caused me to shudder, without knowing why.

"No, nothing *peculiar*," I said, "nothing more, at least, than we both saw stated in the paper."

"'Le Tribunal,'" he replied, "has not entered, I fear, into the unusual horror of the thing. But we will not revert to the idle opinions of this print. It appears to me that this mystery is considered insoluble, for the very reason which should cause it to be regarded as easy of solution—I mean for the *outré*[23] character of its features. The police are confounded by the seeming absence of motive—not for the murder itself—but for the atrocity of the murder. They are puzzled by the seeming impossibility of reconciling the voices heard in contention, with the facts that no one was discovered up stairs but the assassinated Mademoiselle L'Espanaye, and that there were no means of egress without the notice of the party ascending. The wild disorder of the room; the corpse thrust, with the head downward up the chimney; the frightful mutilation of the body of the old lady; these considerations, with those just mentioned, and others which I need not mention, have sufficed to paralyze the powers, by putting completely at fault the boasted acumen, of the government agents. They have fallen into the gross but common error of confounding the unusual with the abstruse. But it is by these deviations from the plane of the ordinary, that reason feels its way, if at all, in its search for the true. In investigations such as we are now pursuing, it should not be so much asked 'what has occurred,' as 'what has occurred which has never occurred before.' In fact, the facility with which I shall arrive, or have arrived, at the solution of this mystery, is in ratio with its apparent insolubility in the eyes of the police."

I stared at the speaker in mute astonishment. He continued.

"I am now awaiting," continued he, looking toward the door of our apartment—"I am now awaiting a person who, although perhaps not the perpetrator of these butcheries, must have been in some measure implicated in their perpetration. Of the worst portion of the crimes committed it is probable that he is innocent. I hope that I am right in this supposition; for upon it I build my expectation of reading the entire

[22]*I handled them with tact.* [23]*Strange, unusual.*

riddle. I look for the man here — in this room — every moment. It is true that he may not arrive; but the probability is that he will. Should he come, it will be necessary to detain him. Here are pistols; and we both know how to use them when occasion demands their use."

I took the pistols, scarcely knowing what I did, or believing what I heard, while Dupin went on, very much as if in a soliloquy. I have already spoken of his abstract manner at such times. His discourse was addressed to myself; but his voice, although by no means loud, had that intonation which is commonly employed in speaking to some one at a great distance. His eyes, vacant in expression, regarded only the wall.

"That the voices heard in contention," he said, "by the party upon the stairs, were not the voices of the women themselves, was fully proved by the evidence. This relieves us of all doubt upon the question whether the old lady could have first destroyed the daughter, and afterward have committed suicide. I speak of this point chiefly for the sake of method; for the strength of Madame L'Espanaye would have been utterly unequal to the task of thrusting her daughter's corpse up the chimney as it was found; and the nature of the wounds upon her own person entirely preclude the idea of self-destruction. Murder, then, has been committed by some third party; and the voices of this third party were those heard in contention. Let me now advert — not to the whole testimony respecting these voices — but to what was peculiar in that testimony. Did you observe any thing peculiar about it?"

I remarked that, while all the witnesses agreed in supposing the gruff voice to be that of a Frenchman, there was much disagreement in regard to the shrill, or as one individual termed it, the harsh voice.

"That was the evidence itself," said Dupin, "but it was not the peculiarity of the evidence. You have observed nothing distinctive. Re-employing my own words, I may say that you have pointed out no prominence above the plane of the ordinary, by which reason may feel its way. Yet there *was* something to be pointed out. The witnesses, as you remark, agreed about the gruff voice; they were here unanimous. But in regard to the shrill voice, the peculiarity is — not that they disagreed — but that, while an Italian, an Englishman, a Spaniard, a Hollander, and a Frenchman attempted to describe it, each one spoke of it as that *of a foreigner*. Each is sure that it was not the voice of one of his own countrymen. Each likens it — not to the voice of an individual of any nation with whose language he is conversant — but the converse. The Frenchman supposes it the voice of a Spaniard, and 'might have distinguished some words *had he been acquainted with the Spanish*.' The Dutchman maintains it to have been that of a Frenchman; but we find it stated that '*not understanding French this witness was examined through an interpreter*.' The Englishman thinks it the voice of a German, and '*does not understand German*.' The Spaniard 'is sure' that it was that of an Englishman, but 'judges by the intonation' altogether, '*as he has no knowledge of the English*.' The Italian believes it the voice of a Russian, but '*has never conversed with a native of Russia*.' A second Frenchman differs, moreover, with the first, and is positive that the voice is that of an Italian; but, *not being cognizant of that tongue*, is, like the Spaniard, 'convinced by the intonation.' Now, how strangely unusual must that voice have really been, about which such testimony as this *could* have been elicited!— in whose *tones*, even, denizens of the five great divisions of Europe could recognize nothing familiar! You will say that it might have been the voice of an Asiatic — of an African. Neither Asiatics nor Africans abound in Paris; but, without denying the inference, I will just now merely call your attention to three points which have relation to this topic. The voice is termed by one witness 'harsh rather than shrill.' It is represented by two others to have been 'quick and *unequal*.' No words — no sounds resembling words — were by any witness mentioned as distinguishable.

"I know not," continued Dupin, "what impression I may have made, so far, upon your own understanding; but I do not hesitate to say that legitimate deductions even from this portion of the testimony — the portion respecting the gruff and shrill voices — are in themselves sufficient to engender a suspicion which should bias, or give direction to all farther progress in the investigation of the mystery. I said 'legitimate deductions;' but my meaning is not thus fully expressed. I designed to imply that the deductions were the *sole* proper ones, and that the suspicion arises *inevitably* from them as the single result. What the suspicion is, however, I will not say just yet. I merely wish you to bear in mind that with myself it was sufficiently forcible to give a definite form — a certain tendency — to my inquiries in the chamber.

"Let us now transport ourselves, in fancy, to this chamber. What shall we first seek here? The means of egress employed by the murderers. It is not too much to say that neither of us believe in præternatural events. Madame and Mademoiselle L'Espanaye were not destroyed by spirits. The doers of the dark deed were material, and escaped materially. Then how? Fortunately, there is but one mode of reasoning upon the point, and that mode *must* lead us to a definite decision. Let us examine, each by each, the possible means of egress. It is clear that the assassins were in the room where Mademoiselle L'Espanaye was found, or at least in the room adjoining, when the party ascended the stairs. It is then only from these two apartments that we have to seek for issues. The police have laid bare the floors, the ceilings, and the masonry of the walls, in every direction. No *secret* issues could have escaped their vigilance. But, not trusting to their eyes, I examined with my own. There were, then, *no* secret issues. Both doors leading from the rooms into the passage were securely locked, with the keys inside. Let us turn to the chimneys. These, although of ordinary width for some eight or ten feet above the hearths, will not admit, throughout their extent, the body of a large cat. The impossibility of egress, by means already stated, being thus absolute, we are reduced to the windows. Through those of the front room no one could have escaped without notice from the crowd in the street. The murderers *must* have passed, then, through those of the back room. Now, brought to this conclusion in so unequivocal a manner as we are, it is not our part, as reasoners, to reject it on account of apparent impossibilities. It is only left for us to prove that these 'apparent impossibilities' are, in reality, not such.

"There are two windows in the chamber. One of them is unobstructed by furniture, and is wholly visible. The lower portion of the other is hidden from view by the head of the unwieldy bedstead which is thrust close up against it. The former was found securely fastened from within. It resisted the utmost force of those who endeavored to raise it. A large gimlet-hole had been pierced in its frame to the left, and a very stout nail was found fitted therein, nearly to the head. Upon examining the other window, a similar nail was seen similarly fitted in it; and a vigorous attempt to raise this sash failed also. The police were now entirely satisfied that egress had not been in these directions. And, *therefore*, it was thought a matter of supererogation to withdraw the nails and open the windows.

"My own examination was somewhat more particular, and was so for the reason I have just given — because here it was, I knew, that all apparent impossibilities *must* be proved to be not such in reality.

"I proceeded to think thus — *a posteriori*.[24] The murderers *did* escape from one of these windows. This being so, they could not have refastened the sashes from the inside, as they were found fastened, — (the consideration which put a stop, through its obviousness, to the scrutiny of the police in this quarter). Yet the sashes *were* fastened. They *must*, then, have the power of fastening themselves. There was no escape from this conclusion. I stepped to the unobstructed casement, withdrew the nail with some difficulty, and attempted to raise the sash. It resisted all my efforts, as I had anticipated. A concealed spring must, I now knew, exist; and this corroboration of my idea convinced me that my premises, at least, were correct, however mysterious still appeared the circumstances attending the nails. A careful search soon brought to light the hidden spring. I pressed it, and, satisfied with the discovery, forbore to upraise the sash.

"I now replaced the nail and regarded it attentively. A person passing out through this window might have reclosed it, and the spring would have caught — but the nail could not have been replaced. The conclusion was plain, and again narrowed in the field of my investigations. The assassins *must* have escaped through the other window. Supposing, then, the springs upon each sash to be the same, as was probable, there *must* be found a difference between the nails, or at least between the modes of their fixture. Getting upon the sacking of the bedstead, I looked over the head-board minutely at the second casement. Passing my hand down behind the board I readily discovered and pressed the spring, which was, as I had supposed, identical in character with its neighbor. I now looked at the nail. It was as stout as the other, and apparently fitted in the same manner — driven in nearly up to the head.

"You will say that I was puzzled; but, if you think so, you must have misunder-

[24]*Retrospectively, after the fact.*

stood the nature of the inductions. To use a sporting phrase, I had not been once 'at fault.' The scent had never for an instant been lost. There was no flaw in any link of the chain. I had traced the secret to its ultimate result — and that result was *the nail.* It had, I say, in every respect, the appearance of its fellow in the other window; but this fact was an absolute nullity (conclusive as it might seem to be) when compared with the consideration that here, at this point, terminated the clew. 'There *must* be something wrong,' I said, 'about the nail.' I touched it; and the head, with about a quarter of an inch of the shank, came off in my fingers. The rest of the shank was in the gimlet-hole, where it had been broken off. The fracture was an old one (for its edges were incrusted with rust) and had apparently been accomplished by the blow of a hammer, which had partially imbedded, in the top of the bottom sash, the head portion of the nail. I now carefully replaced this head portion in the indentation whence I had taken it, and the resemblance to a perfect nail was complete. [Pressing the spring,] I gently raised the sash for a few inches; the head went up with it, remaining firm in its bed. I closed the window, and the semblance of the whole nail was again perfect.

"The riddle, so far, was now unriddled. The assassins had escaped through the window which looked upon the bed. Dropping of its own accord upon their exit (or perhaps purposely closed by them) it had become fastened by the spring; and it was the retention of this spring which had been mistaken by the police for that of the nail — farther inquiry being thus considered unnecessary.

"The next question is that of the mode of descent. Upon this point I had been satisfied in my walk with you around the building. About five feet and a half from the casement in question there ran a lightning-rod. From this rod it would have been impossible for any one to reach the window itself, to say nothing of entering it. I observed, however, that the shutters of the fourth story were of the peculiar kind called by Parisian carpenters *ferrades*— a kind rarely employed at the present day, but frequently seen upon very old mansions at Lyons and Bourdeaux. They are in the form of an ordinary door, (a single, not a folding door) except that the lower half is latticed or worked in open trellis — thus affording an excellent hold for the hands. In the present instance these shutters are fully three feet and a half broad. When we saw them from the rear of the house, they were both about half open — that is to say they stood off at right angles from the wall. It is probable that the police, as well as myself, examined the back of the tenement; but, if so, in looking at these *ferrades* in the line of their breadth (as they must have done), they did not perceive this great breadth itself, or, at all events, failed to take it into due consideration. In fact, having once satisfied themselves that no egress could have been made in this quarter, they would naturally bestow here a very cursory examination. It was clear to me, however, that the shutter belonging to the window at the head of the bed, would, if swung fully back to the wall, reach to within two feet of the lightning-rod. It was also evident that, by exertion of a very unusual degree of activity and courage, an entrance into the window, from the rod, might have been thus effected. By reaching to the distance of two feet and a half (we now suppose the shutter open to its whole extent) a robber might have taken a firm grasp upon the trellis-work. Letting go, then, his hold upon the rod, placing his feet securely against the wall, and springing boldly from it, he might have swung the shutter so as to close it, and, if we imagine the window open at the time, might even have swung himself into the room.

"I wish you to bear especially in mind that I have spoken of a *very* unusual degree of activity as requisite to success in so hazardous and so difficult a feat. It is my design to show you, first, that the thing might possibly have been accomplished:—but, secondly and *chiefly*, I wish to impress upon your understanding the *very extraordinary*—the almost præternatural character of that agility which could have accomplished it.

"You will say, no doubt, using the language of the law, that 'to make out my case,' I should rather undervalue, than insist upon a full estimation of the activity required in this matter. This may be the practice in law, but it is not the usage of reason. My ultimate object is only the truth. My immediate purpose is to lead you to place in juxta-position, that *very unusual* activity of which I have just spoken, with that *very peculiar* shrill (or harsh) and *unequal* voice, about whose nationality no two persons could be found to agree, and in whose utterance no syllabification could be detected."

At these words a vague and half-formed conception of the meaning of Dupin flitted over my mind. I seemed to be upon the verge of comprehension without power to comprehend—as men, at times, find themselves upon the brink of remembrance, without being able, in the end, to remember. My friend went on with his discourse.

"You will see," he said, "that I have shifted the question from the mode of egress to that of ingress. It was my design to convey the idea that both were effected in the same manner, at the same point. Let us now revert in fancy to the interior of the room. Let us survey the appearances here. The drawers of the bureau, it is said, had been rifled, although many articles of apparel still remained within them. The conclusion here is absurd. It is a mere guess—a very silly one—and no more. How are we to know that the articles found in the drawers were not all these drawers had originally contained? Madame L'Espanaye and her daughter lived an exceedingly retired life—saw no company—seldom went out—had little use for numerous changes of habiliment. Those found were at least of as good quality as any likely to be possessed by these ladies. If a thief had taken any, why did he not take the best—why did he not take all? In a word why did he abandon four thousand francs in gold to encumber himself with a bundle of linen? The gold *was* abandoned. Nearly the whole sum mentioned by Monsieur Mignaud, the banker, was discovered, in bags, upon the floor. I wish you, therefore, to discard from your thoughts the blundering idea of *motive* engendered in the brains of the police by that portion of the evidence which speaks of money delivered at the door of the house. Coincidences ten times as remarkable as this (the delivery of the money, and murder committed within three days upon the party receiving it), happen to all of us every hour of our lives, without attracting even a momentary notice. Coincidences in general are great stumbling-blocks in the way of that class of thinkers who have been educated to know nothing, and care less, of the theory of probabilities — that theory to which the most glorious objects of human research are indebted for the most glorious of illustration. In the present instance, had the gold been gone, the fact of its delivery three days before would have formed something more than a coincidence. It would have been corroborative of this idea of motive. But, under the real circumstances of the case, if we are to suppose gold the motive of this outrage, we must also imagine the perpetrator so vacillating an idiot as to have abandoned his gold and his motive together.

"Keeping now steadily in mind the points to which I have drawn your attention — that peculiar voice, that unusual agility, and that startling absence of motive in a murder so singularly atrocious as this — let us glance at the butchery itself. Here is a woman strangled to death by manual strength, and thrust up a chimney, head downward. Ordinary assassins employ no such modes of murder as this. Least of all, do they thus dispose of the murdered. In the manner of thrusting the corpse up the chimney, you will admit that there was something *excessively outré*— something altogether irreconcilable with our common notions of human action, even when we suppose the actors the most depraved of men. Think, too, what must have been the degree of that strength which could have thrust the body *up* such an aperture so forcibly that the united vigor of several persons was found barely sufficient to drag it *down!* Turn now to other indications of the employment of a vigor most marvellous. On the hearth were thick tresses — very thick tresses — of grey human hair. These had been *torn out by the roots*. You are aware of the great force necessary in tearing thus from the head even twenty or thirty hairs together. You saw the locks in question as well as myself. Their roots (a hideous sight!) were clotted with fragments of the flesh of the scalp — sure token of the prodigious power which had been exerted in uprooting perhaps a million of hairs at a time. The throat of the old lady was not merely cut, but the head absolutely severed from the body. The instrument was a mere razor. Here again we have evidence of that vastness of strength upon which I would fix your attention. I wish you also to look, and look steadily, at the *brutal* ferocity of these deeds. Of the bruises upon the body of Madame L'Espanaye I do not speak. Monsieur Dumas, and his worthy coadjutor, Monsieur Etienne, have pronounced that they were inflicted by some obtuse instrument; and so far these gentlemen are very correct. The obtuse instrument was clearly the stone pavement in the yard, upon which the victim had fallen from the window which looked in upon the bed. This idea, however simple it may now seem, escaped the police for the same reason that the breadth of the shutters escaped them — because, by the affair of the nails, their perceptions had been hermetically sealed against the possibility of the windows having ever been opened at all.

"If now, in addition to all these things, you have properly reflected upon the odd disorder of the chamber, we have gone so far as to combine the ideas of a strength superhuman, an agility astounding, a ferocity brutal, a butchery without motive, a *grotesquerie* in horror absolutely alien from humanity, and a voice foreign in tone to the ears of men of many nations, and devoid of all distinct or intelligible syllabification. What result, then, has ensued? What impression have I made upon your fancy?"

I shuddered as Dupin asked me the question. "A madman," I said, "has done this deed — some raving maniac, escaped from a neighboring *Maison de Santé.*"

"In some respects," he replied, "your idea is not irrelevant. But the voices of madmen, even in their wildest paroxysms, are never found to tally with that peculiar voice heard upon the stairs. Madmen are of some nation, and their language, however incoherent in its words, has always the coherence of syllabification. Besides, the hair of a madman is not such hair as I now hold in my hand. I disentangled this little tuft from among the tresses remaining upon the head of Madame L'Espanaye. Tell me what you can make of it."

"Good God," I said, completely unnerved, "this hair is most unusual — this is no *human* hair."

"I have not asserted that it was," said he; "but, before we decide this point, I wish you to glance at the little sketch which I have here traced upon this paper. It is a fac-simile drawing of what has been described in one portion of the testimony as 'dark bruises, and deep indentations of finger nails,' upon the throat of Mademoiselle L'Espanaye, and in another (by Messrs. Dumas and Etienne,) as a 'series of livid spots, evidently the impression of fingers.'

"You will perceive," continued my friend, spreading out the paper upon the table before us, "you will perceive that this drawing gives the idea of a firm and fixed hold. There is no *slipping* apparent. Each finger has retained — possibly until the death of the victim — the fearful grasp by which it originally imbedded itself. Attempt, now, to place all your fingers, at one and the same time, in the impressions as you see them."

I made the attempt in vain.

"We are possibly not giving this matter a fair trial," he said. "The paper is spread out upon a plane surface; but the human throat is cylindrical. Here is a billet of wood, the circumference of which is about that of the throat. Wrap the drawing around it, and try the experiment again."

I did so; but the difficulty was even more obvious than before. "This," I said, "is the mark of no human hand."

"Assuredly it is not," replied Dupin; "read now this passage from Cuvier."[25]

It was a minute anatomical and generally descriptive account of the large fulvous

[25]*Georges Cuvier, French naturalist.*

Ourang-Outang of the East Indian Islands. The gigantic stature, the prodigious strength and activity, the wild ferocity, and the imitative propensities of these mammalia are sufficiently well known to all. I understood the full horrors of the murder at once.

"The description of the digits," said I, as I made an end of reading, "is in exact accordance with this drawing. I see that no animal but an Ourang-Outang, of the species here mentioned, could have impressed the indentations as you have traced them. This tuft of yellow hair is identical in character with that of the beast of Cuvier. But I cannot possibly comprehend the particulars of this frightful mystery. Besides, there were two voices heard in contention, and one of them was unquestionably the voice of a Frenchman."

"True; and you will remember an expression attributed almost unanimously, by the evidence, to this voice,—the expression, '*mon Dieu!*' This, under the circumstances, has been justly characterized by one of the witnesses (Montani, the confectioner), as an expression of remonstrance or expostulation. Upon these two words, therefore, I have mainly built my hopes of a full solution of the riddle. A Frenchman was cognizant of the murder. It is possible—indeed it is far more than probable—that he was innocent of all participation in the bloody transactions which took place. The Ourang-Outang may have escaped from him. He may have traced it to this chamber; but, under the agitating circumstances which ensued, he could never have re-captured it. It is still at large. I will not pursue these guesses—for I have no right to call them more than guesses—since the shades of reflection upon which they are based are scarcely of sufficient depth to be appreciable by my own intellect, and since I could not pretend to make them intelligible to the understanding of another than myself. We will call them guesses then, and speak of them as such. If the Frenchman in question is indeed, as I suppose, innocent of this atrocity, this advertisement, which I left last night, upon our return home, at the office of 'Le Monde,' (a paper devoted to the shipping interest, and much sought for by sailors), will bring him to our residence."

He handed me a paper, and I read thus:

CAUGHT—*In the Bois de Boulogne, early in the morning of the _____ inst.* (the morning of the murder,) *a very large, tawny-colored Ourang-Outang of the Bornese species. The owner (who is ascertained to be a sailor, belonging to a Maltese vessel,) may have the animal again, upon identifying it satisfactorily, and paying a few charges arising from its capture and keeping. Call at No. _____, Rue _____, Faubourg St. Germain—au troisieme.*[26]

"How was it possible," I asked, "that you should know the man to be a sailor, and belonging to a Maltese vessel?"

"I do *not* know it," said Dupin. "I am not *sure* of it. Here, however, is a small

[26]*On the fourth floor.*

piece of ribbon, which has evidently, from its form, and from its greasy appearance, been used in tying the hair in one of those long *queues* of which sailors are so fond. Moreover, this knot is one which few besides sailors can tie, and is peculiar to the Maltese. I picked the ribbon up at the foot of the lightning-rod. It could not have belonged to either of the deceased. Now if, after all, I am wrong in my induction from this ribbon, that the Frenchman was a sailor belonging to a Maltese vessel, still I can have done no harm in stating what I did in the advertisement. If I am in error, he will merely suppose that I have been misled by some circumstance into which he will not take the trouble to inquire. But if I am right — a great point is gained. Cognizant of the murder, although not guilty, the Frenchman will naturally hesitate about replying to the advertisement — about demanding the Ourang-Outang. He will reason thus: — 'I am innocent; I am poor; my Ourang-Outang is of great value — to one in my circumstances a fortune of itself — why should I lose it through idle apprehensions of danger? Here it is within my grasp. It was found in the Bois de Boulogne — at a vast distance from the scene of that butchery. How can it ever be suspected that a brute beast should have done the deed? The police are at fault — they have failed to procure the slightest clew. Should they even trace the animal, it would be impossible to prove me cognizant of the murder, or to implicate me in guilt on account of that cognizance. Above all, *I am known.* The advertiser designates me as the possessor of the beast. I am not sure to what limit his knowledge may extend. Should I avoid claiming a property of so great value, which it is known that I possess, I will render the animal at least, liable to suspicion. It is not my policy to attract attention either to myself or to the beast. I will answer the advertisement — get the Ourang-Outang, and keep it close until this matter has blown over.'"

At this moment we heard a step upon the stairs.

"Be ready," said Dupin, "with your pistols, but neither use them nor show them until at a signal from myself."

The front door of the house had been left open, and the visiter had entered without ringing or rapping, and advanced several steps upon the staircase. Now, however, he seemed to hesitate. Presently we heard him descending. Dupin was moving quickly to the door, when we again heard him coming up. He did not turn back a second time, but stepped up quickly, and rapped at the door of our chamber.

"Come in," said Dupin, in a cheerful and hearty tone.

The visiter entered. He was a sailor, evidently — a tall, stout, and muscular-looking man, with a certain dare-devil expression of countenance, not altogether unprepossessing. His face, greatly sunburnt, was more than half hidden by a world of whisker and *mustachio.* He had with him a huge oaken cudgel, but appeared to be otherwise unarmed. He bowed awkwardly, and bade us "good evening," in French accents, which, although somewhat Neufchatel-ish, were still sufficiently indicative of a Parisian origin.

"Sit down, my friend," said Dupin, "I suppose you have called about the Ourang-

Outang. Upon my word, I almost envy you the possession of him; a remarkably fine, and no doubt a very valuable animal. How old do you suppose him to be?"

The sailor drew a long breath, with the air of a man relieved of some intolerable burden, and then replied, in an assured tone,—

"I have no way of telling—but he can't be more than four or five years old. Have you got him here?"

"Oh no—we had no conveniences for keeping him here. He is at a livery stable in the Rue Dubourg, just by. You can get him in the morning. Of course you are prepared to identify the property?"

"To be sure I am, sir."

"I shall be sorry to part with him," said Dupin.

"I don't mean that you should be at all this trouble for nothing, sir," said the man. "Couldn't expect it. Am very willing to pay a reward for the finding of the animal—that is to say, any reward in reason."

"Well," replied my friend, "that is all very fair, to be sure. Let me think!—what ought I to have? Oh! I will tell you. My reward shall be this. You shall give me all the information in your power about that affair of the murder in the Rue Morgue."

Dupin said the last words in a very low tone, and very quietly. Just as quietly, too, he walked towards the door, locked it, and put the key in his pocket. He then drew a pistol from his bosom and placed it, without the least flurry, upon the table.

The sailor's face flushed up with an ungovernable tide of crimson. He started to his feet and grasped his cudgel; but the next moment he fell back into his seat, trembling convulsively, and with the countenance of death itself. He spoke not a single word. I pitied him from the bottom of my heart.

"My friend," said Dupin, in a kind tone, "you are alarming yourself unnecessarily—you are indeed. We mean you no harm whatever. I pledge you the honor of a gentleman, and of a Frenchman, that we intend you no injury. I perfectly well know that you are innocent of the atrocities in the Rue Morgue. It will not do, however, to deny that you are in some measure implicated in them. From what I have already said, you must know that I have had means of information about this matter—means of which you could never have dreamed. Now the thing stands thus. You have done nothing which you could have avoided—nothing certainly which renders you culpable. You were not even guilty of robbery, when you might have robbed with impunity. You have nothing to conceal. You have no reason for concealment. On the other hand, you are bound by every principle of honor to confess all you know. An innocent man is now imprisoned, charged with that crime of which you can point out the perpetrator."

The sailor had recovered his presence of mind in a great measure, while Dupin uttered these words; but his original boldness of bearing was all gone.

"So help me God," said he, after a brief pause, "I *will* tell you all I that know about this affair;—but I do not expect you to believe one half that I say—I would be a fool indeed if I did. Still, I *am* innocent, and I will make a clean breast if I die for it."

I do not propose to follow the man in the circumstantial narrative which he now detailed. What he stated was, in substance, this. He had lately made a voyage to the Indian Archipelago. A party, of which he formed one, landed at Borneo, and passed into the interior on an excursion of pleasure. Himself and a companion had captured the Ourang-Outang. This companion dying, the animal fell into his own exclusive possession. After great trouble, occasioned by the intractable ferocity of his captive during the home voyage, he at length succeeded in lodging it safely at his own residence in Paris, where, not to attract towards himself the unpleasant curiosity of his neighbors, he kept it carefully secluded, until such time as it should recover from a wound in the foot, received from a splinter on board ship. His ultimate design was to sell it.

Returning home from some sailors' frolic on the night, or rather in the morning of the murder, he found his prisoner occupying his own bed-room, into which he had broken from a closet adjoining, where he had been, as it was thought, securely confined. The beast, razor in hand, and fully lathered, was sitting before a looking-glass attempting the operation of shaving, in which he had no doubt previously watched his master through the key-hole of the closet. Terrified at the sight of so dangerous a weapon in the possession of an animal so ferocious, and so well able to use it, the man, for some moments, was at a loss what to do. He had been accustomed, however, to quiet the creature, even in its fiercest moods, by the use of a strong waggoner's whip, and to this he now resorted. Upon sight of it, the Ourang-Outang sprang at once through the door of the chamber, down the stairs, and thence, through a window, unfortunately open, into the street.

The Frenchman followed in despair; the ape, razor still in hand, occasionally stopping to look back and gesticulate at his pursuer, until the latter had nearly come up with him. He then again made off. In this manner the chase continued for a long time. The streets were profoundly quiet, as it was nearly three o'clock in the morning. In passing down an alley in the rear of the Rue Morgue, the fugitive's attention was arrested by a light gleaming from the open window of Madame L'Espanaye's chamber, in the fourth story of her house. Rushing to the building, he perceived the lightning-rod, clambered up with inconceivable agility, grasped the shutter, which was thrown fully back against the wall, and, by its means, swung himself directly upon the headboard of the bed. The whole feat did not occupy a minute. The shutter was kicked open again by the Ourang-Outang as he entered the room.

The sailor, in the meantime, was both rejoiced and perplexed. He had strong hopes of now recapturing the ape, as it could scarcely escape from the trap into which it had ventured, except by the rod, where it might be intercepted as it came down. On the other hand, there was much cause for anxiety as to what the brute might do in the house. This latter reflection urged the man still to follow the fugitive. A lightning-rod is ascended without difficulty, especially by a sailor; but, when he had arrived as high as the window, which lay far to his left, his career was stopped; the most that he could accomplish was to reach over so as to obtain a glimpse of the interior of the room. At this glimpse he nearly fell from his hold through excess of horror. Now it was that those hideous shrieks arose upon the night, which had startled from slumber the inmates of the Rue Morgue. Madame L'Espanaye and her daughter, habited in their night clothes, had apparently been occupied in arranging some papers in the iron chest already mentioned, which had been wheeled into the middle of the room. It was open, and its contents lay beside it on the floor. Their backs must have been towards the window; and, from the time elapsing between the screams and the ingress of the ape, it seems probable that he was not immediately perceived. The flapping-to of the shutter would naturally have been attributed to the wind.

As the sailor looked in, the gigantic beast had seized Madame L'Espanaye by the hair (which was loose, as she had been combing it,) and was flourishing the razor about her face, in imitation of the motions of a barber. The daughter lay prostrate and motionless; she had swooned. The screams and struggles of the old lady (during which the hair was torn from her head) had the effect of changing the probably pacific purposes of the Ourang-Outang into those of wrath. With one determined sweep of his muscular arm he nearly severed her head from her body. The sight of blood inflamed his anger into phrenzy. Gnashing his teeth, and flashing fire from his eyes, he flew upon the body of the girl, and imbedded his fearful talons in her throat, retaining his grasp until she expired. His wandering and wild glances fell at this moment upon the head of the bed, over which those of his master, glazed in horror, were just discernible. The fury of the beast, who no doubt bore still in mind the dreaded whip, was instantly converted into dread. Conscious of having deserved punishment, he seemed desirous of concealing his bloody deeds, and skipped about the chamber in an apparent agony of nervous agitation, throwing down and breaking the furniture as he moved, and dragging the bed from the bedstead. In conclusion, he seized first the corpse of the daughter, and thrust it up the chimney, as it was found; then that of the old lady, with which he rushed to the window, precipitating it immediately therefrom.

As the ape approached him with his mutilated burden, the sailor shrank aghast to the rod, and rather gliding than clambering down it, hurried at once home—dreading the consequences of the butchery, and gladly abandoning, in his terror, all solicitude about the fate of the Ourang-Outang. The words heard by the party upon the staircase were the Frenchman's exclamations of horror and affright, commingled with the fiendish jabberings of the brute.

I have scarcely anything to add. The Ourang-Outang must have escaped from the chamber, by the rod, just before the breaking of the door. He must have closed the window as he passed through it. He was subsequently caught by the owner himself, who obtained for him a very large sum at the *Jardin des Plantes.* Le Bon was instantly released, upon our narration of the circumstances (with some comments from Dupin) at the *bureau* of the *Préfet de police*. This functionary, however well disposed to my friend, could not altogether conceal his chagrin at the turn which affairs had taken, and was fain to indulge in a sarcasm or two, in regard to the propriety of every person minding his own business.

"Let him talk," said Dupin, who had not thought it necessary to reply. "Let him discourse; it will ease his conscience. I am satisfied with having defeated him in his own castle. In truth, he is too cunning to be acute. There is no *stamen* in his wisdom. It is all head and no body—like the pictures of the Goddess Laverna[27]—or at least all head and shoulders, like a codfish. But he is a good fellow, after all. I like him especially for one master stroke of cant, by which he has attained that reputation for ingenuity which he possesses. I mean the way he has '*de nier ce qui est, et d'expliquer ce qui n'est pas.*'"[28]

[27]*Patroness of thieves in Roman myth.* [28]*Of denying what is, and explaining what isn't.*

The Purloined Letter
by Edgar Allan Poe
(1844)[1]

At Paris, just after dark one gusty evening in the autumn of 18 —, I was enjoying the twofold luxury of meditation and a meerschaum, in company with my friend C. Auguste Dupin, in his little back library, or book-closet, *au troisiême*, No. 33, *Rue Dunôt, Faubourg St. Germain*. For one hour at least we had maintained a profound silence; while each, to any casual observer, might have seemed intently and exclusively occupied with the curling eddies of smoke that oppressed the atmosphere of the chamber. For myself, however, I was mentally discussing certain topics which had formed matter for conversation between us at an earlier period of the evening; I mean the affair of the Rue Morgue, and the mystery attending the murder of Marie Roget. I looked upon it, therefore, as something of a coincidence, when the door of our apartment was thrown open and admitted our old acquaintance, Monsieur G_____, the Prefect of the Parisian police.

We gave him a hearty welcome; for there was nearly half as much of the entertaining as of the contemptible about the man, and we had not seen him for several years. We had been sitting in the dark, and Dupin now arose for the purpose of lighting a lamp, but sat down again, without doing so, upon G.'s saying that he had called to consult us, or rather to ask the opinion of my friend, about some official business which had occasioned a great deal of trouble.

"If it is any point requiring reflection," observed Dupin, as he forebore to enkindle the wick, "we shall examine it to better purpose in the dark."

"That is another of your odd notions," said the Prefect, who had a fashion of calling every thing "odd" that was beyond his comprehension, and thus lived amid an absolute legion of "oddities."

"Very true," said Dupin, as he supplied his visiter with a pipe, and rolled towards him a comfortable chair.

[1]In later versions of the story, Poe included the epigraph "Nil sapientiae odiosius acumine nimio" ("Nothing is more odious to wisdom than too much cunning"), which he attributes to Seneca.

"And what is the difficulty now?" I asked. "Nothing more in the assassination way, I hope?"

"Oh no; nothing of that nature. The fact is, the business is *very* simple indeed, and I make no doubt that we can manage it sufficiently well ourselves; but then I thought Dupin would like to hear the details of it, because it is so excessively *odd.*"

"Simple and odd," said Dupin.

"Why, yes; and not exactly that, either. The fact is, we have all been a good deal puzzled because the affair *is* so simple, and yet baffles us altogether."

"Perhaps it is the very simplicity of the thing which puts you at fault," said my friend.

"What nonsense you *do* talk!" replied the Prefect, laughing heartily.

"Perhaps the mystery is a little *too* plain," said Dupin.

"Oh, good heavens! who ever heard of such an idea?"

"A little *too* self-evident."

"Ha! ha! ha!—ha! ha! ha!—ho! ho! ho!" roared our visiter, profoundly amused, "oh, Dupin, you will be the death of me yet!"

"And what, after all, *is* the matter on hand?" I asked.

"Why, I will tell you," replied the Prefect, as he gave a long, steady, and contemplative puff, and settled himself in his chair. "I will tell you in a few words; but, before I begin, let me caution you that this is an affair demanding the greatest secrecy, and that I should most probably lose the position I now hold, were it known that I confided it to any one."

"Proceed," said I.

"Or not," said Dupin.

"Well, then; I have received personal information, from a very high quarter, that a certain document of the last importance, has been purloined from the royal apartments. The individual who purloined it is known; this beyond a doubt; he was seen to take it. It is known, also, that it still remains in his possession."

"How is this known?" asked Dupin.

"It is clearly inferred," replied the Prefect, "from the nature of the document, and from the non-appearance of certain results which would at once arise from its passing *out* of the robber's possession;—that is to say, from his employing it as he must design in the end to employ it."

"Be a little more explicit," I said.

"Well, I may venture so far as to say that the paper gives its holder a certain power in a certain quarter where such power is immensely valuable." The Prefect was fond of the cant of diplomacy.

"Still I do not quite understand," said Dupin.

"No? Well; the disclosure of the document to a third person, who shall be nameless, would bring in question the honor of a personage of most exalted station; and this fact gives the holder of the document an ascendancy over the illustrious personage whose honor and peace are so jeopardized."

"But this ascendancy," I interposed, "would depend upon the robber's knowledge of the loser's knowledge of the robber. Who would dare—"

"The thief," said G., "is the—Minister D_____, who dares all things, those unbecoming as well as those becoming a man. The method of the theft was not less ingenious than bold. The document in question—a letter, to be frank—had been received by the personage robbed while alone in the royal *boudoir*. During its perusal she was suddenly interrupted by the entrance of the other exalted personage from whom especially it was her wish to conceal it. After a hurried and vain endeavor to thrust it in a drawer, she was forced to place it, open as it was, upon a table. The address, however, was uppermost, and, the contents thus unexposed, the letter escaped notice. At this juncture enters the Minister D_____. His lynx eye immediately perceives the paper, recognizes the handwriting of the address, observes the confusion of the personage addressed, and fathoms her secret. After some business transactions, hurried through in his ordinary manner, he produces a letter somewhat similar to the one in question, opens it, pretends to read it, and then places it in close juxtaposition to the other. Again he converses, for some fifteen minutes, upon the public affairs. At length, in taking leave, he takes also from the table the letter to which he had no claim. Its rightful owner saw, but, of course, dared not call attention to the act, in the presence of the third personage who stood at her elbow. The minister decamped; leaving his own letter—one of no importance—upon the table."

"Here, then," said Dupin to me, "you have precisely what you demand to make the ascendancy complete—the robber's knowledge of the loser's knowledge of the robber."

"Yes," replied the Prefect; "and the power thus attained has, for some months past, been wielded, for political purposes, to a very dangerous extent. The personage robbed is more thoroughly convinced, every day, of the necessity of reclaiming her letter. But this, of course, cannot be done openly. In fine, driven to despair, she has committed the matter to me."

"Than whom," said Dupin, amid a perfect whirlwind of smoke, "no more sagacious agent could, I suppose, be desired, or even imagined."

"You flatter me," replied the Prefect; "but it is possible that some such opinion may have been entertained."

"It is clear," said I, "as you observe, that the letter is still in possession of the minister; since it is this possession, and not any employment, of the letter, which bestows the power. With the employment the power departs."

"True," said G_____; "and upon this conviction I proceeded. My first care was to make thorough search of the minister's hotel; and here my chief embarrassment lay in the necessity of searching without his knowledge. Beyond all things, I have been warned of the danger which would result from giving him reason to suspect our design."

"But," said I, "you are quite *au fait*[2] in these investigations. The Parisian police have done this thing often before."

"O yes; and for this reason I did not despair. The habits of the minister gave me, too, a great advantage. He is frequently absent from home all night. His servants are by no means numerous. They sleep at a distance from their master's apartment, and, being chiefly Neapolitans, are readily made drunk. I have keys, as you know, with which I can open any chamber or cabinet in Paris. For three months a night has not passed, during the greater part of which I have not been engaged, personally, in ransacking the D_____ Hotel. My honor is interested, and, to mention a great secret, the reward is enormous. So I did not abandon the search until I had become fully satisfied that the thief is a more astute man than myself. I fancy that I have investigated every nook and corner of the premises in which it is possible that the paper can be concealed."

"But is it not possible," I suggested, "that although the letter may be in possession of the minister, as it unquestionably is, he may have concealed it elsewhere than upon his own premises?"

"This is barely possible," said Dupin. "The present peculiar condition of affairs at court, and especially of those intrigues in which D_____ is known to be involved, would render the instant availability of the document—its susceptibility of being produced at a moment's notice—a point of nearly equal importance with its possession."

"Its susceptibility of being produced?" said I.

"That is to say, of being *destroyed*," said Dupin.

"True," I observed; "the paper is clearly then upon the premises. As for its being upon the person of the minister, we may consider that as out of the question."

"Entirely," said the Prefect. "He has been twice waylaid, as if by footpads, and his person rigorously searched under my own inspection."

"You might have spared yourself this trouble," said Dupin. "D_____, I presume, is not altogether a fool, and, if not, must have anticipated these waylayings, as a matter of course."

"Not *altogether* a fool," said G_____, "but then he's a poet, which I take to be only one remove from a fool."

"True;" said Dupin, after a long and thoughtful whiff from his meerschaum, "although I have been guilty of certain doggrel myself."

"Suppose you detail," said I, "the particulars of your search."

"Why the fact is, we took our time, and we searched *every where*. I have had long experience in these affairs. I took the entire building, room by room; devoting the nights of a whole week to each. We examined, first, the furniture of each apartment. We opened every possible drawer; and I presume you know that, to a properly

[2]*Expert, competent.*

trained police agent, such a thing as a *secret* drawer is impossible. Any man is a dolt who permits a 'secret' drawer to escape him in a search of this kind. The thing is *so* plain. There is a certain amount of bulk — of space — to be accounted for in every cabinet. Then we have accurate rules. The fiftieth part of a line could not escape us. After the cabinets we took the chairs. The cushions we probed with the fine long needles you have seen me employ. From the tables we removed the tops."

"Why so?"

"Sometimes the top of a table, or other similarly arranged piece of furniture, is removed by the person wishing to conceal an article; then the leg is excavated, the article deposited within the cavity, and the top replaced. The bottoms and tops of bedposts are employed in the same way."

"But could not the cavity be detected by sounding?" I asked.

"By no means, if, when the article is deposited, a sufficient wadding of cotton be placed around it. Besides, in our case, we were obliged to proceed without noise."

"But you could not have removed — you could not have taken to pieces *all* articles of furniture in which it would have been possible to make a deposit in the manner you mention. A letter may be compressed into a thin spiral roll, not differing much in shape or bulk from a large knitting-needle, and in this form it might be inserted into the rung of a chair, for example. You did not take to pieces all the chairs?"

"Certainly not; but we did better — we examined the rungs of every chair in the hotel, and, indeed the jointings of every description of furniture, by the aid of a most powerful microscope.[3] Had there been any traces of recent disturbance we should not have failed to detect it *instanter*. A single grain of gimlet-dust, or saw-dust, for example, would have been as obvious as an apple. Any disorder in the glueing — any unusual gaping in the joints — would have sufficed to insure detection."

"Of course you looked to the mirrors, between the boards and the plates, and you probed the beds and the bed-clothes, as well as the curtains and carpets."

"That of course; and when we had absolutely completed every particle of the furniture in this way, then we examined the house itself. We divided its entire surface into compartments, which we numbered, so that none might be missed; then we scrutinized each individual square inch throughout the premises, including the two houses immediately adjoining, with the microscope, as before."

"The two houses adjoining!" I exclaimed; "you must have had a great deal of trouble."

"We had; but the reward offered is prodigious."

"You include the *grounds* about the houses?"

"All the grounds are paved with brick. They gave us comparatively little trouble. We examined the moss between the bricks, and found it undisturbed."

[3]*Magnifying glass.*

"You looked among D_____'s papers, of course, and into the books of the library?"

"Certainly; we opened every package and parcel; we not only opened every book, but we turned over every leaf in each volume, not contenting ourselves with a mere shake, according to the fashion of some of our police officers. We also measured the thickness of every book-*cover*, with the most accurate admeasurement, and applied to each the most jealous scrutiny of the microscope. Had any of the bindings been recently meddled with, it would have been utterly impossible that the fact should have escaped observation. Some five or six volumes, just from the hands of the binder, we carefully probed, longitudinally, with the needles."

"You explored the floors beneath the carpets?"

"Beyond doubt. We removed every carpet, and examined the boards with the microscope."

"And the paper on the walls?"

"Yes."

"You looked into the cellars?"

"We did; and, as time and labour were no objects, we dug up every one of them to the depth of four feet."

"Then," I said, "you have been making a miscalculation, and the letter is *not* upon the premises, as you suppose."

"I fear you are right there," said the Prefect. "And now, Dupin, what would you advise me to do?"

"To make a thorough re-search of the premises."

"That is absolutely needless," replied G_____. "I am not more sure that I breathe than I am that the letter is not at the Hotel."

"I have no better advice to give you," said Dupin. "You have, of course, an accurate description of the letter?"

"Oh yes!"—And here the Prefect, producing a memorandum-book proceeded to read aloud a minute account of the internal, and especially of the external, appearance of the missing document. Soon after finishing the perusal of this description, he took his departure, more entirely depressed in spirits than I had ever known the good gentleman before.

In about a month afterwards he paid us another visit, and found us occupied very nearly as before. He took a pipe and a chair and entered into some ordinary conversation. At length I said,—

"Well, but G_____, what of the purloined letter? I presume you have at last made up your mind that there is no such thing as overreaching the Minister?"

"Confound him, say I—yes; I made the re-examination, however, as Dupin suggested—but it was all labour lost, as I knew it would be."

"How much was the reward offered, did you say?" asked Dupin.

"Why, a very great deal—a *very* liberal reward—I don't like to say how much, precisely; but one thing I *will* say, that I wouldn't mind giving my individual check for fifty thousand francs to any one who could obtain me that letter. The fact is, it is becoming of more and more importance every day; and the reward has been lately doubled. If it were trebled, however, I could do no more than I have done."

"Why, yes," said Dupin, drawlingly, between the whiffs of his meerschaum, "I really — think, G_____, you have not exerted yourself— to the utmost in this matter. You might — do a little more, I think, eh?"

"How?— in what way?'

"Why — puff, puff— you might — puff, puff— employ counsel in the matter, eh?— puff, puff, puff. Do you remember the story they tell of Abernethy?"

"No; hang Abernethy!"

"To be sure! hang him and welcome. But, once upon a time, a certain rich miser conceived the design of sponging upon this Abernethy for a medical opinion. Getting up, for this purpose, an ordinary conversation in a private company, he insinuated his case to the physician, as that of an imaginary individual.

"'We will suppose,' said the miser, 'that his symptoms are such and such; now, doctor, what would you have directed him to take?'

"'Take!' said Abernethy, 'why, take *advice*, to be sure.'"

"But," said the Prefect, a little discomposed, "*I* am *perfectly* willing to take advice, and to pay for it. I would *really* give fifty thousand francs, every *centime* of it, to any one who would aid me in the matter!"

"In that case," replied Dupin, opening a drawer, and producing a check-book, "you may as well fill me up a check for the amount mentioned. When you have signed it, I will hand you the letter."

I was astounded. The Prefect appeared absolutely thunder-stricken. For some minutes he remained speechless and motionless, looking incredulously at my friend with open mouth, and eyes that seemed starting from their sockets; then, apparently recovering himself in some measure, he seized a pen, and after several pauses and vacant stares, finally filled up and signed a check for fifty thousand francs, and handed it across the table to Dupin. The latter examined it carefully and deposited it in his pocket-book; then, unlocking an *escritoire*,[4] took thence a letter and gave it to the Prefect. This functionary grasped it in a perfect agony of joy, opened it with a trembling hand, cast a rapid glance at its contents, and then, scrambling and struggling to the door, rushed at length unceremoniously from the room and from the house, without having uttered a syllable since Dupin had requested him to fill up the check.

When he had gone, my friend entered into some explanations.

"The Parisian police," he said, "are exceedingly able in their way. They are persevering, ingenious, cunning, and thoroughly versed in the knowledge which their duties seem chiefly to demand. Thus, when G_____ detailed to us his mode of search-

[4] *Writing desk.*

ing the premises at the Hotel D_____, I felt entire confidence in his having made a satisfactory investigation — so far as his labours extended."

"So far as his labours extended?" said I.

"Yes," said Dupin. "The measures adopted were not only the best of their kind, but carried out to absolute perfection. Had the letter been deposited within the range of their search, these fellows would, beyond a question, have found it."

I merely laughed — but he seemed quite serious in all that he said.

"The measures, then," he continued, "were good in their kind, and well executed; their defect lay in their being inapplicable to the case, and to the man. A certain set of highly ingenious resources are, with the Prefect, a sort of Procrustean[5] bed, to which he forcibly adapts his designs. But he perpetually errs by being too deep or too shallow, for the matter in hand; and many a schoolboy is a better reasoner than he. I knew one about eight years of age, whose success at guessing in the game of 'even and odd' attracted universal admiration. This game is simple, and is played with marbles. One player holds in his hand a number of these toys, and demands of another whether that number is even or odd. If the guess is right, the guesser wins one; if wrong, he loses one. The boy to whom I allude won all the marbles of the school. Of course he had some principle of guessing; and this lay in mere observation and admeasurement of the astuteness of his opponents. For example, an arrant simpleton is his opponent, and, holding up his closed hand, asks, 'are they even or odd?' Our schoolboy replies, 'odd,' and loses; but upon the second trial he wins, for he then says to himself, 'the simpleton had them even upon the first trial, and his amount of cunning is just sufficient to make him have them odd upon the second; I will therefore guess odd;' — he guesses odd, and wins. Now, with a simpleton a degree above the first, he would have reasoned thus: 'This fellow finds that in the first instance I guessed odd, and, in the second, he will propose to himself, upon the first impulse, a simple variation from even to odd, as did the first simpleton; but then a second thought will suggest that this is too simple a variation, and finally he will decide upon putting it even as before. I will therefore guess even;' — he guesses even, and wins. Now this mode of reasoning in the schoolboy, whom his fellows termed 'lucky,' — what, in its last analysis, is it?"

"It is merely," I said, "an identification of the reasoner's intellect with that of his opponent."

"It is," said Dupin; "and, upon inquiring of the boy by what means he effected the *thorough* identification in which his success consisted, I received answer as follows: 'When I wish to find out how wise, or how stupid, or how good, or how wicked is any one, or what are his thoughts at the moment, I fashion the expression of my face, as accurately as possible, in accordance with the expression of his, and then wait to see what thoughts or sentiments arise in my mind or heart, as if to match or correspond

[5]*In Greek myth, Procrustes stretched or cut off the limbs of his victims so that they would fit his bed.*

with the expression.' This response of the schoolboy lies at the bottom of all the spurious profundity which has been attributed to Rochefoucault, to La Bougive, to Machiavelli, and to Campanella."

"And the identification," I said, "of the reasoner's intellect with that of his opponent, depends, if I understand you aright, upon the accuracy with which the opponent's intellect is admeasured."

"For its practical value it depends upon this," replied Dupin; "and the Prefect and his cohort fail so frequently, first, by default of this identification, and, secondly, by ill-admeasurement, or rather through non-admeasurement, of the intellect with which they are engaged. They consider only their *own* ideas of ingenuity; and, in searching for anything hidden, advert only to the modes in which *they* would have hidden it. They are right in this much — that their own ingenuity is a faithful representative of that of *the mass*; but when the cunning of the individual felon is diverse in character from their own, the felon foils them, of course. This always happens when it is above their own, and very usually when it is below. They have no variation of principle in their investigations; at best, when urged by some unusual emergency — by some extraordinary reward — they extend or exaggerate their old modes of *practice*, without touching their principles. What, for example, in this case of D_____, has been done to vary the principle of action? What is all this boring, and probing, and sounding, and scrutinizing with the microscope, and dividing the surface of the building into registered square inches — what is it all but an exaggeration *of the application* of the one principle or set of principles of search, which are based upon the one set of notions regarding human ingenuity, to which the Prefect, in the long routine of his duty, has been accustomed? Do you not see he has taken it for granted that *all* men proceed to conceal a letter,— not exactly in a gimlet-hole bored in a chair-leg — but, at least, in *some* out-of-the-way hole or corner suggested by the same tenor of thought which would urge a man to secrete a letter in a gimlet-hole bored in a chair-leg? And do you not see also, that such *recherches*[6] nooks for concealment are adapted only for ordinary occasions, and would be adopted only by ordinary intellects; for, in all cases of concealment, a disposal of the article concealed — a disposal of it in this *recherché* manner,— is, in the very first instance, presumed and presumable; and thus its discovery depends, not at all upon the acumen, but altogether upon the mere care, patience, and determination of the seekers; and where the case is of importance — or, what amounts to the same thing in the policial eyes, when the reward is of magnitude,— the qualities in question have *never* been known to fail. You will now understand what I meant in suggesting that, had the purloined letter been hidden any where within the limits of the Prefect's examination — in other words, had the principle of its concealment been comprehended within the principles of the Prefect — its discovery would have been a matter altogether beyond question. This func-

[6]*Out of the way.*

tionary, however, has been thoroughly mystified; and the remote source of his defeat lies in the supposition that the Minister is a fool, because he has acquired renown as a poet. All fools are poets; this the Prefect *feels*; and he is merely guilty of a *non distributio medii*[7] in thence inferring that all poets are fools."

"But is this really the poet?" I asked. "There are two brothers, I know; and both have attained reputation in letters. The Minister I believe has written learnedly on the Differential Calculus. He is a mathematician, and no poet."

"You are mistaken; I know him well; he is both. As poet *and* mathematician, he would reason well; as a poet, profoundly; as a mere mathematician, he could not have reasoned at all, and thus would have been at the mercy of the Prefect."

"You surprise me," I said, "by these opinions, which have been contradicted by the voice of the world. You do not mean to set at naught the well-digested idea of centuries. The mathematical reason has long been regarded as *the* reason *par excellence*."

"'Il y a à parièr,'" replied Dupin, quoting from Chamfort, "'que toute idée publique, toute convention reçue, est une sottise, car elle a convenue au plus grand nombre.'[8] The mathematicians, I grant you, have done their best to promulgate the popular error to which you allude, and which is none the less an error for its promulgation as truth. With an art worthy a better cause, for example, they have insinuated the term 'analysis' into application to algebra. The French are the originators of this particular deception; but if a term is of any importance — if words derive any value from applicability — then 'analysis' conveys 'algebra' about as much as, in Latin, '*ambitus*' implies 'ambition,' '*religio*' 'religion,' or '*homines honesti*,' a set of *honorable* men."

"You have a quarrel on hand, I see," said I, "with some of the algebraists of Paris; but proceed."

"I dispute the availability, and thus the value, of that reason which is cultivated in any especial form other than the abstractly logical. I dispute, in particular, the reason educed by mathematical study. The mathematics are the science of form and quantity; mathematical reasoning is merely logic applied to observation upon form and quantity. The great error lies in supposing that even the truths of what is called *pure* algebra, are abstract or general truths. And this error is so egregious that I am confounded at the universality with which it has been received. Mathematical axioms are *not* axioms of general truth. What is true of *relation*— of form and quantity — is often grossly false in regard to morals, for example. In this latter science it is very usually *un*true that the aggregated parts are equal to the whole. In chemistry also the axiom fails. In the consideration of motive it fails; for two motives, each of a given value, have not, necessarily, a value when united, equal to the sum of their values apart. There are numerous other mathematical truths which are only truths within

[7]*Undistributed middle — a logical fallacy.*
[8]*It's certain that all commonly held opinions are worthless because so many people accept them.*

the limits of *relation*. But the mathematician argues, from his *finite truths*, through habit, as if they were of an absolutely general applicability—as the world indeed imagines them to be. Bryant, in his very learned 'Mythology,' mentions an analogous source of error, when he says that 'although the Pagan fables are not believed, yet we forget ourselves continually, and make inferences from them as existing realities.'[9] With the algebraists, however, who are Pagans themselves, the 'Pagan fables' *are* believed, and the inferences are made, not so much through lapse of memory, as through an unaccountable addling of the brains. In short, I never yet encountered the mere mathematician who could be trusted out of equal roots, or one who did not clandestinely hold it as a point of his faith that $x^2 + px$ was absolutely and unconditionally equal to q. Say to one of these gentlemen, by way of experiment, if you please, that you believe occasions may occur where $x^2 + px$ is *not* altogether equal to q, and, having made him understand what you mean, get out of his reach as speedily as convenient, for, beyond doubt, he will endeavor to knock you down.

"I mean to say," continued Dupin, while I merely laughed at his last observations, "that if the Minister had been no more than a mathematician, the Prefect would have been under no necessity of giving me this check. Had he been no more than a poet, I think it probable that he would have fooled us all. I knew him, however, as both mathematician and poet, and my measures were adapted to his capacity, with reference to the circumstances by which he was surrounded. I knew him as a courtier, too, and as a bold *intriguant*. Such a man, I considered, could not fail to be aware of the ordinary policial modes of action. He could not have failed to anticipate—and events have proved that he did not fail to anticipate—the waylayings to which he was subjected. He must have foreseen, I reflected, the secret investigations of his premises. His frequent absences from home at night, which were hailed by the Prefect as certain aids to his success, I regarded only as *ruses*, to afford opportunity for thorough search to the police, and thus the sooner to impress them with the conviction to which G_____, in fact, did finally arrive—the conviction that the letter was not upon the premises. I felt, also, that the whole train of thought, which I was at some pains in detailing to you just now, concerning the invariable principle of policial action in searches for articles concealed—I felt that this whole train of thought would necessarily pass through the mind of the Minister. It would imperatively lead him to despise all the ordinary *nooks* of concealment. *He* could not, I reflected, be so weak as not to see that the most intricate and remote recess of his hotel would be as open as his commonest closets to the eyes, to the probes, to the gimlets, and to the microscopes of the Prefect. I saw, in fine, that he would be driven, as a matter of course, to *simplicity*, if not deliberately induced to it as a matter of choice. You will remember, perhaps, how desperately the Prefect laughed when I suggested, upon our first interview, that it was just possible this mystery troubled him so much on account of its being so *very* self-evident."

[9]*From Jacob Bryant's* A New System *or* An Analysis of Ancient Mythology.

"Yes," said I, "I remember his merriment well. I really thought he would have fallen into convulsions."

"The material world," continued Dupin, "abounds with very strict analogies to the immaterial; and thus some color of truth has been given to the rhetorical dogma, that metaphor, or simile, may be made to strengthen an argument, as well as to embellish a description. The principle of the *vis inertiæ*,[10] for example, with the amount of *momentum* proportionate with it and consequent upon it, seems to be identical in physics and metaphysics. It is not more true in the former, that a large body is with more difficulty set in motion than a smaller one, and that its subsequent *impetus* is commensurate with this difficulty, than it is, in the latter, that intellects of the vaster capacity, while more forcible, more constant, and more eventful in their movements than those of inferior grade, are yet the less readily moved, and more embarrassed and full of hesitation in the first few steps of their progress. Again: have you ever noticed which of the street signs, over the shop-doors, are the most attractive of attention?"

"I have never given the matter a thought," I said.

"There is a game of puzzles," he resumed, "which is played upon a map. One party playing requires another to find a given word — the name of town, river, state or empire — any word, in short, upon the motley and perplexed surface of the chart. A novice in the game generally seeks to embarrass his opponents by giving them the most minutely lettered names; but the adept selects such words as stretch, in large characters, from one end of the chart to the other. These, like the over-largely lettered signs and placards of the street, escape observation by dint of being excessively obvious; and here the physical oversight is precisely analogous with the moral inapprehension by which the intellect suffers to pass unnoticed those considerations which are too obtrusively and too palpably self-evident. But this is a point, it appears, somewhat above or beneath the understanding of the Prefect. He never once thought it probable, or possible, that the Minister had deposited the letter immediately beneath the nose of the whole world, by way of best preventing any portion of that world from perceiving it.

"But the more I reflected upon the daring, dashing, and discriminating ingenuity of D_____; upon the fact that the document must always have been *at hand*, if he intended to use it to good purpose; and upon the decisive evidence, obtained by the Prefect, that it was not hidden within the limits of that dignitary's ordinary search — the more satisfied I became that, to conceal this letter, the Minister had resorted to the comprehensive and sagacious expedient of not attempting to conceal it at all.

"Full of these ideas, I prepared myself with a pair of green spectacles, and called one fine morning, quite by accident, at the ministerial hotel. I found D_____ at home, yawning, lounging, and dawdling as usual, and pretending to be in the last

[10] *Force of inertia.*

extremity of *ennui*. He is, perhaps, the most really energetic human being now alive — but that is only when nobody sees him.

"To be even with him, I complained of my weak eyes, and lamented the necessity of the spectacles, under cover of which I cautiously and thoroughly surveyed the whole apartment, while seemingly intent only upon the conversation of my host.

"I paid especial attention to a large writing-table near which he sat, and upon which lay confusedly, some miscellaneous letters and other papers, with one or two musical instruments and a few books. Here, however, after a long and very deliberate scrutiny, I saw nothing to excite particular suspicion.

"At length my eyes, in going the circuit of the room, fell upon a trumpery filigree card-rack of pasteboard, that hung dangling by a dirty blue riband, from a little brass knob just beneath the middle of the mantel-piece. In this rack, which had three or four compartments, were five or six visiting cards and a solitary letter. This last was much soiled and crumpled. It was torn nearly in two, across the middle — as if a design, in the first instance, to tear it entirely up as worthless, had been altered, or stayed, in the second. It had a large black seal, bearing the D_____ cipher *very* conspicuously, and was addressed, in a diminutive female hand, to D_____, the minister, himself. It was thrust carelessly, and even, as it seemed, contemptuously, into one of the uppermost divisions of the rack.

"No sooner had I glanced at this letter, than I concluded it to be that of which I was in search. To be sure, it was, to all appearance, radically different from the one of which the Prefect had read us so minute a description. Here the seal was large and black, with the D____ cipher; there, it was small and red, with the ducal arms of the S_____ family. Here, the address, to the Minister, was diminutive and feminine; there the superscription, to a certain royal personage, was markedly bold and decided; the size alone formed a point of correspondence. But, then, the *radicalness* of these differences, which was excessive; the dirt, the soiled and torn condition of the paper, so inconsistent with the *true* methodical habits of D_____, and so suggestive of a design to delude the beholder into an idea of the worthlessness of the document; these things, together with the hyper-obtrusive situation of this document, full in the view of every visiter, and thus exactly in accordance with the conclusions to which I had previously arrived; these things, I say, were strongly corroborative of suspicion, in one who came with the intention to suspect.

"I protracted my visit as long as possible, and, while I maintained a most animated discussion with the Minister, upon a topic which I knew well had never failed to interest and excite him, I kept my attention really riveted upon the letter. In this examination, I committed to memory its external appearance and arrangement in the rack; and also fell, at length, upon a discovery which set at rest whatever trivial doubt I might have entertained. In scrutinizing the edges of the paper, I observed them to be more *chafed* than seemed necessary. They presented the *broken* appearance which is manifested when a stiff paper, having been once folded and pressed with a folder, is refolded in a reversed direction, in the same creases or edges which had formed the original fold. This discovery was sufficient. It was clear to me that the letter had been turned, as a glove, inside out, re-directed, and re-sealed. I bade the Minister good morning, and took my departure at once, leaving a gold snuff-box upon the table.

"The next morning I called for the snuff-box, when we resumed, quite eagerly, the conversation of the preceding day. While thus engaged, however, a loud report, as if of a pistol, was heard immediately beneath the windows of the hotel, and was succeeded by a series of fearful screams, and the shoutings of a terrified mob. D_____ rushed to a casement, threw it open, and looked out. In the meantime, I stepped to the card-rack, took the letter, put it in my pocket, and replaced it by a *fac-simile*, which I had carefully prepared at my lodgings — imitating the D_____ cipher, very readily, by means of a seal formed of bread.

"The disturbance in the street had been occasioned by the frantic behavior of a man with a musket. He had fired it among a crowd of women and children. It proved, however, to have been without ball, and the fellow was suffered to go his way as a lunatic or a drunkard. When he had gone, D_____ came from the window, whither I had followed him immediately upon securing the object in view. Soon afterwards I bade him farewell. The pretended lunatic was a man in my own pay."

"But what purpose had you," I asked, "in replacing the letter by a *fac-simile*? Would it not have been better, at the first visit, to have seized it openly, and departed?"

"D_____," replied Dupin, "is a desperate man, and a man of nerve. His hotel, too, is not without attendants devoted to his interests. Had I made the wild attempt you suggest, I might never have left the ministerial presence alive. The good people of Paris might have heard of me no more. But I had an object apart from these considerations. You know my political prepossessions. In this matter, I act as a partisan of the lady concerned. For eighteen months the Minister has had her in his power. She has now him in hers — since, being unaware that the letter is not in his possession, he will proceed with his exactions as if it was. Thus will he inevitably commit himself, at once, to his political destruction. His downfall, too, will not be more precipitate than awkward. It is all very well to talk about the *facilis descensus Averni*[11]; but in all kinds of climbing, as Catalani said of singing, it is far more easy to get up than to come down. In the present instance I have no sympathy — at least no pity — for him who descends. He is that *monstrum horrendum*,[12] an unprincipled man of genius. I confess, however, that I should like very well to know the precise character of his thoughts, when, being defied by her whom the Prefect terms 'a certain personage,' he is reduced to opening the letter which I left for him in the card-rack."

"How? did you put any thing particular in it?"

[11]*Easy descent to hell (Virgil).*
[12]*Horrible monster (Virgil).*

"Why — it did not seem altogether right to leave the interior blank — that would have been insulting. To be sure, D_____, at Vienna once, did me an evil turn, which I told him, quite good-humoredly, that I should remember. So, as I knew he would feel some curiosity in regard to the identity of the person who had outwitted him, I thought it a pity not to give him a clue. He is well acquainted with my MS., and I just copied into the middle of the blank sheet the words —

"'_____*Un dessein si funeste,*
S'il n'est digne d'Atrée, est digne de Thyeste.'[13]

They are to be found in Crébillon's 'Atrée.'"[14]

[13]A scheme so infernal, / If not worthy of Atreus, is worthy of Thyestes. *In Greek myth, Atreus and Thyestes were brothers who committed horrible crimes against each other.*
[14]*Dupin refers to Prosper Jolyot de Crébillon's play* Atrée et Thyeste.

The Gold-Bug

by Edgar Allan Poe

(1843)

What ho! what ho! this fellow is dancing mad!
He hath been bitten by the Tarantula.
All in the Wrong.

Many years ago, I contracted an intimacy with a Mr. William Legrand. He was of an ancient Huguenôt[1] family, and had once been wealthy; but a series of misfortunes had reduced him to want. To avoid the mortification consequent upon his disasters, he left New Orleans, the city of his forefathers, and took up his residence at Sullivan's Island, near Charleston, South Carolina.

This Island is a very singular one. It consists of little else than the sea sand, and is about three miles long. Its breadth at no point exceeds a quarter of a mile. It is separated from the main land by a scarcely perceptible creek, oozing its way through a wilderness of reeds and slime, a favorite resort of the marsh-hen. The vegetation, as might be supposed, is scant, or at least dwarfish. No trees of any magnitude are to be seen. Near the western extremity, where Fort Moultrie stands, and where are some miserable frame buildings, tenanted, during summer, by the fugitives from Charleston dust and fever, may be found, indeed, the bristly palmetto; but the whole island, with the exception of this western point, and a line of hard, white beach on the seacoast, is covered with a dense undergrowth of the sweet myrtle, so much prized by the horticulturists of England. The shrub here often attains the height of fifteen or twenty feet, and forms an almost impenetrable coppice, burthening the air with its fragrance.

In the inmost recesses of this coppice, not far from the eastern or more remote end of the island, Legrand had built himself a small hut, which he occupied when I first, by mere accident, made his acquaintance. This soon ripened into friendship—for there was much in the recluse to excite interest and esteem. I found him well educated, with unusual powers of mind, but infected with misanthropy, and subject to perverse moods of alternate enthusiasm and melancholy. He had with him many

[1]*French Protestant.*

books, but rarely employed them. His chief amusements were gunning and fishing, or sauntering along the beach and through the myrtles, in quest of shells or entomological specimens;—his collection of the latter might have been envied by a Swammerdamm.[2] In these excursions he was usually accompanied by an old negro, called Jupiter, who had been manumitted before the reverses of the family, but who could be induced, neither by threats nor by promises, to abandon what he considered his right of attendance upon the footsteps of his young "Massa Will." It is not improbable that the relatives of Legrand, conceiving him to be somewhat unsettled in intellect, had contrived to instill this obstinacy into Jupiter, with a view to the supervision and guardianship of the wanderer.

The winters in the latitude of Sullivan's Island are seldom very severe, and, in the fall of the year, it is a rare event indeed when a fire is considered necessary. About the middle of October, 18 —, there occurred, however, a day of remarkable chilliness. Just before sunset I scrambled my way through the evergreens to the hut of my friend, whom I had not visited for several weeks;—my residence being, at that time, in Charleston, a distance of nine miles from the Island, while the facilities of passage and re-passage were very far behind those of the present day. Upon reaching the hut I rapped, as was my custom, and getting no reply, sought for the key where I knew it was secreted, unlocked the door and went in. A fine fire was blazing upon the hearth. It was a novelty and by no means an ungrateful one. I threw off an overcoat, took an arm-chair by the crackling logs, and waited patiently the arrival of my hosts.

Soon after dark they arrived, and gave me a most cordial welcome. Jupiter, grinning from ear to ear, bustled about to prepare some marsh-hens for supper. Legrand was in one of his fits—how else shall I term them?—of enthusiasm. He had found an unknown bivalve, forming a new genus, and, more than this, he had hunted down and secured, with Jupiter's assistance, a *scarabæus*[3] which he believed to be totally new, but in respect to which he wished to have my opinion on the morrow.

"And why not to-night?" I asked, rubbing my hands over the blaze, and wishing the whole tribe of *scarabæi* at the devil.

"Ah, if I had only known you were here!" said Legrand, "but it's so long since I saw you; and how could I foresee that you would pay me a visit this very night of all others? As I was coming home I met Lieutenant G_____, from the fort, and, very foolishly, I lent him the bug; so it will be impossible for you to see it until the morning. Stay here to-night, and I will send Jup down for it at sunrise. It is the loveliest thing in creation!"

"What?—sunrise?"

"Nonsense! no!—the bug. It is of a brilliant gold color—about the size of a large hickory-nut—with two jet black spots near one extremity of the back, and another, somewhat longer, at the other. The *antennæ* are—"

[2]Jan Swammerdamm, a Dutch entomologist. [3]Scarab, beetle.

"Dey aint *no* tin in him, Massa Will, I keep a tellin on you," here interrupted Jupiter; "de bug is a goole bug, solid, ebery bit of him, inside and all, sep him wing—neber feel half so hebby a bug in my life."

"Well, suppose it is, Jup," replied Legrand, somewhat more earnestly, it seemed to me, than the case demanded, "is that any reason for your letting the birds burn? The color"—here he turned to me—"is really almost enough to warrant Jupiter's idea. You never saw a more brilliant metallic lustre than the scales emit—but of this you cannot judge till to-morrow. In the mean time I can give you some idea of the shape." Saying this, he seated himself at a small table, on which were a pen and ink, but no paper. He looked for some in a drawer, but found none.

"Never mind," said he at length, "this will answer"; and he drew from his waistcoat pocket a scrap of what I took to be very dirty foolscap,[4] and made upon it a rough drawing with the pen. While he did this I retained my seat by the fire, for I was still chilly. When the design was complete he handed it to me without rising. As I received it a loud growl was heard, succeeded by a scratching at the door. Jupiter opened it, and a large Newfoundland, belonging to Legrand, rushed in, leaped upon my shoulders, and loaded me with caresses; for I had shown him much attention during previous visits. When his gambols were over, I looked at the paper, and, to speak the truth, found myself not a little puzzled at what my friend had depicted.

"Well!" I said, after contemplating it for some minutes, "this *is* a strange *scarabæus*, I must confess: new to me: never saw anything like it before—unless it was a skull, or a death's-head—which it more nearly resembles than anything else that has come under *my* observation."

"A death's-head!" echoed Legrand—"Oh—yes—well, it has something of that appearance upon paper, no doubt. The two upper black spots look like eyes, eh? and the longer one at the bottom like a mouth—and then the shape of the whole is oval."

"Perhaps so," said I; "but, Legrand, I fear you are no artist. I must wait until I see the beetle itself, if I am to form any idea of its personal appearance."

"Well, I don't know," said he, a little nettled, "I draw tolerably—*should* do it at least—have had good masters, and flatter myself that I am not quite a blockhead."

"But, my dear fellow, you are joking then," said I, "this is a very passable *skull*—indeed, I may say that it is a very *excellent* skull, according to the vulgar notions about such specimens of physiology—and your *scarabæus* must be the queerest *scarabæus* in the world if it resembles it. Why we may get up a very thrilling bit of superstition upon this hint. I presume you will call the bug *scarabæus caput hominis*, or something of that kind—there are many similar titles in the Natural Histories. But where are the *antennæ* you spoke of?"

"The *antennæ*!" said Legrand, who seemed to be getting unaccountably warm

[4] *Writing paper.*

upon the subject; "I am sure you must see the *antennæ*. I made them as distinct as they are in the original insect, and I presume that is sufficient."

"Well, well," I said, "perhaps you have — still I don't see them"; and I handed him the paper without additional remark, not wishing to ruffle his temper; but I was much surprised at the turn affairs had taken; his ill humor puzzled me — and, as for the drawing of the beetle, there were positively *no antennæ* visible, and the whole *did* bear a very close resemblance to the ordinary cuts of a death's-head.

He received the paper very peevishly, and was about to crumple it, apparently to throw it in the fire, when a casual glance at the design seemed suddenly to rivet his attention. In an instant his face grew violently red — in another as excessively pale. For some minutes he continued to scrutinize the drawing minutely where he sat. At length he arose, took a candle from the table, and proceeded to seat himself upon a sea-chest in the farthest corner of the room. Here again he made an anxious examination of the paper; turning it in all directions. He said nothing, however, and his conduct greatly astonished me; yet I thought it prudent not to exacerbate the growing moodiness of his temper by any comment. Presently he took from his coat pocket a wallet, placed the paper carefully in it, and deposited both in a writing-desk, which he locked. He now grew more composed in his demeanor; but his original air of enthusiasm had quite disappeared. Yet he seemed not so much sulky as abstracted. As the evening wore away he became more and more absorbed in reverie, from which no sallies of mine could arouse him. It had been my intention to pass the night at the hut, as I had frequently done before, but, seeing my host in this mood, I deemed it proper to take leave. He did not press me to remain, but, as I departed, he shook my hand with even more than his usual cordiality.

It was about a month after this (and during the interval I had seen nothing of Legrand) when I received a visit, at Charleston, from his man, Jupiter. I had never seen the good old negro look so dispirited, and I feared that some serious disaster had befallen my friend.

"Well, Jup," said I, "what is the matter now? — how is your master?"

"Why, to speak de troof, massa, him not so berry well as mought be."

"Not well! I am truly sorry to hear it. What does he complain of?"

"Dar! dat's it! — him neber plain of notin — but him berry sick for all dat."

"*Very* sick, Jupiter! — why didn't you say so at once? Is he confined to bed?"

"No, dat he aint! — he aint find nowhar — dat's just whar de shoe pinch — my mind is got to be berry hebby bout poor Massa Will."

"Jupiter, I should like to understand what it is you are talking about. You say your master is sick. Hasn't he told you what ails him?"

"Why, massa, taint worf while for to git mad about de matter — Massa Will say noffin at all aint de matter wid him — but den what make him go about looking dis here way, wid he head down and he soldiers up, and as white as a gose? And den he keep a syphon all de time — "

"Keeps a what, Jupiter?"

"Keeps a syphon wid de figgurs on de slate — de queerest figgurs I ebber did see. Ise gittin to be skeered, I tell you. Hab for to keep mighty tight eye pon him noovers. Todder day he gib me slip fore de sun up and was gone de whole ob de blessed day. I had a big stick ready cut for to gib him d — n good beating when he did come — but Ise sich a fool dat I hadn't de heart arter all — he look so berry poorly."

"Eh? — what? — ah yes! — upon the whole I think you had better not be too severe with the poor fellow — don't flog him, Jupiter — he can't very well stand it — but can you form no idea of what has occasioned this illness, or rather this change of conduct? Has anything unpleasant happened since I saw you?"

"No, massa, dey aint bin noffin unpleasant *since* den — 'twas *fore* den I'm feared — 'twas de berry day you was dare."

"How? what do you mean?"

"Why, massa, I mean de bug — dare now."

"The what?"

"De bug, — I'm berry sartain dat Massa Will bin bit somewhere bout de head by dat d — n goole-bug."

"And what cause have you, Jupiter, for such a supposition?"

"Claws enuff, massa, and mouff too. I nebber did see sich a d — n bug — he kick and he bite ebery ting what cum near him. Massa Will cotch him fuss, but had for to let him go gin mighty quick, I tell you — den was de time he must ha got de bite. I didn't like de look ob de bug mouff, myself, no how, so I wouldn't take hold ob him wid my finger, but I cotch him wid a piece ob paper dat I found. I rap him up in de paper and stuff piece ob it in he mouff— dat was de way."

"And you think, then, that your master was really bitten by the beetle, and that the bite made him sick?"

"I don't tink noffin about it — I nose it. What make him dream bout de goole so much, if taint cause he bit by de goole-bug? Ise heerd bout dem goole-bugs fore dis."

"But how do you know he dreams about gold?"

"How I know? — why cause he talk about it in he sleep — dat's how I nose."

"Well, Jup, perhaps you are right; but to what fortunate circumstance am I to attribute the honor of a visit from you to-day?"

"What de matter, massa?"

"Did you bring any message from Mr. Legrand?"

"No, massa, I bring dis here pissel"; and here Jupiter handed me a note which ran thus:

MY DEAR ______,

Why have I not seen you for so long a time? I hope you have not been so foolish as to take offence at any little *brusquerie* of mine; but no, that is improbable.

Since I saw you I have had great cause for anxiety. I have something to tell you, yet scarcely know how to tell it, or whether I should tell it at all.

I have not been quite well for some days past, and poor old Jup annoys me, almost beyond endurance, by his well-meant attentions. Would you believe it?—he had prepared a huge stick, the other day, with which to chastise me for giving him the slip, and spending the day, *solus*, among the hills on the main land. I verily believe that my ill looks alone saved me a flogging.

I have made no addition to my cabinet since we met.

If you can, in any way, make it convenient, come over with Jupiter. Do come. I wish to see you, *to-night*, upon business of importance. I assure you that it is of the *highest* importance.

Ever, yours, WILLIAM LEGRAND.

There was something in the tone of this note which gave me great uneasiness. Its whole style differed materially from that of Legrand. What could he be dreaming of? What new crotchet[5] possessed his excitable brain? What "business of the highest importance" could *he* possibly have to transact? Jupiter's account of him boded no good. I dreaded lest the continued pressure of misfortune had, at length, fairly unsettled the reason of my friend. Without a moment's hesitation, therefore, I prepared to accompany the negro.

Upon reaching the wharf, I noticed a scythe and three spades, all apparently new, lying in the bottom of the boat in which we were to embark.

"What is the meaning of all this, Jup?" I inquired.

"Him syfe, massa, and spade."

"Very true; but what are they doing here?"

"Him de syfe and de spade what Massa Will sis pon my buying for him in de town, and de debbil's own lot of money I had to gib for em."

"But what, in the name of all that is mysterious, is your 'Massa Will' going to do with scythes and spades?"

"Dat's more dan *I* know, and debbil take me if I don't blieve tis more dan he know, too. But it's all cum ob de bug."

Finding that no satisfaction was to be obtained of Jupiter, whose whole intellect seemed to be absorbed by "de bug," I now stepped into the boat and made sail. With a fair and strong breeze we soon ran into the little cove to the northward of Fort Moultrie, and a walk of some two miles brought us to the hut. It was about three in the afternoon when we arrived. Legrand had been awaiting us in eager expectation. He grasped my hand with a nervous *empressement* which alarmed me and strengthened the suspicions already entertained. His countenance was pale even to ghastliness, and his deep-set eyes glared with unnatural lustre. After some inquiries respecting his health, I asked him, not knowing what better to say, if he had yet obtained the *scarabæus* from Lieutenant G_____.

"Oh, yes," he replied, coloring violently, "I got it from him the next morning.

[5]*Strange attitude or habit.*

Nothing should tempt me to part with that *scarabæus*. Do you know that Jupiter is quite right about it?"

"In what way?" I asked, with a sad foreboding at heart.

"In supposing it to be a bug of *real gold*." He said this with an air of profound seriousness, and I felt inexpressibly shocked.

"This bug is to make my fortune," he continued, with a triumphant smile, "to re-instate me in my family possessions. Is it any wonder, then, that I prize it? Since Fortune has thought fit to bestow it upon me, I have only to use it properly and I shall arrive at the gold of which it is the index. Jupiter, bring me that *scarabæus*!"

"What! de bug, massa? I'd rudder not go fer trubble dat bug—you mus git him for your own self." Hereupon Legrand arose, with a grave and stately air, and brought me the beetle from a glass case in which it was enclosed. It was a beautiful *scarabæus*, and, at that time, unknown to naturalists—of course a great prize in a scientific point of view. There were two round, black spots near one extremity of the back, and a long one near the other. The scales were exceedingly hard and glossy, with all the appearance of burnished gold. The weight of the insect was very remarkable, and, taking all things into consideration, I could hardly blame Jupiter for his opinion respecting it; but what to make of Legrand's concordance with that opinion, I could not, for the life of me, tell.

"I sent for you," said he, in a grandiloquent tone, when I had completed my examination of the beetle, "I sent for you, that I might have your counsel and assistance in furthering the views of Fate and of the bug"—

"My dear Legrand," I cried, interrupting him, "you are certainly unwell, and had better use some little precautions. You shall go to bed, and I will remain with you a few days, until you get over this. You are feverish and"—

"Feel my pulse," said he.

I felt it, and, to say the truth, found not the slightest indication of fever.

"But you may be ill and yet have no fever. Allow me this once to prescribe for you. In the first place, go to bed. In the next"—

"You are mistaken," he interposed, "I am as well as I can expect to be under the excitement which I suffer. If you really wish me well, you will relieve this excitement."

"And how is this to be done?"

"Very easily. Jupiter and myself are going upon an expedition, into the hills, upon the main land, and, in this expedition we shall need the aid of some person in whom we can confide. You are the only one we can trust. Whether we succeed or fail, the excitement which you now perceive in me will be equally allayed."

"I am anxious to oblige you in any way," I replied; "but do you mean to say that this infernal beetle has any connection with your expedition into the hills?"

"It has."

"Then, Legrand, I can become a party to no such absurd proceeding."

"I am sorry—very sorry—for we shall have to try it by ourselves."

"Try it by yourselves! The man is surely mad!—but stay!—how long do you propose to be absent?"

"Probably all night. We shall start immediately, and be back, at all events, by sunrise."

"And will you promise me, upon your honor, that when this freak of yours is over, and the bug business (good God!) settled to your satisfaction, you will then return home and follow my advice implicitly, as that of your physician?"

"Yes; I promise; and now let us be off, for we have no time to lose."

With a heavy heart I accompanied my friend. We started about four o'clock—Legrand, Jupiter, the dog, and myself. Jupiter had with him the scythe and spades—the whole of which he insisted upon carrying—more through fear, it seemed to me, of trusting either of the implements within reach of his master, than from any excess of industry or complaisance. His demeanor was dogged in the extreme, and "dat d—n bug" were the sole words which escaped his lips during the journey. For my own part, I had charge of a couple of dark lanterns,[6] while Legrand contented himself with the *scarabæus*, which he carried attached to the end of a bit of whip-cord; twirling it to and fro, with the air of a conjuror, as he went. When I observed this last plain evidence of my friend's aberration of mind, I could scarcely refrain from tears. I thought it best, however, to humor his fancy, at least for the present, or until I could adopt some more energetic measures with a chance of success. In the mean time I endeavored, but all in vain, to sound him in regard to the object of the expedition. Having succeeded in inducing me to accompany him, he seemed unwilling to hold conversation upon any topic of minor importance, and to all my questions vouchsafed no other reply than "we shall see!"

We crossed the creek at the head of the island by means of a skiff, and, ascending the high grounds on the shore of the main land, proceeded in a northwesterly direction, through a tract of country excessively wild and desolate, where no trace of a human footstep was to be seen. Legrand led the way with decision; pausing only for an instant, here and there, to consult what appeared to be certain landmarks of his own contrivance upon a former occasion.

In this manner we journeyed for about two hours, and the sun was just setting when we entered a region infinitely more dreary than any yet seen. It was a species of table-land, near the summit of an almost inaccessible hill, densely wooded from base to pinnacle, and interspersed with huge crags that appeared to lie loosely upon the soil, and in many cases were prevented from precipitating themselves into the valleys below merely by the support of the trees against which they reclined. Deep ravines, in various directions, gave an air of still sterner solemnity to the scene.

[6]*Lanterns having shutters that can be slid across the opening to direct or conceal light.*

The natural platform to which we had clambered was thickly overgrown with brambles, through which we soon discovered that it would have been impossible to force our way but for the scythe; and Jupiter, by direction of his master, proceeded to clear for us a path to the foot of an enormously tall tulip-tree, which stood, with some eight or ten oaks, upon the level, and far surpassed them all, and all other trees which I had then ever seen, in the beauty of its foliage and form, in the wide spread of its branches, and in the general majesty of its appearance. When we reached this tree, Legrand turned to Jupiter, and asked him if he thought he could climb it. The old man seemed a little staggered by the question, and for some moments made no reply. At length he approached the tree, walked slowly around its huge trunk, and examined it with minute attention. When he had completed his scrutiny, he merely said,

"Yes, massa, Jup climb any tree he ebber see in he life."

"Then up with you as soon as possible, for it will soon be too dark to see what we are about."

"How far mus go up, massa?" inquired Jupiter.

"Get up the main trunk first, and then I will tell you which way to go — and here — stop! — take this beetle with you."

"De bug, Massa Will! — de goole bug!" cried the negro, drawing back in dismay — "what for mus tote de bug way up de tree? — d — n if I do!"

"If you are afraid, Jup, a great big negro like you, to take hold of a harmless little dead beetle, why you can carry it up by this string — but, if you do not take it up with you in some way, I shall be under the necessity of breaking your head with this shovel."

"What de matter now, massa?" said Jup, evidently shamed into compliance; "always want for to raise fuss wid old nigger. Was only funnin any how. *Me* feered de bug! what I keer for de bug?" Here he took cautiously hold of the extreme end of the string, and, maintaining the insect as far from his person as circumstances would permit, prepared to ascend the tree.

In youth, the tulip-tree, or *Liriodendron Tulipferum*, the most magnificent of American foresters, has a trunk peculiarly smooth, and often rises to a great height without lateral branches; but, in its riper age, the bark becomes gnarled and uneven, while many short limbs make their appearance on the stem. Thus the difficulty of ascension, in the present case, lay more in semblance than in reality. Embracing the huge cylinder, as closely as possible, with his arms and knees, seizing with his hands some projections, and resting his naked toes upon others, Jupiter, after one or two narrow escapes from falling, at length wriggled himself into the first great fork, and seemed to consider the whole business as virtually accomplished. The *risk* of the achievement was, in fact, now over, although the climber was some sixty or seventy feet from the ground.

"Which way mus go now, Massa Will?" he asked.

"Keep up the largest branch — the one on this side," said Legrand. The negro obeyed him promptly, and apparently with but little trouble; ascending higher and higher, until no glimpse of his squat figure could be obtained through the dense foliage which enveloped it. Presently his voice was heard in a sort of halloo.

"How much fudder is got for go?"

"How high up are you?" asked Legrand.

"Ebber so fur," replied the negro; "can see de sky fru de top ob de tree."

"Never mind the sky, but attend to what I say. Look down the trunk and count the limbs below you on this side. How many limbs have you passed?"

"One, two, tree, four, fibe — I done pass fibe big limb, massa, pon dis side."

"Then go one limb higher."

In a few minutes the voice was heard again, announcing that the seventh limb was attained.

"Now, Jup," cried Legrand, evidently much excited, "I want you to work your way out upon that limb as far as you can. If you see anything strange, let me know."

By this time what little doubt I might have entertained of my poor friend's insanity, was put finally at rest. I had no alternative but to conclude him stricken with lunacy, and I became seriously anxious about getting him home. While I was pondering upon what was best to be done, Jupiter's voice was again heard.

"Mos feerd for to ventur pon dis limb berry far — tis dead limb putty much all de way."

"Did you say it was a *dead* limb, Jupiter?" cried Legrand in a quavering voice.

"Yes, massa, him dead as de door-nail — done up for sartain — done departed dis here life."

"What in the name of heaven shall I do?" asked Legrand, seemingly in the greatest distress.

"Do!" said I, glad of an opportunity to interpose a word, "why come home and go to bed. *Do*—that's a fine fellow. It's getting late, and, besides, you remember your promise."

"Jupiter," cried he, without heeding me in the least, "do you hear me?"

"Yes, Massa Will, hear you ebber so plain."

"Try the wood well, then, with your knife, and see if you think it *very* rotten."

"Him rotten, massa, sure nuff," replied the negro in a few moments, "but not so berry rotten as mought be. Mought ventur out leetle way pon de limb by myself, dat's true."

"By yourself!— what do you mean?"

"Why I mean de bug. Tis *berry* hebby bug. Spose I drop him down fuss, and den de limb won't break wid just de weight ob one nigger."

"You infernal scoundrel!" cried Legrand, apparently much relieved, "what do you mean by telling me such nonsense as that? As sure as you drop that beetle I'll break your neck. Look here, Jupiter, do you hear me?"

"Yes, massa, needn't hollo at poor nigger dat style."

"Well! now listen!— if you will venture out on the limb as far as you think safe, and not let go the beetle, I'll make you a present of a silver dollar as soon as you get down."

"I'm gwine, Massa Will — deed I is," replied the negro very promptly — "mos out to the eend now."

"*Out to the end!*" here fairly screamed Legrand, "do you say you are out to the end of that limb?"

"Soon be to de eend, massa, — o-o-o-o-oh! Lor-gol-a-marcy! what *is* dis here pon de tree?"

"Well!" cried Legrand, highly delighted, "what is it?"

"Why taint noffin but a skull — somebody bin lef him head up de tree, and de crows done gobble ebery bit ob de meat off."

"A skull, you say!— very well!— how is it fastened to the limb?— what holds it on?"

"Sure nuff, massa; mus look. Why dis berry curous sarcumstance, pon my word — dare's a great big nail in de skull, what fastens ob it on to de tree."

"Well now, Jupiter, do exactly as I tell you — do you hear?"

"Yes, massa."

"Pay attention, then!—find the left eye of the skull."

"Hum! hoo! dat's good! why dare aint no eye lef at all."

"Curse your stupidity! Do you know your right hand from your left?"

"Yes, I nose dat — nose all bout dat — tis my lef hand what I chops de wood wid."

"To be sure! you are left-handed; and your left eye is on the same side as your left hand. Now, I suppose, you can find the left eye of the skull, or the place where the left eye has been. Have you found it?"

Here was a long pause. At length the negro asked,

"Is de lef eye of de skull pon de same side as de lef hand of de skull, too?— cause de skull aint got not a bit ob a hand at all — nebber mind! I got de lef eye now — here de lef eye! what mus do wid it?"

"Let the beetle drop through it, as far as the string will reach — but be careful and not let go your hold of the string."

"All dat done, Massa Will; mighty easy ting for to put de bug fru de hole — look out for him dare below!"

"Very well!— now just keep as you are for a few minutes."

During this colloquy no portion of Jupiter's person could be seen; but the beetle, which he had suffered to descend, was now visible at the end of the string, and glistened, like a globe of burnished gold, in the last rays of the setting sun, some of which still faintly illumined the eminence upon which we stood. The *scarabæus* hung quite clear of any branches, and, if allowed to fall, would have fallen at our feet. Legrand immediately took the scythe, and cleared with it a circular space, three or four yards in diameter, just beneath the insect, and, having accomplished this, ordered Jupiter to let go the string and come down from the tree.

Driving a peg, with great nicety, into the ground, at the precise spot where the beetle lay, my friend now produced from his pocket a tape-measure. Fastening one end of this at that point of the trunk of the tree which was nearest the peg, he unrolled it till it reached the peg, and thence farther unrolled it, in the direction already established by the two points of the tree and the peg, for the distance of fifty feet — Jupiter clearing away the brambles with the scythe. At the spot thus attained a second peg was driven, and about this, as a centre, a rude circle, about four feet in diameter, described. Taking now a spade himself, and giving one to Jupiter and one to me, Legrand begged us to set about digging as quickly as possible. To speak the truth, I had no especial relish for such amusement at any time, and, at that particular moment, would most willingly have declined it; for the night was coming on, and I felt much fatigued with the exercise already taken; but I saw no mode of escape, and was fearful of disturbing my poor friend's equanimity by a refusal. Could I have depended, indeed, upon Jupiter's aid, I would have had no hesitation in attempting to get the lunatic home by force; but I was too well assured of the old negro's disposition, to hope that he would assist me, under any circumstances, in a personal contest with his master. I made no doubt that the latter had been infected with some of the innumerable Southern superstitions about money buried, and that his fantasy had received confirmation by the finding of the *scarabæus*, or, perhaps, by Jupiter's obstinacy in maintaining it to be "a bug of real gold." A mind disposed to lunacy would readily be led away by such suggestions — especially if chiming in with favorite preconceived ideas — and then I called to mind the poor fellow's speech about the beetle's being "the index of his fortune." Upon the whole, I was sadly vexed and puzzled, but, at length, I concluded to make a virtue of necessity — to dig with a good will, and thus the sooner to convince him, by ocular demonstration, of the fallacy of the opinions he entertained.

The lanterns having been lit, we all fell to work with a zeal worthy a more rational cause; and, as the glare fell upon our persons and implements, I could not help thinking how picturesque a group we composed, and how strange and suspicious our labors must have appeared to any interloper who, by chance, might have stumbled upon our whereabouts.

We dug very steadily for two hours. Little was said; and our chief embarrassment lay in the yelpings of the dog, who took exceeding interest in our proceedings. He, at length, became so obstreperous that we grew fearful of his giving the alarm to some stragglers in the vicinity; — or, rather, this was the apprehension of Legrand; — for myself, I should have rejoiced at any interruption which might have enabled me to get the wanderer home. The noise was, at length, very effectually silenced by Jupiter, who, getting out of the hole with a dogged air of deliberation, tied the brute's mouth up with one of his suspenders, and then returned, with a grave chuckle, to his task.

When the time mentioned had expired, we had reached a depth of five feet, and yet no signs of any treasure became manifest. A general pause ensued, and I began to hope that the farce was at an end. Legrand, however, although evidently much disconcerted, wiped his brow thoughtfully and recommenced. We had excavated the entire circle of four feet diameter, and now we slightly enlarged the limit, and went to the farther depth of two feet. Still nothing appeared. The gold-seeker, whom I sincerely pitied, at length clambered from the pit, with the bitterest disappointment imprinted upon every feature, and proceeded, slowly and reluctantly, to put on his coat, which he had thrown off at the beginning of his labor. In the mean time I made no remark. Jupiter, at a signal from his master, began to gather up his tools. This done, and the dog having been unmuzzled, we turned in profound silence towards home.

We had taken, perhaps, a dozen steps in this direction, when, with a loud oath, Legrand strode up to Jupiter, and seized him by the collar. The astonished negro opened his eyes and mouth to the fullest extent, let fall the spades, and fell upon his knees.

"You scoundrel," said Legrand, hissing out the syllables from between his clenched teeth—"you infernal black villain!—speak, I tell you!—answer me this instant, without prevarication!—which—which is your left eye?"

"Oh, my Golly, Massa Will! aint dis here my lef eye for sartain?" roared the terrified Jupiter, placing his hand upon his *right* organ of vision, and holding it there with a desperate pertinacity, as if in immediate dread of his master's attempt at a gouge.

"I thought so!—I knew it!—hurrah!" vociferated Legrand, letting the negro go, and executing a series of curvets and caracols,[7] much to the astonishment of his valet, who, arising from his knees, looked, mutely, from his master to myself, and then from myself to his master.

"Come! we must go back," said the latter, "the game's not up yet"; and he again led the way to the tulip-tree.

"Jupiter," said he, when we reached its foot, "come here! was the skull nailed to the limb with the face outwards, or with the face to the limb?"

"De face was out, massa, so dat de crows could get at de eyes good, widout any trubble."

"Well, then, was it this eye or that through which you dropped the beetle?"—here Legrand touched each of Jupiter's eyes.

"Twas dis eye, massa—de lef eye—jis as you tell me," and here it was his right eye that the negro indicated.

"That will do—we must try it again."

Here my friend, about whose madness I now saw, or fancied that I saw, certain indications of method, removed the peg which marked the spot where the beetle fell, to a spot about three inches to the westward of its former position. Taking, now, the

[7]*Leaping half turns.*

tape-measure from the nearest point of the trunk to the peg, as before, and continuing the extension in a straight line to the distance of fifty feet, a spot was indicated, removed, by several yards, from the point at which we had been digging.

Around the new position a circle, somewhat larger than in the former instance, was now described, and we again set to work with the spades. I was dreadfully weary, but, scarcely understanding what had occasioned the change in my thoughts, I felt no longer any great aversion from the labor imposed. I had become most unaccountably interested — nay, even excited. Perhaps there was something, amid all the extravagant demeanor of Legrand — some air of forethought, or of deliberation, which impressed me. I dug eagerly, and now and then caught myself actually looking, with something that very much resembled expectation, for the fancied treasure, the vision of which had demented my unfortunate companion. At a period when such vagaries of thought most fully possessed me, and when we had been at work perhaps an hour and a half, we were again interrupted by the violent howlings of the dog. His uneasiness, in the first instance, had been, evidently, but the result of playfulness or caprice, but he now assumed a bitter and serious tone. Upon Jupiter's again attempting to muzzle him, he made furious resistance, and, leaping into the hole, tore up the mould frantically with his claws. In a few seconds he had uncovered a mass of human bones, forming two complete skeletons, intermingled with several buttons of metal, and what appeared to be the dust of decayed woollen. One or two strokes of a spade upturned the blade of a large Spanish knife, and, as we dug farther, three or four loose pieces of gold and silver coin came to light.

At sight of these the joy of Jupiter could scarcely be restrained, but the countenance of his master wore an air of extreme disappointment. He urged us, however, to continue our exertions, and the words were hardly uttered when I stumbled and fell forward, having caught the toe of my boot in a large ring of iron that lay half buried in the loose earth.

We now worked in good earnest, and never did I pass ten minutes of more intense excitement. During this interval we had fairly unearthed an oblong chest of wood, which, from its perfect preservation and wonderful hardness, had plainly been subjected to some mineralizing process — perhaps that of the Bi-chloride of Mercury. This box was three feet and a half long, three feet broad, and two and a half feet deep. It was firmly secured by bands of wrought iron, riveted, and forming a kind of open trellis-work over the whole. On each side of the chest, near the top, were three rings of iron — six in all — by means of which a firm hold could be obtained by six persons. Our utmost united endeavors served only to disturb the coffer very slightly in its bed. We at once saw the impossibility of removing so great a weight. Luckily, the sole fastenings of the lid consisted of two sliding bolts. These we drew back — trembling and panting with anxiety. In an instant, a treasure of incalculable value lay gleaming before us. As the rays of the lanterns fell within the pit, there flashed upwards a glow and a glare, from a confused heap of gold and of jewels, that absolutely dazzled our eyes.

I shall not pretend to describe the feelings with which I gazed. Amazement was, of course, predominant. Legrand appeared exhausted with excitement, and spoke very few words. Jupiter's countenance wore, for some minutes, as deadly a pallor as it is possible, in the nature of things, for any negro's visage to assume. He seemed stupefied — thunderstricken. Presently he fell upon his knees in the pit, and, burying his naked arms up to the elbows in gold, let them there remain, as if enjoying the luxury of a bath. At length, with a deep sigh, he exclaimed, as if in a soliloquy,

"And dis all cum ob de goole-bug! de putty goole bug! de poor little goole-bug, what I boosed in dat sabage kind ob style! Aint you shamed ob yourself, nigger?— answer me dat!"

It became necessary, at last, that I should arouse both master and valet to the expediency of removing the treasure. It was growing late, and it behooved us to make exertion, that we might get every thing housed before daylight. It was difficult to say what should be done, and much time was spent in deliberation — so confused were the ideas of all. We, finally, lightened the box by removing two thirds of its contents, when we were enabled, with some trouble, to raise it from the hole. The articles taken out were deposited among the brambles, and the dog left to guard them, with strict orders from Jupiter neither, upon any pretence, to stir from the spot, nor to open his mouth until our return. We then hurriedly made for home with the chest; reaching the hut in safety, but after excessive toil, at one o'clock in the morning. Worn out as we were, it was not in human nature to do more immediately. We rested until two, and had supper; starting for the hills immediately afterwards, armed with three stout sacks, which, by good luck, were upon the premises. A little before four we arrived at the pit, divided the remainder of the booty, as equally as might be, among us, and, leaving the holes unfilled, again set out for the hut, at which, for the second time, we deposited our golden burthens, just as the first faint streaks of the dawn gleamed from over the tree-tops in the East.

We were now thoroughly broken down; but the intense excitement of the time denied us repose. After an unquiet slumber of some three or four hours' duration, we arose, as if by preconcert, to make examination of our treasure.

The chest had been full to the brim, and we spent the whole day, and the greater part of the next night, in a scrutiny of its contents. There had been nothing like order or arrangement. Every thing had been heaped in promiscuously. Having assorted all with care, we found ourselves possessed of even vaster wealth than we had at first supposed. In coin there was rather more than four hundred and fifty thousand dollars — estimating the value of the pieces, as accurately as we could, by the tables of the period. There was not a particle of silver. All was gold of antique date and of great variety — French, Spanish, and German money, with a few English guineas, and some counters, of which we had never seen specimens before. There were several very large and heavy coins, so worn that we could make nothing of their inscriptions. There was no American money. The value of the jewels we found more difficulty in estimating. There were diamonds — some of them exceedingly large and fine — a hundred and ten in all, and not one of them small; eighteen rubies of remarkable brilliancy;— three hundred and ten emeralds, all very beautiful; and twenty-one sapphires, with an opal. These stones had all been broken from their settings and thrown loose in the chest. The settings themselves, which we picked out from among the other gold, appeared to have been beaten up with hammers, as if to prevent identification. Besides all this, there was a vast quantity of solid gold ornaments;— nearly two hundred massive finger and earrings;— rich chains — thirty of these, if I remember;— eighty-three very large and heavy crucifixes;—five gold censers of great value;— a prodigious golden punch-bowl, ornamented with richly chased vine-leaves and Bacchanalian figures; with two sword-handles exquisitely embossed, and many other smaller articles which I cannot recollect. The weight of these valuables exceeded three hundred and fifty pounds avoirdupois; and in this estimate I have not included one hundred and ninety-seven superb gold watches; three of the number being worth each five hundred dollars, if one. Many of them were very old, and as time keepers valueless; the works having suffered, more or less, from corrosion — but all were richly jeweled and in cases of great worth. We estimated the entire contents of the chest, that night, at a million and a half of dollars; and, upon the subsequent disposal of the trinkets and jewels (a few being retained for our own use) it was found that we had greatly undervalued the treasure.

When, at length, we had concluded our examination, and the intense excitement of the time had, in some measure, subsided, Legrand, who saw that I was dying with impatience for a solution of this most extraordinary riddle, entered into a full detail of all the circumstances connected with it.

"You remember," said he, "the night when I handed you the rough sketch I had made of the *scarabæus*. You recollect, also, that I became quite vexed at you for insisting that my drawing resembled a death's-head. When you first made this assertion I thought you were jesting; but afterwards I called to mind the peculiar spots on the back of the insect, and admitted to myself that your remark had some little foundation in fact. Still, the sneer at my graphic powers irritated me — for I am considered a good artist — and, therefore, when you handed me the scrap of parchment, I was about to crumple it up and throw it angrily into the fire."

"The scrap of paper, you mean," said I.

"No; it had much of the appearance of paper, and at first, I supposed it to be such, but, when I came to draw upon it, I discovered it, at once, to be a piece of very thin parchment. It was quite dirty, you remember. Well, as I was in the very act of crumpling it up, my glance fell upon the sketch at which you had been looking, and you may imagine my astonishment when I perceived, in fact, the figure of a death's-head just where, it seemed to me, I had made the drawing of the beetle. For a moment I was too much amazed to think with accuracy. I knew that my design was very different in detail from this — although there was a certain similarity in general outline.

Presently I took a candle, and seating myself at the other end of the room, proceeded to scrutinize the parchment more closely. Upon turning it over, I saw my own sketch upon the reverse, just as I had made it. My first idea, now, was mere surprise at the really remarkable similarity of outline — at the singular coincidence involved in the fact, that, unknown to me, there should have been a skull upon the other side of the parchment, immediately beneath my figure of the *scarabæus*, and that this skull, not only in outline, but in size, should so closely resemble my drawing. I say the singularity of this coincidence absolutely stupefied me for a time. This is the usual effect of such coincidences. The mind struggles to establish a connection — a sequence of cause and effect — and, being unable to do so, suffers a species of temporary paralysis. But, when I recovered from this stupor, there dawned upon me gradually a conviction which startled me even far more than the coincidence. I began distinctly, positively, to remember that there had been *no* drawing upon the parchment when I made my sketch of the *scarabæus*. I became perfectly certain of this; for I recollected turning up first one side and then the other, in search of the cleanest spot. Had the skull been then there, of course I could not have failed to notice it. Here was indeed a mystery which I felt it impossible to explain; but, even at that early moment, there seemed to glimmer, faintly, within the most remote and secret chambers of my intellect, a glow-worm-like conception of that truth which last night's adventure brought to so magnificent a demonstration. I arose at once, and putting the parchment securely away, dismissed all farther reflection until I should be alone.

"When you had gone, and when Jupiter was fast asleep, I betook myself to a more methodical investigation of the affair. In the first place I considered the manner in which the parchment had come into my possession. The spot where we discovered the *scarabæus* was on the coast of the main land, about a mile eastward of the island, and but a short distance above high water mark. Upon my taking hold of it, it gave me a sharp bite, which caused me to let it drop. Jupiter, with his accustomed caution, before seizing the insect, which had flown towards him, looked about him for a leaf, or something of that nature, by which to take hold of it. It was at this moment that his eyes, and mine also, fell upon the scrap of parchment, which I then supposed to be paper. It was lying half buried in the sand, a corner sticking up. Near the spot where we found it, I observed the remnants of the hull of what appeared to have been a ship's long boat. The wreck seemed to have been there for a very great while; for the resemblance to boat timbers could scarcely be traced.

"Well, Jupiter picked up the parchment, wrapped the beetle in it, and gave it to me. Soon afterwards we turned to go home, and on the way met Lieutenant G_____. I showed him the insect, and he begged me to let him take it to the fort. Upon my consenting, he thrust it forthwith into his waistcoat pocket, without the parchment in which it had been wrapped, and which I had continued to hold in my hand during his inspection. Perhaps he dreaded my changing my mind, and thought it best to make sure of the prize at once — you know how enthusiastic he is on all subjects connected with Natural History. At the same time, without being conscious of it, I must have deposited the parchment in my own pocket.

"You remember that when I went to the table, for the purpose of making a sketch of the beetle, I found no paper where it was usually kept. I looked in the drawer and found none there. I searched my pockets, hoping to find an old letter, when my hand fell upon the parchment. I thus detail the precise mode in which it came into my possession; for the circumstances impressed me with peculiar force.

"No doubt you will think me fanciful — but I had already established a kind of *connection.* I had put together two links of a great chain. There was a boat lying upon a sea-coast, and not far from the boat was a parchment —*not a paper*—with a skull depicted upon it. You will, of course, ask 'where is the connection?' I reply that the skull, or death's-head, is the well-known emblem of the pirate. The flag of the death's-head is hoisted in all engagements.

"I have said that the scrap was parchment, and not paper. Parchment is durable — almost imperishable. Matters of little moment are rarely consigned to parchment; since, for the mere ordinary purposes of drawing or writing, it is not nearly so well adapted as paper. This reflection suggested some meaning — some relevancy — in the death's-head. I did not fail to observe, also, the *form* of the parchment. Although one of its corners had been, by some accident, destroyed, it could be seen that the original form was oblong. It was just such a slip, indeed, as might have been chosen for a memorandum — for a record of something to be long remembered and carefully preserved."

"But," I interposed, "you say that the skull was *not* upon the parchment when you made the drawing of the beetle. How then do you trace any connection between the boat and the skull — since this latter, according to your own admission, must have been designed (God only knows how or by whom) at some period subsequent to your sketching the *scarabæus*?"

"Ah, hereupon turns the whole mystery; although the secret, at this point, I had comparatively little difficulty in solving. My steps were sure, and could afford but a single result. I reasoned, for example, thus: When I drew the *scarabæus*, there was no skull apparent upon the parchment. When I had completed the drawing I gave it to you, and observed you narrowly until you returned it. *You*, therefore, did not design the skull, and no one else was present to do it. Then it was not done by human agency. And nevertheless it was done.

"At this stage of my reflections I endeavored to remember, and *did* remember, with entire distinctness, every incident which occurred about the period in question. The weather was chilly (oh rare and happy accident!) and a fire was blazing upon the hearth. I was heated with exercise and sat near the table. You, however, had drawn a chair close to the chimney. Just as I placed the parchment in your hand, and as you were in the act of inspecting it, Wolf, the Newfoundland, entered, and leaped upon your shoulders. With your left hand you caressed him and kept him off, while your right, holding the parchment, was permitted to fall listlessly between your knees, and in close proximity to the fire. At one moment I thought the blaze had caught it, and was about to caution you, but, before I could speak, you had withdrawn it, and were engaged in its examination. When I considered all these particulars, I doubted not for a moment that *heat* had been the agent in bringing to light, upon the parchment, the skull which I saw designed upon it. You are well aware that chemical preparations exist, and have existed time out of mind, by means of which it is possible to write upon either paper or vellum, so that the characters shall become visible only when subjected to the action of fire.

"I now scrutinized the death's-head with care. Its outer edges — the edges of the drawing nearest the edge of the vellum — were far more *distinct* than the others. It was clear that the action of the caloric had been imperfect or unequal. I immediately kindled a fire, and subjected every portion of the parchment to a glowing heat. At first, the only effect was the strengthening of the faint lines in the skull; but, upon persevering in the experiment, there became visible, at the corner of the slip, diagonally opposite to the spot in which the death's-head was delineated, the figure of what I at first supposed to be a goat. A closer scrutiny, however, satisfied me that it was intended for a kid."

"Ha! ha!" said I, "to be sure I have no right to laugh at you — a million and a half of money is too serious a matter for mirth — but you are not about to establish a third link in your chain — you will not find any especial connection between your pirates and a goat — pirates, you know, have nothing to do with goats; they appertain to the farming interest."

"But I have just said that the figure was *not* that of a goat."

"Well, a kid then — pretty much the same thing."

"Pretty much, but not altogether," said Legrand. "You may have heard of one *Captain* Kidd.[8] I at once looked upon the figure of the animal as a kind of punning or hieroglyphical signature. I say signature; because its position upon the vellum suggested this idea. The death's-head at the corner diagonally opposite, had, in the same manner, the air of a stamp, or seal. But I was sorely put out by the absence of all else — of the body to my imagined instrument — of the text for my context."

"I presume you expected to find a letter between the stamp and the signature."

"Something of that kind. The fact is, I felt irresistibly impressed with a presentiment of some vast good fortune impending. I can scarcely say why. Perhaps, after all, it was rather a desire than an actual belief; — but do you know that Jupiter's silly words, about the bug being of solid gold, had a remarkable effect upon my fancy? And then the series of accidents and coincidences — these were so *very* extraordinary. Do you observe how mere an accident it was that these events should have occurred upon the *sole* day of all the year in which it has been, or may be, sufficiently cool for

[8] *William "Captain" Kidd, Scotsman executed for piracy.*

fire, and that without the fire, or without the intervention of the dog at the precise moment in which he appeared, I should never have become aware of the death's-head, and so never the possessor of the treasure?"

"But proceed — I am all impatience."

"Well; you have heard, of course, the many stories current — the thousand vague rumors afloat about money buried, somewhere upon the Atlantic coast, by Kidd and his associates. These rumors must have had some foundation in fact. And that the rumors have existed so long and so continuously, could have resulted, it appeared to me, only from the circumstance of the buried treasure still *remaining* entombed. Had Kidd concealed his plunder for a time, and afterwards reclaimed it, the rumors would scarcely have reached us in their present unvarying form. You will observe that the stories told are all about money-seekers, not about money-finders. Had the pirate recovered his money, there the affair would have dropped. It seemed to me that some accident — say the loss of a memorandum indicating its locality — had deprived him of the means of recovering it, and that this accident had become known to his followers, who otherwise might never have heard that treasure had been concealed at all, and who, busying themselves in vain, because unguided attempts, to regain it, had given first birth, and then universal currency, to the reports which are now so common. Have you ever heard of any important treasure being unearthed along the coast?"

"Never."

"But that Kidd's accumulations were immense, is well known. I took it for granted, therefore, that the earth still held them; and you will scarcely be surprised when I tell you that I felt a hope, nearly amounting to certainty, that the parchment so strangely found, involved a lost record of the place of deposit."

"But how did you proceed?"

"I held the vellum again to the fire, after increasing the heat; but nothing appeared. I now thought it possible that the coating of dirt might have something to do with the failure; so I carefully rinsed the parchment by pouring warm water over it, and, having done this, I placed it in a tin pan, with the skull downwards, and put the pan upon a furnace of lighted charcoal. In a few minutes, the pan having become thoroughly heated, I removed the slip, and, to my inexpressible joy, found it spotted, in several places, with what appeared to be figures arranged in lines. Again I placed it in the pan, and suffered it to remain another minute. Upon taking it off, the whole was just as you see it now."

Here Legrand, having re-heated the parchment, submitted it to my inspection. The following characters were rudely traced, in a red tint, between the death's-head and the goat:

53‡‡†305))6*;4826)4‡.)4‡);806*;48†8¶60))85;1‡
(;:‡*8†83(88)5*†;46(;88*96*?;8)*‡(;485);5*†2:*‡
(;4956*2(5*—4)8¶8*;4069285);)6†8)4‡‡;1(‡9;480

81;8:8‡1;48†85;4)485†528806*81(‡9;48;88;4(‡?34;
48)4‡;161;:188;‡?;

"But," said I, returning him the slip, "I am as much in the dark as ever. Were all the jewels of Golconda[9] awaiting me upon my solution of this enigma, I am quite sure that I should be unable to earn them."

"And yet," said Legrand, "the solution is by no means so difficult as you might be lead to imagine from the first hasty inspection of the characters. These characters, as any one might readily guess, form a cipher—that is to say, they convey a meaning; but then, from what is known of Kidd, I could not suppose him capable of constructing any of the more abstruse cryptographs. I made up my mind, at once, that this was of a simple species—such, however, as would appear, to the crude intellect of the sailor, absolutely insoluble without the key."

"And you really solved it?"

"Readily; I have solved others of an abstruseness ten thousand times greater. Circumstances, and a certain bias of mind, have led me to take interest in such riddles, and it may well be doubted whether human ingenuity can construct an enigma of the kind which human ingenuity may not, by proper application, resolve. In fact, having once established connected and legible characters, I scarcely gave a thought to the mere difficulty of developing their import.

"In the present case—indeed in all cases of secret writing—the first question regards the *language* of the cipher; for the principles of solution, so far, especially, as the more simple ciphers are concerned, depend upon, and are varied by, the genius of the particular idiom. In general, there is no alternative but experiment (directed by probabilities) of every tongue known to him who attempts the solution, until the true one be attained. But, with the cipher now before us, all difficulty was removed by the signature. The pun upon the word 'Kidd' is appreciable in no other language than the English. But for this consideration I should have begun my attempts with the Spanish and French, as the tongues in which a secret of this kind would most naturally have been written by a pirate of the Spanish main. As it was, I assumed the cryptograph to be English.

"You observe there are no divisions between the words. Had there been divisions, the task would have been comparatively easy. In such case I should have commenced with a collation and analysis of the shorter words, and, had a word of a single letter occurred, as is most likely, (*a* or *I*, for example), I should have considered the solution as assured. But, there being no division, my first step was to ascertain the predominant letters, as well as the least frequent. Counting all, I constructed a table, thus:

Of the character 8 there are 33.

;	"	26.
4	"	19.

[9]*City in India famous for its diamond cutting.*

‡)	"	16.
*	"	13.
5	"	12.
6	"	11.
†1	"	8.
0	"	6.
9 2	"	5.
: 3	"	4.
?	"	3.
¶	"	2.
—.	"	1.

"Now, in English, the letter which most frequently occurs is e. Afterwards, the succession runs thus: *a o i d h n r s t u y c f g l m w b k p q x z*. *E* predominates so remarkably that an individual sentence of any length is rarely seen, in which it is not the prevailing character.

"Here, then, we have, in the very beginning, the groundwork for something more than a mere guess. The general use which may be made of the table is obvious — but, in this particular cipher, we shall only very partially require its aid. As our predominant character is 8, we will commence by assuming it as the *e* of the natural alphabet. To verify the supposition, let us observe if the 8 be seen often in couples — for *e* is doubled with great frequency in English — in such words, for example, as 'meet,' 'fleet,' 'speed,' 'seen,' been,' 'agree,' &c. In the present instance we see it doubled no less than five times, although the cryptograph is brief.

"Let us assume 8, then, as *e*. Now, of all *words* in the language, 'the' is most usual; let us see, therefore, whether there are not repetitions of any three characters, in the same order of collocation, the last of them being 8. If we discover repetitions of such letters, so arranged, they will most probably represent the word 'the.' Upon inspection, we find no less than seven such arrangements, the characters being ;48. We may, therefore, assume that ; represents *t*, 4 represents *h*, and 8 represents *e*— the last being now well confirmed. Thus a great step has been taken.

"But, having established a single word, we are enabled to establish a vastly important point; that is to say, several commencements and terminations of other words. Let us refer, for example, to the last instance but one, in which the combination ;48 occurs — not far from the end of the cipher. We know that the ; immediately ensuing is the commencement of a word, and, of the six characters succeeding this 'the,' we are cognizant of no less than five. Let us set these characters down, thus, by the letters we know them to represent, leaving a space for the unknown —

t eeth.

"Here we are enabled, at once, to discard the '*th*,' as forming no portion of the word commencing with the first *t*; since, by experiment of the entire alphabet for a letter adapted to the vacancy, we perceive that no word can be formed of which this *th* can be a part. We are thus narrowed into

t ee,

and, going through the alphabet, if necessary, as before, we arrive at the word 'tree,' as the sole possible reading. We thus gain another letter, *r*, represented by (, with the words 'the tree' in juxtaposition.

"Looking beyond these words, for a short distance, we again see the combination ;48, and employ it by way of *termination* to what immediately precedes. We have thus this arrangement:

the tree ;4(‡?34 the,

or, substituting the natural letters, where known, it reads thus:

the tree thr‡?3h the.

"Now, if, in place of the unknown characters, we leave blank spaces, or substitute dots, we read thus:

the tree thr...h the,

when the word '*through*' makes itself evident at once. But this discovery gives us three new letters, *o*, *u* and *g*, represented by ‡ ? and 3.

"Looking, now, narrowly, through the cipher for combinations of known characters, we find, not very far from the beginning, this arrangement,

83(88, or egree,

which, plainly, is the conclusion of the word 'degree,' and gives us another letter, *d*, represented by †.

"Four letters beyond the word 'degree,' we perceive the combination

;46(;88*.

"Translating the known characters, and representing the unknown by dots, as before, we read thus:

th.rtee.

an arrangement immediately suggestive of the word 'thirteen,' and again furnishing us with two new characters, *i* and *n*, represented by 6 and *.

"Referring, now, to the beginning of the cryptograph, we find the combination,

53‡‡†.

"Translating, as before, we obtain

.good,

which assures us that the first letter is *A*, and that the first two words are 'A good.'

"It is now time that we arrange our key, as far as discovered, in a tabular form, to avoid confusion. It will stand thus:

5	represents	a
†	"	d
8	"	e
3	"	g
4	"	h

6	"	i
*	"	n
‡	"	o
(	"	r
;	"	t

"We have, therefore, no less than ten of the most important letters represented, and it will be unnecessary to proceed with the details of the solution. I have said enough to convince you that ciphers of this nature are readily soluble, and to give you some insight into the *rationale* of their development. But be assured that the specimen before us appertains to the very simplest species of cryptograph. It now only remains to give you the full translation of the characters upon the parchment, as unriddled. Here it is:

'A good glass in the bishop's hostel in the devil's seat forty-one degrees and thirteen minutes northeast and by north main branch seventh limb east side shoot from the left eye of the death's-head a bee line from the tree through the shot fifty feet out.'"

"But," said I, "the enigma seems still in as bad a condition as ever. How is it possible to extort a meaning from all this jargon about 'devil's seats,' 'death's heads,' and 'bishop's hotels?'"

"I confess," replied Legrand, "that the matter still wears a serious aspect, when regarded with a casual glance. My first endeavor was to divide the sentence into the natural division intended by the cryptographist."

"You mean, to punctuate it?"

"Something of that kind."

"But how was it possible to effect this?"

"I reflected that it had been a *point* with the writer to run his words together without division, so as to increase the difficulty of solution. Now, a not over-acute man, in pursuing such an object, would be nearly certain to overdo the matter. When, in the course of his composition, he arrived at a break in his subject which would naturally require a pause, or a point, he would be exceedingly apt to run his characters, at this place, more than usually close together. If you will observe the MS., in the present instance, you will easily detect five such cases of unusual crowding. Acting upon this hint, I made the division thus:

'A good glass in the Bishop's hostel in the Devil's seat—forty-one degrees and thirteen minutes—northeast and by north—main branch seventh limb east side—shoot from the left eye of the death's-head—a bee-line from the tree through the shot fifty feet out.'"

"Even this division," said I, "leaves me still in the dark."

"It left me also in the dark," replied Legrand, "for a few days; during which I made diligent inquiry, in the neighborhood of Sullivan's Island, for any building which went by the name of the 'Bishop's Hotel;' for, of course, I dropped the obsolete word 'hostel.' Gaining no information on the subject, I was on the point of extending my sphere of search, and proceeding in a more systematic manner, when, one morning, it entered into my head, quite suddenly, that this 'Bishop's Hostel' might have some reference to an old family, of the name of Bessop, which, time out of mind, had held possession of an ancient manor-house, about four miles to the northward of the Island. I accordingly went over to the plantation, and re-instituted my inquiries among the older negroes of the place. At length one of the most aged of the women said that she had heard of such a place as *Bessop's Castle*, and thought that she could guide me to it, but that it was not a castle, nor a tavern, but a high rock.

"I offered to pay her well for her trouble, and, after some demur, she consented to accompany me to the spot. We found it without much difficulty, when, dismissing her, I proceeded to examine the place. The 'castle' consisted of an irregular assemblage of cliffs and rocks — one of the latter being quite remarkable for its height as well as for its insulated and artificial appearance. I clambered to its apex, and then felt much at a loss as to what should be next done.

"While I was busied in reflection, my eyes fell upon a narrow ledge in the eastern face of the rock, perhaps a yard below the summit upon which I stood. This ledge projected about eighteen inches, and was not more than a foot wide, while a niche in the cliff just above it, gave it a rude resemblance to one of the hollow-backed chairs used by our ancestors. I made no doubt that here was the 'devil's seat' alluded to in the MS., and now I seemed to grasp the full secret of the riddle.

"The 'good glass,' I knew, could have reference to nothing but a telescope; for the word 'glass' is rarely employed in any other sense by seamen. Now here, I at once saw, was a telescope to be used, and a definite point of view, *admitting no variation*, from which to use it. Nor did I hesitate to believe that the phrases, 'forty-one degrees and thirteen minutes,' and 'northeast and by north,' were intended as directions for the leveling of the glass. Greatly excited by these discoveries, I hurried home, procured a telescope, and returned to the rock.

"I let myself down to the ledge, and found that it was impossible to retain a seat upon it except in one particular position. This fact confirmed my preconceived idea. I proceeded to use the glass. Of course, the 'forty-one degrees and thirteen minutes' could allude to nothing but elevation above the visible horizon, since the horizontal direction was clearly indicated by the words, 'northeast and by north.' This latter direction I at once established by means of a pocket-compass; then, pointing the glass as nearly at an angle of forty-one degrees of elevation as I could do it by guess, I moved it cautiously up or down, until my attention was arrested by a circular rift or opening in the foliage of a large tree that overtopped its fellows in the distance. In the centre of this rift I perceived a white spot, but could not, at first, distinguish what it was. Adjusting the focus of the telescope, I again looked, and now made it out to be a human skull.

"Upon this discovery I was so sanguine as to consider the enigma solved; for the phrase 'main branch, seventh limb, east side,' could refer only to the position of the skull upon the tree, while 'shoot from the left eye of the death's head' admitted, also, of but one interpretation, in regard to a search for buried treasure. I perceived that the design was to drop a bullet from the left eye of the skull, and that a bee-line, or, in other words, a straight line, drawn from the nearest point of the trunk through 'the shot,' (or the spot where the bullet fell,) and thence extended to a distance of fifty feet, would indicate a definite point — and beneath this point I thought it at least *possible* that a deposit of value lay concealed."

"All this," I said, "is exceedingly clear, and, although ingenious, still simple and explicit. When you left the Bishop's Hotel, what then?"

"Why, having carefully taken the bearings of the tree, I turned homewards. The instant that I left 'the devil's seat,' however, the circular rift vanished; nor could I get a glimpse of it afterwards, turn as I would. What seems to me the chief ingenuity in this whole business, is the fact (for repeated experiment has convinced me it *is* a fact) that the circular opening in question is visible from no other attainable point of view than that afforded by the narrow ledge upon the face of the rock.

"In this expedition to the 'Bishop's Hotel,' I had been attended by Jupiter, who had, no doubt, observed, for some weeks past, the abstraction of my demeanor, and took especial care not to leave me alone. But, on the next day, getting up very early, I contrived to give him the slip, and went into the hills in search of the tree. After much toil I found it. When I came home at night my valet proposed to give me a flogging. With the rest of the adventure I believe you are as well acquainted as myself."

"I suppose," said I, "you missed the spot, in the first attempt at digging, through Jupiter's stupidity in letting the bug fall through the right instead of through the left eye of the skull."

"Precisely. This mistake made a difference of about two inches and a half in the 'shot' — that is to say, in the position of the peg nearest the tree; and had the treasure been *beneath* the 'shot,' the error would have been of little moment; but 'the shot,' together with the nearest point of the tree, were merely two points for the establishment of a line of direction; of course the error, however trivial in the beginning, increased as we proceeded with the line, and by the time we had gone fifty feet, threw us quite off the scent. But for my deep-seated impressions that treasure was here somewhere actually buried, we might have had all our labor in vain."

"But your grandiloquence, and your conduct in swinging the beetle — how excessively odd! I was sure you were mad. And why did you insist upon dropping the bug, instead of a bullet, from the skull?"

"Why, to be frank, I felt somewhat annoyed by your evident suspicions touching my sanity, and so resolved to punish you quietly, in my own way, by a little bit of sober mystification. For this reason I swung the beetle, and for this reason I dropped it from the tree. An observation of yours about its great weight suggested the latter idea."

"Yes, I perceive — and now there is only one point which puzzles me. What are we to make of the skeletons found in the hole?"

"That is a question I am no more able to answer than yourself. There seems, however, only one plausible way of accounting for them — and yet it is dreadful to believe in such atrocity as my suggestion would imply. It is clear that Kidd — if Kidd indeed secreted this treasure, which I doubt not — it is clear that he must have had assistance in the labor. But this labor concluded, he may have thought it expedient to remove all participants in his secret. Perhaps a couple of blows with a mattock were sufficient, while his coadjutors were busy in the pit; perhaps it required a dozen — who shall tell?"

Variations on Poe, Expansions of the Form

Wilkie Collins (1824–1889)

The author of over twenty-five novels, at least fifty short stories, and several plays, William Wilkie Collins is best known for *The Woman in White* (1860) and *The Moonstone* (1868). Both novels were originally published in *All the Year Round*, a magazine run by his friend, mentor, and frequent collaborator Charles Dickens, whom he met in 1851. Influenced by his reading of gothic fiction and the English Romantic poets in his youth, Collins began his career as a published author in 1843. He has been credited with writing the first British detective story, "A Stolen Letter," in 1854, as well as with making important contributions to the modern English detective novel. In *The Woman in White*, the protagonist, an art teacher, attempts to solve a mystery involving the woman he loves, and, in *The Moonstone*, several sleuths, including the Scotland Yard professional Sergeant Cuff (whom critics regard as a precursor to Sherlock Holmes) try to figure out who stole a huge diamond. Besides being an early humorous tale of detection, following in the footsteps of Poe's "Thou Art the Man" and preceding Twain's "The Stolen White Elephant" by more than two decades, "Who Is the Thief?" uses an epistolary format in which multiple narrators tell the story, a device that Collins would use to great effect in both *The Woman in White* and *The Moonstone*. The year after it appeared in the *Atlantic*, the tale was renamed "The Biter Bit" and incorporated into *The Queen of Hearts* (1859), a series of ten linked short stories narrated by three brothers. In contrast to Poe's Dupin tales, in which an amateur sleuth bests the Police Prefect G_____ in solving mysteries, in "Who Is the Thief?" an inexperienced detective bungles the case, providing readers with an opportunity to finger the true culprit before the professionals step in and sort out the mess created by the self-important and narrow-minded Matthew Sharpin.

Who Is the Thief?

by Wilkie Collins

(1858)

(*Extracted from the Correspondence of the London Police.*)

From Chief Inspector Theakstone, of the Detective Police, to Sergeant Bulmer, of the same force.

London, 4th July, 18—.

SERGEANT BULMER,

This is to inform you that you are wanted to assist in looking up a case of importance, which will require all the attention of an experienced member of the force. The matter of the robbery on which you are now engaged you will please to shift over to the young man who brings you this letter. You will tell him all the circumstances of the case, just as they stand; you will put him up to the progress you have made (if any) towards detecting the person or persons by whom the money has been stolen; and you will leave him to make the best he can of the matter now in your hands. He is to have the whole responsibility of the case, and the whole credit of his success, if he brings it to a proper issue.

So much for the orders that I am desired to communicate to you. A word in your ear, next, about this new man who is to take your place. His name is Matthew Sharpin; and between ourselves, Sergeant, I don't think much of him. He has not served his time among the rank and file of the force. You and I mounted up, step by step, to the places we now fill; but this stranger, it seems, is to have the chance given him of dashing into our office at one jump,—supposing he turns out strong enough to take it. You will naturally ask me how he comes by this privilege. I can only tell you, that he has some uncommonly strong interest to back him in certain high quarters, which you and I had better not mention except under our breaths. He has been a lawyer's clerk; and he looks, to my mind, rather a mean, underhand sample of that sort of man. According to his own account,—by the bye, I forgot to say that he is wonderfully conceited in his opinion of himself, as well as mean and underhand to look at,—according to his own account, he leaves his old trade and joins ours of his own free will and preference. You will no more believe that than I do. My notion is, that he has managed to ferret out some private information, in connection with the affairs of one of his master's clients, which makes him rather an awkward customer to keep in the office for the future, and which, at the same time, gives him hold enough over his employer to make it dangerous to drive him into a corner by turning him away. I think the giving him this unheard-of chance among us is, in plain words, pretty much like giving him hush-money to keep him quiet. However that may be, Mr. Matthew Sharpin is to have the case now in your hands; and if he succeeds with it, he pokes his ugly nose into our office, as sure as fate. You have heard tell of some sad stuff they have been writing lately in the newspapers, about improving the efficiency of the Detective Police by mixing up a sharp lawyer's clerk or two along with them. Well, the experiment is now going to be tried; and Mr. Matthew Sharpin is the first lucky man who has been pitched on for the purpose. We shall see how this precious move succeeds. I put you up to it, Sergeant, so that you may not stand in your own light by giving the new man any cause to complain of you at head-quarters, and remain yours,

FRANCIS THEAKSTONE.

FROM MR. MATTHEW SHARPIN TO CHIEF INSPECTOR THEAKSTONE.

London, 5th July, 18—.

DEAR SIR,

Having now been favored with the necessary instructions from Sergeant Bulmer, I beg to remind you of certain directions which I have received, relating to the report of my future proceedings, which I am to prepare for examination at head-quarters.

The document in question is to be addressed to you. It is to be not only a daily report, but an hourly report as well, when circumstances may require it. All statements which I send to you, in this way, you are, as I understand, expected to examine carefully before you seal them up and send them in to the higher authorities. The object of my writing and of your examining what I have written is, I am informed, to give me, as an untried hand, the benefit of your advice, in case I want it (which I venture to think I shall not) at any stage of my proceedings. As the extraordinary circumstances of the case on which I am now engaged make it impossible for me to absent myself from the place where the robbery was committed, until I have made some progress towards discovering the thief, I am necessarily precluded from consulting you personally. Hence the necessity of my writing down the various details, which might, perhaps, be better communicated by word of mouth. This, if I am not mistaken, is the position in which we are now placed. I state my own impressions on the subject, in writing, in order that we may clearly understand each other at the outset,—and have the honor to remain your obedient servant,

MATTHEW SHARPIN.

FROM CHIEF INSPECTOR THEAKSTONE TO MR. MATTHEW SHARPIN.

London, 5th July, 18—.

SIR,

You have begun by wasting time, ink, and paper. We both of us perfectly well knew the position we stood in towards each other, when I sent you with my letter to Sergeant Bulmer. There was not the least need to repeat it in writing. Be so good as to employ your pen, in future, on the business actually in hand. You have now three separate matters on which to write me. First, you have to draw up a statement of your instructions received from Sergeant Bulmer, in order to show us that nothing has escaped your memory, and that you are thoroughly acquainted with all the circumstances of the case which has been entrusted to you. Secondly, you are to inform me what it is you propose to do. Thirdly, you are to report every inch of your progress, (if you make any,) from day to day, and, if need be, from hour to hour as well. This is your duty. As to what *my* duty may be, when I want you to remind me of it, I will write and tell you so. In the mean time I remain yours,

FRANCIS THEAKSTONE.

FROM MR. MATTHEW SHARPIN TO CHIEF INSPECTOR THEAKSTONE.

London, 6th July, 18—.

SIR,

You are rather an elderly person, and, as such, naturally inclined to be a little jealous of men like me, who are in the prime of their lives and their faculties. Under these circumstances, it is my duty to be considerate towards you, and not to bear too hardly on your small failings. I decline, therefore, altogether, to take offense at the tone of your letter; I give you the full benefit of the natural generosity of my nature; I sponge the very existence of your surly communication out of my memory; in short, Chief Inspector Theakstone, I forgive you, and proceed to business.

My first duty is to draw up a full statement of the instructions I have received from Sergeant Bulmer. Here they are at your service, according to my version of them.

At Number Thirteen, Rutherford Street, Soho, there is a stationer's shop. It is kept by one Mr. Yatman. He is a married man, but has no family. Besides Mr. and Mrs. Yatman, the other inmates of the house are a lodger, a young single man named Jay, who occupies the front room on the second floor,—a shopman, who sleeps in one of the attics,—and a servant-of-all-work, whose bed is in the back-kitchen. Once a week a charwoman comes to help this servant. These are all the persons who, on ordinary occasions, have means of access to the interior of the house, placed, as a matter of course, at their disposal.

Mr. Yatman has been in business for many years,—carrying on his affairs prosperously enough to realize a handsome independence for a person in his position. Unfortunately for himself, he endeavored to increase the amount of his property by speculating. He ventured boldly in his investments, luck went against him, and rather less than two years ago he found himself a poor man again. All that was saved out of the wreck of his property was the sum of two hundred pounds.

Although Mr. Yatman did his best to meet his altered circumstances, by giving up many of the luxuries and comforts to which he and his wife had been accustomed, he found it impossible to retrench so far as to allow of putting by any money from the income produced by his shop. The business has been declining of late years,—the cheap advertising stationers having done it injury with the public. Consequently, up to the last week, the only surplus property possessed by Mr. Yatman consisted of the two hundred pounds which had been recovered from the wreck of his fortune. This sum was placed as a deposit in a joint-stock bank of the highest possible character.

Eight days ago, Mr. Yatman and his lodger, Mr. Jay, held a conversation together on the subject of the commercial difficulties, which are hampering trade in all directions at the present time. Mr. Jay (who lives by supplying the newspapers with short paragraphs relating to accidents, offenses, and brief records of remarkable occurrences in general,—who is, in short, what they call a penny-a-liner) told his landlord that he had been in the city that day, and heard unfavorable rumors on the subject of the joint-stock banks. The rumors to which he alluded had already reached the ears of

Mr. Yatman from other quarters; and the confirmation of them by his lodger had such an effect on his mind,—predisposed, as it was, to alarm, by the experience of his former losses,—that he resolved to go at once to the bank and withdraw his deposit. It was then getting on toward the end of the afternoon; and he arrived just in time to receive his money before the bank closed.

He received the deposit in bank-notes of the following amounts:—one fifty-pound note, three twenty-pound notes, six ten-pound notes, and six five-pound notes. His object in drawing the money in this form was to have it ready to lay out immediately in trifling loans, on good security, among the small tradespeople of his district,—some of whom are sorely pressed for the very means of existence at the present time. Investments of this kind seemed to Mr. Yatman to be the most safe and the most profitable on which he could now venture.

He brought the money back in an envelope placed in his breast pocket; and asked his shopman, on getting home, to look for a small flat tin cash-box, which had not been used for years, and which, as Mr. Yatman remembered it, was exactly of the right size to hold the bank-notes. For some time the cash-box was searched for in vain. Mr. Yatman called to his wife to know if she had any idea where it was. The question was overheard by the servant-of-all-work, who was taking up the tea-tray at the time, and by Mr. Jay, who was coming down stairs on his way out to the theatre. Ultimately the cash-box was found by the shopman. Mr. Yatman placed the bank-notes in it, secured them by a padlock, and put the box in his coat pocket. It stuck out of the coat pocket a very little, but enough to be seen. Mr. Yatman remained at home, up stairs, all that evening. No visitors called. At eleven o'clock he went to bed, and put the cash-box under his pillow.

When he and his wife woke the next morning, the box was gone. Payment of the notes was immediately stopped at the Bank of England; but no news of the money has been heard of since that time.

So far, the circumstances of the case are perfectly clear. They point unmistakably to the conclusion that the robbery must have been committed by some person living in the house. Suspicion falls, therefore, upon the servant-of-all-work, upon the shopman, and upon Mr. Jay. The two first knew that the cash-box was being inquired for by their master, but did not know what it was he wanted to put into it. They would assume, of course, that it was money. They both had opportunities (the servant, when she took away the tea,—and the shopman, when he came, after shutting up, to give the keys of the till to his master) of seeing the cash-box in Mr. Yatman's pocket, and of inferring naturally, from its position there, that he intended to take it into his bedroom with him at night.

Mr. Jay, on the other hand, had been told, during the afternoon's conversation on the subject of joint-stock banks, that his landlord had a deposit of two hundred pounds in one of them. He also knew that Mr. Yatman left him with the intention of drawing that money out; and he heard the inquiry for the cash-box, afterwards, when he was coming down stairs. He must, therefore, have inferred that the money was in the house, and that the cash-box was the receptacle intended to contain it. That he could have had any idea, however, of the place in which Mr. Yatman intended to keep it for the night is impossible, seeing that he went out before the box was found, and did not return till his landlord was in bed. Consequently, if he committed the robbery, he must have gone into the bedroom purely on speculation.

Speaking of the bedroom reminds me of the necessity of noticing the situation of it in the house, and the means that exist of gaining easy access to it at any hour of the night. The room in question is the back room on the first floor. In consequence of Mrs. Yatman's constitutional nervousness on the subject of fire, which makes her apprehend being burnt alive in her room, in case of accident, by the hampering of the lock, if the key is turned in it, her husband has never been accustomed to lock the bedroom door. Both he and his wife are, by their own admission, heavy sleepers. Consequently, the risk to be run by any evil-disposed persons wishing to plunder the bedroom was of the most trifling kind. They could enter the room by merely turning the handle of the door; and if they moved with ordinary caution, there was no fear of their waking the sleepers inside. This fact is of importance. It strengthens our conviction that the money must have been taken by one of the inmates of the house, because it tends to show that the robbery, in this case, might have been committed by persons not possessed of the superior vigilance and cunning of the experienced thief.

Such are the circumstances, as they were related to Sergeant Bulmer, when he was first called in to discover the guilty parties, and, if possible, to recover the lost bank-notes. The strictest inquiry which he could institute failed of producing the smallest fragment of evidence against any of the persons on whom suspicion naturally fell. Their language and behavior, on being informed of the robbery, was perfectly consistent with the language and behavior of innocent people. Sergeant Bulmer felt, from the first, that this was a case for private inquiry and secret observation. He began by recommending Mr. and Mrs. Yatman to affect a feeling of perfect confidence in the innocence of the persons living under their roof; and he then opened the campaign by employing himself in following the goings and comings, and in discovering the friends, the habits, and the secrets of the maid-of-all-work.

Three days and nights of exertion on his own part, and on that of others who were competent to assist his investigations, were enough to satisfy him that there was no sound cause for suspicion against the girl.

He next practised the same precautions in relation to the shopman. There was more difficulty and uncertainty in privately clearing up this person's character without his knowledge, but the obstacles were at last smoothed away with tolerable success; and though there is not the same amount of certainty, in this case, which there was in the case of the girl, there is still fair reason for believing that the shopman has had nothing to do with the robbery of the cash-box.

As a necessary consequence of these proceedings, the range of suspicion now becomes limited to the lodger, Mr. Jay. When I presented your letter of introduction to Sergeant Bulmer, he had already made some inquiries on the subject of this young man. The result, so far, has not been at all favorable. Mr. Jay's habits are irregular; he frequents public houses, and seems to be familiarly acquainted with a great many dissolute characters; he is in debt to most of the tradespeople whom he employs; he has not paid his rent to Mr. Yatman for the last month; yesterday evening he came home excited by liquor, and last week he was seen talking to a prize-fighter. In short, though Mr. Jay does call himself a journalist, in virtue of his penny-a-line contributions to the newspapers, he is a young man of low tastes, vulgar manners, and bad habits. Nothing has yet been discovered, in relation to him, which redounds to his credit in the smallest degree.

I have now reported, down to the very last details, all the particulars communicated to me by Sergeant Bulmer. I believe you will not find an omission anywhere; and I think you will admit, though you are prejudiced against me, that a clearer statement of facts was never laid before you than the statement I have now made. My next duty is to tell you what I propose to do, now that the case is confided to my hands.

In the first place, it is clearly my business to take up the case at the point where Sergeant Bulmer has left it. On his authority, I am justified in assuming that I have no need to trouble myself about the maid-of-all-work and the shopman. Their characters are now to be considered as cleared up. What remains to be privately investigated is the question of the guilt or innocence of Mr. Jay. Before we give up the notes for lost, we must make sure, if we can, that he knows nothing about them.

This is the plan that I have adopted, with the full approval of Mr. and Mrs. Yatman, for discovering whether Mr. Jay is or is not the person who has stolen the cash-box:—

I propose, to-day, to present myself at the house in the character of a young man who is looking for lodgings. The back room on the second floor will be shown to me as the room to let; and I shall establish myself there to-night, as a person from the country, who has come to London to look for a situation in a respectable shop or office. By this means I shall be living next to the room occupied by Mr. Jay. The partition between us is mere lath and plaster. I shall make a small hole in it, near the cornice, through which I can see what Mr. Jay does in his room, and hear every word that is said when any friend happens to call on him. Whenever he is at home, I shall be at my post of observation. Whenever he goes out, I shall be after him. By employing these means of watching him, I believe I may look forward to the discovery of his secret — if he knows anything about the lost bank-notes — as to a dead certainty.

What you may think of my plan of observation I cannot undertake to say. It appears to me to unite the invaluable merits of boldness and simplicity. Fortified by this conviction, I close the present communication with feelings of the most sanguine description in regard to the future, and remain your obedient servant,

MATTHEW SHARPIN.

FROM THE SAME TO THE SAME.

7th July.

SIR,

As you have not honored me with any answer to my last communication, I assume, that, in spite of your prejudices against me, it has produced the favorable impression on your mind which I ventured to anticipate. Gratified and encouraged beyond measure by the token of approval which your eloquent silence conveys to me, I proceed to report the progress that has been made in the course of the last twenty-four hours.

I am now comfortably established next door to Mr. Jay; and I am delighted to say that I have two holes in the partition, instead of one. My natural sense of humor has led me into the pardonable extravagance of giving them both appropriate names. One I call my Peep-Hole, and the other my Pipe-Hole. The name of the first explains itself; the name of the second refers to a small tin pipe, or tube, inserted in the hole, and twisted so that the mouth of it comes close to my ear, when I am standing at my post of observation. Thus, while I am looking at Mr. Jay through my Peep-Hole, I can hear every word that may be spoken in his room through my Pipe-Hole.

Perfect candor — a virtue which I have possessed from my childhood — compels me to acknowledge, before I go any farther, that the ingenious notion of adding a Pipe-Hole to my proposed Peep-Hole originated with Mrs. Yatman. This lady — a most intelligent and accomplished person, simple, and yet distinguished, in her manners — has entered into all my little plans with an enthusiasm and intelligence which I cannot too highly praise. Mr. Yatman is so cast down by his loss, that he is quite incapable of affording me any assistance. Mrs. Yatman, who is evidently most tenderly attached to him, feels her husband's sad condition of mind even more acutely than she feels the loss of the money; and is mainly stimulated to exertion by her desire to assist in raising him from the miserable state of prostration into which he has now fallen. "The money, Mr. Sharpin," she said to me yesterday evening, with tears in her eyes, "the money may be regained by rigid economy and strict attention to business. It is my husband's wretched state of mind that makes me so anxious for the discovery of the thief. I may be wrong, but I felt hopeful of success as soon as you entered the house; and I believe, that, if the wretch who has robbed us is to be found, you are the man to discover him." I accepted this gratifying compliment in the spirit in which it was offered,—firmly believing that I shall be found, sooner or later, to have thoroughly deserved it.

Let me now return to business,— that is to say, to my Peep-Hole and my Pipe-Hole.

I have enjoyed some hours of calm observation of Mr. Jay. Though rarely at home, as I understand from Mrs. Yatman, on ordinary occasions, he has been indoors the whole of this day. That is suspicious, to begin with. I have to report, further, that he rose at a late hour this morning, (always a bad sign in a young man,) and that he lost a great deal of time, after he was up, in yawning and complaining to himself of headache. Like other debauched characters, he ate little or nothing for breakfast. His next proceeding was to smoke a pipe,—a dirty clay pipe, which a gentleman would have been ashamed to put between his lips. When he had done smoking, he took out pen, ink, and paper, and sat down to write, with a groan,—whether of remorse for having taken the bank-notes, or of disgust at the task before him, I am unable to say. After writing a few lines, (too far away from my Peep-Hole to give me a chance of reading over his shoulder,) he bent back in his chair, and amused himself by humming the tunes of popular songs. I recognized "My Mary Anne," "Bobbin' Around," and "Old Dog Tray," among other melodies. Whether these do or do not represent secret signals by which he communicates with his accomplices remains to be seen. After he had amused himself for some time by humming, he got up and began to walk about the room, occasionally stopping to add a sentence to the paper on his desk. Before long, he went to a locked cupboard and opened it. I strained my eyes eagerly, in expectation of making a discovery. I saw him take something carefully out of the cupboard,—he turned round,—it was only a pint-bottle of brandy! Having drunk some of the liquor, this extremely indolent reprobate lay dawn on his bed again, and in five minutes was fast asleep.

After hearing him snoring for at least two hours, I was recalled to my Peep-Hole by a knock at his door. He jumped up and opened it with suspicious activity. A very small boy, with a very dirty face, walked in, said, "Please, Sir, I've come for copy," sat down on a chair with his legs a long way from the ground, and instantly fell asleep! Mr. Jay swore an oath, tied a wet towel round his head, and, sitting down to his paper, began to cover it with writing as fast as his fingers could move the pen. Occasionally getting up to dip the towel in water and tie it on again, he continued at this employment for nearly three hours,—then folded up the leaves of writing, woke the boy, and gave them to him, with this remarkable expression: "Now, then, young sleepy-head, quick, march! If you see the Governor, tell him to have the money ready for me when I call for it." The boy grinned, and disappeared. I was sorely tempted to follow "sleepy-head," but, on reflection, considered it safest still to keep my eye on the proceedings of Mr. Jay.

In half an hour's time, he put on his hat and walked out. Of course, I put on my hat and walked out also. As I went down stairs, I passed Mrs. Yatman going up. The lady has been kind enough to undertake, by previous arrangement between us, to search Mr. Jay's room, while he is out of the way, and while I am necessarily engaged in the pleasing duty of following him wherever he goes. On the occasion to which I now refer, he walked straight to the nearest tavern, and ordered a couple of mutton-chops for his dinner. I placed myself in the next box to him, and ordered a couple of mutton-chops for my dinner. Before I had been in the room a minute, a young man of highly suspicious manners and appearance, sitting at a table opposite, took his glass of porter in his hand and joined Mr. Jay. I pretended to be reading the newspaper, and listened, as in duty bound, with all my might.

"How are you, my boy?" says the young man. "Jack has been here, inquiring after you."

"Did he leave any message?" asks Mr. Jay.

"Yes," says the other. "He told me, if I met with you, to say that he wished very particularly to see you to-night; and that he would give you a look-in, at Rutherford Street, at seven o'clock."

"All right," says Mr. Jay. "I'll get back in time to see him."

Upon this, the suspicious-looking young man finished his porter, and, saying that he was rather in a hurry, took leave of his friend, (perhaps I should not be wrong, if I said his accomplice?) and left the room.

At twenty-five minutes and a half past six,— in these serious cases it is important to be particular about time,— Mr. Jay finished his chops and paid his bill. At twenty-six minutes and three-quarters, I finished my chops and paid mine. In ten minutes more I was inside the house in Rutherford Street, and was received by Mrs. Yatman in the passage. That charming woman's face exhibited an expression of melancholy and disappointment which it quite grieved me to see.

"I am afraid, Ma'am," says I, "that you have not hit on any little criminating discovery in the lodger's room?"

She shook her head and sighed. It was a soft, languid, fluttering sigh,— and, upon my life, it quite upset me. For the moment, I forgot business, and burned with envy of Mr. Yatman.

"Don't despair, Ma'am," I said, with an insinuating mildness which seemed to touch her. "I have heard a mysterious conversation,— I know of a guilty appointment,— and I expect great things from my Peep-Hole and my Pipe-Hole to-night. Pray, don't be alarmed, but I think we are on the brink of a discovery."

Here my enthusiastic devotion to business got the better of my tender feelings. I looked,— winked,— nodded,— left her.

When I got back to my observatory, I found Mr. Jay digesting his mutton-chops in an arm-chair, with his pipe in his mouth. On his table were two tumblers, a jug of water, and the pint-bottle of brandy. It was then close upon seven o'clock. As the hour struck, the person described as "Jack" walked in.

He looked agitated,— I am happy to say he looked violently agitated. The cheerful glow of anticipated success diffused itself (to use a strong expression) all over me, from head to foot. With breathless interest I looked through my Peep-Hole, and saw the visitor— the "Jack" of this delightful case— sit down, facing me, at the opposite side of the table to Mr. Jay. Making allowance for the difference in expression which their countenances just now happened to exhibit, these two abandoned villains were so much alike in other respects as to lead at once to the conclusion that they were brothers. Jack was the cleaner man and the better-dressed of the two. I admit that, at the outset. It is, perhaps, one of my failings to push justice and impartiality to their utmost limits. I am no Pharisee[1]; and where Vice has its redeeming point, I say, let Vice have its due,—yes, yes, by all manner of means, let Vice have its due.

"What's the matter now, Jack?" says Mr. Jay.

"Can't you see it in my face?" says Jack. "My dear fellow, delays are dangerous. Let us have done with suspense, and risk it, the day after to-morrow."

"So soon as that?" cries Mr. Jay, looking very much astonished. "Well, I'm ready, if you are. But, I say, Jack, is Somebody Else ready, too? Are you quite sure of that?"

He smiled,—as he spoke,—a frightful smile, and laid a very strong emphasis on those two words, "Somebody Else." There is evidently a third ruffian, a nameless desperado, concerned in the business.

"Meet us to-morrow," says Jack, "and judge for yourself. Be in the Regent's Park at eleven in the morning, and look out for us at the turning that leads to the Avenue Road."

"I'll be there," says Mr. Jay. "Have a drop of brandy and water. What are you getting up for? You're not going already?"

"Yes, I am," says Jack. "The fact is, I'm so excited and agitated, that I can't sit still anywhere for five minutes together. Ridiculous as it may appear to you, I'm in a perpetual state of nervous flutter. I can't, for the life of me, help fearing that we shall be found out. I fancy that every man who looks twice at me in the street is a spy"—

At those words, I thought my legs would have given way under me. Nothing but strength of mind kept me at my Peep-Hole,—nothing else, I give you my word of honor.

"Stuff and nonsense!" cries Mr. Jay, with all the effrontery of a veteran in crime. "We have kept the secret up to this time, and we will manage cleverly to the end. Have a drop of brandy and water, and you will feel as certain about it as I do."

Jack steadily refused the brandy and water, and steadily persisted in taking his leave. "I must try if I can't walk it off," he said. "Remember to-morrow morning,—eleven o'clock,—Avenue-Road side of the Regent's Park."

With those words he went out. His hardened relative laughed desperately, and resumed the dirty clay pipe.

I sat down on the side of my bed, actually quivering with excitement. It is clear to me that no attempt has yet been made to change the stolen bank-notes; and I may add, that Sergeant Bulmer was of that opinion also, when he left the case in my hands. What is the natural conclusion to draw from the conversation which I have just set down? Evidently, that the confederates meet to-morrow to take their respective shares in the stolen money, and to decide on the safest means of getting the notes changed the day after. Mr. Jay is, beyond a doubt, the leading criminal in this business, and

[1]*Member of a strict, ancient Jewish sect; a self-righteous person.*

he will probably run the chief risk,—that of changing the fifty-pound note. I shall, therefore, still make it my business to follow him,—attending at the Regent's Park to-morrow, and doing my best to hear what is said there. If another appointment is made for the day after, I shall, of course, go to it. In the mean time, I shall want the immediate assistance of two competent persons (supposing the rascals separate after their meeting) to follow the two minor criminals. It is only fair to add, that, if the rogues all retire together, I shall probably keep my subordinates in reserve. Being naturally ambitious, I desire, if possible, to have the whole credit of discovering this robbery to myself.

8th July.

I have to acknowledge, with thanks, the speedy arrival of my two subordinates,—men of very average abilities, I am afraid; but, fortunately, I shall always be on the spot to direct them.

My first business this morning was, necessarily, to prevent possible mistakes, by accounting to Mr. and Mrs. Yatman for the presence of the two strangers on the scene. Mr. Yatman (between ourselves, a poor, feeble man) only shook his head and groaned. Mrs. Yatman (that superior woman) favored me with a charming look of intelligence. "Oh, Mr. Sharpin!" she said, "I am so sorry to see those two men! Your sending for their assistance looks as if you were beginning to be doubtful of success." I privately winked at her, (she is very good in allowing me to do so without taking offence,) and told her, in my facetious way, that she labored under a slight mistake. "It is because I am sure of success, Ma'am, that I send for them. I am determined to recover the money, not for my own sake only, but for Mr. Yatman's sake,—and for yours." I laid a considerable amount of stress on those last three words. She said, "Oh, Mr. Sharpin!" again,—and blushed of a heavenly red,—and looked down at her work. I could go to the world's end with that woman, if Mr. Yatman would only die.

I sent off the two subordinates to wait, until I wanted them, at the Avenue-Road gate of the Regent's Park. Half an hour afterwards I was following the same direction myself, at the heels of Mr. Jay.

The two confederates were punctual to the appointed time. I blush to record it, but it is, nevertheless, necessary to state, that the third rogue—the nameless desperado of my report, or, if you prefer it, the mysterious "Somebody Else" of the conversation between the two brothers—is—a woman! and, what is worse, a young woman! and, what is more lamentable still, a nice-looking woman! I have long resisted a growing conviction, that, wherever there is mischief in this world, an individual of the fair sex is inevitably certain to be mixed up in it. After the experience of this morning, I can struggle against that sad conclusion no longer. I give up the sex,—excepting Mrs. Yatman, I give up the sex.

The man named "Jack" offered the woman his arm. Mr. Jay placed himself on the other side of her. The three then walked away slowly among the trees. I followed them at a respectful distance. My two subordinates, at a respectful distance also, followed me.

It was, I deeply regret to say, impossible to get near enough to them to overhear their conversation, without running too great a risk of being discovered. I could only infer from their gestures and actions that they were all three talking together with extraordinary earnestness on some subject which deeply interested them. After having been engaged in this way a full quarter of an hour, they suddenly turned round to retrace their steps. My presence of mind did not forsake me in this emergency. I signed to the two subordinates to walk on carelessly and pass them, while I myself slipped dexterously behind a tree. As they came by me, I heard "Jack" address these words to Mr. Jay:—

"Let us say half-past ten to-morrow morning. And mind you come in a cab. We had better not risk taking one in this neighborhood."

Mr. Jay made some brief reply, which I could not overhear. They walked back to the place at which they had met, shaking hands there with an audacious cordiality which it quite sickened me to see. Then they separated. I followed Mr. Jay. My subordinates paid the same delicate attention to the other two.

Instead of taking me back to Rutherford Street, Mr. Jay led me to the Strand. He stopped at a dingy, disreputable-looking house, which, according to the inscription over the door, was a newspaper office, but which, in my judgment, had all the external appearance of a place devoted to the reception of stolen goods. After remaining inside for a few minutes, he came out, whistling, with his finger and thumb in his waistcoat pocket. Some men would now have arrested him on the spot. I remembered the necessity of catching the two confederates, and the importance of not interfering with the appointment that had been made for the next morning. Such coolness as this, under trying circumstances, is rarely to be found, I should imagine, in a young beginner, whose reputation as a detective policeman is still to make.

From the house of suspicious appearance Mr. Jay betook himself to a cigar-divan, and read the magazines over a cheroot. I sat at a table near him, and read the magazines, likewise, over a cheroot. From the divan he strolled to the tavern, and had his chops. I strolled to the tavern, and had my chops. When he had done, he went back to his lodging. When I had done, I went back to mine. He was overcome with drowsiness early in the evening, and went to bed. As soon as I heard him snoring, I was overcome with drowsiness, and went to bed also.

Early in the morning, my two subordinates came to make their report. They had seen the man named "Jack" leave the woman at the gate of an apparently respectable villa-residence, not far from the Regent's Park. Left to himself, he took a turning to the right, which led to a sort of suburban street, principally inhabited by shopkeepers. He stopped at the private door of one of the houses, and let himself in with his own key,—looking about him as he opened the door, and staring suspiciously at my men as they lounged along on the opposite side of the way. These were all the particulars which the subordinates had to communicate. I kept them in my room to attend on me, if needful, and mounted to my Peep-Hole to have a look at Mr. Jay.

He was occupied in dressing himself, and was taking extraordinary pains to destroy all traces of the natural slovenliness of his appearance. This was precisely what I expected. A vagabond like Mr. Jay knows the importance of giving himself a respectable look when he is going to run the risk of changing a stolen bank-note. At five minutes past ten o'clock he had given the last brush to his shabby hat and the last scouring with bread-crumb to his dirty gloves. At ten minutes past ten he was in the street, on his way to the nearest cab-stand, and I and my subordinates were close on his heels.

He took a cab, and we took a cab. I had not overheard them appoint a place of meeting, when following them in the Park on the previous day; but I soon found that we were proceeding in the old direction of the Avenue-Road gate. The cab in which Mr. Jay was riding turned into the Park slowly. We stopped outside, to avoid exciting suspicion. I got out to follow the cab on foot. Just as I did so, I saw it stop, and detected the two confederates approaching it from among the trees. They got in, and the cab was turned about directly. I ran back to my own cab, and told the driver to let them pass him, and then to follow as before.

The man obeyed my directions, but so clumsily as to excite their suspicions. We had been driving after them about three minutes, (returning along the road by which we had advanced,) when I looked out of the window to see how far they might be ahead of us. As I did this, I saw two hats popped out of the windows of their cab, and two faces looking back at me. I sank into my place in a cold sweat;—the expression is coarse, but no other form of words can describe my condition at that trying moment.

"We are found out!" I said, faintly, to my two subordinates. They stared at me in astonishment. My feelings changed instantly from the depth of despair to the height of indignation. "It is the cabman's fault. Get out, one of you," I said, with dignity,—"get out, and punch his head."

Instead of following my directions, (I should wish this act of disobedience to be reported at head-quarters,) they both looked out of the window. Before I could pull them back, they both sat down again. Before I could express my just indignation, they both grinned, and said to me, "Please to look out, Sir!"

I did look out. Their cab had stopped. Where? At a church door!

What effect this discovery might have had upon the ordinary run of men, I don't know. Being of a religious turn myself, it filled me with horror. I have often read of the unprincipled cunning of criminal persons; but I never before heard of three thieves attempting to double on their pursuers by entering a church! The sacrilegious audacity of that proceeding is, I should think, unparalleled in the annals of crime.

I checked my grinning subordinates by a frown. It was easy to see what was passing in their superficial minds. If I had not been able to look below the surface, I might, on observing two nicely dressed men and one nicely dressed woman enter a church before eleven in the morning, on a week day, have come to the same hasty conclusion at which my inferiors had evidently arrived. As it was, appearances had no power to impose on *me*. I got out, and, followed by one of my men, entered the church. The other man I sent round to watch the vestry door. You may catch a weasel asleep,—but not your humble servant, Matthew Sharpin!

We stole up the gallery-stairs, diverged to the organ-loft, and peeped through the curtains in front. There they were, all three, sitting in a pew below,—yes, incredible as it may appear, sitting in a pew below!

Before I could determine what to do, a clergyman made his appearance in full canonicals,[2] from the vestry door, followed by a clerk. My brain whirled, and my eyesight grew dim. Dark remembrances of robberies committed in vestries floated through my mind. I trembled for the excellent man in full canonicals;—I even trembled for the clerk.

The clergyman placed himself inside the altar rails. The three desperadoes approached him. He opened his book, and began to read. What?—you will ask.

I answer, without the slightest hesitation; the first lines of the Marriage Service.

My subordinate had the audacity to look at me, and then to stuff his pocket-handkerchief into his mouth. I scorned to pay any attention to him. After my own eyes had satisfied me that there was a parchment license in the clergyman's hand, and that it was consequently useless to come forward and forbid the marriage,—after I had seen this, and after I had discovered that the man "Jack" was the bridegroom, and that the man Jay acted the part of father and gave away the bride, I left the church, followed by my man, and joined the other subordinate outside the vestry door. Some people in my position would now have felt rather crestfallen, and would have begun to think that they had made a very foolish mistake. Not the faintest misgiving of any kind troubled me. I did not feel in the slightest degree depreciated in my own estimation. And even now, after a lapse of three hours, my mind remains, I am happy to say, in the same calm and hopeful condition.

As soon as I and my subordinates were assembled together, outside the church, I intimated my intention of still following the other cab, in spite of what had occurred. My reason for deciding on this course will appear presently. The two subordinates appeared to be astonished at my resolution. One of them had the impertinence to say to me, "If you please, Sir, who is it we are after? A man who has stolen money, or a man who has stolen a wife?" The other low person encouraged him by laughing. Both have deserved an official reprimand; and both, I sincerely trust, will be sure to get it.

[2]*Clothing worn by clergy members during religious ceremonies.*

When the marriage ceremony was over, the three got into their cab; and, once more, our vehicle (neatly hidden round the corner of the church, so that they could not suspect it to be near them) started to follow theirs. We traced them to the terminus of the South-Western Railway. The newly married couple took tickets for Richmond,—paying their fare with a half sovereign,[3] and so depriving me of the pleasure of arresting them, which I should certainly have done, if they had offered a banknote. They parted from Mr. Jay, saying, "Remember the address,—14, Babylon Terrace. You dine with us to-morrow week."[4] Mr. Jay accepted the invitation, and added, jocosely, that he was going home at once to get off his clean clothes, and to be comfortable and dirty again for the rest of the day. I have to report that I saw him home safely, and that he is comfortable and dirty again (to use his own disgraceful language) at the present moment.

Here the affair rests, having by this time reached what I may call its first stage. I know very well what persons of hasty judgments will be inclined to say of my proceedings thus far. They will assert that I have been deceiving myself, all through, in the most absurd way; they will declare that the suspicious conversations which I have reported referred solely to the difficulties and dangers of successfully carrying out a runaway match; and they will appeal to the scene in the church, as offering undeniable proof of the correctness of their assertions. So let it be. I dispute nothing, up to this point. But I ask a question, out of the depths of my own sagacity as a man of the world, which the bitterest of my enemies will not, I think, find it particularly easy to answer. Granted the fact of the marriage, what proof does it afford me of the innocence of the three persons concerned in that clandestine transaction? It gives me none. On the contrary, it strengthens my suspicions against Mr. Jay and his confederates, because it suggests a distinct motive for their stealing the money. A gentleman who is going to spend his honeymoon at Richmond wants money; and a gentleman who is in debt to all his tradespeople wants money. Is this an unjustifiable imputation of bad motives? In the name of outraged Morality, I deny it. These men have combined together, and have stolen a woman. Why should they not combine together and steal a cash-box? I take my stand on the logic of rigid Virtue; and I defy all the sophistry of Vice to move me an inch out of my position.

Speaking of virtue, I may add that I have put this view of the case to Mr. and Mrs. Yatman. That accomplished and charming woman found it difficult, at first, to follow the close chain of my reasoning. I am free to confess that she shook her head, and shed tears, and joined her husband in premature lamentation over the loss of the two hundred pounds. But a little careful explanation on my part, and a little attentive listening on hers, ultimately changed her opinion. She now agrees with me, that there is nothing in this unexpected circumstance of the clandestine marriage which absolutely tends to divert suspicion from Mr. Jay, or Mr. "Jack," or the runaway

[3]British gold coin equal to ten shillings. [4]One week from tomorrow.

lady,—"audacious hussy" was the term my fair friend used in speaking of her, but let that pass. It is more to the purpose to record, that Mrs. Yatman has not lost confidence in me, and that Mr. Yatman promises to follow her example and do his best to look hopefully for future results.

I have now, in the new turn that circumstances have taken, to await advice from your office. I pause for fresh orders with all the composure of a man who has got two strings to his bow. When I traced the three confederates from the church door to the railway terminus, I had two motives for doing so. First, I followed them as a matter of official business, believing them still to have been guilty of the robbery. Secondly, I followed them as a matter of private speculation, with a view of discovering the place of refuge to which the runaway couple intended to retreat, and of making my information a marketable commodity to offer to the young lady's family and friends. Thus, whatever happens, I may congratulate myself beforehand on not having wasted my time. If the office approves of my conduct, I have my plan ready for further proceedings. If the office blames me, I shall take myself off, with my marketable information, to the genteel villa-residence in the neighborhood of the Regent's Park. Any way, the affair puts money into my pocket, and does credit to my penetration, as an uncommonly sharp man.

I have only one word more to add, and it is this:—If any individual ventures to assert that Mr. Jay and his confederates are innocent of all share in the stealing of the cash-box, I, in return, defy that individual—though he may even be Chief Inspector Theakstone himself—to tell me who has committed the robbery at Rutherford Street, Soho.

Strong in that conviction,

I have the honor to be

Your very obedient servant,

MATTHEW SHARPIN.

FROM CHIEF INSPECTOR THEAKSTONE TO SERGEANT BULMER.

Birmingham, July 9th.

SERGEANT BULMER,

That empty-headed puppy, Mr. Matthew Sharpin, has made a mess of the case at Rutherford Street, exactly as I expected he would. Business keeps me in this town; so I write to you to set the matter straight. I enclose, with this, the pages of feeble scribble-scrabble which the creature, Sharpin, calls a report. Look them over; and when you have made your way through all the gabble, I think you will agree with me that the conceited booby has looked for the thief in every direction but the right one. The case is perfectly simple, now. Settle it at once; forward your report to me at this place; and tell Mr. Sharpin that he is suspended till further notice.

Yours,

FRANCIS THEAKSTONE.

FFROM SERGEANT BULMER TO CHIEF INSPECTOR THEAKSTONE.

London, July 10th.

INSPECTOR THEAKSTONE,

Your letter and enclosure came safe to hand. Wise men, they say, may always learn something, even from a fool. By the time I had got through Sharpin's maundering report of his own folly, I saw my way clear enough to the end of the Rutherford-Street case, just as you thought I should. In half an hour's time I was at the house. The first person I saw there was Mr. Sharpin himself.

"Have you come to help me?" says he.

"Not exactly," says I. "I've come to tell you that you are suspended till further notice."

"Very good," says he, not taken down, by so much as a single peg, in his own estimation. "I thought you would be jealous of me. It's very natural; and I don't blame you. Walk in, pray, and make yourself at home. I'm off to do a little detective business on my own account, in the neighborhood of the Regent's Park. Ta-ta, Sergeant, ta-ta!"

With those words he took himself out of my way,—which was exactly what I wanted him to do. As soon as the maid-servant had shut the door, I told her to inform her master that I wanted to say a word to him in private. She showed me into the parlor behind the shop; and there was Mr. Yatman, all alone, reading the newspaper.

"About this matter of the robbery, Sir," says I.

He cut me short, peevishly enough,—being naturally a poor, weak, womanish sort of man. "Yes, yes, I know," says he. "You have come to tell me that your wonderfully clever man, who has bored holes in my second-floor partition, has made a mistake, and is off the scent of the scoundrel who has stolen my money."

"Yes, Sir," says I. "That *is* one of the things I came to tell you. But I have got something else to say, besides that."

"Can you tell me who the thief is?" says he, more pettish than ever.

"Yes, Sir," says I, "I think I can."

He put down the newspaper, and began to look rather anxious and frightened.

"Not my shopman?" says he. "I hope, for the man's own sake, it's not my shopman."

"Guess again, Sir," says I.

"That idle slut, the maid?" says he.

"She is idle, Sir," says I, "and she is also a slut; my first inquiries about her proved as much as that. But she's not the thief."

"Then, in the name of Heaven, who is?" says he.

"Will you please to prepare yourself for a very disagreeable surprise, Sir?" says I. "And in case you lose your temper, will you excuse my remarking, that I am the stronger man of the two, and that, if you allow yourself to lay hands on me, I may unintentionally hurt you, in pure self-defence?"

He turned as pale as ashes, and pushed his chair two or three feet away from me.

"You have asked me to tell you, Sir, who has taken your money," I went on. "If you insist on my giving you an answer"—

"I do insist," he said, faintly. "Who has taken it?"

"Your wife has taken it," I said, very quietly, and very positively at the same time.

He jumped out of the chair as if I had put a knife into him, and struck his fist on the table, so heavily that the wood cracked again.

"Steady, Sir," says I. "Flying into a passion won't help you to the truth."

"It's a lie!" says he, with another smack of his fist on the table,—"a base, vile, infamous lie! How dare you"—

He stopped, and fell back into the chair again, looked about him in a bewildered way, and ended by bursting out crying.

"When your better sense comes back to you, Sir," says I, "I am sure you will be gentleman enough to make me an apology for the language you have just used. In the mean time, please to listen, if you can, to a word of explanation. Mr. Sharpin has sent in a report to our Inspector, of the most irregular and ridiculous kind; setting down, not only all his own foolish doings and sayings, but the doings and sayings of Mrs. Yatman as well. In most cases, such a document would have been fit only for the waste-paper basket; but, in this particular case, it so happens that Mr. Sharpin's budget of nonsense leads to a certain conclusion which the simpleton of a writer has been quite innocent of suspecting from the beginning to the end. Of that conclusion I am so sure, that I will forfeit my place, if it does not turn out that Mrs. Yatman has been practising upon the folly and conceit of this young man, and that she has tried to shield herself from discovery by purposely encouraging him to suspect the wrong persons. I tell you that confidently; and I will even go farther. I will undertake to give a decided opinion as to why Mrs. Yatman took the money, and what she has done with it, or with a part of it. Nobody can look at that lady, Sir, without being struck by the great taste and beauty of her dress"—

As I said those last words, the poor man seemed to find his powers of speech again. He cut me short directly, as haughtily as if he had been a duke instead of a stationer. "Try some other means of justifying your vile calumny against my wife," says he. "Her milliner's bill, for the past year, is on my file of receipted accounts, at this moment."

"Excuse me, Sir," says I, "but that proves nothing. Milliners, I must tell you, have a certain rascally custom which comes within the daily experience of our office. A married lady who wishes it can keep two accounts at her dress-maker's;—one is the account which her husband sees and pays; the other is the private account, which contains all the extravagant items, and which the wife pays secretly, by installments, whenever she can. According to our usual experience, these installments are mostly squeezed out of the housekeeping money. In your case, I suspect no installments have been paid; proceedings have been threatened; Mrs. Yatman, knowing your altered circumstances, has felt herself driven into a corner; and she has paid her private account out of your cashbox."

"I won't believe it!" says he. "Every word you speak is an abominable insult to me and to my wife."

"Are you man enough, Sir," says I, taking him up short, in order to save time and words, "to get that receipted bill you spoke of just now, off the file, and to come with me at once to the milliner's shop where Mrs. Yatman deals?"

He turned red in the face at that, got the bill directly, and put on his hat. I took out of my pocket-book the list containing the numbers of the lost notes, and we left the house together immediately.

Arrived at the milliner's (one of the expensive West-End houses, as I expected,) I asked for a private interview, on important business, with the mistress of the concern. It was not the first time that she and I had met over the same delicate investigation. The moment she set eyes on me, she sent for her husband. I mentioned who Mr. Yatman was, and what we wanted.

"This is strictly private?" says the husband. I nodded my head.

"And confidential?" says the wife. I nodded again.

"Do you see any objection, dear, to obliging the Sergeant with a sight of the books?" says the husband.

"None in the world, love, if you approve of it," says the wife.

All this while poor Mr. Yatman sat looking the picture of astonishment and distress, quite out of place at our polite conference. The books were brought,—and one minute's look at the pages in which Mrs. Yatman's name figured was enough, and more than enough, to prove the truth of every word that I had spoken.

There, in one book, was the husband's account, which Mr. Yatman had settled. And there, in the other, was the private account, crossed off also; the date of settlement being the very day after the loss of the cash-box. This said private account amounted to the sum of a hundred and seventy-five pounds, odd shillings; and it extended over a period of three years. Not a single installment had been paid on it. Under the last line was an entry to this effect: "Written to for the third time, June 23d." I pointed to it, and asked the milliner if that meant "last June." Yes, it did mean last June; and she now deeply regretted to say that it had been accompanied by a threat of legal proceedings.

"I thought you gave good customers more than three years' credit?" says I.

The milliner looks at Mr. Yatman, and whispers to me,—"Not when a lady's husband gets into difficulties."

She pointed to the account as she spoke. The entries after the time when Mr. Yatman's circumstances became involved were just as extravagant, for a person in his wife's situation, as the entries for the year before that period. If the lady had economized in other things, she had certainly not economized in the matter of dress.

There was nothing left now but to examine the cash-book, for form's sake. The money had been paid in notes, the amounts and numbers of which exactly tallied with the figures set down in my list.

After that, I thought it best to get Mr. Yatman out of the house immediately. He was in such a pitiable condition, that I called a cab and accompanied him home in it. At first, he cried and raved like a child; but I soon quieted him,— and I must add, to his credit, that he made me a most handsome apology for his language, as the cab drew up at his house-door. In return, I tried to give him some advice about how to set matters right, for the future, with his wife. He paid very little attention to me, and went up stairs muttering to himself about a separation. Whether Mrs. Yatman will come cleverly out of the scrape or not seems doubtful. I should say, myself, that she will go into screeching hysterics, and so frighten the poor man into forgiving her. But this is no business of ours. So far as we are concerned, the case is now at an end; and the present report may come to a conclusion along with it.

I remain, accordingly, yours to command,

THOMAS BULMER.

P.S.— I have to add, that, on leaving Rutherford Street, I met Mr. Matthew Sharpin coming back to pack up his things.

"Only think!" says he, rubbing his hands in great spirits, "I've been to the genteel villa-residence; and the moment I mentioned my business, they kicked me out directly. There were two witnesses of the assault; and it's worth a hundred pounds to me, if it's worth a farthing."

"I wish you joy of your luck," says I.

"Thank you," says he. "When may I pay you the same compliment on finding the thief?"

"Whenever you like," says I, "for the thief is found."

"Just what I expected," says he. "I've done all the work; and now you cut in, and claim all the credit.— Mr. Jay, of course?"

"No," says I.

"Who is it, then?" says he.

"Ask Mrs. Yatman," says I. "She'll tell you."

"All right! I'd much rather hear it from her than from you," says he,— and goes into the house in a mighty hurry.

What do you think of that, Inspector Theakstone? Would you like to stand in Mr. Sharpin's shoes? I shouldn't, I can promise you!

FROM CHIEF INSPECTOR THEAKSTONE TO MR. MATTHEW SHARPIN.

July 12th.

SIR,

Sergeant Bulmer has already told you to consider yourself suspended until further notice. I have now authority to add, that your services as a member of the Detective Police are positively declined. You will please to take this letter as notifying officially your dismissal from the force.

I may inform you, privately, that your rejection is not intended to cast any reflections on your character. It merely implies that you are not quite sharp enough for our purpose. If we are to have a new recruit among us, we should infinitely prefer Mrs. Yatman.

Your obedient servant,

FRANCIS THEAKSTONE.

NOTE ON THE PRECEDING CORRESPONDENCE—The editor is, unfortunately, not in a position to add any explanations of importance to the last of the published letters of Chief Inspector Theakstone. It has been discovered that Mr. Matthew Sharpin left the house in Rutherford Street a quarter of an hour after his interview outside of it with Sergeant Bulmer,—his manner expressing the liveliest emotions of terror and astonishment, and his left cheek displaying a bright patch of red, which looked as if it might have been the result of what is popularly termed a smart box on the ear. He was also heard, by the shopman at Rutherford Street, to use a very shocking expression in reference to Mrs. Yatman; and was seen to clinch his fist vindictively, as he ran round the corner of the street. Nothing more has been heard of him; and it is conjectured that he has left London with the intention of offering his valuable services to the provincial police.

On the interesting domestic subject of Mr. and Mrs. Yatman still less is known. It has, however, been positively ascertained that the medical attendant of the family was sent for in a great hurry on the day when Mr. Yatman returned from the milliner's shop. The neighboring chemist received, soon afterwards, a prescription of a soothing nature to make up for Mrs. Yatman. The day after, Mr. Yatman purchased some smelling-salts at the shop, and afterwards appeared at the circulating library to ask for a novel that would amuse an invalid lady. It has been inferred from these circumstances that he has not thought it desirable to carry out his threat of separating himself from his wife,—at least in the present (presumed) condition of that lady's sensitive nervous system.

Mark Twain (1835–1910)

Samuel Langhorne Clemens was born in Florida, Missouri, and raised in the Mississippi River town of Hannibal. At the age of eleven, when his father died, he quit school to work in a print shop and a few years later began writing. He became a journeyman printer, trained to become a riverboat pilot, briefly served on the Confederate side in the Civil War, and moved west when his brother Orion became an official of the Nevada Territory. In Nevada and later in California, he worked as a newspaper reporter and published humorous pieces under the pseudonym Mark Twain. His breakthrough came with the appearance of "The Celebrated Jumping Frog of Calaveras County" in 1865. Four years later his first book, *The Innocents Abroad*, based on newspaper dispatches about his 1867 journey to Europe and the Holy Land, was a success. He followed this up with *Roughing It* in 1872, *The Gilded Age* (written with Charles Dudley Warner) in 1873, *The Adventures of Tom Sawyer* in 1876, and *A Tramp Abroad* in 1880.

Between 1876 and 1884, he worked on his most famous book and a recognized classic of American literature, *Adventures of Huckleberry Finn*. Although Twain was the most important nineteenth-century American author after Poe to write detection, he clearly had reservations about what he saw as its formulaic nature, remarking in an 1896 notebook entry, "What a curious thing a 'detective' story is. And was there ever one the author needn't be ashamed of, except 'Murders in the Rue Morgue.'" He produced not only inferior detective stories, including "Simon Wheeler, Detective" and *Tom Sawyer, Detective*, but also texts in which elements of detection are subordinate yet nevertheless significantly contribute to the efficacy of the whole, such as "The Facts Concerning the Recent Carnival of Crime in Connecticut" and *Pudd'nhead Wilson* (1894).

Twain seems to have been more comfortable sending up the genre than writing it straight, yet even here the results are mixed. Unlike Bret Harte's "Stolen Cigar Case," Twain's meandering 1902 parody of Sherlock Holmes, "The Double-Barreled Detective Story," is only intermittently entertaining. In contrast, "The Stolen White Elephant," published two decades earlier, is a brilliant, funny parody of not only real-life detectives, including the New York Police Department and the nineteenth century's best-known private investigator Allan Pinkerton, but also dime novels and Poe's originary stories. In "The Stolen White Elephant" Twain burlesques specific types of detective fiction invented by Poe — the locked-room mystery, armchair detection, the stolen property tale, and the cryptographic story — and even alludes to one of the theories about the mysterious death of Poe himself.

The Stolen White Elephant

by Mark Twain

(1882)[1]

I.

The following curious history was related to me by a chance railway acquaintance. He was a gentleman more than seventy years of age, and his thoroughly good and gentle face and earnest and sincere manner imprinted the unmistakable stamp of truth upon every statement which fell from his lips. He said:—

You know in what reverence the royal white elephant of Siam is held by the people of that country. You know it is sacred to kings, only kings may possess it, and that it is, indeed, in a measure even superior to kings, since it receives not merely honor but worship. Very well; five years ago, when the troubles concerning the frontier line arose between Great Britain and Siam, it was presently manifest that Siam had been in the wrong. Therefore every reparation was quickly made, and the British representative stated that he was satisfied and the past should be forgotten. This greatly relieved the King of Siam, and partly as a token of gratitude, partly also, perhaps, to wipe out any little remaining vestige of unpleasantness which England might feel toward him, he wished to send the Queen a present,— the sole sure way of propitiating an enemy, according to Oriental ideas. This present ought not only to be a royal one, but transcendently royal. Wherefore, what offering could be so meet as that of a white elephant? My position in the Indian civil service was such that I was deemed peculiarly worthy of the honor of conveying the present to her Majesty. A ship was fitted out for me and my servants and the officers and attendants of the elephant, and in due time I arrived in New York harbor and placed my royal charge in admirable quarters in Jersey City. It was necessary to remain awhile in order to recruit the animal's health before resuming the voyage.

All went well during a fortnight,— then my calamities began. The white elephant was stolen! I was called up at dead of night and informed of this fearful misfortune. For some moments I was beside myself with terror and anxiety; I was helpless. Then I grew calmer and collected my faculties. I soon saw my course,— for, indeed, there was but the one course for an intelligent man to pursue. Late as it was, I flew to New York and got a policeman to conduct me to the headquarters of the detective force. Fortunately I arrived in time, though the chief of the force, the celebrated Inspector

[1]*Left out of "A Tramp Abroad," because it was feared that some of the particulars had been exaggerated, and that others were not true. Before these suspicions had been proven groundless, the book had gone to press.— M. T.*

Blunt, was just on the point of leaving for his home. He was a man of middle size and compact frame, and when he was thinking deeply he had a way of knitting his brows and tapping his forehead reflectively with his finger, which impressed you at once with the conviction that you stood in the presence of a person of no common order. The very sight of him gave me confidence and made me hopeful. I stated my errand. It did not flurry him in the least; it had no more visible effect upon his iron self-possession than if I had told him somebody had stolen my dog. He motioned me to a seat, and said, calmly,—

"Allow me to think a moment, please."

So saying, he sat down at his office table and leaned his head upon his hand. Several clerks were at work at the other end of the room; the scratching of their pens was all the sound I heard during the next six or seven minutes. Meantime the inspector sat there, buried in thought. Finally he raised his head, and there was that in the firm lines of his face which showed me that his brain had done its work and his plan was made. Said he,—and his voice was low and impressive,—

"This is no ordinary case. Every step must be warily taken; each step must be made sure before the next is ventured. And secrecy must be observed,—secrecy profound and absolute. Speak to no one about the matter, not even the reporters. I will take care of *them*; I will see that they get only what it may suit my ends to let them know." He touched a bell; a youth appeared. "Alaric, tell the reporters to remain for the present." The boy retired. "Now let us proceed to business,—and systematically. Nothing can be accomplished in this trade of mine without strict and minute method."

He took a pen and some paper. "Now—name of the elephant?"

"Hassan Ben Ali Ben Selim Abdallah Mohammed Moisé Alhammal Jamsetjejeebhoy Dhuleep Sultan Ebu Bhudpoor."

"Very well. Given name?"

"Jumbo."

"Very well. Place of birth?"

"The capital city of Siam."

"Parents living?"

"No,—dead."

"Had they any other issue besides this one?"

"None. He was an only child."

"Very well. These matters are sufficient under that head. Now please describe the elephant, and leave out no particular, however insignificant,—that is, insignificant from *your* point of view. To me in my profession there *are* no insignificant particulars; they do not exist."

I described,—he wrote. When I was done, he said,—

"Now listen. If I have made any mistakes, correct me."

He read as follows:—

"Height, 19 feet; length from apex of forehead to insertion of tail, 26 feet; length of trunk, 16 feet; length of tail, 6 feet; total length, including trunk, and tail, 48 feet; length of tusks, 9½ feet; ears in keeping with these dimensions; footprint resembles the mark left when one up-ends a barrel in the snow; the color of the elephant, a dull white; has a hole the size of a plate in each ear for the insertion of jewelry and possesses the habit in a remarkable degree of squirting water upon spectators and of maltreating with his trunk not only such persons as he is acquainted with, but even entire strangers; limps slightly with his right hind leg, and has a small scar in his left armpit caused by a former boil; had on, when stolen, a castle containing seats for fifteen persons, and a gold-cloth saddle-blanket the size of an ordinary carpet."

There were no mistakes. The inspector touched the bell, handed the description to Alaric, and said:—

"Have fifty thousand copies of this printed at once and mailed to every detective office and pawnbroker's shop on the continent." Alaric retired. "There,—so far, so good. Next, I must have a photograph of the property."

I gave him one. He examined it critically, and said—

"It must do, since we can do no better; but he has his trunk curled up and tucked into his mouth. That is unfortunate, and is calculated to mislead, for of course he does not usually have it in that position." He touched his bell.

"Alaric, have fifty thousand copies of this photograph made the first thing in the morning, and mail them with the descriptive circulars."

Alaric retired to execute his orders. The inspector said,—

"It will be necessary to offer a reward, of course. Now as to the amount?"

"What sum would you suggest?"

"To *begin* with, I should say,—well, twenty-five thousand dollars. It is an intricate and difficult business; there are a thousand avenues of escape and opportunities of concealment. These thieves have friends and pals everywhere—"

"Bless me, do you know who they are?"

The wary face, practised in concealing the thoughts and feelings within, gave me no token, nor yet the replying words, so quietly uttered:—

"Never mind about that. I may, and I may not. We generally gather a pretty shrewd inkling of who our man is by the manner of his work and the size of the game he goes after. We are not dealing with a pickpocket or a hall thief, now, make up your mind to that. This property was not 'lifted' by a novice. But, as I was saying, considering the amount of travel which will have to be done, and the diligence with which the thieves will cover up their traces as they move along, twenty-five thousand may be too small a sum to offer, yet I think it worth while to start with that."

So we determined upon that figure as a beginning. Then this man, whom nothing escaped which could by any possibility be made to serve as a clew, said:—

"There are cases in detective history to show that criminals have been detected through peculiarities in their appetites. Now, what does this elephant eat, and how much?"

"Well, as to *what* he eats,—he will eat *anything*. He will eat a man, he will eat a Bible—he will eat anything *between* a man and a Bible."

"Good,—very good, indeed, but too general. Details are necessary,—details are the only valuable things in our trade. Very well,—as to men. At one meal,—or, if you prefer, during one day,—how many men will he eat, if fresh?"

"He would not care whether they were fresh or not; at a single meal he would eat five ordinary men."

"Very good; five men; we will put that down. What nationalities would he prefer?"

"He is indifferent about nationalities. He prefers acquaintances, but is not prejudiced against strangers."

"Very good. Now, as to Bibles. How many Bibles would he eat at a meal?"

"He would eat an entire edition."

"It is hardly succinct enough. Do you mean the ordinary octavo,[2] or the family illustrated?"

"I think he would be indifferent to illustrations; that is, I think he would not value illustrations above simple letter-press."

"No, you do not get my idea. I refer to bulk. The ordinary octavo Bible weighs about two pounds and a half, while the great quarto[3] with the illustrations weighs ten or twelve. How many Doré Bibles[4] would he eat at a meal?"

"If you knew this elephant, you could not ask. He would take what they had."

"Well, put it in dollars and cents, then. We must get at it somehow. The Doré costs a hundred dollars a copy, Russia leather, beveled."

"He would require about fifty thousand dollars' worth,—say an edition of five hundred copies."

"Now that is more exact. I will put that down. Very well; he likes men and Bibles; so far, so good. What else will he eat? I want particulars."

"He will leave Bibles to eat bricks, he will leave bricks to eat bottles, he will leave bottles to eat clothing, he will leave clothing to eat cats, he will leave cats to eat oysters, he will leave oysters to eat ham, he will leave ham to eat sugar, he will leave sugar to eat pie, he will leave pie to eat potatoes, he will leave potatoes to eat bran; he will leave bran to eat hay, he will leave hay to eat oats, he will leave oats to eat rice, for he was mainly raised on it. There is nothing whatever that he will not eat but European butter, and he would eat that if he could taste it."

"Very good. General quantity at a meal,—say about—"

"Well, anywhere from a quarter to half a ton."

"And he drinks—"

"Everything that is fluid. Milk, water, whisky, molasses, castor oil, camphene, carbolic acid,—it is no use to go into particulars; whatever fluid occurs to you set it down. He will drink anything that is fluid, except European coffee."

[2]A book size of approximately 6 × 9 in. [3]A book size of approximately 9½ × 12 in. [4]A bible illustrated by Gustave Doré.

"Very good. As to quantity?"

"Put it down five to fifteen barrels,—his thirst varies; his other appetites do not."

"These things are unusual. They ought to furnish quite good clews toward tracing him."

He touched the bell.

"Alaric, summon Captain Burns."

Burns appeared. Inspector Blunt unfolded the whole matter to him, detail by detail. Then he said in the clear, decisive tones of a man whose plans are clearly defined in his head, and who is accustomed to command,—

"Captain Burns, detail Detectives Jones, Davis, Halsey, Bates, and Hackett to shadow the elephant."

"Yes, sir."

"Detail Detectives Moses, Dakin, Murphy, Rogers, Tupper, Higgins, and Bartholomew to shadow the thieves."

"Yes, sir."

"Place a strong guard—a guard of thirty picked men, with a relief of thirty—over the place from whence the elephant was stolen, to keep strict watch there night and day, and allow none to approach—except reporters—without written authority from me."

"Yes, sir."

"Place detectives in plain clothes in the railway, steamship, and ferry depots, and upon all roadways leading out of Jersey City, with orders to search all suspicious persons."

"Yes, sir."

"Furnish all these men with photograph and accompanying description of the elephant, and instruct them to search all trains and outgoing ferryboats and other vessels."

"Yes, sir."

"If the elephant should be found, let him be seized, and the information forwarded to me by telegraph."

"Yes, sir."

"Let me be informed at once if any clews should be found,—footprints of the animal, or anything of that kind."

"Yes, sir."

"Get an order commanding the harbor police to patrol the frontages vigilantly."

"Yes, sir."

"Dispatch detectives in plain clothes over all the railways, north as far as Canada, west as far as Ohio, south as far as Washington."

"Yes, sir."

"Place experts in all the telegraph offices to listen in to all messages; and let them require that all cipher dispatches be interpreted to them."

"Yes, sir."

"Let all these things be done with the utmost's secrecy,— mind, the most impenetrable secrecy."

"Yes, sir."

"Report to me promptly at the usual hour."

"Yes, Sir."

"Go!"

"Yes, sir."

He was gone.

Inspector Blunt was silent and thoughtful a moment, while the fire in his eye cooled down and faded out. Then he turned to me and said in a placid voice,—

"I am not given to boasting, it is not my habit; but—we shall find the elephant."

I shook him warmly by the hand and thanked him; and I *felt* my thanks, too. The more I had seen of the man the more I liked him, and the more I admired him and marveled over the mysterious wonders of his profession. Then we parted for the night, and I went home with a far happier heart than I had carried with me to his office.

II.

Next morning it was all in the newspapers, in the minutest detail. It even had additions,— consisting of Detective This, Detective That, and Detective The Other's "Theory" as to how the robbery was done, who the robbers were, and whither they had flown with their booty. There were eleven of these theories, and they covered all the possibilities; and this single fact shows what independent thinkers detectives are. No two theories were alike, or even much resembled each other, save in one striking particular, and in that one all the eleven theories were absolutely agreed. That was, that although the rear of my building was torn out and the only door remained locked, the elephant had not been removed through the rent, but by some other (undiscovered) outlet. All agreed that the robbers had made that rent only to mislead the detectives. That never would have occurred to me or to any other layman, perhaps, but it had not deceived the detectives for a moment. Thus, what I had supposed was the only thing that had no mystery about it was in fact the very thing I had gone furthest astray in. The eleven theories all named the supposed robbers, but no two named the same robbers; the total number of suspected persons was thirty-seven. The various newspaper accounts all closed with the most important opinion of all,— that of Chief Inspector Blunt. A portion of this statement read as follows:—

> "The chief knows who the two principals are, namely, 'Brick' Duffy and 'Red' McFadden. Ten days before the robbery was achieved he was already aware that it was

to be attempted, and had quietly proceeded to shadow these two noted villains; but unfortunately on the night in question their track was lost, and before it could be found again the bird was flown,—that is, the elephant.

"Duffy and McFadden are the boldest scoundrels in the profession; the chief has reasons for believing that they are the men who stole the stove out of the detective headquarters on a bitter night last winter,—in consequence of which the chief and every detective present were in the hands of the physicians before morning, some with frozen feet, others with frozen fingers, ears, and other members."

When I read the first half of that I was more astonished than ever at the wonderful sagacity of this strange man. He not only saw everything in the present with a clear eye, but even the future could not be hidden from him. I was soon at his office, and said I could not help wishing he had had those men arrested, and so prevented the trouble and loss; but his reply was simple and unanswerable:—

"It is not our province to prevent crime, but to punish it. We cannot punish it until it is committed."

I remarked that the secrecy with which we had begun had been marred by the newspapers; not only all our facts but all our plans and purposes had been revealed; even all the suspected persons had been named; these would doubtless disguise themselves now, or go into hiding.

"Let them. They will find that when I am ready for them my hand will descend upon them, in their secret places, as unerringly as the hand of fate. As to the newspapers, we *must* keep in with them. Fame, reputation, constant public mention,—these are the detective's bread and butter. He must publish his facts, else he will be supposed to have none; he must publish his theory, for nothing is so strange or striking as a detective's theory, or brings him so much wonderful respect; we must publish our plans, for these the journals insist upon having, and we could not deny them without offending. We must constantly show the public what we are doing, or they will believe we are doing nothing. It is much pleasanter to have a newspaper say, 'Inspector Blunt's ingenious and extraordinary theory is as follows,' than to have it say some harsh thing, or, worse still, some sarcastic one."

"I see the force of what you say. But I noticed that in one part of your remarks in the papers this morning you refused to reveal your opinion upon a certain minor point."

"Yes, we always do that; it has a good effect. Besides, I had not formed any opinion on that point, anyway."

I deposited a considerable sum of money with the inspector, to meet current expenses, and sat down to wait for news. We were expecting the telegrams to begin to arrive at any moment now. Meantime I reread the newspapers and also our descriptive circular, and observed that our $25,000 reward seemed to be offered only to detectives. I said I thought it ought to be offered to anybody who would catch the elephant. The inspector said:—

"It is the detectives who will find the elephant; hence the reward will go to the right place. If other people found the animal, it would only be by watching the detectives and taking advantage of clews and indications stolen from them, and that would entitle the detectives to the reward, after all. The proper office of a reward is to stimulate the men who deliver up their time and their trained sagacities to this sort of work, and not to confer benefits upon chance citizens who stumble upon a capture without having earned the benefits by their own merits and labors."

This was reasonable enough, certainly. Now the telegraphic machine in the corner began to click, and the following dispatch was the result:—

> FLOWER STATION, N. Y., 7.30 A.M.
>
> Have got a clew. Found a succession of deep tracks across a farm near here. Followed them two miles east without result; think elephant went west. Shall now shadow him in that direction.
>
> DARLEY, *Detective.*

"Darley's one of the best men on the force," said the inspector. "We shall hear from him again before long."

Telegram No. 2 came:—

> BARKER'S, N. J., 7.40 A.M.
>
> Just arrived. Glass factory broken open here during night, and eight hundred bottles taken. Only water in large quantity near here is five miles distant. Shall strike for there. Elephant will be thirsty. Bottles were empty.
>
> BAKER, *Detective.*

"That promises well, too," said the inspector. "I told you the creature's appetites would not be bad clews."

Telegram No. 3:—

> TAYLORVILLE, L. I. 8.15 A.M.
>
> A haystack near here disappeared during night. Probably eaten. Have got a clew, and am off.
>
> HUBBARD, *Detective.*

"How he does move around!" said the inspector. "I knew we had a difficult job on hand, but we shall catch him yet."

> FLOWER STATION, N. Y., 9 A.M.
>
> Shadowed the tracks three miles westward. Large, deep, and ragged. Have just met a farmer who says they are not elephant tracks. Says they are holes where he dug up saplings for shade-trees when ground was frozen last winter. Give me orders how to proceed.
>
> DARLEY, *Detective.*

"Aha! a confederate of the thieves! The thing, grows warm," said the inspector. He dictated the following telegram to Darley:—

Arrest the man and force him to name his pals. Continue to follow the tracks,—to the Pacific, if necessary.

Chief BLUNT.

Next telegram:—

CONEY POINT, PA., 8.45 A.M.

Gas office broken open here during night and three months' unpaid gas bills taken. Have got a clew and am away.

MURPHY, *Detective.*

"Heavens!" said the inspector; "would he eat gas bills?"

"Through ignorance,—yes; but they cannot support life. At least, unassisted."

Now came this exciting telegram:—

IRONVILLE, N. Y., 9.30 A.M.

Just arrived. This village in consternation. Elephant passed through here at five this morning. Some say he went east, some say west, some north, some south,—but all say they did not wait to notice, particularly. He killed a horse; have secure a piece of it for a clew. Killed it with his trunk; from style of blow, think he struck it left-handed. From position in which horse lies, think elephant traveled northward along line Berkley Railway. Has four and a half hours' start, but I move on his track at once.

HAWES, *Detective.*

I uttered exclamations of joy. The inspector was as self-contained as a graven image. He calmly touched his bell.

"Alaric, send Captain Burns here."

Burns appeared.

"How many men are ready for instant orders?"

"Ninety-six, sir."

"Send them north at once. Let them concentrate along the line of the Berkley road north of Ironville."

"Yes, sir."

"Let them conduct their movements with the utmost secrecy. As fast as others are at liberty, hold them for orders."

"Yes, sir."

"Go!"

"Yes, sir."

Presently came another telegram:—

SAGE CORNERS, N. Y., 10.30.

Just arrived. Elephant passed through here at 8.15. All escaped from the town but a policeman. Apparently elephant did not strike at policeman, but at the lamp-post. Got both. I have secured a portion of the policeman as clew.

STUMM, *Detective.*

"So the elephant has turned westward," said the inspector. "However, he will not escape, for my men are scattered all over that region."

The next telegram said:—

GLOVER'S, 11.15.

Just arrived. Village deserted, except sick and aged. Elephant passed through three quarters of an hour ago. The anti-temperance mass meeting was in session; he put his trunk in at a window and washed it out with water from cistern. Some swallowed it—since dead; several drowned. Detectives Cross and O'Shaughnessy were passing through town, but going south,—so missed elephant. Whole region for many miles around in terror,—people flying from their homes. Wherever they turn they meet elephant, and many are killed.

BRANT, *Detective.*

I could have shed tears, this havoc so distressed me. But the inspector only said,—

"You see,—we are closing in on him. He feels our presence; he has turned eastward again."

Yet further troublous news was in store for us. The telegraph brought this:—

HOGANPORT, 12.19.

Just arrived. Elephant passed through half an hour ago, creating wildest fright and excitement. Elephant raged around streets; two plumbers going by, killed one—other escaped. Regret general.

O'FLAHERTY, *Detective.*

"Now he is right in the midst of my men," said the inspector. "Nothing can save him."

A succession of telegrams came from detectives who were scattered through New Jersey and Pennsylvania, and who were following clews consisting of ravaged barns, factories, and Sunday school libraries, with high hopes,—hopes amounting to certainties, indeed. The inspector said,—

"I wish I could communicate with them and order them north, but that is impossible. A detective only visits a telegraph office to send his report; then he is off again, and you don't know where to put your hand on him."

Now came this despatch:—

BRIDGEPORT, CT., 12.15.

Barnum[5] offers rate of $4,000 a year for exclusive privilege of using elephant as traveling advertising medium from now till detectives find him. Wants to paste circus-posters on him. Desires immediate answer.

BOGGS, *Detective.*

"That is perfectly absurd!" I exclaimed.

[5]*American showman who bought a huge elephant named Jumbo from the London Zoo and exhibited it widely in the United States and Canada.*

"Of course it is," said the inspector. "Evidently Mr. Barnum, who thinks he is so sharp, does not know me,—but I know him."

Then he dictated this answer to the despatch:—

> Mr. Barnum's offer declined. Make it $7,000 or nothing.
>
> *Chief* BLUNT.

"There. We shall not have to wait long for an answer. Mr. Barnum is not at home; he is in the telegraph office,—it is his way when he has business on hand. Inside of three—"

> DONE.—P. T. BARNUM.

So interrupted the clicking telegraphic instrument. Before I could make a comment upon this extraordinary episode, the following despatch carried my thoughts into another and very distressing channel:—

> BOLIVIA, N. Y., 12.50.
>
> Elephant arrived here from the south and passed through toward the forest at 11.50, dispersing a funeral on the way, and diminishing the mourners by two. Citizens fired some small cannon-balls into him, and they fled. Detective Burke and I arrived ten minutes later, from the north, but mistook some excavations for footprints, and so lost a good deal of time; but at last we struck the right trail and followed it to the woods. We then got down on our hands and knees and continued to keep a sharp eye on the track, and so shadowed it into the brush. Burke was in advance. Unfortunately the animal had stopped to rest; therefore, Burke having his head down, intent upon the track, butted up against the elephant's hind legs before he was aware of his vicinity. Burke instantly arose to his feet, seized the tail, and exclaimed joyfully, "I claim the re—" but got no further, for a single blow of the huge trunk laid the brave fellow's fragments low in death. I fled rearward, and the elephant turned and shadowed me to the edge of the wood, making tremendous speed, and I should inevitably have been lost, but that the remains of the funeral providentially intervened again and diverted his attention. I have just learned that nothing of that funeral is now left; but this is no loss, for there is abundance of material for another. Meantime, the elephant has disappeared again.
>
> MULROONEY, *Detective.*

We heard no news except from the diligent and confident detectives scattered about New Jersey, Pennsylvania, Delaware, and Virginia,—who were all following fresh and encouraging clews,—until shortly after 2 P.M., when this telegram came:—

> BAXTER CENTRE, 2.15.
>
> Elephant been here, plastered over with circus-bills, and broke up a revival, striking down and damaging many who were on the point of entering upon a better life. Citizens penned him up and established a guard. When Detective Brown and I arrived, some time after, we entered enclosure and proceeded to identify elephant by photograph and description. All marks tallied exactly except one, which we could not see,—the boil-scar under armpit. To make sure, Brown crept under to look, and was immediately brained,—that is, head crushed and destroyed, though nothing issued from debris. All fled; so did elephant, striking right and left with much effect. He

escaped, but left bold blood-track from cannon-wounds. Rediscovery certain. He broke southward, through a dense forest.

BRENT, *Detective.*

That was the last telegram. At nightfall a fog shut down which was so dense that objects but three feet away could not be discerned. This lasted all night. The ferry-boats and even the omnibuses had to stop running.

III.

Next morning the papers were as full of detective theories as before; they had all our tragic facts in detail also, and a great many more which they had received from their telegraphic correspondents. Column after column was occupied, a third of its way down, with glaring head-lines, which it made my heart sick to read. Their general tone was like this:—

"THE WHITE ELEPHANT AT LARGE! HE MOVES UPON HIS FATAL MARCH! WHOLE VILLAGES DESERTED BY THEIR FRIGHT-STRICKEN OCCUPANTS! PALE TERROR GOES BEFORE HIM, DEATH AND DEVASTATION FOLLOW AFTER! AFTER THESE, THE DETECTIVES! BARNS DESTROYED, FACTORIES GUTTED, HARVESTS DEVOURED, PUBLIC ASSEMBLAGES DISPERSED, ACCOMPANIED BY SCENES OF CARNAGE IMPOSSIBLE TO DESCRIBE! THEORIES OF THIRTY-FOUR OF THE MOST DISTINGUISHED DETECTIVES ON THE FORCE! THEORY OF CHIEF BLUNT!"

"There!" said Inspector Blunt, almost betrayed into excitement, "this is magnificent! This is the greatest windfall that any detective organization ever had. The fame of it will travel to the ends of the earth, and endure to the end of time, and my name with it."

But there was no joy for me. I felt as if I had committed all those red crimes, and that the elephant was only my irresponsible agent. And how the list had grown! In one place he had "interfered with an election and killed five repeaters." He had followed this act with the destruction of two pool fellows, named O'Donohue and McFlannigan, who had "found a refuge in the home of the oppressed of all lands only the day before, and were in the act of exercising for the first time the noble right of American citizens at the polls, when stricken down by the relentless hand of the Scourge of Siam." In another, he had "found a crazy sensation-preacher preparing his next season's heroic attacks on the dance, the theater, and other things which can't strike back, and had stepped on him." And in still another place he had "killed a lightning-rod agent." And so the list went on, growing redder and redder, and more and more heart-breaking. Sixty persons had been killed, and two hundred and forty wounded. All the accounts bore just testimony to the activity and devotion of the detectives, and all closed with the remark that "three hundred thousand citizens and four detectives saw the dread creature, and two of the latter he destroyed."

I dreaded to hear the telegraphic instrument begin to click again. By and by the messages began to pour in, but I was happily disappointed in their nature. It was soon apparent that all trace of the elephant was lost. The fog had enabled him to search out a good hiding-place unobserved. Telegrams from the most absurdly distant points reported that a dim vast mass had been glimpsed there through the fog at such and such an hour, and was "undoubtedly the elephant." This dim vast mass had been glimpsed in New Haven, in New Jersey, in Pennsylvania, in interior New York, in Brooklyn, and even in the city of New York itself! But in all cases the dim vast mass had vanished quickly and left no trace. Every detective of the large force scattered over this huge extent of country sent his hourly report, and each and every one of them had a clew, and was shadowing something, and was hot upon the heels of it.

But the day passed without other result.

The next day the same.

The next just the same.

The newspaper reports began to grow monotonous with facts that amounted to nothing, clews which led to nothing, and theories which had nearly exhausted the elements which surprise and delight and dazzle.

By advice of the inspector I doubled the reward.

Four more dull days followed. Then came a bitter blow to the poor, hard-working detectives,—the journalists declined to print their theories, and coldly said, "Give us a rest."

Two weeks after the elephant's disappearance I raised the reward to $75,000 by the inspector's advice. It was a great sum, but I felt that I would rather sacrifice my whole private fortune than lose my credit with my government. Now that the detectives were in adversity, the newspapers turned upon them, and began to fling the most stinging sarcasms at them. This gave the minstrels an idea, and they dressed themselves as detectives and hunted the elephant on the stage in the most extravagant way. The caricaturists made pictures of detectives scanning the country with spy-glasses, while the elephant, at their backs, stole apples out of their pockets. And they made all sorts of ridiculous pictures of the detective badge,—you have seen that badge printed in gold on the back of detective novels, no doubt,—it is a wide-staring eye, with the legend, "WE NEVER SLEEP."[6] When detectives called for a drink, the would-be facetious bar-keeper resurrected an obsolete form of expression and said, "Will you have an eye-opener?" All the air was thick with sarcasms.

But there was one man who moved calm, untouched, unaffected, through it all. It was that heart of oak, the chief inspector. His brave eye never drooped, his serene confidence never wavered. He always said,—

"Let them rail on; he laughs best who laughs last."

My admiration for the man grew into a species of worship. I was at his side

[6] *Motto of the Pinkerton Detective Agency accompanied by a widely opened eye that was featured on the back of a series of books, supposedly written by Allan Pinkerton himself, detailing the agency's exploits.*

One of several logos used by the Pinkerton Detective Agency during the nineteenth century.

always. His office had become an unpleasant place to me, and now became daily more and more so. Yet if he could endure it I meant to do so also; at least, as long as I could. So I came regularly, and stayed,—the only outsider who seemed to be capable of it. Everybody wondered how I could; and often it seemed to me that I must desert, but at such times I looked into that calm and apparently unconscious face, and held my ground.

About three weeks after the elephant's disappearance I was about to say, one morning, that I should *have* to strike my colors and retire, when the great detective arrested the thought by proposing one more superb and masterly move.

This was to compromise with the robbers. The fertility of this man's invention exceeded anything I have ever seen, and I have had a wide intercourse with the world's finest minds. He said he was confident he could compromise for $100,000 and recover the elephant. I said I believed I could scrape the amount together, but what would become of the poor detectives who had worked so faithfully? He said:—

"In compromises they always get half."

This removed my only objection. So the inspector wrote two notes, in this form:—

> DEAR MADAM,—Your husband can make a large sum of money (and be entirely protected from the law) by making an immediate appointment with me.
>
> *Chief* BLUNT.

He sent one of these by his confidential messenger to the "reputed wife" of Brick Duffy, and the other to the reputed wife of Red McFadden.

Within the hour these offensive answers came:—

> YE OWLD FOOL: brick McDuffys bin ded 2 yere.
>
> BRIDGET MAHONEY.

> CHIEF BAT,—Red McFadden is hung and in heving 18 month. Any Ass but a detective know that.
>
> MARY O'HOOLIGAN.

"I had long suspected these facts," said the inspector; "this testimony proves the unerring accuracy of my instinct."

The moment one resource failed him he was ready with another. He immediately wrote an advertisement for the morning papers, and I kept a copy of it:—

> A.—xwblv. 242 N. Tjnd—fz328wmlg. Ozpo—; 2 m! ogw. Mum.

He said that if the thief was alive this would bring him to the usual rendezvous. He further explained that the usual rendezvous was a place where all business affairs between detectives and criminals were conducted. This meeting would take place at twelve the next night.

We could do nothing till then, and I lost no time in getting out of the office, and was grateful indeed for the privilege.

At 11 the next night I brought $100,000 in bank-notes and put them into the chief's hands, and shortly afterward he took his leave, with the brave old undimmed confidence in his eye. An almost intolerable hour dragged to a close; then I heard his welcome tread, and rose gasping and tottered to meet him. How his fine eyes flamed with triumph! He said,—

"We've compromised! The jokers will sing a different tune to-morrow! Follow me!"

He took a lighted candle and strode down into the vast vaulted basement where sixty detectives always slept, and where a score were now playing cards to while the time. I followed close after him. He walked swiftly down to the dim and remote end of the place, and just as I succumbed to the pangs of suffocation and was swooning away he stumbled and fell over the outlying members of a mighty object, and I heard him exclaim as he went down:

"Our noble profession is vindicated. Here is your elephant!"

I was carried to the office above and restored with carbolic acid. The whole detective force swarmed in, and such another season of triumphant rejoicing ensued as I had never witnessed before. The reporters were called, baskets of champagne were opened, toasts were drunk, the handshakings and congratulations were continuous and enthusiastic. Naturally the chief was the hero of the hour, and his happiness was so complete and had been so patiently and worthily and bravely won that it made me happy to see it, though I stood there a homeless beggar, my priceless charge dead, and my position in my country's service lost to me through what would always seem my fatally careless execution of a great trust. Many an eloquent eye testified its deep admiration for the chief, and many a detective's voice murmured, "Look at him,—just the king of the profession,—only give him a clew, it's all he wants, and there ain't anything hid that he can't find." The dividing of the $50,000 made great pleasure; when it was finished the chief made a little speech while he put his share in his pocket, in which he said, "Enjoy it, boys, for you've earned it; and, more than that, you've earned for the detective profession undying fame."

A telegram arrived, which read:

> MONROE, MICH., 10 P.M.
>
> First time I've struck a telegraph office in over three weeks. Have followed those footprints, horseback, through the woods, a thousand miles to here, and they get stronger and bigger and fresher every day. Don't worry—inside of another week I'll have the elephant. This is dead sure.
>
> DARLEY, *Detective.*

The chief ordered three cheers for "Darley, one of the finest minds on the force," and then commanded that he be telegraphed to come home and receive his share of the reward.

So ended that marvellous episode of the stolen elephant. The newspapers were pleasant with praises once more, the next day, with one contemptible exception. This sheet said, "Great is the detective! He may be a little slow in finding a little thing like a mislaid elephant,—he may hunt him all day and sleep with his rotting carcass all night for three weeks, but he will find him at last—if he can get the man who mislaid him to show him the place!"

Poor Hassan was lost to me forever. The cannon-shots had wounded him fatally, he had crept to that unfriendly place in the fog, and there, surrounded by his enemies and in constant danger of detection, he had wasted away with hunger and suffering till death gave him peace.

The compromise cost me $100,000; my detective expenses were $42,000 more; I never applied for a place again under my government; I am a ruined man and a wanderer on the earth,—but my admiration for that man, whom I believe to be the greatest detective the world has ever produced, remains undimmed to this day, and will so remain unto the end.

G. K. CHESTERTON (1874–1936)

A journalist, playwright, poet, novelist, illustrator, critic, and much more, the prolific Gilbert Keith Chesterton was born in London and studied at the University College, London, and the Slade School of Art. His career as an author began in 1900 with a collection of poetry, and he would go on to write over one hundred books and thousands of essays. His published works include the 1908 novel *The Man Who Was Thursday* and critical studies of Thomas Aquinas, St. Francis of Assisi, William Blake, Robert Browning, Geoffrey Chaucer, Charles Dickens, Samuel Johnson, George Bernard Shaw, and Robert Louis Stevenson. The first Father Brown story, "The Blue Cross," appeared in 1910 and was reprinted in *The Innocence of Father Brown* the following year. Three more collections about the unassuming priest would follow: *The Wisdom of Father Brown* in 1914, *The Incredulity of Father Brown* in 1926, and *The Secret of Father Brown* in 1927. In his *Autobiography* Chesterton pinpoints the origins of his clerical detective to an encounter with Father John O'Connor at a lecture, which provided him with the idea of "constructing a comedy in which a priest should appear to know nothing and in fact know more about crime than the criminals." Chesterton and O'Connor became close friends, and the former converted to Catholicism in 1922. In 1923 Chesterton published a collection of non–Brown detective stories entitled *The Man Who Knew Too Much*. He also wrote critical essays about detection, including "A Defence of Detective Stories," in which he sees the genre as being capable of serving a moral purpose and calls it "the earliest and only form of popular literature in which is expressed some sense of the poetry of modern life." "The Blue Cross" served as the basis of two films, *Father Brown, Detective* in 1934 and *Father Brown* (also known as *The Detective)*, starring Alec Guinness, in 1954. Like "The Purloined Letter," the story pits a French master criminal against a legendary Parisian detective. However, with the frequently underestimated Brown, Chesterton introduces something new into detection: a man of God who cares more about saving souls than solving crimes, punishing lawbreakers, and outwitting opponents.

The Blue Cross
by G. K. Chesterton

(1910)

Between the silver ribbon of morning and the green glittering ribbon of sea, the boat touched Harwich and let loose a swarm of folk like flies, among whom the man we must follow was by no means conspicuous—nor wished to be. There was nothing notable about him, except a slight contrast between the holiday gaiety of his clothes and the official gravity of his face. His clothes included a slight, pale grey jacket, a white waistcoat, and a silver straw hat with a grey-blue ribbon. His lean face was dark by contrast, and ended in a curt black beard that looked Spanish and suggested an Elizabethan ruff. He was smoking a cigarette with the seriousness of an idler. There was nothing about him to indicate the fact that the grey jacket covered a loaded revolver, that the white waistcoat covered a police card, or that the straw hat covered one of the most powerful intellects in Europe. For this was Valentin himself, the head of the Paris police and the most famous investigator of the world; and he was coming from Brussels to London to make the greatest arrest of the century.

Flambeau was in England. The police of three countries had tracked the great criminal at last from Ghent to Brussels, from Brussels to the Hook of Holland; and it was conjectured that he would take some advantage of the unfamiliarity and confusion of the Eucharistic Congress, then taking place in London. Probably he would travel as some minor clerk or secretary connected with it; but, of course, Valentin could not be certain; nobody could be certain about Flambeau.

It is many years now since this colossus of crime suddenly ceased keeping the world in a turmoil; and when he ceased, as they said after the death of Roland,[1] there was a great quiet upon the earth. But in his best days (I mean, of course, his worst) Flambeau was a figure as statuesque and international as the Kaiser. Almost every morning the daily paper announced that he had escaped the consequences of one extraordinary crime by committing another. He was a Gascon[2] of gigantic stature and bodily daring; and the wildest tales were told of his outbursts of athletic humour; how he turned the *juge d'instruction*[3] upside down and stood him on his head, "to clear his mind"; how he ran down the Rue de Rivoli with a policeman under each arm. It is due to him to say that his fantastic physical strength was generally employed in such bloodless though undignified scenes; his real crimes were chiefly those of ingenious and wholesale robbery. But each of his thefts was almost a new sin, and would make a story by itself. It was he who ran the great Tyrolean Dairy Company in London, with no dairies, no cows, no carts, no milk, but with some thousand subscribers. These he served by the simple operation of moving the little milk cans outside people's doors to the doors of his own customers. It was he who had kept up an unaccountable and close correspondence with a young lady whose whole letter-bag was intercepted, by the extraordinary trick of photographing his messages infinitesimally small upon the slides of a microscope. A sweeping simplicity, however, marked many of his experiments. It is said that he once repainted all the numbers in a street in the dead of night merely to divert one traveller into a trap. It is quite certain that he

[1]*French hero of medieval legend who appears in the epic* The Song of Roland.
[2]*Boastful and swaggering person.*
[3]*Magistrate in France responsible for conducting the investigative hearing that precedes a criminal trial.*

invented a portable pillar-box,[4] which he put up at corners in quiet suburbs on the chance of strangers dropping postal orders into it. Lastly, he was known to be a startling acrobat; despite his huge figure, he could leap like a grasshopper and melt into the tree-tops like a monkey. Hence the great Valentin, when he set out to find Flambeau, was perfectly aware that his adventures would not end when he had found him.

But how was he to find him? On this the great Valentin's ideas were still in process of settlement.

There was one thing which Flambeau, with all his dexterity of disguise, could not cover, and that was his singular height. If Valentin's quick eye had caught a tall apple-woman, a tall grenadier, or even a tolerably tall duchess, he might have arrested them on the spot. But all along his train there was nobody that could be a disguised Flambeau, any more than a cat could be a disguised giraffe. About the people on the boat he had already satisfied himself; and the people picked up at Harwich or on the journey limited themselves with certainty to six. There was a short railway official travelling up to the terminus, three fairly short market gardeners picked up two stations afterwards, one very short widow lady going up from a small Essex town, and a very short Roman Catholic priest going up from a small Essex village. When it came to the last case, Valentin gave it up and almost laughed. The little priest was so much the essence of those Eastern flats; he had a face as round and dull as a Norfolk dumpling; he had eyes as empty as the North Sea; he had several brown paper parcels, which he was quite incapable of collecting. The Eucharistic Congress had doubtless sucked out of their local stagnation many such creatures, blind and helpless, like moles disinterred. Valentin was a skeptic in the severe style of France, and could have no love for priests. But he could have pity for them, and this one might have provoked pity in anybody. He had a large, shabby umbrella, which constantly fell on the floor. He did not seem to know which was the right end of his return ticket. He explained with a moon-calf simplicity to everybody in the carriage that he had to be careful, because he had something made of real silver "with blue stones" in one of his brown-paper parcels. His quaint blending of Essex flatness with saintly simplicity continuously amused the Frenchman till the priest arrived (somehow) at Tottenham with all his parcels, and came back for his umbrella. When he did the last, Valentin even had the good nature to warn him not to take care of the silver by telling everybody about it. But to whomever he talked, Valentin kept his eye open for someone else; he looked out steadily for anyone, rich or poor, male or female, who was well up to six feet; for Flambeau was four inches above it.

He alighted at Liverpool Street, however, quite conscientiously secure that he had not missed the criminal so far. He then went to Scotland Yard to regularise his position and arrange for help in case of need; he then lit another cigarette and went for a long stroll in the streets of London. As he was walking in the streets and squares

[4] *Pillar-shaped mailbox.*

beyond Victoria, he paused suddenly and stood. It was a quaint, quiet square, very typical of London, full of an accidental stillness. The tall, flat houses round looked at once prosperous and uninhabited; the square of shrubbery in the centre looked as deserted as a green Pacific islet. One of the four sides was much higher than the rest, like a daïs; and the line of this side was broken by one of London's admirable accidents — a restaurant that looked as if it had strayed from Soho. It was an unreasonably attractive object, with dwarf plants in pots and long, striped blinds of lemon yellow and white. It stood specially high above the street, and in the usual patchwork way of London, a flight of steps from the street ran up to meet the front door almost as a fire-escape might run up to a first-floor window. Valentin stood and smoked in front of the yellow-white blinds and considered them long.

The most incredible thing about miracles is that they happen. A few clouds in heaven do come together into the staring shape of one human eye. A tree does stand up in the landscape of a doubtful journey in the exact and elaborate shape of a note of interrogation. I have seen both these things myself within the last few days. Nelson[5] does die in the instant of victory; and a man named Williams does quite accidentally murder a man named Williamson; it sounds like a sort of infanticide. In short, there is in life an element of elfin coincidence which people reckoning on the prosaic may perpetually miss. As it has been well expressed in the paradox of Poe, wisdom should reckon on the unforeseen.

Aristide Valentin was unfathomably French; and the French intelligence is intelligence specially and solely. He was not "a thinking machine"; for that is a brainless phrase of modern fatalism and materialism. A machine only is a machine because it cannot think. But he was a thinking man, and a plain man at the same time. All his wonderful successes, that looked like conjuring, had been gained by plodding logic, by clear and commonplace French thought. The French electrify the world not by starting any paradox, they electrify it by carrying out a truism. They carry a truism so far — as in the French Revolution. But exactly because Valentin understood reason, he understood the limits of reason. Only a man who knows nothing of motors talks of motoring without petrol; only a man who knows nothing of reason talks of reasoning without strong, undisputed first principles. Here he had no strong first principles. Flambeau had been missed at Harwich; and if he was in London at all, he might be anything from a tall tramp on Wimbledon Common to a tall toast-master at the Hotel Metropole. In such a naked state of nescience,[6] Valentin had a view and a method of his own.

In such cases he reckoned on the unforeseen. In such cases, when he could not follow the train of the reasonable, he coldly and carefully followed the train of the unreasonable. Instead of going to the right places — banks, police stations, rendezvous — he systematically went to the wrong places; knocked at every empty house,

[5]Horatio Nelson, British naval hero killed in the Battle of Trafalgar. [6]Ignorance.

turned down every *cul de sac*, went up every lane blocked with rubbish, went round every crescent that led him uselessly out of the way. He defended this crazy course quite logically. He said that if one had a clue this was the worst way; but if one had no clue at all it was the best, because there was just the chance that any oddity that caught the eye of the pursuer might be the same that had caught the eye of the pursued. Somewhere a man must begin, and it had better be just where another man might stop. Something about that flight of steps up to the shop, something about the quietude and quaintness of the restaurant, roused all the detective's rare romantic fancy and made him resolve to strike at random. He went up the steps, and sitting down at a table by the window, asked for a cup of black coffee.

It was half-way through the morning, and he had not breakfasted; the slight litter of other breakfasts stood about on the table to remind him of his hunger; and adding a poached egg to his order, he proceeded musingly to shake some white sugar into his coffee, thinking all the time about Flambeau. He remembered how Flambeau had escaped, once by a pair of nail scissors, and once by a house on fire; once by having to pay for an unstamped letter, and once by getting people to look through a telescope at a comet that might destroy the world. He thought his detective brain as good as the criminal's, which was true. But he fully realised the disadvantage. "The criminal is the creative artist; the detective only the critic," he said with a sour smile, and lifted his coffee cup to his lips slowly, and put it down very quickly. He had put salt in it.

He looked at the vessel from which the silvery powder had come; it was certainly a sugar-basin; as unmistakably meant for sugar as a champagne-bottle for champagne. He wondered why they should keep salt in it. He looked to see if there were any more orthodox vessels. Yes; there were two salt-cellars quite full. Perhaps there was some specialty in the condiment in the salt-cellars. He tasted it; it was sugar. Then he looked round at the restaurant with a refreshed air of interest, to see if there were any other traces of that singular artistic taste which puts the sugar in the salt-cellars and the salt in the sugar-basin. Except for an odd splash of some dark fluid on one of the white-papered walls, the whole place appeared neat, cheerful and ordinary. He rang the bell for the waiter.

When that official hurried up, fuzzy-haired and somewhat blear-eyed at that early hour, the detective (who was not without an appreciation of the simpler forms of humour) asked him to taste the sugar and see if it was up to the high reputation of the hotel. The result was that the waiter yawned suddenly and woke up.

"Do you play this delicate joke on your customers every morning?" inquired Valentin. "Does changing the salt and sugar never pall on you as a jest?"

The waiter, when this irony grew clearer, stammeringly assured him that the establishment had certainly no such intention; it must be a most curious mistake. He picked up the sugar-basin and looked at it; he picked up the salt-cellar and looked at that, his face growing more and more bewildered. At last he abruptly excused himself, and hurrying away, returned in a few seconds with the proprietor. The proprietor also examined the sugar-basin and then the salt-cellar; the proprietor also looked bewildered.

Suddenly the waiter seemed to grow inarticulate with a rush of words.

"I zink," he stuttered eagerly, "I zink it is those two clergy-men."

"What two clergymen?"

"The two clergymen," said the waiter, "that threw soup at the wall."

"Threw soup at the wall?" repeated Valentin, feeling sure this must be some singular Italian metaphor.

"Yes, yes," said the attendant excitedly, and pointed at the dark splash on the white paper; "threw it over there on the wall."

Valentin looked his query at the proprietor, who came to his rescue with fuller reports.

"Yes, sir," he said, "it's quite true, though I don't suppose it has anything to do with the sugar and salt. Two clergymen came in and drank soup here very early, as soon as the shutters were taken down. They were both very quiet, respectable people; one of them paid the bill and went out; the other, who seemed a slower coach altogether, was some minutes longer getting his things together. But he went at last. Only, the instant before he stepped into the street he deliberately picked up his cup, which he had only half emptied, and threw the soup slap on the wall. I was in the back room myself, and so was the waiter; so I could only rush out in time to find the wall splashed and the shop empty. It don't do any particular damage, but it was confounded cheek; and I tried to catch the men in the street. They were too far off though; I only noticed they went round the next corner into Carstairs Street."

The detective was on his feet, hat settled and stick in hand. He had already decided that in the universal darkness of his mind he could only follow the first odd finger that pointed; and this finger was odd enough. Paying his bill and clashing the glass doors behind him, he was soon swinging round into the other street.

It was fortunate that even in such fevered moments his eye was cool and quick. Something in a shop-front went by him like a mere flash; yet he went back to look at it. The shop was a popular greengrocer and fruiterer's, an array of goods set out in the open air and plainly ticketed with their names and prices. In the two most prominent compartments were two heaps, of oranges and of nuts respectively. On the heap of nuts lay a scrap of cardboard, on which was written in bold, blue chalk, "Best tangerine oranges, two a penny." On the oranges was the equally clear and exact description, "Finest Brazil nuts, 4d. a lb." M. Valentin looked at these two placards and fancied he had met this highly subtle form of humour before, and that somewhat recently. He drew the attention of the red-faced fruiterer, who was looking rather sullenly up and down the street, to this inaccuracy in his advertisements. The fruiterer said nothing, but sharply put each card into its proper place. The detective, leaning elegantly on his walking-cane, continued to scrutinize the shop. At last he said, "Pray excuse my apparent irrelevance, my good sir, but I should like to ask you a question in experimental psychology and the association of ideas."

The red-faced shopman regarded him with an eye of menace; but he continued gaily, swinging his cane, "Why," he pursued, "why are two tickets wrongly placed in a greengrocer's shop like a shovel hat that has come to London for a holiday? Or, in case I do not make myself clear, what is the mystical association which connects the idea of nuts marked as oranges with the idea of two clergymen, one tall and the other short?"

The eyes of the tradesman stood out of his head like a snail's; he really seemed for an instant likely to fling himself upon the stranger. At last he stammered angrily: "I don't know what you 'ave to do with it, but if you're one of their friends, you can tell 'em from me that I'll knock their silly 'eads off, parsons or no parsons, if they upset my apples again."

"Indeed?" asked the detective, with great sympathy. "Did they upset your apples?"

"One of 'em did," said the heated shopman; "rolled 'em all over the street. I'd 'ave caught the fool but for havin' to pick 'em up."

"Which way did these parsons go?" asked Valentin.

"Up that second road on the left-hand side, and then across the square," said the other promptly.

"Thanks," replied Valentin, and vanished like a fairy. On the other side of the second square he found a policeman, and said: "This is urgent, constable; have you seen two clergymen in shovel hats?"

The policeman began to chuckle heavily. "I 'ave, sir; and if you arst me, one of 'em was drunk. He stood in the middle of the road that bewildered that —"

"Which way did they go?" snapped Valentin.

"They took one of them yellow buses over there," answered the man; "them that go to Hampstead."

Valentin produced his official card and said very rapidly: "Call up two of your men to come with me in pursuit," and crossed the road with such contagious energy that the ponderous policeman was moved to almost agile obedience. In a minute and a half the French detective was joined on the opposite pavement by an inspector and a man in plain clothes.

"Well, sir," began the former, with smiling importance, "and what may —?"

Valentin pointed suddenly with his cane. "I'll tell you on the top of that omnibus," he said, and was darting and dodging across the tangle of the traffic. When all three sank panting on the top seats of the yellow vehicle, the inspector said: "We could go four times as quick in a taxi."

"Quite true," replied their leader placidly, "if we only had an idea of where we were going."

"Well, where *are* you going?" asked the other, staring.

Valentin smoked frowningly for a few seconds; then, removing his cigarette, he said: "If you *know* what a man's doing, get in front of him; but if you want to guess what he's doing, keep behind him. Stray when he strays; stop when he stops; travel as slowly as he. Then you may see what he saw and may act as he acted. All we can do is to keep our eyes skinned for a queer thing."

"What sort of queer thing do you mean?" asked the inspector.

"Any sort of queer thing," answered Valentin, and relapsed into obstinate silence.

The yellow omnibus crawled up the northern roads for what seemed like hours on end; the great detective would not explain further, and perhaps his assistants felt a silent and growing doubt of his errand. Perhaps, also, they felt a silent and growing desire for lunch, for the hours crept long past the normal luncheon hour, and the long roads of the North London suburbs seemed to shoot out into length after length like an infernal telescope. It was one of those journeys on which a man perpetually feels that now at last he must have come to the end of the universe, and then finds he has only come to the beginning of Tufnell Park. London died away in draggled taverns and dreary scrubs, and then was unaccountably born again in blazing high streets and blatant hotels. It was like passing through thirteen separate vulgar cities all just touching each other. But though the winter twilight was already threatening the road ahead of them, the Parisian detective still sat silent and watchful, eyeing the frontage of the streets that slid by on either side. By the time they had left Camden Town behind, the policemen were nearly asleep; at least, they gave something like a jump as Valentin leapt erect, struck a hand on each man's shoulder, and shouted to the driver to stop.

They tumbled down the steps into the road without realizing why they had been dislodged; when they looked round for enlightenment they found Valentin triumphantly pointing his finger towards a window on the left side of the road. It was a large window, forming part of the long façade of a gilt and palatial public-house; it was the part reserved for respectable dining, and labeled "Restaurant." This window, like all the rest along the frontage of the hotel, was of frosted and figured glass; but in the middle of it was a big, black smash, like a star in the ice.

"Our cue at last," cried Valentin, waving his stick; "the place with the broken window."

"What window? What cue?" asked his principal assistant. "Why, what proof is there that this has anything to do with them?"

Valentin almost broke his bamboo stick with rage.

"Proof!" he cried. "Good God! The man is looking for proof! Why, of course, the chances are twenty to one that it has nothing to do with them. But what else can we do? Don't you see we must either follow one wild possibility or else go home to bed?" He banged his way into the restaurant, followed by his companions, and they were soon seated at a late luncheon at a little table, and looked at the star of smashed glass from the inside. Not that it was very informative to them even then.

"Got your window broken, I see," said Valentin to the waiter as he paid the bill.

"Yes, sir," answered the attendant, bending busily over the change, to which Valentin silently added an enormous tip. The waiter straightened himself with mild but unmistakable animation.

"Ah, yes, sir," he said. "Very odd thing, that, sir."

"Indeed? Tell us about it," said the detective with careless curiosity.

"Well, two gents in black came in," said the waiter; "two of those foreign parsons that are running about. They had a cheap and quiet little lunch, and one of them paid for it and went out. The other was just going out to join him when I looked at my change again and found he'd paid me more than three times too much. 'Here,' I says to the chap who was nearly out of the door, 'you've paid too much.' 'Oh,' he says, very cool, 'have we?' 'Yes,' I says, and picks up the bill to show him. Well, that was a knock-out."

"What do you mean?" asked his interlocutor.

"Well, I'd have sworn on seven Bibles that I'd put 4s. on that bill. But now I saw I'd put 14s., as plain as paint."

"Well?" cried Valentin, moving slowly, but with burning eyes, "and then?"

"The parson at the door he says all serene, 'Sorry to confuse your accounts, but it'll pay for the window.' 'What window?' I says. 'The one I'm going to break,' he says, and smashed that blessed pane with his umbrella."

All three inquirers made an exclamation; and the inspector said under his breath, "Are we after escaped lunatics?" The waiter went on with some relish for the ridiculous story:

"I was so knocked silly for a second, I couldn't do anything. The man marched out of the place and joined his friend just round the corner. Then they went so quick up Bullock Street that I couldn't catch them, though I ran round the bars to do it."

"Bullock Street," said the detective, and shot up that thoroughfare as quickly as the strange couple he pursued.

Their journey now took them through bare brick ways like tunnels; streets with few lights and even with few windows; streets that seemed built out of the blank backs of everything and everywhere. Dusk was deepening, and it was not easy even for the London policemen to guess in what exact direction they were treading. The inspector, however, was pretty certain that they would eventually strike some part of Hampstead Heath. Abruptly one bulging gas-lit window broke the blue twilight like a bull's-eye lantern[7]; and Valentin stopped an instant before a little garish sweetstuff shop. After an instant's hesitation he went in; he stood amid the gaudy colors of the confectionery with entire gravity and bought thirteen chocolate cigars with a certain care. He was clearly preparing an opening; but he did not need one.

An angular, elderly young woman in the shop had regarded his elegant appear-

[7]*Multipurpose dark lantern used by both policemen and criminals.*

ance with a merely automatic inquiry; but when she saw the door behind him blocked with the blue uniform of the inspector, her eyes seemed to wake up.

"Oh," she said, "if you've come about that parcel, I've sent it off already."

"Parcel?" repeated Valentin; and it was his turn to look inquiring.

"I mean the parcel the gentleman left — the clergyman gentleman."

"For goodness' sake," said Valentin, leaning forward with his first real confession of eagerness, "for Heaven's sake tell us what happened exactly."

"Well," said the woman a little doubtfully, "the clergymen came in about half an hour ago and bought some peppermints and talked a bit, and then went off towards the Heath. But a second after, one of them runs back into the shop and says, 'Have I left a parcel!' Well, I looked everywhere and couldn't see one; so he says, 'Never mind; but if it should turn up, please post it to this address,' and he left me the address and a shilling for my trouble. And sure enough, though I thought I'd looked everywhere, I found he'd left a brown paper parcel, so I posted it to the place he said. I can't remember the address now; it was somewhere in Westminster. But as the thing seemed so important, I thought perhaps the police had come about it."

"So they have," said Valentin shortly. "Is Hampstead Heath near here?"

"Straight on for fifteen minutes," said the woman, "and you'll come right out on the open." Valentin sprang out of the shop and began to run. The other detectives followed him at a reluctant trot.

The street they threaded was so narrow and shut in by shadows that when they came out unexpectedly into the void common and vast sky they were startled to find the evening still so light and clear. A perfect dome of peacock-green sank into gold amid the blackening trees and the dark violet distances. The glowing green tint was just deep enough to pick out in points of crystal one or two stars. All that was left of the daylight lay in a golden glitter across the edge of Hampstead and that popular hollow which is called the Vale of Health. The holiday makers who roam this region had not wholly dispersed; a few couples sat shapelessly on benches; and here and there a distant girl still shrieked in one of the swings. The glory of heaven deepened and darkened around the sublime vulgarity of man; and standing on the slope and looking across the valley, Valentin beheld the thing which he sought.

Among the black and breaking groups in that distance was one especially black which did not break — a group of two figures clerically clad. Though they seemed as small as insects, Valentin could see that one of them was much smaller than the other. Though the other had a student's stoop and an inconspicuous manner, he could see that the man was well over six feet high. He shut his teeth and went forward, whirling his stick impatiently. By the time he had substantially diminished the distance and magnified the two black figures as in a vast microscope, he had perceived something else; something which startled him, and yet which he had somehow expected. Whoever was the tall priest, there could be no doubt about the identity of the short one.

It was his friend of the Harwich train, the stumpy little *cure* of Essex whom he had warned about his brown paper parcels.

Now, so far as this went, everything fitted in finally and rationally enough. Valentin had learned by his inquiries that morning that a Father Brown from Essex was bringing up a silver cross with sapphires, a relic of considerable value, to show some of the foreign priests at the congress. This undoubtedly was the "silver with blue stones"; and Father Brown undoubtedly was the little greenhorn in the train. Now there was nothing wonderful about the fact that what Valentin had found out Flambeau had also found out; Flambeau found out everything. Also there was nothing wonderful in the fact that when Flambeau heard of a sapphire cross he should try to steal it; that was the most natural thing in all natural history. And most certainly there was nothing wonderful about the fact that Flambeau should have it all his own way with such a silly sheep as the man with the umbrella and the parcels. He was the sort of man whom anybody could lead on a string to the North Pole; it was not surprising that an actor like Flambeau, dressed as another priest, could lead him to Hampstead Heath. So far the crime seemed clear enough; and while the detective pitied the priest for his helplessness, he almost despised Flambeau for condescending to so gullible a victim. But when Valentin thought of all that had happened in between, of all that had led him to his triumph, he racked his brains for the smallest rhyme or reason in it. What had the stealing of a blue-and-silver cross from a priest from Essex to do with chucking soup at wall paper? What had it to do with calling nuts oranges, or with paying for windows first and breaking them afterwards? He had come to the end of his chase; yet somehow he had missed the middle of it. When he failed (which was seldom), he had usually grasped the clue, but nevertheless missed the criminal. Here he had grasped the criminal, but still he could not grasp the clue.

The two figures that they followed were crawling like black flies across the huge green contour of a hill. They were evidently sunk in conversation, and perhaps did not notice where they were going; but they were certainly going to the wilder and more silent heights of the Heath. As their pursuers gained on them, the latter had to use the undignified attitudes of the deer-stalker, to crouch behind clumps of trees and even to crawl prostrate in deep grass. By these ungainly ingenuities the hunters even came close enough to the quarry to hear the murmur of the discussion, but no word could be distinguished except the word "reason" recurring frequently in a high and almost childish voice. Once over an abrupt dip of land and a dense tangle of thickets, the detectives actually lost the two figures they were following. They did not find the trail again for an agonising ten minutes, and then it led round the brow of a great dome of hill overlooking an amphitheatre of rich and desolate sunset scenery. Under a tree in this commanding yet neglected spot was an old ramshackle wooden seat. On this seat sat the two priests still in serious speech together. The gorgeous green and gold still clung to the darkening horizon; but the dome above was turning slowly from peacock-green to peacock-blue, and the stars detached themselves more and more like solid jewels. Mutely motioning to his followers, Valentin contrived to creep up behind the big branching tree, and, standing there in deathly silence, heard the words of the strange priests for the first time.

After he had listened for a minute and a half, he was gripped by a devilish doubt. Perhaps he had dragged the two English policemen to the wastes of a nocturnal heath on an errand no saner than seeking figs on its thistles. For the two priests were talking exactly like priests, piously, with learning and leisure, about the most aerial enigmas of theology. The little Essex priest spoke the more simply, with his round face turned to the strengthening stars; the other talked with his head bowed, as if he were not even worthy to look at them. But no more innocently clerical conversation could have been heard in any white Italian cloister or black Spanish cathedral.

The first he heard was the tail of one of Father Brown's sentences, which ended: "...what they really meant in the Middle Ages by the heavens being incorruptible."

The taller priest nodded his bowed head and said:

"Ah, yes, these modern infidels appeal to their reason; but who can look at those millions of worlds and not feel that there may well be wonderful universes above us where reason is utterly unreasonable?"

"No," said the other priest; "reason is always reasonable, even in the last limbo, in the lost borderland of things. I know that people charge the Church with lowering reason, but it is just the other way. Alone on earth, the Church makes reason really supreme. Alone on earth, the Church affirms that God himself is bound by reason."

The other priest raised his austere face to the spangled sky and said:

"Yet who knows if in that infinite universe—?"

"Only infinite physically," said the little priest, turning sharply in his seat, "not infinite in the sense of escaping from the laws of truth."

Valentin behind his tree was tearing his fingernails with silent fury. He seemed almost to hear the sniggers of the English detectives whom he had brought so far on a fantastic guess only to listen to the metaphysical gossip of two mild old parsons. In his impatience he lost the equally elaborate answer of the tall cleric, and when he listened again it was again Father Brown who was speaking:

"Reason and justice grip the remotest and the loneliest star. Look at those stars. Don't they look as if they were single diamonds and sapphires? Well, you can imagine any mad botany or geology you please. Think of forests of adamant with leaves of brilliants. Think the moon is a blue moon, a single elephantine sapphire. But don't fancy that all that frantic astronomy would make the smallest difference to the reason and justice of conduct. On plains of opal, under cliffs cut out of pearl, you would still find a notice-board, 'Thou shalt not steal.'"

Valentin was just in the act of rising from his rigid and crouching attitude and creeping away as softly as might be, felled by the one great folly of his life. But something in the very silence of the tall priest made him stop until the latter spoke. When at last he did speak, he said simply, his head bowed and his hands on his knees:

"Well, I think that other worlds may perhaps rise higher than our reason. The mystery of heaven is unfathomable, and I for one can only bow my head."

Then, with brow yet bent and without changing by the faintest shade his attitude or voice, he added:

"Just hand over that sapphire cross of yours, will you? We're all alone here, and I could pull you to pieces like a straw doll."

The utterly unaltered voice and attitude added a strange violence to that shocking change of speech. But the guarder of the relic only seemed to turn his head by the smallest section of the compass. He seemed still to have a somewhat foolish face turned to the stars. Perhaps he had not understood. Or, perhaps, he had understood and sat rigid with terror.

"Yes," said the tall priest, in the same low voice and in the same still posture, "yes, I am Flambeau."

Then, after a pause, he said:

"Come, will you give me that cross?"

"No," said the other, and the monosyllable had an odd sound.

Flambeau suddenly flung off all his pontifical pretensions. The great robber leaned back in his seat and laughed low but long.

"No," he cried, "you won't give it me, you proud prelate. You won't give it me, you little celibate simpleton. Shall I tell you why you won't give it me? Because I've got it already in my own breast-pocket."

The small man from Essex turned what seemed to be a dazed face in the dusk, and said, with the timid eagerness of "The Private Secretary":[8]

"Are — are you sure?"

Flambeau yelled with delight.

"Really, you're as good as a three-act farce," he cried. "Yes, you turnip, I am quite sure. I had the sense to make a duplicate of the right parcel, and now, my friend, you've got the duplicate and I've got the jewels. An old dodge, Father Brown — a very old dodge."

"Yes," said Father Brown, and passed his hand through his hair with the same strange vagueness of manner. "Yes, I've heard of it before."

The colossus of crime leaned over to the little rustic priest with a sort of sudden interest.

"You have heard of it?" he asked. "Where have you heard of it?"

"Well, I mustn't tell you his name, of course," said the little man simply. "He was a penitent, you know. He had lived prosperously for about twenty years entirely on duplicate brown paper parcels. And so, you see, when I began to suspect you, I thought of this poor chap's way of doing it at once."

"Began to suspect me?" repeated the outlaw with increased intensity. "Did you

[8]*Popular three-act farce by Sir Charles Henry Hawtrey.*

really have the gumption to suspect me just because I brought you up to this bare part of the heath?"

"No, no," said Brown with an air of apology. "You see, I suspected you when we first met. It's that little bulge up the sleeve where you people have the spiked bracelet."

"How in Tartarus,"[9] cried Flambeau, "did you ever hear of the spiked bracelet?"

"Oh, one's little flock, you know!" said Father Brown, arching his eyebrows rather blankly. "When I was a curate in Hartlepool, there were three of them with spiked bracelets. So, as I suspected you from the first, don't you see, I made sure that the cross should go safe, anyhow. I'm afraid I watched you, you know. So at last I saw you change the parcels. Then, don't you see, I changed them back again. And then I left the right one behind."

"Left it behind?" repeated Flambeau, and for the first time there was another note in his voice beside his triumph.

"Well, it was like this," said the little priest, speaking in the same unaffected way. "I went back to that sweet-shop and asked if I'd left a parcel, and gave them a particular address if it turned up. Well, I knew I hadn't; but when I went away again I did. So, instead of running after me with that valuable parcel, they have sent it flying to a friend of mine in Westminster." Then he added rather sadly: "I learnt that, too, from a poor fellow in Hartlepool. He used to do it with handbags he stole at railway stations, but he's in a monastery now. Oh, one gets to know, you know," he added, rubbing his head again with the same sort of desperate apology. "We can't help being priests. People come and tell us these things."

Flambeau tore a brown-paper parcel out of his inner pocket and rent it in pieces. There was nothing but paper and sticks of lead inside it. He sprang to his feet with a gigantic gesture, and cried:

"I don't believe you. I don't believe a bumpkin like you could manage all that. I believe you've still got the stuff on you, and if you don't give it up — why, we're all alone, and I'll take it by force!"

"No," said Father Brown simply, and stood up also, "you won't take it by force. First, because I really haven't still got it. And, second, because we are not alone."

Flambeau stopped in his stride forward.

"Behind that tree," said Father Brown, pointing, "are two strong policemen and the greatest detective alive. How did they come here, do you ask? Why, I brought them, of course! How did I do it? Why, I'll tell you if you like! Lord bless you, we have to know twenty such things when we work among the criminal classes! Well, I wasn't sure you were a thief, and it would never do to make a scandal against one of our own clergy. So I just tested you to see if anything would make you show yourself. A man generally makes a small scene if he finds salt in his coffee; if he doesn't, he has some reason for keeping quiet. I changed the salt and sugar, and you kept quiet. A

[9]*Dark and gloomy place.*

man generally objects if his bill is three times too big. If he pays it, he has some motive for passing unnoticed. I altered your bill, and you paid it."

The world seemed waiting for Flambeau to leap like a tiger. But he was held back as by a spell; he was stunned with the utmost curiosity.

"Well," went on Father Brown, with lumbering lucidity, "as you wouldn't leave any tracks for the police, of course somebody had to. At every place we went to, I took care to do something that would get us talked about for the rest of the day. I didn't do much harm — a splashed wall, spilt apples, a broken window; but I saved the cross, as the cross will always be saved. It is at Westminster by now. I rather wonder you didn't stop it with the Donkey's Whistle."

"With the what?" asked Flambeau.

"I'm glad you've never heard of it," said the priest, making a face. "It's a foul thing. I'm sure you're too good a man for a Whistler. I couldn't have countered it even with the Spots[10] myself; I'm not strong enough in the legs."

"What on earth are you talking about?" asked the other.

"Well, I did think you'd know the Spots," said Father Brown, agreeably surprised. "Oh, you can't have gone so very wrong yet!"

"How in blazes do you know all these horrors?" cried Flambeau.

The shadow of a smile crossed the round, simple face of his clerical opponent.

"Oh, by being a celibate simpleton, I suppose," he said. "Has it never struck you that a man who does next to nothing but hear men's real sins is not likely to be wholly unaware of human evil? But, as a matter of fact, another part of my trade, too, made me sure you weren't a priest."

"What?" asked the thief, almost gaping.

"You attacked reason," said Father Brown. "It's bad theology."

And even as he turned away to collect his property, the three policemen came out from under the twilight trees. Flambeau was an artist and a sportsman. He stepped back and swept Valentin a great bow.

"Do not bow to me, *mon ami*," said Valentin with silver clearness. "Let us both bow to our master."

And they both stood an instant uncovered while the little Essex priest blinked about for his umbrella.

[10]Donkey's Whistle and Spots are terms made up by Chesterton to suggest Father Brown's familiarity with the activities of criminals.

The World's Most Celebrated Detective

Arthur Conan Doyle (1859–1930)

Aficionados of the world's best-known detective can join Sherlock Holmes societies and read journals devoted to the character. In London, they can visit the Sherlock Holmes Museum and the Sherlock Holmes Memorabilia Shop, take a look at the statue of the crime solver on Marylebone Road, quaff a pint of Sherlock Holmes Ale and consume a Holmes themed meal at the Sherlock Holmes Pub, and even spend the night at the Park Plaza Sherlock Holmes Hotel. First appearing in Arthur Conan Doyle's short novels *A Study in Scarlet* in 1887 and *The Sign of Four* in 1889, the character did not immediately become an iconic figure. It was the publication of *The Adventures of Sherlock Holmes* in the *Strand* magazine in 1891 and 1892 that led to the character's enduring popularity. Born in Edinburgh, Scotland, Conan Doyle attended a Jesuit boarding school for seven years, studied medicine at the University of Edinburgh, and established a private practice in Southsea, Portsmouth, in 1882. He published his first story in 1879 and began writing novels in the mid–1880s. In addition to acknowledging the considerable influence Poe had upon him, Conan Doyle credited a medical school professor with inspiring him to write detection: "I thought of my old teacher Joe Bell, of his eagle face, of his curious ways, of his eerie trick of spotting details. If he were a detective he would surely reduce this fascinating but unorganized business to something nearer to an exact science." Critics have identified several factors that make the Sherlock Holmes stories so memorable. First and foremost, with Holmes Conan Doyle created an unusual but nevertheless believable character of unimpeachable morality whose deductive skills astound readers. In addition, because each man compensates for what the other lacks and holds the other in high esteem, Holmes and Watson combine to form one of the greatest teams in all of fiction. Rejecting, like Poe, the idea of having his sleuth narrate his own adventures, Conan Doyle created what he termed "a commonplace comrade as a foil — an educated man of action who could both join the exploits and narrate them" and chose "a drab, quiet name for this unostentatious man." Moreover, the stories feature language that is striking yet accessible. Even Raymond Chandler, hardly a fan of Conan Doyle, grudgingly observed, "Sherlock Holmes is after all mostly an attitude and a few dozen lines of unforgettable dialogue." It is precisely the specificity of the stories, their depiction of credible people performing true-to-life actions in vividly drawn and readily identifiable locations, that has made them so timeless. Each of the three Holmes stories included here has its own distinctive features. The first installment in *The Adventures of Sherlock Holmes*, "A Scandal in Bohemia" establishes the long-term friendship and successful working relationship between Holmes and Watson, deftly highlights issues of gender, and ingeniously humanizes Holmes by making him fallible. Conan Doyle identified "The Adventure of the Speckled Band" as his own personal favorite, an opinion that was shared by readers of the *Strand* and has been confirmed by more recent polls. Although people have pointed out various mistakes of fact that Conan Doyle incorporates into the tale, the high level of suspense that he achieves and the confrontation between Holmes and an evil killer that concludes the story no doubt account for its popularity. Similar to Poe's "The Purloined Letter," "The Final Problem" pits a brilliant detective against a criminal mastermind. By 1893 when *The Memoirs of Sherlock Holmes* was appearing in the *Strand*, the Holmes stories had become such a sensation that they made Conan Doyle uncomfortable. Because he did not wish to be thoroughly identified with what he considered "a lower stratum of literary achievement," he felt compelled to kill off his detective in the final installment of the series, which was published in December 1893. Of the intense public outcry that ensued Conan Doyle remarked, "They say that a man is never properly appreciated until he is dead, and the general protest against my summary execution of Holmes taught me how many and how numerous were his friends. 'You brute' was the beginning of the letter of remonstrance which one lady sent me, and I expect she spoke for others beside herself. I heard of many who wept." In 1902 Conan Doyle brought Holmes back in *The Hound of the Baskervilles*, which takes place before the events in "The Final Problem," and a year later resurrected him in "The Empty House." Although he wrote several fictional works in which Holmes does not appear, only with *The Lost World* in 1912 did Conan Doyle approach the success of his detective stories.

A Scandal in Bohemia
by Sir Arthur Conan Doyle

(1891)

I.

To Sherlock Holmes she is always *the* woman. I have seldom heard him mention her under any other name. In his eyes she eclipses and predominates the whole of her sex. It was not that he felt any emotion akin to love for Irene Adler. All emotions, and that one particularly, were abhorrent to his cold, precise, but admirably balanced life. He was, I take it, the most perfect reasoning and observing machine that the world has ever seen; but, as a lover, he would have placed himself in a false position. He never spoke of the softer passions, save with a gibe and a sneer. They were admirable things for the observer — excellent for drawing the veil from men's motives and actions. But for the trained reasoner to admit such intrusions into his own delicate and finely adjusted temperament was to introduce a distracting factor which might throw a doubt upon all his mental results. Grit in a sensitive instrument, or a crack in one of his own high-power lenses, would not be more disturbing than a strong emotion in a nature such as his. And yet there was but one woman to him, and that woman was the late Irene Adler, of dubious and questionable memory.

I had seen little of Holmes lately. My marriage had drifted us away from each other. My own complete happiness, and the home-centred interests which rise up around the man who first finds himself master of his own establishment, were sufficient to absorb all my attention; while Holmes, who loathed every form of society with his whole Bohemian soul, remained in our lodgings in Baker Street, buried among his old books, and alternating from week to week between cocaine and ambition, the drowsiness of the drug, and the fierce energy of his own keen nature. He was still, as ever, deeply attracted by the study of crime, and occupied his immense faculties and extraordinary powers of observation in following out those clues, and clearing up those mysteries, which had been abandoned as hopeless by the official police. From time to time I heard some vague account of his doings: of his summons to Odessa in the case of the Trepoff murder, of his clearing up of the singular tragedy of the Atkinson brothers at Trincomalee, and finally of the mission which he had accomplished so delicately and successfully for the reigning family of Holland. Beyond these signs of his activity, however, which I merely shared with all the readers of the daily press, I knew little of my former friend and companion.

One night — it was on the 20th of March, 1888 — I was returning from a journey to a patient (for I had now returned to civil practice), when my way led me through Baker Street. As I passed the well-remembered door, which must always be associated in my mind with my wooing, and with the dark incidents of the Study in Scarlet, I was seized with a keen desire to see Holmes again, and to know how he was employing his extraordinary powers. His rooms were brilliantly lit, and, even as I looked up, I saw his tall spare figure pass twice in a dark silhouette against the blind. He was pacing the room swiftly, eagerly, with his head sunk upon his chest, and his hands clasped behind him. To me, who knew his every mood and habit, his attitude and manner told their own story. He was at work again. He had arisen out of his drug-created dreams, and was hot upon the scent of some new problem. I rang the bell, and was shown up to the chamber which had formerly been in part my own.

His manner was not effusive. It seldom was; but he was glad, I think, to see me. With hardly a word spoken, but with a kindly eye, he waved me to an armchair, threw across his case of cigars, and indicated a spirit case and a gasogene[1] in the corner. Then he stood before the fire, and looked me over in his singular introspective fashion.

"Wedlock suits you," he remarked. "I think, Watson, that you have put on seven and a half pounds since I saw you."

"Seven," I answered.

"Indeed, I should have thought a little more. Just a trifle more, I fancy, Watson. And in practice again, I observe. You did not tell me that you intended to go into harness."

"Then, how do you know?"

"I see it, I deduce it. How do I know that you have been getting yourself very wet lately, and that you have a most clumsy and careless servant girl?"

[1]*Device for producing carbonated water.*

"My dear Holmes," said I, "this is too much. You would certainly have been burned, had you lived a few centuries ago. It is true that I had a country walk on Thursday and came home in a dreadful mess; but, as I have changed my clothes I can't imagine how you deduce it. As to Mary Jane, she is incorrigible, and my wife has given her notice; but there, again, I fail to see how you work it out."

He chuckled to himself and rubbed his long, nervous hands together.

"It is simplicity itself," said he; "my eyes tell me that on the inside of your left shoe, just where the firelight strikes it, the leather is scored by six almost parallel cuts. Obviously they have been caused by someone who has very carelessly scraped round the edges of the sole in order to remove crusted mud from it. Hence, you see, my double deduction that you had been out in vile weather, and that you had a particularly malignant boot-slitting specimen of the London slavey. As to your practice, if a gentleman walks into my rooms smelling of iodoform, with a black mark of nitrate of silver upon his right fore-finger, and a bulge on the right side of his top-hat to show where he has secreted his stethoscope, I must be dull, indeed, if I do not pronounce him to be an active member of the medical profession."

I could not help laughing at the ease with which he explained his process of deduction. "When I hear you give your reasons," I remarked, "the thing always appears to me to be so ridiculously simple that I could easily do it myself, though at each successive instance of your reasoning I am baffled, until you explain your process. And yet I believe that my eyes are as good as yours."

"Quite so," he answered, lighting a cigarette, and throwing himself down into an armchair. "You see, but you do not observe. The distinction is clear. For example, you have frequently seen the steps which lead up from the hall to this room."

"Frequently."

"How often?"

"Well, some hundreds of times."

"Then how many are there?"

"How many? I don't know."

"Quite so! You have not observed. And yet you have seen. That is just my point. Now, I know that there are seventeen steps, because I have both seen and observed. By the way, since you are interested in these little problems, and since you are good enough to chronicle one or two of my trifling experiences, you may be interested in this." He threw over a sheet of thick, pink-tinted notepaper which had been lying open upon the table. "It came by the last post," said he. "Read it aloud."

The note was undated, and without either signature or address.

"There will call upon you to-night, at a quarter to eight o'clock," it said, "a gentleman who desires to consult you upon a matter of the very deepest moment. Your recent services to one of the royal houses of Europe have shown that you are one who may safely be trusted with matters which are of an importance which can hardly be exaggerated. This account of you we have from all quarters received. Be in your chamber then at that hour, and do not take it amiss if your visitor wears a mask."

"This is indeed a mystery," I remarked. "What do you imagine that it means?"

"I have no data yet. It is a capital mistake to theorise before one has data. Insensibly one begins to twist facts to suit theories, instead of theories to suit facts. But the note itself. What do you deduce from it?"

I carefully examined the writing, and the paper upon which it was written.

"The man who wrote it was presumably well to do," I remarked, endeavouring to imitate my companion's processes. "Such paper could not be bought under half a crown a packet. It is peculiarly strong and stiff."

"Peculiar — that is the very word," said Holmes. "It is not an English paper at all. Hold it up to the light."

I did so, and saw a large "*E*" with a small "*g*," a "*P*," and a large "*G*" with a small "*t*" woven into the texture of the paper.

"What do you make of that?" asked Holmes.

"The name of the maker, no doubt; or his monogram, rather."

"Not at all. The '*G*' with the small '*t*' stands for 'Gesellschaft,' which is the German for 'Company.' It is a customary contraction like our 'Co.' '*P*,' of course, stands for 'Papier.' Now for the '*Eg*.' Let us glance at our Continental Gazetteer." He took down a heavy brown volume from his shelves. "Eglow, Eglonitz — here we are, Egria. It is in a German-speaking country — in Bohemia, not far from Carlsbad. 'Remarkable as being the scene of the death of Wallenstein,[2] and for its numerous glass factories and paper mills.' Ha, ha, my boy, what do you make of that?" His eyes sparkled, and he sent up a great blue triumphant cloud from his cigarette.

"The paper was made in Bohemia," I said.

"Precisely. And the man who wrote the note is a German. Do you note the peculiar construction of the sentence — 'This account of you we have from all quarters received.' A Frenchman or Russian could not have written that. It is the German who is so uncourteous to his verbs. It only remains, therefore, to discover what is wanted by this German who writes upon Bohemian paper and prefers wearing a mask to showing his face. And here he comes, if I am not mistaken, to resolve all our doubts."

As he spoke there was the sharp sound of horses' hoofs and grating wheels against the curb, followed by a sharp pull at the bell. Holmes whistled.

"A pair, by the sound," said he. "Yes," he continued, glancing out of the window. "A nice little brougham[3] and a pair of beauties. A hundred and fifty guineas apiece. There's money in this case, Watson, if there is nothing else."

"I think that I had better go, Holmes."

[2]*Born in Bohemia, Albrecht Wenzel Eusebius von Wallenstein, Duke of Friedland, was assassinated during the Thirty Years' War.*

[3]*Four-wheeled carriage with an outdoor driver's seat.*

"Not a bit, Doctor. Stay where you are. I am lost without my Boswell.[4] And this promises to be interesting. It would be a pity to miss it."

"But your client —"

"Never mind him. I may want your help, and so may he. Here he comes. Sit down in that armchair, Doctor, and give us your best attention."

A slow and heavy step, which had been heard upon the stairs and in the passage, paused immediately outside the door. Then there was a loud and authoritative tap.

"Come in!" said Holmes.

A man entered who could hardly have been less than six feet six inches in height, with the chest and limbs of a Hercules. His dress was rich with a richness which would, in England, be looked upon as akin to bad taste. Heavy bands of Astrakhan were slashed across the sleeves and fronts of his double-breasted coat, while the deep blue cloak which was thrown over his shoulders was lined with flame-coloured silk and secured at the neck with a brooch which consisted of a single flaming beryl. Boots which extended halfway up his calves, and which were trimmed at the tops with rich brown fur, completed the impression of barbaric opulence which was suggested by his whole appearance. He carried a broad-brimmed hat in his hand, while he wore across the upper part of his face, extending down past the cheekbones, a black vizard mask, which he had apparently adjusted that very moment, for his hand was still raised to it as he entered. From the lower part of the face he appeared to be a man of strong character, with a thick, hanging lip, and a long, straight chin suggestive of resolution pushed to the length of obstinacy.

"You had my note?" he asked with a deep harsh voice and a strongly marked German accent. "I told you that I would call." He looked from one to the other of us, as if uncertain which to address.

"Pray take a seat," said Holmes. "This is my friend and colleague, Dr. Watson, who is occasionally good enough to help me in my cases. Whom have I the honour to address?"

"You may address me as the Count Von Kramm, a Bohemian nobleman. I understand that this gentleman, your friend, is a man of honour and discretion, whom I may trust with a matter of the most extreme importance. If not, I should much prefer to communicate with you alone."

I rose to go, but Holmes caught me by the wrist and pushed me back into my chair. "It is both, or none," said he. "You may say before this gentleman anything which you may say to me."

The Count shrugged his broad shoulders. "Then I must begin," said he, "by binding you both to absolute secrecy for two years; at the end of that time the matter will be of no importance. At present it is not too much to say that it is of such weight it may have an influence upon European history."

[4]*James Boswell, famous biographer of Samuel Johnson.*

"I promise," said Holmes.

"And I."

"You will excuse this mask," continued our strange visitor. "The august person who employs me wishes his agent to be unknown to you, and I may confess at once that the title by which I have just called myself is not exactly my own."

"I was aware of it," said Holmes drily.

"The circumstances are of great delicacy, and every precaution has to be taken to quench what might grow to be an immense scandal and seriously compromise one of the reigning families of Europe. To speak plainly, the matter implicates the great House of Ormstein, hereditary kings of Bohemia."

"I was also aware of that," murmured Holmes, settling himself down in his armchair and closing his eyes.

Our visitor glanced with some apparent surprise at the languid, lounging figure of the man who had been no doubt depicted to him as the most incisive reasoner and most energetic agent in Europe. Holmes slowly reopened his eyes and looked impatiently at his gigantic client.

"If your Majesty would condescend to state your case," he remarked, "I should be better able to advise you."

The man sprang from his chair and paced up and down the room in uncontrollable agitation. Then, with a gesture of desperation, he tore the mask from his face and hurled it upon the ground. "You are right," he cried; "I am the King. Why should I attempt to conceal it?"

"Why, indeed?" murmured Holmes. "Your Majesty had not spoken before I was aware that I was addressing Wilhelm Gottsreich Sigismond von Ormstein, Grand Duke of Cassel-Felstein, and hereditary King of Bohemia."

"But you can understand," said our strange visitor, sitting down once more and passing his hand over his high white forehead, "you can understand that I am not accustomed to doing such business in my own person. Yet the matter was so delicate that I could not confide it to an agent without putting myself in his power. I have come *incognito* from Prague for the purpose of consulting you."

"Then, pray consult," said Holmes, shutting his eyes once more.

"The facts are briefly these: Some five years ago, during a lengthy visit to Warsaw, I made the acquaintance of the well-known adventuress Irene Adler. The name is no doubt familiar to you."

"Kindly look her up in my index, Doctor," murmured Holmes without opening his eyes. For many years he had adopted a system of docketing all paragraphs concerning men and things, so that it was difficult to name a subject or a person on which he could not at once furnish information. In this case I found her biography sandwiched in between that of a Hebrew rabbi and that of a staff-commander who had written a monograph upon the deep sea fishes.

"Let me see!" said Holmes. "Hum! Born in New Jersey in the year 1858. Contralto — hum! La Scala, hum! Prima donna Imperial Opera of Warsaw — Yes! Retired from operatic stage — ha! Living in London — quite so! Your Majesty, as I understand, became entangled with this young person, wrote her some compromising letters, and is now desirous of getting those letters back."

"Precisely so. But how —"

"Was there a secret marriage?"

"None."

"No legal papers or certificates?"

"None."

"Then I fail to follow your Majesty. If this young person should produce her letters for blackmailing or other purposes, how is she to prove their authenticity?"

"There is the writing."

"Pooh, pooh! Forgery."

"My private note-paper."

"Stolen."

"My own seal."

"Imitated."

"My photograph."

"Bought."

"We were both in the photograph."

"Oh, dear! That is very bad! Your Majesty has indeed committed an indiscretion."

"I was mad — insane."

"You have compromised yourself seriously."

"I was only Crown Prince then. I was young. I am but thirty now."

"It must be recovered."

"We have tried and failed."

"Your Majesty must pay. It must be bought."

"She will not sell."

"Stolen, then."

"Five attempts have been made. Twice burglars in my pay ransacked her house. Once we diverted her luggage when she travelled. Twice she has been waylaid. There has been no result."

"No sign of it?"

"Absolutely none."

Holmes laughed. "It is quite a pretty little problem," said he.

"But a very serious one to me," returned the King reproachfully.

"Very, indeed. And what does she propose to do with the photograph?"

"To ruin me."

"But how?"

"I am about to be married."

"So I have heard."

"To Clotilde Lothman von Saxe-Meningen, second daughter of the King of Scandinavia. You may know the strict principles of her family. She is herself the very soul of delicacy. A shadow of a doubt as to my conduct would bring the matter to an end."

"And Irene Adler?"

"Threatens to send them the photograph. And she will do it. I know that she will do it. You do not know her, but she has a soul of steel. She has the face of the most beautiful of women, and the mind of the most resolute of men. Rather than I should marry another woman, there are no lengths to which she would not go — none."

"You are sure that she has not sent it yet?"

"I am sure."

"And why?"

"Because she has said that she would send it on the day when the betrothal was publicly proclaimed. That will be next Monday."

"Oh, then we have three days yet," said Holmes with a yawn. "That is very fortunate, as I have one or two matters of importance to look into just at present. Your Majesty will, of course, stay in London for the present?"

"Certainly. You will find me at the Langham under the name of the Count Von Kramm."

"Then I shall drop you a line to let you know how we progress."

"Pray do so. I shall be all anxiety."

"Then, as to money?"

"You have *carte blanche*."

"Absolutely?"

"I tell you that I would give one of the provinces of my kingdom to have that photograph."

"And for present expenses?"

The King took a heavy chamois leather bag from under his cloak and laid it on the table.

"There are three hundred pounds in gold and seven hundred in notes," he said.

Holmes scribbled a receipt upon a sheet of his note-book and handed it to him.

"And Mademoiselle's address?" he asked.

"Is Briony Lodge, Serpentine Avenue, St. John's Wood."

Holmes took a note of it. "One other question," said he. "Was the photograph a cabinet?"[5]

"It was."

"Then, good night, your Majesty, and I trust that we shall soon have some good news for you. And good night, Watson," he added, as the wheels of the royal brougham

[5]*Photograph of approximately 4 × 6 inches suitable for framing or mounting.*

rolled down the street. "If you will be good enough to call to-morrow afternoon at three o'clock I should like to chat this little matter over with you."

II.

At three o'clock precisely I was at Baker Street, but Holmes had not yet returned. The landlady informed me that he had left the house shortly after eight o'clock in the morning. I sat down beside the fire, however, with the intention of awaiting him, however long he might be. I was already deeply interested in his inquiry, for, though it was surrounded by none of the grim and strange features which were associated with the two crimes which I have already recorded,[6] still, the nature of the case and the exalted station of his client gave it a character of its own. Indeed, apart from the nature of the investigation which my friend had on hand, there was something in his masterly grasp of a situation, and his keen, incisive reasoning, which made it a pleasure to me to study his system of work, and to follow the quick, subtle methods by which he disentangled the most inextricable mysteries. So accustomed was I to his invariable success that the very possibility of his failing had ceased to enter into my head.

It was close upon four before the door opened, and a drunken-looking groom, ill-kempt and side-whiskered, with an inflamed face and disreputable clothes, walked into the room. Accustomed as I was to my friend's amazing powers in the use of disguises, I had to look three times before I was certain that it was indeed he. With a nod he vanished into the bedroom, whence he emerged in five minutes tweed-suited and respectable, as of old. Putting his hands into his pockets, he stretched out his legs in front of the fire and laughed heartily for some minutes.

"Well, really!" he cried, and then he choked; and laughed again until he was obliged to lie back, limp and helpless, in the chair.

"What is it?"

"It's quite too funny. I am sure you could never guess how I employed my morning, or what I ended by doing."

"I can't imagine. I suppose that you have been watching the habits, and perhaps the house, of Miss Irene Adler."

"Quite so, but the sequel was rather unusual. I will tell you, however. I left the house a little after eight o'clock this morning in the character of a groom out of work. There is a wonderful sympathy and freemasonry among horsey men. Be one of them, and you will know all that there is to know. I soon found Briony Lodge. It is a *bijou* villa, with a garden at the back, but built out in front right up to the road, two stories. Chubb lock to the door. Large sitting-room on the right side, well furnished, with long windows almost to the floor, and those preposterous English window fasteners

[6]A Study in Scarlet *and* The Sign of Four, *which preceded* The Adventures of Sherlock Holmes.

which a child could open. Behind there was nothing remarkable, save that the passage window could be reached from the top of the coach-house. I walked round it and examined it closely from every point of view, but without noting anything else of interest.

"I then lounged down the street and found, as I expected, that there was a mews in a lane which runs down by one wall of the garden. I lent the ostlers a hand in rubbing down their horses, and I received in exchange twopence, a glass of half-and-half, two fills of shag tobacco, and as much information as I could desire about Miss Adler, to say nothing of half a dozen other people in the neighbourhood in whom I was not in the least interested, but whose biographies I was compelled to listen to."

"And what of Irene Adler?" I asked.

"Oh, she has turned all the men's heads down in that part. She is the daintiest thing under a bonnet on this planet. So say the Serpentine-mews, to a man. She lives quietly, sings at concerts, drives out at five every day, and returns at seven sharp for dinner. Seldom goes out at other times, except when she sings. Has only one male visitor, but a good deal of him. He is dark, handsome, and dashing; never calls less than once a day, and often twice. He is a Mr. Godfrey Norton, of the Inner Temple. See the advantages of a cabman as a confidant. They had driven him home a dozen times from Serpentine-mews, and knew all about him. When I had listened to all they had to tell, I began to walk up and down near Briony Lodge once more, and to think over my plan of campaign.

"This Godfrey Norton was evidently an important factor in the matter. He was a lawyer. That sounded ominous. What was the relation between them, and what the object of his repeated visits? Was she his client, his friend, or his mistress? If the former, she had probably transferred the photograph to his keeping. If the latter, it was less likely. On the issue of this question depended whether I should continue my work at Briony Lodge, or turn my attention to the gentleman's chambers in the Temple. It was a delicate point, and it widened the field of my inquiry. I fear that I bore you with these details, but I have to let you see my little difficulties, if you are to understand the situation."

"I am following you closely," I answered.

"I was still balancing the matter in my mind when a hansom cab[7] drove up to Briony Lodge, and a gentleman sprang out. He was a remarkably handsome man, dark, aquiline, and moustached — evidently the man of whom I had heard. He appeared to be in a great hurry, shouted to the cabman to wait, and brushed past the maid who opened the door with the air of a man who was thoroughly at home.

"He was in the house about half an hour, and I could catch glimpses of him in the windows of the sitting-room, pacing up and down, talking excitedly, and waving his arms. Of her I could see nothing. Presently he emerged, looking even more flurried

[7] *Two-wheeled, two-passenger carriage.*

than before. As he stepped up to the cab, he pulled a gold watch from his pocket and looked at it earnestly, 'Drive like the devil,' he shouted, 'first to Gross & Hankey's in Regent Street, and then to the Church of St. Monica in the Edgeware Road. Half a guinea if you do it in twenty minutes!'

"Away they went, and I was just wondering whether I should not do well to follow them when up the lane came a neat little landau,[8] the coachman with his coat only half-buttoned, and his tie under his ear, while all the tags of his harness were sticking out of the buckles. It hadn't pulled up before she shot out of the hall door and into it. I only caught a glimpse of her at the moment, but she was a lovely woman, with a face that a man might die for.

"'The Church of St. Monica, John,' she cried, 'and half a sovereign if you reach it in twenty minutes.'

"This was quite too good to lose, Watson. I was just balancing whether I should run for it, or whether I should perch behind her landau when a cab came through the street. The driver looked twice at such a shabby fare; but I jumped in before he could object. 'The Church of St. Monica,' said I, 'and half a sovereign if you reach it in twenty minutes.' It was twenty-five minutes to twelve, and of course it was clear enough what was in the wind.

"My cabby drove fast. I don't think I ever drove faster, but the others were there before us. The cab and the landau with their steaming horses were in front of the door when I arrived. I paid the man, and hurried into the church. There was not a soul there save the two whom I had followed and a surpliced clergyman, who seemed to be expostulating with them. They were all three standing in a knot in front of the altar. I lounged up the side aisle like any other idler who has dropped into a church. Suddenly, to my surprise, the three at the altar faced round to me, and Godfrey Norton came running as hard as he could towards me.

"'Thank God,' he cried. 'You'll do. Come! Come!'

"'What then?' I asked.

"'Come, man, come, only three minutes, or it won't be legal.'

"I was half dragged up to the altar, and, before I knew where I was, I found myself mumbling responses which were whispered in my ear, and vouching for things of which I knew nothing, and generally assisting in the secure tying up of Irene Adler, spinster, to Godfrey Norton, bachelor. It was all done in an instant, and there was the gentleman thanking me on the one side and the lady on the other, while the clergyman beamed on me in front. It was the most preposterous position in which I ever found myself in my life, and it was the thought of it that started me laughing just now. It seems that there had been some informality about their license, that the clergyman absolutely refused to marry them without a witness of some sort, and that my lucky appearance saved the bridegroom from having to sally out into the streets

[8] *Four-wheeled, two- or four-horse, covered carriage capable of carrying four people.*

in search of a best man. The bride gave me a sovereign, and I mean to wear it on my watch chain in memory of the occasion."

"This is a very unexpected turn of affairs," said I; "and what then?"

"Well, I found my plans very seriously menaced. It looked as if the pair might take an immediate departure, and so necessitate very prompt and energetic measures on my part. At the church door, however, they separated, he driving back to the Temple, and she to her own house. 'I shall drive out in the park at five as usual,' she said as she left him. I heard no more. They drove away in different directions, and I went off to make my own arrangements."

"Which are?"

"Some cold beef and a glass of beer," he answered, ringing the bell. "I have been too busy to think of food, and I am likely to be busier still this evening. By the way, Doctor, I shall want your co-operation."

"I shall be delighted."

"You don't mind breaking the law?"

"Not in the least."

"Nor running a chance of arrest?"

"Not in a good cause."

"Oh, the cause is excellent!"

"Then I am your man."

"I was sure that I might rely on you."

"But what is it you wish?"

"When Mrs. Turner has brought in the tray I will make it clear to you. Now," he said as he turned hungrily on the simple fare that our landlady had provided, "I must discuss it while I eat, for I have not much time. It is nearly five now. In two hours we must be on the scene of action. Miss Irene, or Madame, rather, returns from her drive at seven. We must be at Briony Lodge to meet her."

"And what then?"

"You must leave that to me. I have already arranged what is to occur. There is only one point on which I must insist. You must not interfere, come what may. You understand?"

"I am to be neutral?"

"To do nothing whatever. There will probably be some small unpleasantness. Do not join in it. It will end in my being conveyed into the house. Four or five minutes afterwards the sitting-room window will open. You are to station yourself close to that open window."

"Yes."

"You are to watch me, for I will be visible to you."

"Yes."

"And when I raise my hand — so — you will throw into the room what I give you to throw, and will, at the same time, raise the cry of fire. You quite follow me?"

"Entirely."

"It is nothing very formidable," he said, taking a long cigar-shaped roll from his pocket. "It is an ordinary plumber's smoke-rocket, fitted with a cap at either end to make it self-lighting. Your task is confined to that. When you raise your cry of fire, it will be taken up by quite a number of people. You may then walk to the end of the street, and I will rejoin you in ten minutes. I hope that I have made myself clear?"

"I am to remain neutral, to get near the window, to watch you, and, at the signal, to throw in this object, then to raise the cry of fire, and to await you at the corner of the street."

"Precisely."

"Then you may entirely rely on me."

"That is excellent. I think, perhaps, it is almost time that I prepare for the new *rôle* I have to play."

He disappeared into his bedroom, and returned in a few minutes in the character of an amiable and simple-minded Nonconformist clergyman. His broad black hat, his baggy trousers, his white tie, his sympathetic smile, and general look of peering and benevolent curiosity were such as Mr. John Hare[9] alone could have equalled. It was not merely that Holmes changed his costume. His expression, his manner, his very soul seemed to vary with every fresh part that he assumed. The stage lost a fine actor, even as science lost an acute reasoner, when he became a specialist in crime.

It was a quarter past six when we left Baker Street, and it still wanted ten minutes to the hour when we found ourselves in Serpentine Avenue. It was already dusk, and the lamps were just being lighted as we paced up and down in front of Briony Lodge, waiting for the coming of its occupant. The house was just such as I had pictured it from Sherlock Holmes' succinct description, but the locality appeared to be less private than I expected. On the contrary, for a small street in a quiet neighbourhood, it was remarkably animated. There was a group of shabbily dressed men smoking and laughing in a corner, a scissors grinder with his wheel, two guardsmen who were flirting with a nurse-girl, and several well-dressed young men who were lounging up and down with cigars in their mouths.

"You see," remarked Holmes, as we paced to and fro in front of the house, "this marriage rather simplifies matters. The photograph becomes a double-edged weapon now. The chances are that she would be as averse to its being seen by Mr. Godfrey Norton, as our client is to its coming to the eyes of his princess. Now the question is — Where are we to find the photograph?"

"Where, indeed?"

"It is most unlikely that she carries it about with her. It is cabinet size. Too large

[9]*Famous English actor.*

for easy concealment about a woman's dress. She knows that the King is capable of having her waylaid and searched. Two attempts of the sort have already been made. We may take it, then, that she does not carry it about with her."

"Where, then?"

"Her banker or her lawyer. There is that double possibility. But I am inclined to think neither. Women are naturally secretive, and they like to do their own secreting. Why should she hand it over to anyone else? She could trust her own guardianship, but she could not tell what indirect or political influence might be brought to bear upon a business man. Besides, remember that she had resolved to use it within a few days. It must be where she can lay her hands upon it. It must be in her own house."

"But it has twice been burgled."

"Pshaw! They did not know how to look."

"But how will you look?"

"I will not look."

"What then?"

"I will get her to show me."

"But she will refuse."

"She will not be able to. But I hear the rumble of wheels. It is her carriage. Now carry out my orders to the letter."

As he spoke the gleam of the side-lights of a carriage came round the curve of the avenue. It was a smart little landau which rattled up to the door of Briony Lodge. As it pulled up, one of the loafing men at the corner dashed forward to open the door in the hope of earning a copper, but was elbowed away by another loafer, who had rushed up with the same intention. A fierce quarrel broke out, which was increased by the two guardsmen, who took sides with one of the loungers, and by the scissors grinder, who was equally hot upon the other side. A blow was struck, and in an instant the lady, who had stepped from her carriage, was the centre of a little knot of flushed and struggling men, who struck savagely at each other with their fists and sticks. Holmes dashed into the crowd to protect the lady; but just as he reached her, he gave a cry and dropped to the ground, with the blood running freely down his face. At his fall the guardsmen took to their heels in one direction and the loungers in the other, while a number of better dressed people, who had watched the scuffle without taking part in it, crowded in to help the lady and to attend to the injured man. Irene Adler, as I will still call her, had hurried up the steps; but she stood at the top with her superb figure outlined against the lights of the hall, looking back into the street.

"Is the poor gentleman much hurt?" she asked.

"He is dead," cried several voices.

"No, no, there's life in him!" shouted another. "But he'll be gone before you can get him to hospital."

"He's a brave fellow," said a woman. "They would have had the lady's purse and watch if it hadn't been for him. They were a gang, and a rough one, too. Ah, he's breathing now."

"He can't lie in the street. May we bring him in, marm?"

"Surely. Bring him into the sitting-room. There is a comfortable sofa. This way, please!"

Slowly and solemnly he was borne into Briony Lodge and laid out in the principal room, while I still observed the proceedings from my post by the window. The lamps had been lit, but the blinds had not been drawn, so that I could see Holmes as he lay upon the couch. I do not know whether he was seized with compunction at that moment for the part he was playing, but I know that I never felt more heartily ashamed of myself in my life than when I saw the beautiful creature against whom I was conspiring, or the grace and kindliness with which she waited upon the injured man. And yet it would be the blackest treachery to Holmes to draw back now from the part which he had entrusted to me. I hardened my heart, and took the smoke-rocket from under my ulster. After all, I thought, we are not injuring her. We are but preventing her from injuring another.

Holmes had sat up upon the couch, and I saw him motion like a man who is in need of air. A maid rushed across and threw open the window. At the same instant I saw him raise his hand and at the signal I tossed my rocket into the room with a cry of "Fire!" The word was no sooner out of my mouth than the whole crowd of spectators, well dressed and ill — gentlemen, ostlers, and servant-maids — joined in a general shriek of "Fire!" Thick clouds of smoke curled through the room and out at the open window. I caught a glimpse of rushing figures, and a moment later the voice of Holmes from within assuring them that it was a false alarm. Slipping through the shouting crowd I made my way to the corner of the street, and in ten minutes was rejoiced to find my friend's arm in mine, and to get away from the scene of uproar. He walked swiftly and in silence for some few minutes until we had turned down one of the quiet streets which lead towards the Edgeware Road.

"You did it very nicely, Doctor," he remarked. "Nothing could have been better. It is all right."

"You have the photograph?"

"I know where it is."

"And how did you find out?"

"She showed me, as I told you she would."

"I am still in the dark."

"I do not wish to make a mystery," said he laughing. "The matter was perfectly simple. You, of course, saw that everyone in the street was an accomplice. They were all engaged for the evening."

"I guessed as much."

"Then, when the row broke out, I had a little moist red paint in the palm of my hand. I rushed forward, fell down, clapped my hand to my face, and became a piteous spectacle. It is an old trick."

"That also I could fathom."

"Then they carried me in. She was bound to have me in. What else could she do? And into her sitting-room, which was the very room which I suspected. It lay between that and her bedroom, and I was determined to see which. They laid me on a couch, I motioned for air, they were compelled to open the window, and you had your chance."

"How did that help you?"

"It was all-important. When a woman thinks that her house is on fire, her instinct is at once to rush to the thing which she values most. It is a perfectly overpowering impulse, and I have more than once taken advantage of it. In the case of the Darlington Substitution Scandal it was of use to me, and also in the Arnsworth Castle business. A married woman grabs at her baby — an unmarried one reaches for her jewel-box. Now it was clear to me that our lady of to-day had nothing in the house more precious to her than what we are in quest of. She would rush to secure it. The alarm of fire was admirably done. The smoke and shouting were enough to shake nerves of steel. She responded beautifully. The photograph is in a recess behind a sliding panel just above the right bell-pull. She was there in an instant, and I caught a glimpse of it as she half-drew it out. When I cried out that it was a false alarm, she replaced it, glanced at the rocket, rushed from the room, and I have not seen her since. I rose, and, making my excuses, escaped from the house. I hesitated whether to attempt to secure the photograph at once; but the coachman had come in, and, as he was watching me narrowly, it seemed safer to wait. A little over-precipitance may ruin all."

"And now?" I asked.

"Our quest is practically finished. I shall call with the King to-morrow, and with you, if you care to come with us. We will be shown into the sitting-room to wait for the lady, but it is probable that when she comes she may find neither us nor the photograph. It might be a satisfaction to his Majesty to regain it with his own hands."

"And when will you call?"

"At eight in the morning. She will not be up, so that we shall have a clear field. Besides, we must be prompt, for this marriage may mean a complete change in her life and habits. I must wire to the King without delay."

We had reached Baker Street and had stopped at the door. He was searching his pockets for the key when someone passing said:—

"Good-night, Mister Sherlock Holmes."

There were several people on the pavement at the time, but the greeting appeared to come from a slim youth in an ulster who had hurried by.

"I've heard that voice before," said Holmes, staring down the dimly lit street. "Now, I wonder who the deuce that could have been."

III.

I slept at Baker Street that night, and we were engaged upon our toast and coffee in the morning when the King of Bohemia rushed into the room.

"You have really got it!" he cried, grasping Sherlock Holmes by either shoulder and looking eagerly into his face.

"Not yet."

"But you have hopes?"

"I have hopes."

"Then, come. I am all impatience to be gone."

"We must have a cab."

"No, my brougham is waiting."

"Then that will simplify matters." We descended, and started off once more for Briony Lodge.

"Irene Adler is married," remarked Holmes.

"Married! When?"

"Yesterday."

"But to whom?"

"To an English lawyer named Norton."

"But she could not love him."

"I am in hopes that she does."

"And why in hopes?"

"Because it would spare your Majesty all fear of future annoyance. If the lady loves her husband, she does not love your Majesty. If she does not love your Majesty, there is no reason why she should interfere with your Majesty's plan."

"It is true. And yet—! Well! I wish she had been of my own station! What a queen she would have made!" He relapsed into a moody silence which was not broken until we drew up in Serpentine Avenue.

The door of Briony Lodge was open, and an elderly woman stood upon the steps. She watched us with a sardonic eye as we stepped from the brougham.

"Mr. Sherlock Holmes, I believe?" said she.

"I am Mr. Holmes," answered my companion, looking at her with a questioning and rather startled gaze.

"Indeed! My mistress told me that you were likely to call. She left this morning with her husband, by the 5:15 train from Charing Cross, for the Continent."

"What!" Sherlock Holmes staggered back, white with chagrin and surprise. "Do you mean that she has left England?"

"Never to return."

"And the papers?" asked the King hoarsely. "All is lost."

"We shall see." He pushed past the servant, and rushed into the drawing-room, followed by the King and myself. The furniture was scattered about in every direction, with dismantled shelves and open drawers, as if the lady had hurriedly ransacked them before her flight. Holmes rushed at the bell-pull, tore back a small sliding shutter, and, plunging in his hand, pulled out a photograph and a letter. The photograph was of Irene Adler herself in evening dress, the letter was superscribed to "Sherlock Holmes, Esq. To be left till called for." My friend tore it open and we all three read it together. It was dated at midnight of the preceding night and ran in this way:—

"MY DEAR MR. SHERLOCK HOLMES,—You really did it very well. You took me in completely. Until after the alarm of fire, I had not a suspicion. But then, when I found how I had betrayed myself, I began to think. I had been warned against you months ago. I had been told that, if the King employed an agent, it would certainly be you. And your address had been given me. Yet, with all this, you made me reveal what you wanted to know. Even after I became suspicious, I found it hard to think evil of such a dear, kind old clergyman. But, you know, I have been trained as an actress myself. Male costume is nothing new to me. I often take advantage of the freedom which it gives. I sent John, the coachman, to watch you, ran up stairs, got into my walking-clothes, as I call them, and came down just as you departed.

"Well, I followed you to your door, and so made sure that I was really an object of interest to the celebrated Mr. Sherlock Holmes. Then I, rather imprudently, wished you good-night, and started for the Temple to see my husband.

"We both thought the best resource was flight, when pursued by so formidable an antagonist; so you will find the nest empty when you call to-morrow. As to the photograph, your client may rest in peace. I love and am loved by a better man than he. The King may do what he will without hindrance from one whom he has cruelly wronged. I keep it only to safeguard myself, and to preserve a weapon which will always secure me from any steps which he might take in the future. I leave a photograph which he might care to possess; and I remain, dear Mr. Sherlock Holmes, very truly yours,

"IRENE NORTON, *née* ADLER."

"What a woman—oh, what a woman!" cried the King of Bohemia, when we had all three read this epistle. "Did I not tell you how quick and resolute she was? Would she not have made an admirable queen? Is it not a pity that she was not on my level?"

"From what I have seen of the lady she seems, indeed, to be on a very different level to your Majesty," said Holmes, coldly. "I am sorry that I have not been able to bring your Majesty's business to a more successful conclusion."

"On the contrary, my dear sir," cried the King. "Nothing could be more successful. I know that her word is inviolate. The photograph is now as safe as if it were in the fire."

"I am glad to hear your Majesty say so."

"I am immensely indebted to you. Pray tell me in what way I can reward you. This ring—." He slipped an emerald snake ring from his finger and held it out upon the palm of his hand.

"Your Majesty has something which I should value even more highly," said Holmes.

"You have but to name it."

"This photograph!"

The King stared at him in amazement.

"Irene's photograph!" he cried. "Certainly, if you wish it."

"I thank your Majesty. Then there is no more to be done in the matter. I have the honour to wish you a very good-morning." He bowed, and, turning away without observing the hand which the King had stretched out to him, he set off in my company for his chambers.

And that was how a great scandal threatened to affect the kingdom of Bohemia, and how the best plans of Mr. Sherlock Holmes were beaten by a woman's wit. He used to make merry over the cleverness of women, but I have not heard him do it of late. And when he speaks of Irene Adler, or when he refers to her photograph, it is always under the honourable title of *the* woman.

The Adventure of the Speckled Band

by Sir Arthur Conan Doyle

(1892)

On glancing over my notes of the seventy odd cases in which I have during the last eight years studied the methods of my friend Sherlock Holmes, I find many tragic, some comic, a large number merely strange, but none commonplace; for, working as he did rather for the love of his art than for the acquirement of wealth, he refused to associate himself with any investigation which did not tend towards the unusual, and even the fantastic. Of all these varied cases, however, I cannot recall any which presented more singular features than that which was associated with the well-known Surrey family of the Roylotts of Stoke Moran. The events in question occurred in the early days of my association with Holmes, when we were sharing rooms as bachelors in Baker Street. It is possible that I might have placed them upon record before, but a promise of secrecy was made at the time, from which I have only been freed during the last month by the untimely death of the lady to whom the pledge was given. It is perhaps as well that the facts should now come to light, for I have reasons to know that there are widespread rumours as to the death of Dr. Grimesby Roylott which tend to make the matter even more terrible than the truth.

It was early in April in the year '83 that I woke one morning to find Sherlock Holmes standing, fully dressed, by the side of my bed. He was a late riser, as a rule, and, as the clock on the mantelpiece showed me that it was only a quarter-past seven, I blinked up at him in some surprise, and perhaps just a little resentment, for I was myself regular in my habits.

"Very sorry to knock you up, Watson," said he, "but it's the common lot this morning. Mrs. Hudson has been knocked up, she retorted upon me, and I on you."

"What is it, then — a fire?"

"No; a client. It seems that a young lady has arrived in a considerable state of excitement, who insists upon seeing me. She is waiting now in the sitting-room. Now, when young ladies wander about the Metropolis at this hour of the morning, and knock sleepy people up out of their beds, I presume that it is something very pressing which they have to communicate. Should it prove to be an interesting case, you would, I am sure, wish to follow it from the outset. I thought, at any rate, that I should call you and give you the chance."

"My dear fellow, I would not miss it for anything."

I had no keener pleasure than in following Holmes in his professional investigations, and in admiring the rapid deductions, as swift as intuitions, and yet always founded on a logical basis, with which he unravelled the problems which were submitted to him. I rapidly threw on my clothes, and was ready in a few minutes to accompany my friend down to the sitting-room. A lady dressed in black and heavily veiled, who had been sitting in the window, rose as we entered.

"Good morning, madam," said Holmes cheerily. "My name is Sherlock Holmes. This is my intimate friend and associate, Dr. Watson, before whom you can speak as freely as before myself. Ha, I am glad to see that Mrs. Hudson has had the good sense to light the fire. Pray draw up to it, and I shall order you a cup of hot coffee, for I observe that you are shivering."

"It is not cold which makes me shiver," said the woman in a low voice, changing her seat as requested.

"What, then?"

"It is fear, Mr. Holmes. It is terror." She raised her veil as she spoke, and we could see that she was indeed in a pitiable state of agitation, her face all drawn and grey, with restless frightened eyes, like those of some hunted animal. Her features and figure were those of a woman of thirty, but her hair was shot with premature grey, and her expression was weary and haggard. Sherlock Holmes ran her over with one of his quick, all-comprehensive glances.

"You must not fear," said he, soothingly, bending forward and patting her forearm. "We shall soon set matters right, I have no doubt. You have come in by train this morning, I see."

"You know me, then?"

"No, but I observe the second half of a return ticket in the palm of your left glove. You must have started early, and yet you had a good drive in a dog-cart, along heavy roads, before you reached the station."

The lady gave a violent start and stared in bewilderment at my companion.

"There is no mystery, my dear madam," said he, smiling. "The left arm of your jacket is spattered with mud in no less than seven places. The marks are perfectly fresh. There is no vehicle save a dog-cart[1] which throws up mud in that way, and then only when you sit on the left-hand side of the driver."

"Whatever your reasons may be, you are perfectly correct," said she. "I started from home before six, reached Leatherhead at twenty past, and came in by the first train to Waterloo. Sir, I can stand this strain no longer; I shall go mad if it continues.

[1]*Open two-wheeled carriage.*

I have no one to turn to — none, save only one, who cares for me, and he, poor fellow, can be of little aid. I have heard of you, Mr. Holmes; I have heard of you from Mrs. Farintosh, whom you helped in the hour of her sore need. It was from her that I had your address. Oh, sir, do you not think that you could help me, too, and at least throw a little light through the dense darkness which surrounds me? At present it is out of my power to reward you for your services, but in a month or six weeks I shall be married, with the control of my own income, and then at least you shall not find me ungrateful."

Holmes turned to his desk and, unlocking it, drew out a small case-book, which he consulted.

"Farintosh," said he. "Ah yes, I recall the case; it was concerned with an opal tiara. I think it was before your time, Watson. I can only say, madam, that I shall be happy to devote the same care to your case as I did to that of your friend. As to reward, my profession is its own reward; but you are at liberty to defray whatever expenses I may be put to, at the time which suits you best. And now I beg that you will lay before us everything that may help us in forming an opinion upon the matter."

"Alas!" replied our visitor, "the very horror of my situation lies in the fact that my fears are so vague, and my suspicions depend so entirely upon small points, which might seem trivial to another, that even he to whom of all others I have a right to look for help and advice looks upon all that I tell him about it as the fancies of a nervous woman. He does not say so, but I can read it from his soothing answers and averted eyes. But I have heard, Mr. Holmes, that you can see deeply into the manifold wickedness of the human heart. You may advise me how to walk amid the dangers which encompass me."

"I am all attention, madam."

"My name is Helen Stoner, and I am living with my stepfather, who is the last survivor of one of the oldest Saxon families in England, the Roylotts of Stoke Moran, on the western border of Surrey."

Holmes nodded his head. "The name is familiar to me," said he.

"The family was at one time among the richest in England, and the estates extended over the borders into Berkshire in the north, and Hampshire in the west. In the last century, however, four successive heirs were of a dissolute and wasteful disposition, and the family ruin was eventually completed by a gambler in the days of the Regency.[2] Nothing was left save a few acres of ground, and the two-hundred-year-old house, which is itself crushed under a heavy mortgage. The last squire dragged out his existence there, living the horrible life of an aristocratic pauper; but his only son, my stepfather, seeing that he must adapt himself to the new conditions, obtained an advance from a relative, which enabled him to take a medical degree and went out

[2]*1811–1820.*

to Calcutta, where, by his professional skill and his force of character, he established a large practice. In a fit of anger, however, caused by some robberies which had been perpetrated in the house, he beat his native butler to death and narrowly escaped a capital sentence. As it was, he suffered a long term of imprisonment, and afterwards returned to England a morose and disappointed man.

"When Dr. Roylott was in India he married my mother, Mrs. Stoner, the young widow of Major-General Stoner, of the Bengal Artillery. My sister Julia and I were twins, and we were only two years old at the time of my mother's re-marriage. She had a considerable sum of money, not less than a thousand a year, and this she bequeathed to Dr. Roylott entirely while we resided with him, with a provision that a certain annual sum should be allowed to each of us in the event of our marriage. Shortly after our return to England my mother died — she was killed eight years ago in a railway accident near Crewe. Dr. Roylott then abandoned his attempts to establish himself in practice in London and took us to live with him in the old ancestral house at Stoke Moran. The money which my mother had left was enough for all our wants, and there seemed to be no obstacle to our happiness.

"But a terrible change came over our stepfather about this time. Instead of making friends and exchanging visits with our neighbours, who had at first been overjoyed to see a Roylott of Stoke Moran back in the old family seat, he shut himself up in his house and seldom came out save to indulge in ferocious quarrels with whoever might cross his path. Violence of temper approaching to mania has been hereditary in the men of the family, and in my stepfather's case it had, I believe, been intensified by his long residence in the tropics. A series of disgraceful brawls took place, two of which ended in the police-court, until at last he became the terror of the village, and the folks would fly at his approach, for he is a man of immense strength, and absolutely uncontrollable in his anger.

"Last week he hurled the local blacksmith over a parapet into a stream, and it was only by paying over all the money which I could gather together that I was able to avert another public exposure. He had no friends at all save the wandering gipsies, and he would give these vagabonds leave to encamp upon the few acres of bramble-covered land which represent the family estate, and would accept in return the hospitality of their tents, wandering away with them sometimes for weeks on end. He has a passion also for Indian animals, which are sent over to him by a correspondent, and he has at this moment a cheetah and a baboon, which wander freely over his grounds, and are feared by the villagers almost as much as their master.

"You can imagine from what I say that my poor sister Julia and I had no great pleasure in our lives. No servant would stay with us, and for a long time we did all the work of the house. She was but thirty at the time of her death, and yet her hair had already begun to whiten, even as mine has."

"Your sister is dead, then?"

"She died just two years ago, and it is of her death that I wish to speak to you.

You can understand that, living the life which I have described, we were little likely to see anyone of our own age and position. We had, however, an aunt, my mother's maiden sister, Miss Honoria Westphail, who lives near Harrow, and we were occasionally allowed to pay short visits at this lady's house. Julia went there at Christmas two years ago, and met there a half-pay major of Marines, to whom she became engaged. My stepfather learned of the engagement when my sister, returned and offered no objection to the marriage; but within a fortnight of the day which had been fixed for the wedding, the terrible event occurred which has deprived me of my only companion."

Sherlock Holmes had been leaning back in his chair with his eyes closed and his head sunk in a cushion, but he half opened his lids now and glanced across at his visitor.

"Pray be precise as to details," said he.

"It is easy for me to be so, for every event of that dreadful time is seared into my memory. The manor-house is, as I have already said, very old, and only one wing is now inhabited. The bedrooms in this wing are on the ground floor, the sitting-rooms being in the central block of the buildings. Of these bedrooms the first is Dr. Roylott's, the second my sister's, and the third my own. There is no communication between them, but they all open out into the same corridor. Do I make myself plain?"

"Perfectly so."

"The windows of the three rooms open out upon the lawn. That fatal night Dr. Roylott had gone to his room early, though we knew that he had not retired to rest, for my sister was troubled by the smell of the strong Indian cigars which it was his custom to smoke. She left her room, therefore, and came into mine, where she sat for some time, chatting about her approaching wedding. At eleven o'clock she rose to leave me, but she paused at the door and looked back.

"'Tell me, Helen,' said she, 'have you ever heard anyone whistle in the dead of the night?'

"'Never,' said I.

"'I suppose that you could not possibly whistle, yourself, in your sleep?'

"'Certainly not. But why?'

"'Because during the last few nights I have always, about three in the morning, heard a low, clear whistle. I am a light sleeper, and it has awakened me. I cannot tell where it came from — perhaps from the next room, perhaps from the lawn. I thought that I would just ask you whether you had heard it.'

"'No, I have not. It must be those wretched gipsies in the plantation.'

"'Very likely. And yet if it were on the lawn, I wonder that you did not hear it also.'

"'Ah, but I sleep more heavily than you.'

"'Well, it is of no great consequence, at any rate.' She smiled back at me, closed my door, and a few moments later I heard her key turn in the lock."

"Indeed," said Holmes. "Was it your custom always to lock yourselves in at night?"

"Always."

"And why?"

"I think that I mentioned to you that the doctor kept a cheetah and a baboon. We had no feeling of security unless our doors were locked."

"Quite so. Pray proceed with your statement."

"I could not sleep that night. A vague feeling of impending misfortune impressed me. My sister and I, you will recollect, were twins, and you know how subtle are the links which bind two souls which are so closely allied. It was a wild night. The wind was howling outside, and the rain was beating and splashing against the windows. Suddenly, amid all the hubbub of the gale, there burst forth the wild scream of a terrified woman. I knew that it was my sister's voice. I sprang from my bed, wrapped a shawl round me, and rushed into the corridor. As I opened my door I seemed to hear a low whistle, such as my sister described, and a few moments later a clanging sound, as if a mass of metal had fallen. As I ran down the passage, my sister's door was unlocked, and revolved slowly upon its hinges. I stared at it horror-stricken, not knowing what was about to issue from it. By the light of the corridor-lamp I saw my sister appear at the opening, her face blanched with terror, her hands groping for help, her whole figure swaying to and fro like that of a drunkard. I ran to her and threw my arms round her, but at that moment her knees seemed to give way and she fell to the ground. She writhed as one who is in terrible pain, and her limbs were dreadfully convulsed. At first I thought that she had not recognised me, but as I bent over her she suddenly shrieked out in a voice which I shall never forget, 'Oh, my God! Helen! It was the band! The speckled band!' There was something else which she would fain have said, and she stabbed with her finger into the air in the direction of the doctor's room, but a fresh convulsion seized her and choked her words. I rushed out, calling loudly for my stepfather, and I met him hastening from his room in his dressing-gown. When he reached my sister's side she was unconscious, and though he poured brandy down her throat and sent for medical aid from the village, all efforts were in vain, for she slowly sank and died without having recovered her consciousness. Such was the dreadful end of my beloved sister."

"One moment," said Holmes, "are you sure about this whistle and metallic sound? Could you swear to it?"

"That was what the county coroner asked me at the inquiry. It is my strong impression that I heard it, and yet, among the crash of the gale and the creaking of an old house, I may possibly have been deceived."

"Was your sister dressed?"

"No, she was in her nightdress. In her right hand was found the charred stump of a match, and in her left a matchbox."

"Showing that she had struck a light and looked about her when the alarm took place. That is important. And what conclusions did the coroner come to?"

"He investigated the case with great care, for Dr. Roylott's conduct had long been notorious in the county, but he was unable to find any satisfactory cause of death. My evidence showed that the door had been fastened upon the inner side, and the windows were blocked by old-fashioned shutters with broad iron bars, which were secured every night. The walls were carefully sounded, and were shown to be quite solid all round, and the flooring was also thoroughly examined, with the same result. The chimney is wide, but is barred up by four large staples. It is certain, therefore, that my sister was quite alone when she met her end. Besides, there were no marks of any violence upon her."

"How about poison?"

"The doctors examined her for it, but without success."

"What do you think that this unfortunate lady died of, then?"

"It is my belief that she died of pure fear and nervous shock, though what it was that frightened her I cannot imagine."

"Were there gipsies in the plantation at the time?"

"Yes, there are nearly always some there."

"Ah, and what did you gather from this allusion to a band — a speckled band?"

"Sometimes I have thought that it was merely the wild talk of delirium, sometimes that it may have referred to some band of people, perhaps to these very gipsies in the plantation. I do not know whether the spotted handkerchiefs which so many of them wear over their heads might have suggested the strange adjective which she used."

Holmes shook his head like a man who is far from being satisfied.

"These are very deep waters," said he; "pray go on with your narrative."

"Two years have passed since then, and my life has been until lately lonelier than ever. A month ago, however, a dear friend, whom I have known for many years, has done me the honour to ask my hand in marriage. His name is Armitage — Percy Armitage — the second son of Mr. Armitage, of Crane Water, near Reading. My stepfather has offered no opposition to the match, and we are to be married in the course of the spring. Two days ago some repairs were started in the west wing of the building, and my bedroom wall has been pierced, so that I have had to move into the chamber in which my sister died, and to sleep in the very bed in which she slept. Imagine, then, my thrill of terror when last night, as I lay awake, thinking over her terrible fate, I suddenly heard in the silence of the night the low whistle which had been the herald of her own death. I sprang up and lit the lamp, but nothing was to be seen in the room. I was too shaken to go to bed again, however, so I dressed, and as soon as it was daylight I slipped down, got a dog-cart at the 'Crown' Inn, which is opposite, and drove to Leatherhead, from whence I have come on this morning with the one object of seeing you and asking your advice."

"You have done wisely," said my friend. "But have you told me all?"

"Yes, all."

"Miss Roylott, you have not. You are screening your stepfather."

"Why, what do you mean?"

For answer Holmes pushed back the frill of black lace which fringed the hand that lay upon our visitor's knee. Five little livid spots, the marks of four fingers and a thumb, were printed upon the white wrist.

"You have been cruelly used," said Holmes.

The lady coloured deeply and covered over her injured wrist. "He is a hard man," she said, "and perhaps he hardly knows his own strength."

There was a long silence, during which Holmes leaned his chin upon his hands and stared into the crackling fire.

"This is a very deep business," he said at last. "There are a thousand details which I should desire to know before I decide upon our course of action. Yet we have not a moment to lose. If we were to come to Stoke Moran to-day, would it be possible for us to see over these rooms without the knowledge of your stepfather?"

"As it happens, he spoke of coming into town to-day upon some most important business. It is probable that he will be away all day, and that there would be nothing to disturb you. We have a housekeeper now, but she is old and foolish, and I could easily get her out of the way."

"Excellent. You are not averse to this trip, Watson?"

"By no means."

"Then we shall both come. What are you going to do yourself?"

"I have one or two things which I would wish to do now that I am in town. But I shall return by the twelve o'clock train, so as to be there in time for your coming."

"And you may expect us early in the afternoon. I have myself some small business matters to attend to. Will you not wait and breakfast?"

"No, I must go. My heart is lightened already since I have confided my trouble to you. I shall look forward to seeing you again this afternoon." She dropped her thick black veil over her face and glided from the room.

"And what do you think of it all, Watson?" asked Sherlock Holmes, leaning back in his chair.

"It seems to me to be a most dark and sinister business."

"Dark enough, and sinister enough."

"Yet if the lady is correct in saying that the flooring and walls are sound, and that the door, window, and chimney are impassable, then her sister must have been undoubtedly alone when she met her mysterious end."

"What becomes, then, of these nocturnal whistles, and what of the very peculiar words of the dying woman?"

"I cannot think."

"When you combine the ideas of whistles at night, the presence of a band of gipsies who are on intimate terms with this old doctor, the fact that we have every reason to believe that the doctor has an interest in preventing his stepdaughter's marriage, the dying allusion to a band, and, finally, the fact that Miss Helen Stoner heard a metallic clang, which might have been caused by one of those metal bars that secured the shutters falling back into its place, I think that there is good ground to think that the mystery may be cleared along those lines."

"But what, then, did the gipsies do?"

"I cannot imagine."

"I see many objections to any such theory."

"And so do I. It is precisely for that reason that we are going to Stoke Moran this day. I want to see whether the objections are fatal, or if they may be explained away. But what, in the name of the devil!"

The ejaculation had been drawn from my companion by the fact that our door had been suddenly dashed open, and that a huge man had framed himself in the aperture. His costume was a peculiar mixture of the professional and of the agricultural, having a black top hat, a long frock coat, and a pair of high gaiters, with a hunting crop swinging in his hand. So tall was he that his hat actually brushed the cross bar of the doorway, and his breadth seemed to span it across from side to side. A large face, seared with a thousand wrinkles, burned yellow with the sun, and marked with every evil passion, was turned from one to the other of us, while his deep-set, bile-shot eyes, and his high, thin, fleshless nose, gave him somewhat the resemblance to a fierce old bird of prey.

"Which of you is Holmes?" asked this apparition.

"My name, sir; but you have the advantage of me," said my companion quietly.

"I am Dr. Grimesby Roylott, of Stoke Moran."

"Indeed, Doctor," said Holmes blandly. "Pray take a seat."

"I will do nothing of the kind. My stepdaughter has been here. I have traced her. What has she been saying to you?"

"It is a little cold for the time of the year," said Holmes.

"What has she been saying to you?" screamed the old man furiously.

"But I have heard that the crocuses promise well," continued my companion imperturbably.

"Ha! You put me off, do you?" said our new visitor, taking a step forward and shaking his hunting crop.

"I know you, you scoundrel! I have heard of you before. You are Holmes, the meddler."

My friend smiled.

"Holmes the busybody!"

His smile broadened.

"Holmes the Scotland Yard Jack-in-office!"

Holmes chuckled heartily. "Your conversation is most entertaining," said he. "When you go out close the door, for there is a decided draught."

"I will go when I have said my say. Don't you dare to meddle with my affairs. I know that Miss Stoner has been here — I traced her! I am a dangerous man to fall foul of! See here." He stepped swiftly forward, seized the poker, and bent it into a curve with his huge brown hands.

"See that you keep yourself out of my grip," he snarled, and hurling the twisted poker into the fireplace, he strode out of the room.

"He seems a very amiable person," said Holmes, laughing. "I am not quite so bulky, but if he had remained I might have shown him that my grip was not much more feeble than his own." As he spoke he picked up the steel poker, and with a sudden effort straightened it out again.

"Fancy his having the insolence to confound me with the official detective force! This incident gives zest to our investigation, however, and I only trust that our little friend will not suffer from her imprudence in allowing this brute to trace her. And now, Watson, we shall order breakfast, and afterwards I shall walk down to Doctors' Commons, where I hope to get some data which may help us in this matter."

It was nearly one o'clock when Sherlock Holmes returned from his excursion. He held in his hand a sheet of blue paper, scrawled over with notes and figures.

"I have seen the will of the deceased wife," said he. "To determine its exact meaning I have been obliged to work out the present prices of the investments with which it is concerned. The total income, which at the time of the wife's death was little short of £1100, is now, through the fall in agricultural prices, not more than £750. Each daughter can claim an income of £250, in case of marriage. It is evident, therefore, that if both girls had married this beauty would have had a mere pittance, while even one of them would cripple him to a very serious extent. My morning's work has not been wasted, since it has proved that he has the very strongest motives for standing in the way of anything of the sort. And now, Watson, this is too serious for dawdling, especially as the old man is aware that we are interesting ourselves in his affairs; so if you are ready, we shall call a cab and drive to Waterloo. I should be very much obliged if you would slip your revolver into your pocket. An Eley's No. 2[3] is an excellent argument with gentlemen who can twist steel pokers into knots. That and a tooth-brush are, I think, all that we need."

At Waterloo we were fortunate in catching a train for Leatherhead, where we hired a trap[4] at the station inn and drove for four or five miles through the lovely Surrey lanes. It was a perfect day, with a bright sun and a few fleecy clouds in the heavens. The trees and wayside hedges were just throwing out their first green shoots, and the air was full of the pleasant smell of the moist earth. To me at least there was a strange contrast between the sweet promise of the spring and this sinister quest

[3] *Type of bullet for a Webley handgun.*
[4] *Two-wheeled, one-horse carriage.*

upon which we were engaged. My companion sat in the front of the trap, his arms folded, his hat pulled down over his eyes, and his chin sunk upon his breast, buried in the deepest thought. Suddenly, however, he started, tapped me on the shoulder, and pointed over the meadows.

"Look there!" said he.

A heavily timbered park stretched up in a gentle slope, thickening into a grove at the highest point. From amid the branches there jutted out the grey gables and high roof-tree of a very old mansion.

"Stoke Moran?" said he.

"Yes, sir, that be the house of Dr. Grimesby Roylott," remarked the driver.

"There is some building going on there," said Holmes; "that is where we are going."

"There's the village," said the driver, pointing to a cluster of roofs some distance to the left; "but if you want to get to the house, you'll find it shorter to get over this stile, and so by the foot-path over the fields. There it is, where the lady is walking."

"And the lady, I fancy, is Miss Stoner," observed Holmes, shading his eyes. "Yes, I think we had better do as you suggest."

We got off, paid our fare, and the trap rattled back on its way to Leatherhead.

"I thought it as well," said Holmes as we climbed the stile, "that this fellow should think we had come here as architects, or on some definite business. It may stop his gossip. Good-afternoon, Miss Stoner. You see that we have been as good as our word."

Our client of the morning had hurried forward to meet us with a face which spoke her joy. "I have been waiting so eagerly for you," she cried, shaking hands with us warmly. "All has turned out splendidly. Dr. Roylott has gone to town, and it is unlikely that he will be back before evening."

"We have had the pleasure of making the doctor's acquaintance," said Holmes, and in a few words he sketched out what had occurred. Miss Stoner turned white to the lips as she listened.

"Good heavens!" she cried, "he has followed me, then."

"So it appears."

"He is so cunning that I never know when I am safe from him. What will he say when he returns?"

"He must guard himself, for he may find that there is someone more cunning than himself upon his track. You must lock yourself up from him to-night. If he is violent, we shall take you away to your aunt's at Harrow. Now, we must make the best use of our time, so kindly take us at once to the rooms which we are to examine."

The building was of grey, lichen-blotched stone, with a high central portion and two curving wings, like the claws of a crab, thrown out on each side. In one of these wings the windows were broken and blocked with wooden boards, while the roof was partly caved in, a picture of ruin. The central portion was in little better repair, but the right-hand block was comparatively modern, and the blinds in the windows, with the blue smoke curling up from the chimneys, showed that this was where the family resided. Some scaffolding had been erected against the end wall, and the stone-work had been broken into, but there were no signs of any workmen at the moment of our visit. Holmes walked slowly up and down the ill-trimmed lawn and examined with deep attention the outsides of the windows.

"This, I take it, belongs to the room in which you used to sleep, the centre one to your sister's, and the one next to the main building to Dr. Roylott's chamber?"

"Exactly so. But I am now sleeping in the middle one."

"Pending the alterations, as I understand. By the way, there does not seem to be any very pressing need for repairs at that end wall."

"There were none. I believe that it was an excuse to move me from my room."

"Ah! that is suggestive. Now, on the other side of this narrow wing runs the corridor from which these three rooms open. There are windows in it, of course?"

"Yes, but very small ones. Too narrow for anyone to pass through."

"As you both locked your doors at night, your rooms were unapproachable from that side. Now, would you have the kindness to go into your room and bar your shutters?"

Miss Stoner did so, and Holmes, after a careful examination through the open window, endeavoured in every way to force the shutter open, but without success. There was no slit through which a knife could be passed to raise the bar. Then with his lens he tested the hinges, but they were of solid iron, built firmly into the massive masonry. "Hum!" said he, scratching his chin in some perplexity, "my theory certainly presents some difficulties. No one could pass these shutters if they were bolted. Well, we shall see if the inside throws any light upon the matter."

A small side door led into the whitewashed corridor from which the three bedrooms opened. Holmes refused to examine the third chamber, so we passed at once to the second, that in which Miss Stoner was now sleeping, and in which her sister had met with her fate. It was a homely little room, with a low ceiling and a gaping fireplace, after the fashion of old country-houses. A brown chest of drawers stood in one corner, a narrow white-counterpaned bed in another, and a dressing-table on the left-hand side of the window. These articles, with two small wickerwork chairs, made up all the furniture in the room save for a square of Wilton carpet in the centre. The boards round and the panelling of the walls were of brown, worm-eaten oak, so old and discoloured that it may have dated from the original building of the house. Holmes drew one of the chairs into a corner and sat silent, while his eyes travelled round and round and up and down, taking in every detail of the apartment.

"Where does that bell communicate with?" he asked at last, pointing to a thick bell-rope which hung down beside the bed, the tassel actually lying upon the pillow.

"It goes to the housekeeper's room."

"It looks newer than the other things?"

"Yes, it was only put there a couple of years ago."

"Your sister asked for it, I suppose?"

"No, I never heard of her using it. We used always to get what we wanted for ourselves."

"Indeed, it seemed unnecessary to put so nice a bell-pull there. You will excuse me for a few minutes while I satisfy myself as to this floor." He threw himself down upon his face with his lens in his hand and crawled swiftly backward and forward, examining minutely the cracks between the boards. Then he did the same with the woodwork with which the chamber was panelled. Finally he walked over to the bed and spent some time in staring at it, and in running his eye up and down the wall. Finally he took the bell-rope in his hand and gave it a brisk tug.

"Why, it's a dummy," said he.

"Won't it ring?"

"No, it is not even attached to a wire. This is very interesting. You can see now that it is fastened to a hook just above where the little opening for the ventilator is."

"How very absurd! I never noticed that before."

"Very strange!" muttered Holmes, pulling at the rope. "There are one or two very singular points about this room. For example, what a fool a builder must be to open a ventilator into another room, when, with the same trouble, he might have communicated with the outside air!"

"That is also quite modern," said the lady.

"Done about the same time as the bell-rope?" remarked Holmes.

"Yes, there were several little changes carried out about that time."

"They seem to have been of a most interesting character — dummy bell-ropes, and ventilators which do not ventilate. With your permission, Miss Stoner, we shall now carry our researches into the inner apartment."

Dr. Grimesby Roylott's chamber was larger than that of his step-daughter, but was as plainly furnished. A camp bed, a small wooden shelf full of books, mostly of a technical character, an armchair beside the bed, a plain wooden chair against the wall, a round table, and a large iron safe were the principal things which met the eye. Holmes walked slowly round and examined each and all of them with the keenest interest.

"What's in here?" he asked, tapping the safe.

"My stepfather's business papers."

"Oh! you have seen inside, then?"

"Only once, some years ago. I remember that it was full of papers."

"There isn't a cat in it, for example?"

"No. What a strange idea!"

"Well, look at this!" He took up a small saucer of milk which stood on the top of it.

"No; we don't keep a cat. But there is a cheetah and a baboon."

"Ah, yes, of course! Well, a cheetah is just a big cat, and yet a saucer of milk does not go very far in satisfying its wants, I daresay. There is one point which I should wish to determine." He squatted down in front of the wooden chair, and examined the seat of it with the greatest attention.

"Thank you. That is quite settled," said he, rising and putting his lens in his pocket. "Hullo! Here is something interesting!"

The object which had caught his eye was a small dog lash hung on one corner of the bed. The lash, however, was curled upon itself, and tied so as to make a loop of whipcord.

"What do you make of that, Watson?"

"It's a common enough lash. But I don't know why it should be tied."

"That is not quite so common, is it? Ah, me! it's a wicked world, and when a clever man turns his brains to crime it is the worst of all. I think that I have seen enough now, Miss Stoner, and with your permission we shall walk out upon the lawn."

I had never seen my friend's face so grim, or his brow so dark, as it was when we turned from the scene of this investigation. We had walked several times up and down the lawn, neither Miss Stoner nor myself liking to break in upon his thoughts, before he roused himself from his reverie.

"It is very essential, Miss Stoner," said he, "that you should absolutely follow my advice in every respect."

"I shall most certainly do so."

"The matter is too serious for any hesitation. Your life may depend upon your compliance."

"I assure you that I am in your hands."

"In the first place, both my friend and I must spend the night in your room."

Both Miss Stoner and I gazed at him in astonishment.

"Yes, it must be so. Let me explain. I believe that that is the village inn over there?"

"Yes, that is the 'Crown.'"

"Very good. Your windows would be visible from there?"

"Certainly."

"You must confine yourself to your room, on pretence of a headache, when your stepfather comes back. Then when you hear him retire for the night, you must open the shutters of your window, undo the hasp, put your lamp there as a signal to us, and then withdraw quietly with everything which you are likely to want into the room which you used to occupy. I have no doubt that, in spite of the repairs, you could manage there for one night."

"Oh, yes, easily."

"The rest you will leave in our hands."

"But what will you do?"

"We shall spend the night in your room, and we shall investigate the cause of this noise which has disturbed you."

"I believe, Mr. Holmes, that you have already made up your mind," said Miss Stoner, laying her hand upon my companion's sleeve.

"Perhaps I have."

"Then, for pity's sake, tell me what was the cause of my sister's death."

"I should prefer to have clearer proofs before I speak."

"You can at least tell me whether my own thought is correct, and if she died from some sudden fright."

"No, I do not think so. I think that there was probably some more tangible cause. And now, Miss Stoner, we must leave you, for if Dr. Roylott returned and saw us, our journey would be in vain. Good-bye, and be brave, for if you will do what I have told you, you may rest assured that we shall soon drive away the dangers that threaten you."

Sherlock Holmes and I had no difficulty in engaging a bedroom and sitting-room at the "Crown" Inn. They were on the upper floor, and from our window we could command a view of the avenue gate, and of the inhabited wing of Stoke Moran Manor House. At dusk we saw Dr. Grimesby Roylott drive past, his huge form looming up beside the little figure of the lad who drove him. The boy had some slight difficulty in undoing the heavy iron gates, and we heard the hoarse roar of the doctor's voice, and saw the fury with which he shook his clinched fists at him. The trap drove on, and a few minutes later we saw a sudden light spring up among the trees as the lamp was lit in one of the sitting-rooms.

"Do you know, Watson," said Holmes, as we sat together in the gathering darkness, "I have really some scruples as to taking you to-night. There is a distinct element of danger."

"Can I be of assistance?"

"Your presence might be invaluable."

"Then I shall certainly come."

"It is very kind of you."

"You speak of danger. You have evidently seen more in these rooms than was visible to me."

"No, but I fancy that I may have deduced a little more. I imagine that you saw all that I did."

"I saw nothing remarkable save the bell-rope, and what purpose that could answer I confess is more than I can imagine."

"You saw the ventilator, too?"

"Yes, but I do not think that it is such a very unusual thing to have a small opening between two rooms. It was so small that a rat could hardly pass through."

"I knew that we should find a ventilator before ever we came to Stoke Moran."

"My dear Holmes!"

"Oh, yes, I did. You remember in her statement she said that her sister could smell Dr. Roylott's cigar. Now, of course that suggested at once that there must be a communication between the two rooms. It could only be a small one, or it would have been remarked upon at the Coroner's inquiry. I deduced a ventilator."

"But what harm can there be in that?"

"Well, there is at least a curious coincidence of dates. A ventilator is made, a cord is hung, and a lady who sleeps in the bed dies. Does not that strike you?"

"I cannot as yet see any connection."

"Did you observe anything very peculiar about that bed?"

"No."

"It was clamped to the floor. Did you ever see a bed fastened like that before?"

"I cannot say that I have."

"The lady could not move her bed. It must always be in the same relative position to the ventilator and to the rope — or so we may call it, since it was clearly never meant for a bell-pull."

"Holmes," I cried, "I seem to see dimly what you are hinting at. We are only just in time to prevent some subtle and horrible crime."

"Subtle enough and horrible enough. When a doctor does go wrong, he is the first of criminals. He has nerve and he has knowledge. Palmer and Pritchard[5] were among the heads of their profession. This man strikes even deeper, but I think, Watson, that we shall be able to strike deeper still. But we shall have horrors enough before the night is over; for goodness' sake let us have a quiet pipe, and turn our minds for a few hours to something more cheerful."

About nine o'clock the light among the trees was extinguished, and all was dark in the direction of the Manor House. Two hours passed slowly away, and then, suddenly, just at the stroke of eleven, a single bright light shone out right in front of us.

"That is our signal," said Holmes, springing to his feet; "it comes from the middle window."

As we passed out he exchanged a few words with the landlord, explaining that we were going on a late visit to an acquaintance, and that it was possible that we might spend the night there. A moment later we were out on the dark road, a chill wind blowing in our faces, and one yellow light twinkling in front of us through the gloom to guide us on our sombre errand.

There was little difficulty in entering the grounds, for unrepaired breaches gaped in the old park wall. Making our way among the trees, we reached the lawn, crossed it, and were about to enter through the window, when out from a clump of laurel

[5]*William Palmer and Edward William Pritchard were doctors found guilty of poisoning people.*

bushes there darted what seemed to be a hideous and distorted child, who threw itself upon the grass with writhing limbs, and then ran swiftly across the lawn into the darkness.

"My God!" I whispered; "did you see it?"

Holmes was for the moment as startled as I. His hand closed like a vice upon my wrist in his agitation. Then he broke into a low laugh, and put his lips to my ear.

"It is a nice household," he murmured. "That is the baboon."

I had forgotten the strange pets which the Doctor affected. There was a cheetah, too; perhaps we might find it upon our shoulders at any moment. I confess that I felt easier in my mind when, after following Holmes' example and slipping off my shoes, I found myself inside the bedroom. My companion noiselessly closed the shutters, moved the lamp onto the table, and cast his eyes round the room. All was as we had seen it in the day-time. Then creeping up to me and making a trumpet of his hand, he whispered into my ear again so gently that it was all that I could do to distinguish the words:

"The least sound would be fatal to our plans."

I nodded to show that I had heard.

"We must sit without light. He would see it through the ventilator."

I nodded again.

"Do not go asleep; your very life may depend upon it. Have your pistol ready in case we should need it. I will sit on the side of the bed, and you in that chair."

I took out my revolver and laid it on the corner of the table.

Holmes had brought up a long thin cane, and this he placed upon the bed beside him. By it he laid the box of matches and the stump of a candle. Then he turned down the lamp, and we were left in darkness.

How shall I ever forget that dreadful vigil? I could not hear a sound, not even the drawing of a breath, and yet I knew that my companion sat open-eyed, within a few feet of me, in the same state of nervous tension in which I was myself. The shutters cut off the least ray of light, and we waited in absolute darkness. From outside came the occasional cry of a night-bird, and once at our very window a long drawn cat-like whine, which told us that the cheetah was indeed at liberty. Far away we could hear the deep tones of the parish clock, which boomed out every quarter of an hour. How long they seemed, those quarters! Twelve struck, and one, and two, and three, and still we sat waiting silently for whatever might befall.

Suddenly there was the momentary gleam of a light up in the direction of the ventilator, which vanished immediately, but was succeeded by a strong smell of burning oil and heated metal. Someone in the next room had lit a dark-lantern.[6] I heard a gentle sound of movement, and then all was silent once more, though the smell grew stronger. For half an hour I sat with straining ears. Then suddenly another

[6]*Lantern with a shutter that can be slid across the opening to direct or conceal light.*

sound became audible—a very gentle, soothing sound, like that of a small jet of steam escaping continually from a kettle. The instant that we heard it, Holmes sprang from the bed, struck a match, and lashed furiously with his cane at the bell-pull.

"You see it, Watson?" he yelled. "You see it?"

But I saw nothing. At the moment when Holmes struck the light I heard a low, clear whistle, but the sudden glare flashing into my weary eyes made it impossible for me to tell what it was at which my friend lashed so savagely. I could, however, see that his face was deadly pale, and filled with horror and loathing.

He had ceased to strike, and was gazing up at the ventilator, when suddenly there broke from the silence of the night the most horrible cry to which I have ever listened. It swelled up louder and louder, a hoarse yell of pain and fear and anger all mingled in the one dreadful shriek. They say that away down in the village, and even in the distant parsonage, that cry raised the sleepers from their beds. It struck cold to our hearts, and I stood gazing at Holmes, and he at me, until the last echoes of it had died away into the silence from which it rose.

"What can it mean?" I gasped.

"It means that it is all over," Holmes answered. "And perhaps, after all, it is for the best. Take your pistol, and we shall enter Dr. Roylott's room."

With a grave face he lit the lamp and led the way down the corridor. Twice he struck at the chamber door without any reply from within. Then he turned the handle and entered, I at his heels, with the cocked pistol in my hand.

It was a singular sight which met our eyes. On the table stood a dark lantern with the shutter half open, throwing a brilliant beam of light upon the iron safe, the door of which was ajar. Beside this table, on the wooden chair, sat Dr. Grimesby Roylott, clad in a long grey dressing-gown, his bare ankles protruding beneath, his feet thrust into red heelless Turkish slippers. Across his lap lay the short stock with the long lash which we had noticed during the day. His chin was cocked upward, and his eyes were fixed in a dreadful rigid stare at the corner of the ceiling. Round his brow he had a peculiar yellow band, with brownish speckles, which seemed to be bound tightly round his head. As we entered he made neither sound nor motion.

"The band! the speckled band!" whispered Holmes.

I took a step forward. In an instant his strange headgear began to move, and there reared itself from among his hair the squat diamond-shaped head and puffed neck of a loathsome serpent.

"It is a swamp adder!"[7] cried Holmes; "the deadliest snake in India. He has died within ten seconds of being bitten. Violence does, in truth, recoil upon the violent, and the schemer falls into the pit which he digs for another.[8] Let us thrust this creature back into its den, and we can then remove Miss Stoner to some place of shelter, and let the county police know what has happened."

[7]*Not a real animal.* [8]*Paraphrase of Ecclesiastes 10:8.*

As he spoke he drew the dog whip swiftly from the dead man's lap, and throwing the noose round the reptile's neck, he drew it from its horrid perch and, carrying it at arm's length, threw it into the iron safe, which he closed upon it.

Such are the true facts of the death of Dr. Grimesby Roylott, of Stoke Moran. It is not necessary that I should prolong a narrative which has already run to too great a length, by telling how we broke the sad news to the terrified girl, how we conveyed her by the morning train to the care of her good aunt at Harrow, of how the slow process of official inquiry came to the conclusion that the doctor met his fate while indiscreetly playing with a dangerous pet. The little which I had yet to learn of the case was told me by Sherlock Holmes as we travelled back next day.

"I had," said he, "come to an entirely erroneous conclusion which shows, my dear Watson, how dangerous it always is to reason from insufficient data. The presence of the gipsies, and the use of the word 'band,' which was used by the poor girl, no doubt, to explain the appearance which she had caught a hurried glimpse of by the light of her match, were sufficient to put me upon an entirely wrong scent. I can only claim the merit that I instantly reconsidered my position when, however, it became clear to me that whatever danger threatened an occupant of the room could not come either from the window or the door. My attention was speedily drawn, as I have already remarked to you, to this ventilator, and to the bell-rope which hung down to the bed. The discovery that this was a dummy, and that the bed was clamped to the floor, instantly gave rise to the suspicion that the rope was there as a bridge for something passing through the hole and coming to the bed. The idea of a snake instantly occurred to me, and when I coupled it with my knowledge that the doctor was furnished with a supply of creatures from India, I felt that I was probably on the right track. The idea of using a form of poison which could not possibly be discovered by any chemical test was just such a one as would occur to a clever and ruthless man who had had an Eastern training. The rapidity with which such a poison would take effect would also, from his point of view, be an advantage. It would be a sharp-eyed coroner, indeed, who could distinguish the two little dark punctures which would show where the poison fangs had done their work. Then I thought of the whistle. Of course he must recall the snake before the morning light revealed it to the victim. He had trained it, probably by the use of the milk which we saw, to return to him when summoned. He would put it through this ventilator at the hour that he thought best, with the certainty that it would crawl down the rope and land on the bed. It might or might not bite the occupant, perhaps she might escape every night for a week, but sooner or later she must fall a victim.

"I had come to these conclusions before ever I had entered his room. An inspection of his chair showed me that he had been in the habit of standing on it, which, of course, would be necessary in order that he should reach the ventilator. The sight of the safe, the saucer of milk, and the loop of whipcord were enough to finally dispel any doubts which may have remained. The metallic clang heard by Miss Stoner was obviously caused by her stepfather hastily closing the door of his safe upon its terrible occupant. Having once made up my mind, you know the steps which I took in order to put the matter to the proof. I heard the creature hiss, as I have no doubt that you did also, and I instantly lit the light and attacked it."

"With the result of driving it through the ventilator."

"And also with the result of causing it to turn upon its master at the other side. Some of the blows of my cane came home, and roused its snakish temper, so that it flew upon the first person it saw. In this way I am no doubt indirectly responsible for Dr. Grimesby Roylott's death, and I cannot say that it is likely to weigh very heavily upon my conscience."

The Adventure of the Final Problem
by Sir Arthur Conan Coyle
(1893)

It is with a heavy heart that I take up my pen to write these the last words in which I shall ever record the singular gifts by which my friend Mr. Sherlock Holmes was distinguished. In an incoherent and, as I deeply feel, an entirely inadequate fashion, I have endeavoured to give some account of my strange experiences in his company from the chance which first brought us together at the period of the "Study in Scarlet," up to the time of his interference in the matter of the "Naval Treaty"[1]— an interference which had the unquestionable effect of preventing a serious international complication. It was my intention to have stopped there, and to have said nothing of that event which has created a void in my life which the lapse of two years has done little to fill. My hand has been forced, however, by the recent letters in which Colonel James Moriarty defends the memory of his brother, and I have no choice but to lay the facts before the public exactly as they occurred. I alone know the absolute truth of the matter, and I am satisfied that the time has come when no good purpose is to be served by its suppression. As far as I know, there have been only three accounts in the public press: that in the *Journal de Genève* on May 6th, 1891, the Reuter's despatch in the English papers on May 7th, and finally the recent letters to which I have alluded. Of these the first and second were extremely condensed, while the last is, as I shall now show, an absolute perversion of the facts. It lies with me to tell for the first time what really took place between Professor Moriarty and Mr. Sherlock Holmes.

It may be remembered that after my marriage, and my subsequent start in private practice, the very intimate relations which had existed between Holmes and myself became to some extent modified. He still came to me from time to time when he desired a companion in his investigation, but these occasions grew more and more seldom, until I find that in the year 1890 there were only three cases of which I retain any record. During the winter of that year and the early spring of 1891, I saw in the papers that he had been engaged by the French government upon a matter of supreme

[1]*The first and last Holmes stories up to this point.*

importance, and I received two notes from Holmes, dated from Narbonne and from Nîmes, from which I gathered that his stay in France was likely to be a long one. It was with some surprise, therefore, that I saw him walk into my consulting-room upon the evening of the 24th of April. It struck me that he was looking even paler and thinner than usual.

"Yes, I have been using myself up rather too freely," he remarked, in answer to my look rather than to my words; "I have been a little pressed of late. Have you any objection to my closing your shutters?"

The only light in the room came from the lamp upon the table at which I had been reading. Holmes edged his way round the wall and flinging the shutters together, he bolted them securely.

"You are afraid of something?" I asked.

"Well, I am."

"Of what?"

"Of air-guns."

"My dear Holmes, what do you mean?"

"I think that you know me well enough, Watson, to understand that I am by no means a nervous man. At the same time, it is stupidity rather than courage to refuse to recognise danger when it is close upon you. Might I trouble you for a match?" He drew in the smoke of his cigarette as if the soothing influence was grateful to him.

"I must apologize for calling so late," said he, "and I must further beg you to be so unconventional as to allow me to leave your house presently by scrambling over your back garden wall."

"But what does it all mean?" I asked.

He held out his hand, and I saw in the light of the lamp that two of his knuckles were burst and bleeding.

"It is not an airy nothing,[2] you see," said he, smiling. "On the contrary, it is solid enough for a man to break his hand over. Is Mrs. Watson in?"

"She is away upon a visit."

"Indeed! You are alone?"

"Quite."

"Then it makes it the easier for me to propose that you should come away with me for a week to the Continent."

"Where?"

"Oh, anywhere. It's all the same to me."

There was something very strange in all this. It was not Holmes's nature to take an aimless holiday, and something about his pale, worn face told me that his nerves were at their highest tension. He saw the question in my eyes, and, putting his finger-tips together and his elbows upon his knees, he explained the situation.

[2]*Allusion to Shakespeare's* A Midsummer's Nights Dream *5.1.17.*

Sherlock Holmes's Baker Street interview with Professor Moriarty, right (Sidney Paget, 1893).

"You have probably never heard of Professor Moriarty?" said he.

"Never."

"Aye, there's the genius and the wonder of the thing!" he cried. "The man pervades London, and no one has heard of him. That's what puts him on a pinnacle in the records of crime. I tell you, Watson, in all seriousness, that if I could beat that man, if I could free society of him, I should feel that my own career had reached its summit, and I should be prepared to turn to some more placid line in life. Between ourselves, the recent cases in which I have been of assistance to the royal family of Scandinavia, and to the French Republic, have left me in such a position that I could continue to live in the quiet fashion which is most congenial to me, and to concentrate my attention upon my chemical researches. But I could not rest, Watson, I could not sit quiet in my chair, if I thought that such a man as Professor Moriarty were walking the streets of London unchallenged."

"What has he done, then?"

"His career has been an extraordinary one. He is a man of good birth and excellent education, endowed by Nature with a phenomenal mathematical faculty. At the age of twenty-one he wrote a treatise upon the Binomial Theorem, which has had a European vogue. On the strength of it he won the Mathematical Chair at one of our smaller Universities, and had, to all appearance, a most brilliant career before him. But the man had hereditary tendencies of the most diabolical kind. A criminal strain ran in his blood, which, instead of being modified, was increased and rendered infinitely more dangerous by his extraordinary mental powers. Dark rumours gathered round him in the University town, and eventually he was compelled to resign his Chair and to come down to London, where he set up as an Army coach. So much is known to the world, but what I am telling you now is what I have myself discovered.

"As you are aware, Watson, there is no one who knows the higher criminal world of London so well as I do. For years past I have continually been conscious of some power behind the malefactor, some deep organizing power which for ever stands in the way of the law, and throws its shield over the wrong-doer. Again and again in cases of the most varying sorts — forgery cases, robberies, murders — I have felt the presence of this force, and I have deduced its action in many of those undiscovered crimes in which I have not been personally consulted. For years I have endeavoured to break through the veil which shrouded it, and at last the time came when I seized my thread and followed it, until it led me, after a thousand cunning windings, to ex–Professor Moriarty of mathematical celebrity.

"He is the Napoleon of crime, Watson. He is the organizer of half that is evil and of nearly all that is undetected in this great city. He is a genius, a philosopher, an abstract thinker. He has a brain of the first order. He sits motionless, like a spider in the centre of its web, but that web has a thousand radiations, and he knows well every quiver of each of them. He does little himself. He only plans. But his agents are numerous and splendidly organized. Is there a crime to be done, a paper to be abstracted, we will say, a house to be rifled, a man to be removed — the word is passed to the Professor, the matter is organized and carried out. The agent may be caught. In that case money is found for his bail or his defence. But the central power which uses the agent is never caught — never so much as suspected. This was the organization which I deduced, Watson, and which I devoted my whole energy to exposing and breaking up.

"But the Professor was fenced round with safeguards so cunningly devised that, do what I would, it seemed impossible to get evidence which would convict in a court of law. You know my powers, my dear Watson, and yet at the end of three months I was forced to confess that I had at last met an antagonist who was my intellectual equal. My horror at his crimes was lost in my admiration at his skill. But at last he made a trip — only a little, little trip — but it was more than he could afford when I was so close upon him. I had my chance, and, starting from that point, I have woven my net round him until now it is all ready to close. In three days, that is to say, on Monday next, matters will be ripe, and the Professor, with all the principal members of his gang, will be in the hands of the police. Then will come the greatest criminal trial of the century, the clearing up of over forty mysteries, and the rope for all of them — but if we move at all prematurely, you understand, they may slip out of our hands even at the last moment.

"Now, if I could have done this without the knowledge of Professor Moriarty, all would have been well. But he was too wily for that. He saw every step which I took to draw my toils round him. Again and again he strove to break away, but I as often headed him off. I tell you, my friend, that if a detailed account of that silent contest could be written, it would take its place as the most brilliant bit of thrust-and-parry work in the history of detection. Never have I risen to such a height, and never have I been so hard pressed by an opponent. He cut deep, and yet I just undercut him. This morning the last steps were taken, and three days only were wanted to complete the business. I was sitting in my room thinking the matter over, when the door opened and Professor Moriarty stood before me.

"My nerves are fairly proof, Watson, but I must confess to a start when I saw the very man who had been so much in my thoughts standing there on my threshold. His appearance was quite familiar to me. He is extremely tall and thin, his forehead domes out in a white curve, and his two eyes are deeply sunken in this head. He is clean-shaven, pale, and ascetic-looking, retaining something of the professor in his features. His shoulders are rounded from much study, and his face protrudes forward, and is for ever slowly oscillating from side to side in a curiously reptilian fashion. He peered at me with great curiosity in his puckered eyes.

"'You have less frontal development that I should have expected,' said he, at last. 'It is a dangerous habit to finger loaded firearms in the pocket of one's dressing-gown.'

"The fact is that upon his entrance I had instantly recognised the extreme personal danger in which I lay. The only conceivable escape for him lay in silencing my tongue. In an instant I had slipped the revolver from the drawer into my pocket, and was covering him through the cloth. At his remark I drew the weapon out and laid it cocked upon the table. He still smiled and blinked, but there was something about his eyes which made me feel very glad that I had it there.

"'You evidently don't know me,' said he.

"'On the contrary,' I answered, 'I think it is fairly evident that I do. Pray take a chair. I can spare you five minutes if you have anything to say.'

"'All that I have to say has already crossed your mind,' said he.

"'Then possibly my answer has crossed yours,' I replied.

"'You stand fast?'

"'Absolutely.'

"He clapped his hand into his pocket, and I raised the pistol from the table. But he merely drew out a memorandum-book in which he had scribbled some dates.

"'You crossed my path on the 4th of January,' said he. 'On the 23rd you incommoded me; by the middle of February I was seriously inconvenienced by you; at the end of March I was absolutely hampered in my plans; and now, at the close of April, I find myself placed in such a position through your continual persecution that I am in positive danger of losing my liberty. The situation is becoming an impossible one.'

"'Have you any suggestion to make?' I asked.

"'You must drop it, Mr. Holmes,' said he, swaying his face about. 'You really must, you know.'

"'After Monday,' said I.

"'Tut, tut,' said he. 'I am quite sure that a man of your intelligence will see that there can be but one outcome to this affair. It is necessary that you should withdraw. You have worked things in such a fashion that we have only one resource left. It has been an intellectual treat to me to see the way in which you have grappled with this affair, and I say, unaffectedly, that it would be a grief to me to be forced to take any extreme measure. You smile, sir, but I assure you that it really would.'

"'Danger is part of my trade,' I remarked.

"'That is not danger,' said he. 'It is inevitable destruction. You stand in the way not merely of an individual, but of a mighty organization, the full extent of which you, with all your cleverness, have been unable to realize. You must stand clear, Mr. Holmes, or be trodden under foot.'

"'I am afraid,' said I, rising, 'that in the pleasure of this conversation I am neglecting business of importance which awaits me elsewhere.'

"He rose also and looked at me in silence, shaking his head sadly.

"'Well, well,' said he, at last. 'It seems a pity, but I have done what I could. I know every move of your game. You can do nothing before Monday. It has been a duel between you and me, Mr. Holmes. You hope to place me in the dock. I tell you that I will never stand in the dock. You hope to beat me. I tell you that you will never beat me. If you are clever enough to bring destruction upon me, rest assured that I shall do as much to you.'

"'You have paid me several compliments, Mr. Moriarty,' said I. 'Let me pay you one in return when I say that if I were assured of the former eventuality I would, in the interests of the public, cheerfully accept the latter.'

"'I can promise you the one, but not the other,' he snarled, and so turned his rounded back upon me, and went peering and blinking out of the room.

"That was my singular interview with Professor Moriarty. I confess that it left an unpleasant effect upon my mind. His soft, precise fashion of speech leaves a conviction of sincerity which a mere bully could not produce. Of course, you will say: 'Why not take police precautions against him?' The reason is that I am well convinced that it is from his agents the blow will fall. I have the best proofs that it would be so."

"You have already been assaulted?"

"My dear Watson, Professor Moriarty is not a man who lets the grass grow under his feet. I went out about mid-day to transact some business in Oxford Street. As I passed the corner which leads from Bentinck Street on to the Welbeck Street crossing a two-horse van furiously driven whizzed round and was on me like a flash. I sprang for the foot-path and saved myself by the fraction of a second. The van dashed round by Marylebone Lane and was gone in an instant. I kept to the pavement after that, Watson, but as I walked down Vere Street a brick came down from the roof of one of the houses, and was shattered to fragments at my feet. I called the police and had the place examined. There were slates and bricks piled up on the roof preparatory to some repairs, and they would have me believe that the wind had toppled over one of these. Of course I knew better, but I could prove nothing. I took a cab after that and reached my brother's rooms in Pall Mall, where I spent the day. Now I have come round to you, and on my way I was attacked by a rough with a bludgeon. I knocked him down, and the police have him in custody; but I can tell you with the most absolute confidence that no possible connection will ever be traced between the gentleman upon whose front teeth I have barked my knuckles and the retiring mathematical coach, who is, I dare say, working out problems upon a black-board ten miles away. You will not wonder, Watson, that my first act on entering your rooms was to close your shutters, and that I have been compelled to ask your permission to leave the house by some less conspicuous exit than the front door."

I had often admired my friend's courage, but never more than now, as he sat quietly checking off a series of incidents which must have combined to make up a day of horror.

"You will spend the night here?" I said.

"No, my friend, you might find me a dangerous guest. I have my plans laid, and all will be well. Matters have gone so far now that they can move without my help as far as the arrest goes, though my presence is necessary for a conviction. It is obvious, therefore, that I cannot do better than get away for the few days which remain before the police are at liberty to act. It would be a great pleasure to me, therefore, if you could come on to the Continent with me."

"The practice is quiet," said I, "and I have an accommodating neighbour. I should be glad to come."

"And to start to-morrow morning?"

"If necessary."

"Oh yes, it is most necessary. Then these are your instructions, and I beg, my dear Watson, that you will obey them to the letter, for you are now playing a double-handed game with me against the cleverest rogue and the most powerful syndicate of criminals in Europe. Now listen! You will despatch whatever luggage you intend to take by a trusty messenger unaddressed to Victoria to-night. In the morning you will send for a hansom,[3] desiring your man to take neither the first nor the second which may present itself. Into this hansom you will jump, and you will drive to the Strand end of the Lowther Arcade, handing the address to the cabman upon a slip of paper, with a request that he will not throw it away. Have your fare ready, and the instant that your cab stops, dash through the Arcade, timing yourself to reach the other side at a quarter-past nine. You will find a small brougham[4] waiting close to the curb, driven by a fellow with a heavy black cloak tipped at the collar with red. Into this you will step, and you will reach Victoria in time for the Continental express."

"Where shall I meet you?"

"At the station. The second first-class carriage from the front will be reserved for us."

"The carriage is our rendezvous, then?"

"Yes."

It was in vain that I asked Holmes to remain for the evening. It was evident to me that he thought he might bring trouble to the roof he was under, and that that was the motive which impelled him to go. With a few hurried words as to our plans for the morrow he rose and came out with me into the garden, clambering over the wall which leads into Mortimer Street, and immediately whistling for a hansom, in which I heard him drive away.

In the morning I obeyed Holmes's injunctions to the letter. A hansom was procured with such precaution as would prevent its being one which was placed ready for us, and I drove immediately after breakfast to the Lowther Arcade, through which I hurried at the top of my speed. A brougham was waiting with a very massive driver wrapped in a dark cloak, who, the instant that I had stepped in, whipped up the horse and rattled off to Victoria Station. On my alighting there he turned the carriage, and dashed away again without so much as a look in my direction.

So far all had gone admirably. My luggage was waiting for me, and I had no difficulty in finding the carriage which Holmes had indicated, the less so as it was the only one in the train which was marked "Engaged." My only source of anxiety now was the non-appearance of Holmes. The station clock marked only seven minutes from the time when we were due to start. In vain I searched among the groups of travellers and leave-takers for the lithe figure of my friend. There was no sign of him. I spent a few minutes in assisting a venerable Italian priest, who was endeavouring to make a porter understand, in his broken English, that his luggage was to be booked through to Paris. Then, having taken another look round, I returned to my carriage,

[3] *Two-wheeled, two-passenger carriage widely used as a public conveyance.*
[4] *Four-wheeled carriage with an outdoor driver's seat.*

where I found that the porter, in spite of the ticket, had given me my decrepit Italian friend as a travelling companion. It was useless for me to explain to him that his presence was an intrusion, for my Italian was even more limited than his English, so I shrugged my shoulders resignedly, and continued to look out anxiously for my friend.

A chill of fear had come over me, as I thought that his absence might mean that some blow had fallen during the night. Already the doors had all been shut and the whistle blown, when —

"My dear Watson," said a voice, "you have not even condescended to say good-morning."

I turned in incontrollable astonishment. The aged ecclesiastic had turned his face towards me. For an instant the wrinkles were smoothed away, the nose drew away from the chin, the lower lip ceased to protrude and the mouth to mumble, the dull eyes regained their fire, the drooping figure expanded. The next the whole frame collapsed again, and Holmes had gone as quickly as he had come.

"Good heavens!" I cried; "how you startled me!"

"Every precaution is still necessary," he whispered. "I have reason to think that they are hot upon our trail. Ah, there is Moriarty himself."

The train had already begun to move as Holmes spoke. Glancing back, I saw a tall man pushing his way furiously through the crowd, and waving his hand as if he desired to have the train stopped. It was too late, however, for we were rapidly gathering momentum, and an instant later had shot clear of the station.

"With all our precautions, you see that we have cut it rather fine," said Holmes, laughing. He rose, and throwing off the black cassock[5] and hat which had formed his disguise, he packed them away in a hand-bag.

"Have you seen the morning paper, Watson?"

"No."

"You haven't seen about Baker Street, then?"

"Baker Street?"

"They set fire to our rooms last night. No great harm was done."

"Good heavens, Holmes! This is intolerable."

"They must have lost my track completely after their bludgeon-man was arrested. Otherwise they could not have imagined that I had returned to my rooms. They have evidently taken the precaution of watching you, however, and that is what has brought Moriarty to Victoria. You could not have made any slip in coming?"

"I did exactly what you advised."

"Did you find your brougham?"

"Yes, it was waiting."

"Did you recognise your coachman?"

"No."

[5]*Long garment worn by members of the clergy.*

"It was my brother Mycroft. It is an advantage to get about in such a case without taking a mercenary into your confidence. But we must plan what we are to do about Moriarty now."

"As this is an express, and as the boat runs in connection with it, I should think we have shaken him off very effectively."

"My dear Watson, you evidently did not realize my meaning when I said that this man may be taken as being quite on the same intellectual plane as myself. You do not imagine that if I were the pursuer I should allow myself to be baffled by so slight an obstacle. Why, then, should you think so meanly of him?"

"What will he do?"

"What I should do?"

"What would you do, then?"

"Engage a special."

"But it must be late."

"By no means. This train stops at Canterbury; and there is always at least a quarter of an hour's delay at the boat. He will catch us there."

"One would think that we were the criminals. Let us have him arrested on his arrival."

"It would be to ruin the work of three months. We should get the big fish, but the smaller would dart right and left out of the net. On Monday we should have them all. No, an arrest is inadmissible."

"What then?"

"We shall get out at Canterbury."

"And then?"

"Well, then we must make a cross-country journey to Newhaven, and so over to Dieppe. Moriarty will again do what I should do. He will get on to Paris, mark down our luggage, and wait for two days at the depôt. In the meantime we shall treat ourselves to a couple of carpet-bags, encourage the manufactures of the countries through which we travel, and make our way at our leisure into Switzerland, via Luxembourg and Basle."

At Canterbury, therefore, we alighted, only to find that we should have to wait an hour before we could get a train to Newhaven.

I was still looking rather ruefully after the rapidly disappearing luggage van which contained my wardrobe, when Holmes pulled my sleeve and pointed up the line.

"Already, you see," said he.

Far away, from among the Kentish woods there rose a thin spray of smoke. A minute later a carriage and engine could be seen flying along the open curve which leads to the station. We had hardly time to take our place behind a pile of luggage when it passed with a rattle and a roar, beating a blast of hot air into our faces.

"There he goes," said Holmes, as we watched the carriage swing and rock over the points. "There are limits, you see, to our friend's intelligence. It would have been a *coup-de-maître*[6] had he deduced what I would deduce and acted accordingly."

"And what would he have done had he overtaken us?"

"There cannot be the least doubt that he would have made a murderous attack upon me. It is, however, a game at which two may play. The question now is whether we should take a premature lunch here, or run our chance of starving before we reach the buffet at Newhaven."

We made our way to Brussels that night and spent two days there, moving on upon the third day as far as Strasburg. On the Monday morning Holmes had telegraphed to the London police, and in the evening we found a reply waiting for us at our hotel. Holmes tore it open, and then with a bitter curse hurled it into the grate.

"I might have known it!" he groaned. "He has escaped!"

"Moriarty?"

"They have secured the whole gang with the exception of him. He has given them the slip. Of course, when I had left the country there was no one to cope with him. But I did think that I had put the game in their hands. I think that you had better return to England, Watson."

"Why?"

"Because you will find me a dangerous companion now. This man's occupation is gone. He is lost if he returns to London. If I read his character right he will devote his whole energies to revenging himself upon me. He said as much in our short interview, and I fancy that he meant it. I should certainly recommend you to return to your practice."

It was hardly an appeal to be successful with one who was an old campaigner[7] as well as an old friend. We sat in the Strasburg *salle-à-manger*[8] arguing the question for half an hour, but the same night we had resumed our journey and were well on our way to Geneva.

For a charming week we wandered up the Valley of the Rhone, and then, branching off at Leuk, we made our way over the Gemmi Pass, still deep in snow, and so, by way of Interlaken, to Meiringen. It was a lovely trip, the dainty green of the spring below, the virgin white of the winter above; but it was clear to me that never for one instant did Holmes forget the shadow which lay across him. In the homely Alpine villages or in the lonely mountain passes, I could tell by his quick glancing eyes and his sharp scrutiny of every face that passed us, that he was well convinced that, walk where we would, we could not walk ourselves clear of the danger which was dogging our footsteps.

Once, I remember, as we passed over the Gemmi, and walked along the border of the melancholy Daubensee, a large rock which had been dislodged from the ridge

[6]*Masterstroke.* [7]*Watson served as an army doctor in the colonies.* [8]*Dining room.*

upon our right clattered down and roared into the lake behind us. In an instant Holmes had raced up on to the ridge, and, standing upon a lofty pinnacle, craned his neck in every direction. It was in vain that our guide assured him that a fall of stones was a common chance in the spring-time at that spot. He said nothing, but he smiled at me with the air of a man who sees the fulfillment of that which he had expected.

And yet for all his watchfulness he was never depressed. On the contrary, I can never recollect having seen him in such exuberant spirits. Again and again he recurred to the fact that if he could be assured that society was freed from Professor Moriarty he would cheerfully bring his own career to a conclusion.

"I think that I may go so far as to say, Watson, that I have not lived wholly in vain," he remarked. "If my record were closed to-night I could still survey it with equanimity. The air of London is the sweeter for my presence. In over a thousand cases I am not aware that I have ever used my powers upon the wrong side. Of late I have been tempted to look into the problems furnished by nature rather than those more superficial ones for which our artificial state of society is responsible. Your memoirs will draw to an end, Watson, upon the day that I crown my career by the capture or extinction of the most dangerous and capable criminal in Europe."

I shall be brief, and yet exact, in the little which remains for me to tell. It is not a subject on which I would willingly dwell, and yet I am conscious that a duty devolves upon me to omit no detail.

It was on the 3rd of May that we reached the little village of Meiringen, where we put up at the Englischer Hof, then kept by Peter Steiler the elder. Our landlord was an intelligent man, and spoke excellent English, having served for three years as waiter at the Grosvenor Hotel in London. At his advice, upon the afternoon of the 4th we set off together, with the intention of crossing the hills and spending the night at the hamlet of Rosenlaui. We had strict injunctions, however, on no account to pass the falls of Reichenbach, which are about half-way up the hill, without making a small detour to see them.

It is, indeed, a fearful place. The torrent, swollen by the melting snow, plunges into a tremendous abyss, from which the spray rolls up like the smoke from a burning house. The shaft into which the river hurls itself is a immense chasm, lined by glistening coal-black rock, and narrowing into a creaming, boiling pit of incalculable depth, which brims over and shoots the stream onward over its jagged lip. The long sweep of green water roaring for ever down, and the thick flickering curtain of spray hissing for ever upward, turn a man giddy with their constant whirl and clamour. We stood near the edge peering down at the gleam of the breaking water far below us against the black rocks, and listening to the half-human shout which came booming up with the spray out of the abyss.

The path has been cut half-way round the fall to afford a complete view, but it ends abruptly, and the traveller has to return as he came. We had turned to do so, when we saw a Swiss lad come running along it with a letter in his hand. It bore the mark of the hotel which we had just left, and was addressed to me by the landlord. It appeared that within a very few minutes of our leaving, an English lady had arrived who was in the last stage of consumption. She had wintered at Davos Platz, and was journeying now to join her friends at Lucerne, when a sudden hemorrhage had overtaken her. It was thought that she could hardly live a few hours, but it would be a great consolation to her to see an English doctor, and, if I would only return, etc., etc. The good Steiler assured me in a postscript that he would himself look upon my compliance as a very great favour, since the lady absolutely refused to see a Swiss physician, and he could not but feel that he was incurring a great responsibility.

The appeal was one which could not be ignored. It was impossible to refuse the request of a fellow-countrywoman dying in a strange land. Yet I had my scruples about leaving Holmes. It was finally agreed, however, that he should retain the young Swiss messenger with him as guide and companion while I returned to Meiringen. My friend would stay some little time at the fall, he said, and would then walk slowly over the hill to Rosenlaui, where I was to rejoin him in the evening. As I turned away I saw Holmes, with his back against a rock and his arms folded, gazing down at the rush of the waters. It was the last that I was ever destined to see of him in this world.

When I was near the bottom of the descent I looked back. It was impossible, from that position, to see the fall, but I could see the curving path which winds over the shoulder of the hill and leads to it. Along this a man was, I remember, walking very rapidly.

I could see his black figure clearly outlined against the green behind him. I noted him, and the energy with which he walked, but he passed from my mind again as I hurried on upon my errand.

It may have been a little over an hour before I reached Meiringen. Old Steiler was standing at the porch of his hotel.

"Well," said I, as I came hurrying up, "I trust that she is no worse?"

A look of surprise passed over his face, and at the first quiver of his eyebrows my heart turned to lead in my breast.

"You did not write this?" I said, pulling the letter from my pocket. "There is no sick Englishwoman in the hotel?"

"Certainly not," he cried. "But it has the hotel mark upon it! Ha, it must have been written by that tall Englishman who came in after you had gone. He said—"

But I waited for none of the landlord's explanations. In a tingle of fear I was already running down the village street, and making for the path which I had so lately descended. It had taken me an hour to come down. For all my efforts two more had passed before I found myself at the fall of Reichenbach once more. There was Holmes's Alpine-stock still leaning against the rock by which I had left him. But there was no sign of him, and it was in vain that I shouted. My only answer was my own voice reverberating in a rolling echo from the cliffs around me.

It was the sight of that Alpine-stock which turned me cold and sick. He had not gone to Rosenlaui, then. He had remained on that three-foot path, with sheer wall on one side and sheer drop on the other, until his enemy had overtaken him. The young Swiss had gone too. He had probably been in the pay of Moriarty, and had left the two men together. And then what had happened? Who was to tell us what had happened then?

I stood for a minute or two to collect myself, for I was dazed with the horror of the thing. Then I began to think of Holmes's own methods and to try to practise them in reading this tragedy. It was, alas, only too easy to do. During our conversation we had not gone to the end of the path, and the Alpine-stock marked the place where we had stood. The blackish soil is kept for ever soft by the incessant drift of spray, and a bird would leave its tread upon it. Two lines of footmarks were clearly marked along the farther end of the path, both leading away from me. There were none returning. A few yards from the end the soil was all ploughed up into a patch of mud, and the branches and ferns which fringed the chasm were torn and bedraggled. I lay upon my face and peered over with the spray spouting up all around me. It had darkened since I left, and now I could only see here and there the glistening of moisture upon the black walls, and far away down at the end of the shaft the gleam of the broken water. I shouted; but only the same half-human cry of the fall was borne back to my ears.

But it was destined that I should after all have a last word of greeting from my friend and comrade. I have said that his Alpine-stock had been left leaning against a rock which jutted on to the path. From the top of this boulder the gleam of something bright caught my eye, and, raising my hand, I found that it came from the silver cigarette-case which he used to carry. As I took it up a small square of paper upon which it had lain fluttered down on to the ground. Unfolding it, I found that it consisted of three pages torn from his note-book and addressed to me. It was characteristic of the man that the direction was as precise, and the writing as firm and clear, as though it had been written in his study.

"My dear Watson," he said, "I write these few lines through the courtesy of Mr. Moriarty, who awaits my convenience for the final discussion of those questions which lie between us. He has been giving me a sketch of the methods by which he avoided the English police and kept himself informed of our movements. They certainly confirm the very high opinion which I had formed of his abilities. I am pleased to think that I shall be able to free society from any further effects of his presence, though I fear that it is at a cost which will give pain to my friends, and especially, my dear Watson, to you. I have already explained to you, however, that my career had in any case reached its crisis, and that no possible conclusion to it could be more congenial to me than this. Indeed, if I may make a full confession to you, I was quite convinced that the letter from Meiringen was a hoax, and I allowed you to depart on that errand under the persuasion that some development of this sort would follow. Tell Inspector Patterson that the papers which he needs to convict the gang are in pigeonhole M., done up in a blue envelope and inscribed 'Moriarty.' I made every disposition of my property before leaving England, and handed it to my brother Mycroft. Pray give my greetings to Mrs. Watson, and believe me to be, my dear fellow,

"Very sincerely yours,
SHERLOCK HOLMES."

A few words may suffice to tell the little that remains. An examination by experts leaves little doubt that a personal contest between the two men ended, as it could hardly fail to end in such a situation, in their reeling over, locked in each other's arms. Any attempt at recovering the bodies was absolutely hopeless, and there, deep down in that dreadful caldron of swirling water and seething foam, will lie for all time the most dangerous criminal and the foremost champion of the law of their generation. The Swiss youth was never found again, and there can be no doubt that he was one of the numerous agents whom Moriarty kept in this employ. As to the gang, it will be within the memory of the public how completely the evidence which Holmes had accumulated exposed their organization, and how heavily the hand of the dead man weighed upon them. Of their terrible chief few details came out during the proceedings, and if I have now been compelled to make a clear statement of his career it is due to those injudicious champions who have endeavoured to clear his memory by attacks upon him whom I shall ever regard as the best and the wisest man whom I have ever known.[9]

[9]*Paraphrase of Plato's words on the occasion of the death of Socrates in the* Phaedo.

Bret Harte (1836–1902)

Bret Harte's life abounds in ironies. He was an Easterner with a penchant for poetry, who gained early fame by writing stories about the rough and tumble life in California. He was a mentor to, early friend of, and collaborator with Mark Twain, who later broke with and spoke bitterly of him. And he was an author credited with originating a quintessential American style, who frequently published parodies of other writers and spent his last two and a half decades abroad. Francis Brett Hart was born and raised in New York state and in his late teens moved to the West coast, where he tutored ranchers' children, worked as a miner and an apothecary, rode shotgun on stagecoaches, and set type in a printing office before becoming a journalist and an author. An early champion of the underdog, he was a lifelong critic of violence and prejudice against Native Americans, Chinese Americans, and African Americans. He enjoyed some success with "The Work on Red Mountain" and other writings he published in the early and mid–1860s, but it was the appearance of his story "The Luck of Roaring Camp" in 1868 that cemented his reputation. He returned to the East in 1871, briefly becoming the highest paid writer in the United States, but found it difficult to sustain his early success. In 1878 he left the United States for Europe, working as American Consul in Krefeld, Germany, and Glasgow, Scotland, prior to settling in London in 1885. Some of Harte's early fame rested on a series of send-ups of writers such as Charles Dickens, Victor Hugo, Charlotte Brontë, and Wilkie Collins, which he called *Condensed Novels.* At the end of his life, he wrote a second series of such works, poking fun at Rudyard Kipling, Arthur Conan Doyle, and other British writers. In 1866, the *North American Review* highly praised Harte as a parodist, an assessment echoed many years later by G. K. Chesterton, who lauded Harte for incorporating a perception of "the real beauty" and "the real ambition" of the authors he lampooned into his *Condensed Novels.* This can certainly be seen in "The Stolen Cigar Case," widely regarded as the best among the legions of Sherlock Holmes parodies.

The Stolen Cigar Case
by A. CO—N D—LE (Bret Harte)

(1900)

I found Hemlock Jones in the old Brook Street lodgings, musing before the fire. With the freedom of an old friend I at once threw myself in my usual familiar attitude at his feet, and gently caressed his boot. I was induced to do this for two reasons: one, that it enabled me to get a good look at his bent, concentrated face, and the other, that it seemed to indicate my reverence for his superhuman insight. So absorbed was he even then, in tracking some mysterious clue, that he did not seem to notice me. But therein I was wrong — as I always was in my attempt to understand that powerful intellect.

"It is raining," he said, without lifting his head.

"You have been out, then?" I said quickly.

"No. But I see that your umbrella is wet, and that your overcoat has drops of water on it."

I sat aghast at his penetration. After a pause he said carelessly, as if dismissing the subject: "Besides, I hear the rain on the window. Listen."

I listened. I could scarcely credit my ears, but there was the soft pattering of drops on the panes. It was evident there was no deceiving this man!

"Have you been busy lately?" I asked, changing the subject. "What new problem — given up by Scotland Yard as inscrutable — has occupied that gigantic intellect?"

He drew back his foot slightly, and seemed to hesitate ere he returned it to its original position. Then he answered wearily: "Mere trifles — nothing to speak of. The Prince Kupoli has been here to get my advice regarding the disappearance of certain rubies from the Kremlin; the Rajah of Pootibad, after vainly beheading his entire bodyguard, has been obliged to seek my assistance to recover a jeweled sword. The Grand Duchess of Pretzel-Brauntswig is desirous of discovering where her husband was on the night of February 14; and last night" — he lowered his voice slightly — "a lodger in this very house, meeting me on the stairs, wanted to know why they didn't answer his bell."

I could not help smiling — until I saw a frown gathering on his inscrutable forehead.

"Pray remember," he said coldly, "that it was through such an apparently trivial question that I found out Why Paul Ferroll Killed His Wife, and What Happened to Jones!"[1]

I became dumb at once. He paused for a moment, and then suddenly changing back to his usual pitiless, analytical style, he said: "When I say these are trifles, they are so in comparison to an affair that is now before me. A crime has been committed, — and, singularly enough, against myself. You start," he said. "You wonder who would have dared to attempt it. So did I; nevertheless, it has been done. *I* have been *robbed*!"

"*You* robbed! You, Hemlock Jones, the Terror of Peculators!" I gasped in amazement, arising and gripping the table as I faced him.

[1]*References to an 1860 novel by Caroline Clive and an 1897 farce by George Broadhurst.*

"Yes! Listen. I would confess it to no other. But *you* who have followed my career, who know my methods; you, for whom I have partly lifted the veil that conceals my plans from ordinary humanity,—you, who have for years rapturously accepted my confidences, passionately admired my inductions and inferences, placed yourself at my beck and call, become my slave, groveled at my feet, given up your practice except those few unremunerative and rapidly decreasing patients to whom, in moments of abstraction over *my* problems, you have administered strychnine for quinine and arsenic for Epsom salts; you, who have sacrificed anything and everybody to me,—*you* I make my confidant!"

I arose and embraced him warmly, yet he was already so engrossed in thought that at the same moment he mechanically placed his hand upon his watch chain as if to consult the time. "Sit down," he said. "Have a cigar?"

"I have given up cigar smoking," I said.

"Why?" he asked.

I hesitated, and perhaps colored. I had really given it up because, with my diminished practice, it was too expensive. I could afford only a pipe. "I prefer a pipe," I said laughingly. "But tell me of this robbery. What have you lost?"

He arose, and planting himself before the fire with his hands under his coattails, looked down upon me reflectively for a moment. "Do you remember the cigar case presented to me by the Turkish Ambassador for discovering the missing favorite of the Grand Vizier in the fifth chorus girl at the Hilarity Theatre? It was that one. I mean the cigar case. It was incrusted with diamonds."

"And the largest one had been supplanted by paste," I said.

"Ah," he said, with a reflective smile, "you know that?"

"You told me yourself. I remember considering it a proof of your extraordinary perception. But, by Jove, you don't mean to say you have lost it?"

He was silent for a moment. "No; it has been stolen, it is true, but I shall still find it. And by myself alone! In your profession, my dear fellow, when a member is seriously ill, he does not prescribe for himself, but calls in a brother doctor. Therein we differ. I shall take this matter in my own hands."

"And where could you find better?" I said enthusiastically. "I should say the cigar case is as good as recovered already."

"I shall remind you of that again," he said lightly. "And now, to show you my confidence in your judgment, in spite of my determination to pursue this alone, I am willing to listen to any suggestions from you."

He drew a memorandum book from his pocket and, with a grave smile, took up his pencil.

I could scarcely believe my senses. He, the great Hemlock Jones, accepting suggestions from a humble individual like myself! I kissed his hand reverently, and began in a joyous tone:—

"First, I should advertise, offering a reward; I should give the same intimation in hand-bills, distributed at the 'pubs' and the pastry-cooks'. I should next visit the different pawnbrokers; I should give notice at the police station. I should examine the servants. I should thoroughly search the house and my own pockets. I speak relatively," I added, with a laugh. "Of course I mean *your* own."

He gravely made an entry of these details.

"Perhaps," I added, "you have already done this?"

"Perhaps," he returned enigmatically. "Now, my dear friend," he continued, putting the note-book in his pocket and rising, "would you excuse me for a few moments? Make yourself perfectly at home until I return; there may be some things," he added with a sweep of his hand toward his heterogeneously filled shelves, "that may interest you and while away the time. There are pipes and tobacco in that corner."

Then nodding to me with the same inscrutable face he left the room. I was too well accustomed to his methods to think much of his unceremonious withdrawal, and made no doubt he was off to investigate some clue which had suddenly occurred to his active intelligence.

Left to myself I cast a cursory glance over his shelves. There were a number of small glass jars containing earthy substances, labeled "Pavement and Road Sweepings," from the principal thoroughfares and suburbs of London, with the sub-directions "for identifying foot-tracks." There were several other jars, labeled "Fluff from Omnibus and Road Car Seats," "Cocoanut Fibre and Rope Strands from Mattings in Public Places," "Cigarette Stumps and Match Ends from Floor of Palace Theatre, Row A, 1 to 50." Everywhere were evidences of this wonderful man's system and perspicacity.

I was thus engaged when I heard the slight creaking of a door, and I looked up as a stranger entered. He was a rough-looking man, with a shabby overcoat and a still more disreputable muffler around his throat and the lower part of his face. Considerably annoyed at his intrusion, I turned upon him rather sharply, when, with a mumbled, growling apology for mistaking the room, he shuffled out again and closed the door. I followed him quickly to the landing and saw that he disappeared down the stairs. With my mind full of the robbery, the incident made a singular impression upon me. I knew my friend's habit of hasty absences from his room in his moments of deep inspiration; it was only too probable that, with his powerful intellect and magnificent perceptive genius concentrated on one subject, he should be careless of his own belongings, and no doubt even forget to take the ordinary precaution of locking up his drawers. I tried one or two and found that I was right, although for some reason I was unable to open one to its fullest extent. The handles were sticky, as if some one had opened them with dirty fingers. Knowing Hemlock's fastidious cleanliness, I resolved to inform him of this circumstance, but I forgot it, alas! until — but I am anticipating my story.

His absence was strangely prolonged. I at last seated myself by the fire, and lulled by warmth and the patter of the rain on the window, I fell asleep. I may have dreamt, for during my sleep I had a vague semi-consciousness as of hands being softly pressed on my pockets — no doubt induced by the story of the robbery. When I came fully to my senses, I found Hemlock Jones sitting on the other side of the hearth, his deeply concentrated gaze fixed on the fire.

"I found you so comfortably asleep that I could not bear to awaken you," he said, with a smile.

I rubbed my eyes. "And what news?" I asked. "How have you succeeded?"

"Better than I expected," he said, "and I think," he added, tapping his note-book, "I owe much to *you*."

Deeply gratified, I awaited more. But in vain. I ought to have remembered that in his moods Hemlock Jones was reticence itself. I told him simply of the strange intrusion, but he only laughed.

Later, when I arose to go, he looked at me playfully. "If you were a married man," he said, "I would advise you not to go home until you had brushed your sleeve. There are a few short brown sealskin hairs on the inner side of your forearm, just where they would have adhered if your arm had encircled a seal-skin coat with some pressure!"

"For once you are at fault," I said triumphantly; "the hair is my own, as you will perceive; I have just had it cut at the hairdresser's, and no doubt this arm projected beyond the apron."

He frowned slightly, yet, nevertheless, on my turning to go he embraced me warmly — a rare exhibition in that man of ice. He even helped me on with my overcoat and pulled out and smoothed down the flaps of my pockets. He was particular, too, in fitting my arm in my overcoat sleeve, shaking the sleeve down from the armhole to the cuff with his deft fingers. "Come again soon!" he said, clapping me on the back.

"At any and all times," I said enthusiastically; "I only ask ten minutes twice a day to eat a crust at my office, and four hours' sleep at night, and the rest of my time is devoted to you always, as you know."

"It is indeed," he said, with his impenetrable smile.

Nevertheless, I did not find him at home when I next called. One afternoon, when nearing my own home, I met him in one of his favorite disguises, — a long blue swallow-tailed coat, striped cotton trousers, large turn-over collar, blacked face, and white hat, carrying a tambourine. Of course to others the disguise was perfect, although it was known to myself, and I passed him — according to an old understanding between us — without the slightest recognition, trusting to a later explanation. At another time, as I was making a professional visit to the wife of a publican at the East End, I saw him, in the disguise of a broken-down artisan, looking into the window of an adjacent pawnshop. I was delighted to see that he was evidently following my suggestions, and in my joy I ventured to tip him a wink; it was abstractedly returned.

Two days later I received a note appointing a meeting at his lodgings that night.

That meeting, alas! was the one memorable occurrence of my life, and the last meeting I ever had with Hemlock Jones! I will try to set it down calmly, though my pulses still throb with the recollection of it.

I found him standing before the fire, with that look upon his face which I had seen only once or twice in our acquaintance — a look which I may call an absolute concatenation of inductive and deductive ratiocination — from which all that was human, tender, or sympathetic was absolutely discharged. He was simply an icy algebraic symbol! Indeed, his whole being was concentrated to that extent that his clothes fitted loosely, and his head was absolutely so much reduced in size by his mental compression that his hat tipped back from his forehead and literally hung on his massive ears.

After I had entered he locked the doors, fastened the windows, and even placed a chair before the chimney. As I watched these significant precautions with absorbing interest, he suddenly drew a revolver and, presenting it to my temple, said in low, icy tones:

"Hand over that cigar case!"

Even in my bewilderment my reply was truthful, spontaneous, and involuntary. "I haven't got it," I said.

He smiled bitterly, and threw down his revolver. "I expected that reply! Then let me now confront you with something more awful, more deadly, more relentless and convincing than that mere lethal weapon,— the damning inductive and deductive proofs of your guilt!" He drew from his pocket a roll of paper and a note-book.

"But surely," I gasped, "you are joking! You could not for a moment believe"—

"Silence! Sit down!" I obeyed.

"You have condemned yourself," he went on pitilessly. "Condemned yourself on my processes,— processes familiar to you, applauded by you, accepted by you for years! We will go back to the time when you first saw the cigar case. Your expressions," he said in cold, deliberate tones, consulting his paper, "were, 'How beautiful! I wish it were mine.' This was your first step in crime — and my first indication. From '*I wish* it were mine' to '*I will* have it mine,' and the mere detail, '*How can* I make it mine?' the advance was obvious. Silence! But as in my methods it was necessary that there should be an overwhelming inducement to the crime, that unholy admiration of yours for the mere trinket itself was not enough. You are a smoker of cigars."

"But," I burst out passionately, "I told you I had given up smoking cigars."

"Fool!" he said coldly, "that is the *second* time you have committed yourself. Of course you told me! What more natural than for you to blazon forth that prepared and unsolicited statement to *prevent* accusation. Yet, as I said before, even that wretched attempt to cover up your tracks was not enough. I still had to find that overwhelming, impelling motive necessary to affect a man like you. That motive I found in the strongest of all impulses — Love, I suppose you would call it," he added bitterly, "that night you called! You had brought the most conclusive proofs of it on your sleeve."

"But—" I almost screamed.

"Silence!" he thundered. "I know what you would say. You would say that even if you had embraced some Young Person in a sealskin coat, what had that to do with the robbery? Let me tell you, then, that that sealskin coat represented the quality and character of your fatal entanglement! You bartered your honor for it—that stolen cigar case was the purchaser of the sealskin coat!

"Silence! Having thoroughly established your motive, I now proceed to the commission of the crime itself. Ordinary people would have begun with that—with an attempt to discover the whereabouts of the missing object. These are not *my* methods."

So overpowering was his penetration that, although I knew myself innocent, I licked my lips with avidity to hear the further details of this lucid exposition of my crime.

"You committed that theft the night I showed you the cigar case, and after I had carelessly thrown it in that drawer. You were sitting in that chair, and I had arisen to take something from that shelf. In that instant you secured your booty without rising. Silence! Do you remember when I helped you on with your overcoat the other night? I was particular about fitting your arm in. While doing so I measured your arm with a spring tape measure, from the shoulder to the cuff. A later visit to your tailor confirmed that measurement. It proved to be *the exact distance between your chair and that drawer!*"

I sat stunned.

"The rest are mere corroborative details! You were again tampering with the drawer when I discovered you doing so! Do not start! The stranger that blundered into the room with a muffler on—was myself! More, I had placed a little soap on the drawer handles when I purposely left you alone. The soap was on your hand when I shook it at parting. I softly felt your pockets, when you were asleep, for further developments. I embraced you when you left—that I might feel if you had the cigar case or any other articles hidden on your body. This confirmed me in the belief that you had already disposed of it in the manner and for the purpose I have shown you. As I still believed you capable of remorse and confession, I twice allowed you to see I was on your track: once in the garb of an itinerant negro minstrel, and the second time as a workman looking in the window of the pawnshop where you pledged your booty."

"But," I burst out, "if you had asked the pawnbroker, you would have seen how unjust"—

"Fool!" he hissed, "that was one of YOUR suggestions—to search the pawnshops! Do you suppose I followed any of your suggestions, the suggestions of the thief? On the contrary, they told me what to avoid."

"And I suppose," I said bitterly, "you have not even searched your drawer?"

"No," he said calmly.

I was for the first time really vexed. I went to the nearest drawer and pulled it out sharply. It stuck as it had before, leaving a part of the drawer unopened. By working it, however, I discovered that it was impeded by some obstacle that had slipped to the upper part of the drawer, and held it firmly fast. Inserting my hand, I pulled out the impeding object. It was the missing cigar case! I turned to him with a cry of joy.

But I was appalled at his expression. A look of contempt was now added to his acute, penetrating gaze. "I have been mistaken," he said slowly; "I had not allowed for your weakness and cowardice! I thought too highly of you even in your guilt! But I see now why you tampered with that drawer the other night. By some inexplicable means — possibly another theft — you took the cigar case out of pawn and, like a whipped hound, restored it to me in this feeble, clumsy fashion. You thought to deceive me, Hemlock Jones! More, you thought to destroy my infallibility. Go! I give you your liberty. I shall not summon the three policemen who wait in the adjoining room — but out of my sight forever!"

As I stood once more dazed and petrified, he took me firmly by the ear and led me into the hall, closing the door behind him. This reopened presently, wide enough to permit him to thrust out my hat, overcoat, umbrella, and overshoes, and then closed against me forever!

I never saw him again. I am bound to say, however, that thereafter my business increased, I recovered much of my old practice, and a few of my patients recovered also. I became rich. I had a brougham[2] and a house in the West End. But I often wondered, pondering on that wonderful man's penetration and insight, if, in some lapse of consciousness, I had not really stolen his cigar case!

[2]*Four-wheeled carriage with an outside driver's seat.*

Gender, Sexuality, and Detection

Mary Wilkins Freeman (1852–1930)

In a prolific career that spanned half a century, Mary Wilkins Freeman made notable contributions to American short fiction. Born in Massachusetts and raised in Vermont, she is best known for her stories set in her native New England. In the words of Mary R. Reichardt, "women's struggles for self-assertion and self-identity in often repressive and impoverished circumstances" stand out as Freeman's "most compelling and characteristic theme." She began publishing in 1882 and reached the height of her popularity with her collections *A Humble Romance and Other Stories* in 1887 and *A New England Nun and Other Stories* in 1891. Popular magazines of the day, including *Harper's* and *Lippincott's,* paid top dollar for her work. Her literary friends included Hamlin Garland, William Dean Howells, Rudyard Kipling, and Julia Ward Howe, and she was acquainted with Sarah Orne Jewett, Mark Twain, and Edith Wharton. In 1926 the American Academy of Arts and Letters awarded her the William Dean Howells Gold Medal for Fiction. Likely inspired, as Lillian Faderman has suggested, by the 1892 case of a mentally limited Tennessee woman named Alice Mitchell, "The Long Arm" appeared in many newspapers after winning the Bacheller Syndicate prize of $2000 in 1895. Despite the critical scrutiny Freeman's fiction has recently received, this story, which was written in collaboration with her journalist friend Joseph Edgar Chamberlain, is largely unknown today. Although Sarah Fairbanks lacks the intuition and analytical ability of subsequent female detectives such as Lady Molly, Violet Strange, and Miss Marple, the blind spots that prevent the protagonist and narrator from solving the case on her own reflect those of late nineteenth-century society generally. Particularly when "The Long Arm" is read in conjunction with more explicitly feminist stories such as Susan Glaspell's "A Jury of Her Peers," its unique combination of boldness and subtlety becomes apparent.

The Long Arm

by Mary Wilkins Freeman

(1895)

CHAPTER I.— The Tragedy.

(*From notes written by Miss Sarah Fairbanks immediately after the report of the Grand Jury.*)

As I take my pen to write this, I have a feeling that I am in the witness-box — for, or against myself, which? The place of the criminal in the dock I will not voluntarily take. I will affirm neither my innocence nor my guilt. I will present the facts of the case as impartially and as coolly as if I had nothing at stake. I will let all who read this judge me as they will.

This I am bound to do, since I am condemned to something infinitely worse than the life-cell or the gallows. I will try my own self in lieu of judge and jury; my guilt or my innocence I will prove to you all, if it be in mortal power. In my despair I am tempted to say, I care not which it may be, so something be proved. Open condemnation could not overwhelm me like universal suspicion.

Now, first, as I have heard is the custom in the courts of law, I will present the case. I am Sarah Fairbanks, a country school teacher, twenty-nine years of age. My mother died when I was twenty-three. Since then, while I have been teaching at Digby, a cousin of my father's, Rufus Bennett, and his wife have lived with my father. During the long summer vacation they returned to their little farm in Vermont, and I kept house for my father.

For five years I have been engaged to be married to Henry Ellis, a young man whom I met in Digby. My father was very much opposed to the match, and has told me repeatedly that if I insisted upon marrying him in his lifetime he would disinherit me. On this account Henry never visited me at my own home. While I could not bring myself to break off my engagement finally, I wished to avoid an open rupture with my father. He was quite an old man, and I was the only one he had left of a large family.

I believe that parents should honour their children, as well as children their parents; but I had arrived at this conclusion: in nine-tenths of the cases wherein children marry against their parents' wishes, even when the parents have no just grounds for opposition, the marriages are unhappy.

I sometimes felt that I was unjust to Henry, and resolved that, if ever I suspected that his fancy turned toward any other girl, I would not hinder it, especially as I was getting older and, I thought, losing my good looks.

A little while ago, a young and pretty girl came to Digby to teach the school in the south district. She boarded in the same house with Henry. I heard that he was somewhat attentive to her, and I made up my mind I would not interfere. At the same time it seemed to me that my heart was breaking. I heard her people had money, too, and she was an only child. I had always felt that Henry ought to marry a wife with money, because he had nothing himself, and was not very strong.

School closed five weeks ago, and I came home for the summer vacation. The night before I left, Henry came to see me, and urged me to marry him. I refused again; but I never before had felt that my father was so hard and cruel as I did that night. Henry said that he should certainly see me during the vacation, and when I replied that he must not come, he was angry, and said — but such foolish things are not worth repeating. Henry has really a very sweet temper, and would not hurt a fly.

The very night of my return home Rufus Bennett and my father had words about some maple sugar which Rufus made on his Vermont farm and sold to father, who made a good trade for it to some people in Boston. That was father's business. He had once kept a store, but had given it up, and sold a few articles that he could make a large profit on here and there at wholesale. He used to send to New Hampshire and Vermont for butter, eggs, and cheese. Cousin Rufus thought father did not allow him enough profit on the maple sugar, and in the dispute father lost his temper, and said that Rufus had given him underweight. At that, Rufus swore an oath, and seized father by the throat. Rufus's wife screamed, "Oh, don't! don't! oh, he'll kill him!"

I went up to Rufus and took hold of his arm.

"Rufus Bennett," said I, "you let go my father!"

But Rufus's eyes glared like a madman's, and he would not let go. Then I went to the desk-drawer where father had kept a pistol since some houses in the village were broken into; I got out the pistol, laid hold of Rufus again, and held the muzzle against his forehead.

"You let go of my father," said I, "or I'll fire!"

Then Rufus let go, and father dropped like a log. He was purple in the face. Rufus's wife and I worked a long time over him to bring him to.

"Rufus Bennett," said I, "go to the well and get a pitcher of water." He went, but when father had revived and got up, Rufus gave him a look that showed he was not over his rage.

"I'll get even with you yet, Martin Fairbanks, old man as you are!" he shouted out, and went into the outer room.

We got father to bed soon. He slept in the bedroom downstairs, out of the sitting-room. Rufus and his wife had the north chamber, and I had the south one. I left my door open that night, and did not sleep. I listened; no one stirred in the night. Rufus and his wife were up very early in the morning, and before nine o'clock left for Vermont. They had a day's journey, and would reach home about nine in the evening. Rufus's wife bade father good-bye, crying, while Rufus was getting their trunk downstairs, but Rufus did not go near father nor me. He ate no breakfast; his very back looked ugly when he went out of the yard.

That very day about seven in the evening, after tea, I had just washed the dishes and put them away, and went out on the north doorstep, where father was sitting, and sat down on the lowest step. There was a cool breeze there; it had been a very hot day.

"I want to know if that Ellis fellow has been to see you any lately?" said father all at once.

"Not a great deal," I answered.

"Did he come to see you the last night you were there?" said father.

"Yes, sir," said I, "he did come."

"If you ever have another word to say to that fellow while I live, I'll kick you out of the house like a dog, daughter of mine though you be," said he. Then he swore a great oath and called God to witness. "Speak to that fellow again, if you dare, while I live!" said he.

I did not say a word; I just looked up at him as I sat there. Father turned pale and shrank back, and put his hand to his throat, where Rufus had clutched him. There were some purple finger-marks there.

"I suppose you would have been glad if he had killed me," father cried out.

"I saved your life," said I.

"What did you do with that pistol?" he asked.

"I put it back in the desk-drawer."

I got up and went around and sat on the west doorstep, which is the front one. As I sat there, the bell rang for the Tuesday evening meeting, and Phœbe Dole and Maria Woods, two old maiden ladies, dressmakers, our next-door neighbours, went past on their way to meeting. Phœbe stopped and asked if Rufus and his wife were gone. Maria went around the house. Very soon they went on, and several other people passed. When they had all gone, it was as still as death.

I sat alone a long time, until I could see by the shadows that the full moon had risen. Then I went to my room and went to bed.

I lay awake a long time, crying. It seemed to me that all hope of marriage between Henry and me was over. I could not expect him to wait for me. I thought of that other girl; I could see her pretty face wherever I looked. But at last I cried myself to sleep.

At about five o'clock I awoke and got up. Father always wanted his breakfast at six o'clock, and I had to prepare it now.

When father and I were alone, he always built the fire in the kitchen stove, but that morning I did not hear him stirring as usual, and I fancied that he must be so out of temper with me, that he would not build the fire.

I went to my closet for a dark blue calico dress which I wore to do housework in. It had hung there during all the school term. As I took it off the hook, my attention was caught by something strange about the dress I had worn the night before. This dress was made of thin summer silk; it was green in colour, sprinkled over with white rings. It had been my best dress for two summers, but now I was wearing it on hot afternoons at home, for it was the coolest dress I had. The night before, too, I had thought of the possibility of Henry's driving over from Digby and passing the house. He had done this sometimes during the last summer vacation, and I wished to look my best if he did.

As I took down the calico dress I saw what seemed to be a stain on the green silk. I threw on the calico hastily, and then took the green silk and carried it over to the window. It was covered with spots — horrible great splashes and streaks down the front. The right sleeve, too, was stained, and all the stains were wet.

"What have I got on my dress?" said I.

It looked like blood. Then I smelled of it, and it was sickening in my nostrils, but I was not sure what the smell of blood was like. I thought I must have got the stains by some accident the night before.

"If that is blood on my dress," I said, "I must do something to get it off at once, or the dress will be ruined."

It came to my mind that I had been told that blood-stains had been removed from cloth by an application of flour paste on the wrong side. I took my green silk, and ran down the back stairs, which lead — having a door at the foot — directly into the kitchen.

There was no fire in the kitchen stove, as I had thought. Everything was very solitary and still, except for the ticking of the clock on the shelf. When I crossed the kitchen to the pantry, however, the cat mewed to be let in from the shed. She had a little door of her own by which she could enter or leave the shed at will, an aperture just large enough for her Maltese body to pass at ease beside the shed door. It had a little lid, too, hung upon a leathern hinge. On my way I let the cat in; then I went into the pantry and got a bowl of flour. This I mixed with water into a stiff paste, and applied to the under surface of the stains on my dress. I then hung the dress up to dry in the dark end of a closet leading out of the kitchen, which contained some old clothes of father's.

Then I made up the fire in the kitchen stove. I made coffee, baked biscuits, and poached some eggs for breakfast.

Then I opened the door into the sitting-room and called, "Father, breakfast is ready." Suddenly I started. There was a red stain on the inside of the sitting-room door. My heart began to beat in my ears. "Father!" I called out — "father!"

There was no answer.

"Father!" I called again, as loud as I could scream. "Why don't you speak? What is the matter?"

The door of his bedroom stood open. I had a feeling that I saw a red reflection in there. I gathered myself together and went across the sitting-room to father's bedroom door. His little looking-glass hung over his bureau opposite his bed, which was reflected in it.

That was the first thing I saw, when I reached the door. I could see father in the looking-glass and the bed. Father was dead there; he had been murdered in the night.

CHAPTER II. — THE KNOT OF RIBBON.

I think I must have fainted away, for presently I found myself on the floor, and for a minute I could not remember what had happened. Then I remembered, and an awful, unreasoning terror seized me. "I must lock all the doors quick," I thought; "quick, or the murderer will come back."

I tried to get up, but I could not stand. I sank down again. I had to crawl out of the room on my hands and knees.

I went first to the front door; it was locked with a key and a bolt. I went next to the north door, and that was locked with a key and bolt. I went to the north shed door, and that was bolted. Then I went to the little-used east door in the shed, beside which the cat had her little passage-way, and that was fastened with an iron hook. It has no latch.

The whole house was fastened on the inside. The thought struck me like an icy hand, "The murderer is in this house!" I rose to my feet then; I unhooked that door, and ran out of the house, and out of the yard, as for my life.

I took the road to the village. The first house, where Phœbe Dole and Maria Woods live, is across a wide field from ours. I did not intend to stop there, for they were only women, and could do nothing; but seeing Phœbe looking out of the window, I ran into the yard.

She opened the window.

"What is it?" said she. "What is the matter, Sarah Fairbanks?"

Maria Woods came and leaned over her shoulder. Her face looked almost as white as her hair, and her blue eyes were dilated. My face must have frightened her.

"Father — father is murdered in his bed!" I said.

There was a scream, and Maria Woods's face disappeared from over Phœbe Dole's shoulder — she had fainted. I do not know whether Phœbe looked paler — she is always very pale — but I saw in her black eyes a look which I shall never forget. I think she began to suspect me at that moment.

Phœbe glanced back at Maria, but she asked me another question.

"Has he had words with anybody?" said she.

"Only with Rufus," I said; "but Rufus is gone."

Phœbe turned away from the window to attend to Maria, and I ran on to the village.

A hundred people can testify what I did next — can tell how I called for the doctor and the deputy-sheriff; how I went back to my own home with the horror-stricken crowd; how they flocked in and looked at poor father; but only the doctor touched him, very carefully, to see if he were quite dead; how the coroner came, and all the rest.

The pistol was in the bed beside father, but it had not been fired; the charge was still in the barrel. It was blood-stained, and there was one bruise on father's head which might have been inflicted by the pistol, used as a club. But the wound which caused his death was in his breast, and made evidently by some cutting instrument, though the cut was not a clean one; the weapon must have been dull.

They searched the house, lest the murderer should be hidden away. I heard Rufus

Bennett's name whispered by one and another. Everybody seemed to know that he and father had had words the night before; I could not understand how, because I had told nobody except Phœbe Dole, who had had no time to spread the news, and I was sure that no one else had spoken of it.

They looked in the closet where my green silk dress hung, and pushed it aside to be sure nobody was concealed behind it, but they did not notice anything wrong about it. It was dark in the closet, and besides, they did not look for anything like that until later.

All these people — the deputy-sheriff, and afterwards the high sheriff, and other out-of-town officers, for whom they had telegraphed, and the neighbours — all hunted their own suspicion, and that was Rufus Bennett. All believed he had come back, and killed my father. They fitted all the facts to that belief. They made him do the deed with a long, slender screw-driver, which he had recently borrowed from one of the neighbours and had not returned. They made his finger-marks, which were still on my father's throat, fit the red prints of the sitting-room door. They made sure that he had returned and stolen into the house by the east door shed, while father and I sat on the doorsteps the evening before; that he had hidden himself away, perhaps in that very closet where my dress hung, and afterwards stolen out and killed my father, and then escaped.

They were not shaken when I told them that every door was bolted and barred that morning. They themselves found all the windows fastened down, except a few which were open on account of the heat, and even these last were raised only the width of the sash, and fastened with sticks, so that they could be raised no higher. Father was very cautious about fastening the house, for he sometimes had considerable sums of money by him. The officers saw all these difficulties in the way, but they fitted them somehow to their theory, and two deputy-sheriffs were at once sent to apprehend Rufus.

They had not begun to suspect me then, and not the slightest watch was kept on my movements. The neighbours were very kind, and did everything to help me, relieving me altogether of all those last offices — in this case so much sadder than usual.

An inquest was held, and I told freely all I knew, except about the blood-stains on my dress. I hardly knew why I kept that back. I had no feeling then that I might have done the deed myself, and I could not bear to convict myself, if I was innocent.

Two of the neighbours, Mrs. Holmes and Mrs. Adams, remained with me all that day. Towards evening, when there were very few in the house, they went into the parlour to put it in order for the funeral, and I sat down alone in the kitchen. As I sat there by the window I thought of my green silk dress, and wondered if the stains were out. I went to the closet and brought the dress out to the light. The spots and streaks had almost disappeared. I took the dress out into the shed, and scraped off the flour paste, which was quite dry; I swept up the paste, burned it in the stove, took the dress upstairs to my own closet, and hung it in its old place. Neighbours remained with me all night.

At three o'clock in the afternoon of the next day, which was Thursday, I went over to Phœbe Dole's to see about a black dress to wear at the funeral. The neighbours had urged me to have my black silk dress altered a little, and trimmed with crape.

I found only Maria Woods at home. When she saw me she gave a little scream, and began to cry. She looked as if she had already been weeping for hours. Her blue eyes were bloodshot.

"Phœbe's gone over to — Mrs. Whitney's to — try on her dress," she sobbed.

"I want to get my black silk dress fixed a little," said I.

"She'll be home — pretty soon," said Maria.

I laid my dress on the sofa and sat down. Nobody ever consults Maria about a dress. She sews well, but Phœbe does all the planning.

Maria Woods continued to sob like a child, holding her little soaked handkerchief over her face. Her shoulders heaved. As for me, I felt like a stone; I could not weep.

"Oh," she gasped out finally, "I knew — I knew! I told Phœbe — I knew just how it would be, I — knew!"

I roused myself at that.

"What do you mean?" said I.

"When Phœbe came home Tuesday night and said she heard your father and Rufus Bennett having words, I knew how it would be," she choked out. "I knew he had a dreadful temper."

"Did Phœbe Dole know Tuesday night that father and Rufus Bennett had words?" said I.

"Yes," said Maria Woods.

"How did she know?"

"She was going through your yard, the short cut to Mrs. Ormsby's, to carry her brown alpaca dress home. She came right home and told me; and she overheard them."

"Have you spoken of it to anybody but me?" said I.

Maria said she didn't know; she might have done so. Then she remembered hearing Phœbe herself speak of it to Harriet Sargent when she came in to try on her dress. It was easy to see how people knew about it.

I did not say any more, but I thought it was strange that Phœbe Dole had asked me if father had had words with anybody when she knew it all the time.

Phœbe came in before long. I tried on my dress, and she made her plan about the alterations, and the trimming. I made no suggestions. I did not care how it was done, but if I had cared it would have made no difference. Phœbe always does things her own way. All the women in the village are in a manner under Phœbe Dole's thumb. The garments are visible proofs of her force of will.

While she was taking up my black silk on the shoulder seams, Phœbe Dole said—"Let me see—you had a green silk made at Digby three summers ago, didn't you?"

"Yes," I said.

"Well," said she, "why don't you have it dyed black? those thin silks dye quite nice. It would make you a good dress."

I scarcely replied, and then she offered to dye it for me herself. She had a recipe which she used with great success. I thought it was very kind of her, but did not say whether I would accept her offer or not. I could not fix my mind upon anything but the awful trouble I was in.

"I'll come over and get it to-morrow morning," said Phœbe.

I thanked her. I thought of the stains, and then my mind seemed to wander again to the one subject. All the time Maria Woods sat weeping. Finally Phœbe turned to her with impatience.

"If you can't keep calmer, you'd better go upstairs, Maria," said she. "You'll make Sarah sick. Look at her! she doesn't give way—and think of the reason she's got."

"I've got reason, too," Maria broke out; then, with a piteous shriek, "Oh, I've got reason."

"Maria Woods, go out of the room!" said Phœbe. Her sharpness made me jump, half dazed as I was.

Maria got up without a word, and went out of the room, bending almost double with convulsive sobs.

"She's been dreadfully worked up over your father's death," said Phœbe calmly, going on with the fitting. "She's terribly nervous. Sometimes I have to be real sharp with her, for her own good."

I nodded. Maria Woods has always been considered a sweet, weakly, dependent woman, and Phœbe Dole is undoubtedly very fond of her. She has seemed to shield her, and take care of her nearly all her life. The two have lived together since they were young girls.

Phœbe is tall, and very pale and thin; but she never had a day's illness. She is plain, yet there is a kind of severe goodness and faithfulness about her colourless face, with the smooth bands of white hair over her ears.

I went home as soon as my dress was fitted. That evening Henry Ellis came over to see me. I do not need to go into details concerning that visit. It seemed enough to say that he tendered the fullest sympathy and protection, and I accepted them. I cried a little, for the first time, and he soothed and comforted me.

Henry had driven over from Digby and tied his horse in the yard. At ten o'clock he bade me good night on the doorstep, and was just turning his buggy around, when Mrs. Adams came running to the door.

"Is this yours?" said she, and she held out a knot of yellow ribbon.

"Why, that's the ribbon you have around your whip, Henry," said I.

He looked at it.

"So it is," he said. "I must have dropped it." He put it into his pocket and drove away.

"He didn't drop that ribbon to-night!" said Mrs. Adams. "I found it Wednesday morning out in the yard. I thought I remembered seeing him have a yellow ribbon on his whip."

CHAPTER III.—SUSPICION IS NOT PROOF.

When Mrs. Adams told me she had picked up Henry's whip-ribbon Wednesday morning, I said nothing, but thought that Henry must have driven over Tuesday evening after all, and even come up into the yard, although the house was shut up, and I in bed, to get a little nearer to me. I felt conscience-stricken, because I could not help a thrill of happiness, when my father lay dead in the house.

My father was buried as privately and as quietly as we could bring it about. But it was a terrible ordeal. Meantime word came from Vermont that Rufus Bennett had been arrested on his farm. He was perfectly willing to come back with the officers, and, indeed, had not the slightest trouble in proving that he was at his home in Vermont when the murder took place. He proved by several witnesses that he was out of the State long before my father and I sat on the steps together that evening, and that he proceeded directly to his home as fast as the train and stage-coach could carry him.

The screw-driver with which the deed was supposed to have been committed was found, by the neighbour from whom it had been borrowed, in his wife's bureau drawer. It had been returned, and she had used it to put a picture-hook in her chamber. Bennett was discharged and returned to Vermont.

Then Mrs. Adams told of the finding of the yellow ribbon from Henry Ellis's whip, and he was arrested, since he was held to have a motive for putting my father out of the world. Father's opposition to our marriage was well known, and Henry was suspected also of having had an eye to his money. It was found, indeed, that my father had more money than I had known myself.

Henry owned to having driven into the yard that night, and to having missed the ribbon from his whip on his return; but one of the hostlers in the livery stables in Digby, where he kept his horse and buggy, came forward and testified to finding the yellow ribbon in the carriage-room that Tuesday night before Henry returned from his drive. There were two yellow ribbons in evidence, therefore, and the one produced by the hostler seemed to fit Henry's whip-stock the more exactly.

Moreover, nearly the exact minute of the murder was claimed to be proved by the post-mortem examination; and by the testimony of the stableman as to the hour of Henry's return and the speed of his horse, he was further cleared of suspicion; for, if the opinion of the medical experts was correct, Henry must have returned to the livery stable too soon to have committed the murder.

He was discharged, at any rate, although suspicion still clung to him. Many people believe now in his guilt — those who do not, believe in mine; and some believe we were accomplices.

After Henry's discharge, I was arrested. There was no one else left to accuse. There must be a motive for the murder; I was the only person left with a motive. Unlike the others, who were discharged after preliminary examination, I was held to the grand jury and taken to Dedham, where I spent four weeks in jail, awaiting the meeting of the grand jury.

Neither at the preliminary examination, nor before the grand jury, was I allowed to make the full and frank statement that I am making here. I was told simply to answer the questions that were put to me, and to volunteer nothing, and I obeyed.

I know nothing about law. I wished to do the best I could — to act in the wisest manner, for Henry's sake and my own. I said nothing about the green silk dress. They searched the house for all manner of things, at the time of my arrest, but the dress was not there — it was in Phœbe Dole's dye-kettle. She had come over after it one day when I was picking beans in the garden, and had taken it out of the closet. She brought it back herself, and told me this, after I had returned from Dedham.

"I thought I'd get it and surprise you," said she. "It's taken a beautiful black."

She gave me a strange look — half as if she would see into my very soul, in spite of me, half as if she were in terror of what she would see there, as she spoke. I do not know just what Phœbe Dole's look meant. There may have been a stain left on that dress after all, and she may have seen it.

I suppose if it had not been for that flour-paste which I had learned to make, I should have hung for the murder of my father. As it was, the grand jury found no bill against me because there was absolutely no evidence to convict me; and I came home a free woman. And if people were condemned for their motives, would there be enough hangmen in the world?

They found no weapon with which I could have done the deed. They found no blood-stains on my clothes. The one thing which told against me, aside from my ever-present motive, was the fact that on the morning after the murder the doors and windows were fastened. My volunteering this information had of course weakened its force as against myself.

Then, too, some held that I might have been mistaken in my terror and excitement, and there was a theory, advanced by a few, that the murderer had meditated making me also a victim, and had locked the doors that he might not be frustrated in his designs, but had lost heart at the last, and had allowed me to escape, and then fled himself. Some held that he had intended to force me to reveal the whereabouts of father's money, but his courage had failed him.

Father had quite a sum in a hiding-place which only he and I knew. But no search for money had been made, as far as any one could see — not a bureau drawer had been disturbed, and father's gold watch was ticking peacefully under his pillow; even his wallet in his vest pocket had not been opened. There was a small roll of bank-notes in it, and some change; father never carried much money. I suppose if father's wallet and watch had been taken, I should not have been suspected at all.

I was discharged, as I have said, from lack of evidence, and have returned to my home — free, indeed, but with this awful burden of suspicion on my shoulders. That brings me up to the present day. I returned yesterday evening. This evening Henry Ellis has been over to see me; he will not come again, for I have forbidden him to do so. This is what I said to him —

"I know you are innocent, you know I am innocent. To all the world beside we are under suspicion — I more than you, but we are both under suspicion. If we are known to be together that suspicion is increased for both of us. I do not care for myself, but I do care for you. Separated from me the stigma attached to you will soon fade away, especially if you should marry elsewhere."

Then Henry interrupted me.

"I will never marry elsewhere," said he.

I could not help being glad that he said it, but I was firm.

"If you should see some good woman whom you could love, it will be better for you to marry elsewhere," said I.

"I never will!" he said again. He put his arms around me, but I had strength to push him away.

"You never need, if I succeed in what I undertake before you meet the other," said I. I began to think he had not cared for that pretty girl who boarded in the same house after all.

"What is that?" he said. "What are you going to undertake?"

"To find my father's murderer," said I.

Henry gave me a strange look; then, before I could stop him, he took me fast in his arms and kissed my forehead.

"As God is my witness, Sarah, I believe in your innocence," he said; and from that minute I have felt sustained and fully confident of my power to do what I had undertaken.

My father's murderer I will find. To-morrow I begin my search. I shall first make an exhaustive examination of the house, such as no officer in the case has yet made, in the hope of finding a clue. Every room I propose to divide into square yards, by line and measure, and every one of these square yards I will study as if it were a problem in algebra.

I have a theory that it is impossible for any human being to enter any house, and commit in it a deed of this kind, and not leave behind traces which are the known quantities in an algebraic equation to those who can use them.

There is a chance that I shall not be quite unaided. Henry has promised not to come again until I bid him, but he is to send a detective here from Boston — one whom he knows. In fact, the man is a cousin of his, or else there would be small hope of our securing him, even if I were to offer him a large price.

The man has been remarkably successful in several cases, but his health is not good; the work is a severe strain upon his nerves, and he is not driven to it from any lack of money. The physicians have forbidden him to undertake any new case, for a year at least, but Henry is confident that we may rely upon him for this.

I will now lay aside this and go to bed. To-morrow is Wednesday; my father will have been dead seven weeks. To-morrow morning I will commence the work, in which, if it be in human power, aided by a higher wisdom, I shall succeed.

CHAPTER IV.—THE BOX OF CLUES.

(*The pages which follow are from Miss Fairbanks's journal, begun after the conclusion of the notes already given to the reader.*)

Wednesday night.—I have resolved to record carefully each day the progress I make in my examination of the house. I began today at the bottom—that is, with the room least likely to contain any clue, the parlour. I took a chalk-line and a yard-stick, and divided the floor into square yards, and every one of these squares I examined on my hands and knees. I found in this way literally nothing on the carpet but dust, lint, two common white pins, and three inches of blue sewing-silk.

At last I got the dustpan and brush, and yard by yard swept the floor. I took the sweepings in a white pasteboard box out into the yard in the strong sunlight, and examined them. There was nothing but dust and lint and five inches of brown woollen thread—evidently a ravelling of some dress material. The blue silk and the brown thread are the only possible clues which I found to-day, and they are hardly possible. Rufus's wife can probably account for them.

Nobody has come to the house all day. I went down to the store this afternoon to get some necessary provisions, and people stopped talking when I came in. The clerk took my money as if it were poison.

Thursday night.—To-day I have searched the sitting-room, out of which my father's bedroom opens. I found two bloody footprints on the carpet which no one had noticed before—perhaps because the carpet itself is red and white. I used a microscope[1] which I had in my school work. The footprints, which are close to the bedroom door, pointing out into the sitting-room, are both from the right foot; one is brighter than the other, but both are faint. The foot was evidently either bare or clad only in a stocking—the prints are so widely spread. They are wider than my father's shoes. I tried one in the brightest print.

I found nothing else new in the sitting-room. The blood-stains on the doors

[1]*Magnifying glass.*

which have been already noted are still there. They had not been washed away, first by order of the sheriff, and next by mine. These stains are of two kinds; one looks as if made by a bloody garment brushing against it; the other, I should say, was made in the first place by the grasp of a bloody hand, and then brushed over with a cloth. There are none of these marks upon the door leading to the bedroom — they are on the doors leading into the front entry and the china closet. The china closet is really a pantry, although I use it only for my best dishes and preserves.

Friday night.— To-day I searched the closet. One of the shelves, which is about as high as my shoulders, was blood-stained. It looked to me as if the murderer might have caught hold of it to steady himself. Did he turn faint after his dreadful deed? Some tumblers of jelly were ranged on that shelf and they had not been disturbed. There was only that bloody clutch on the edge.

I found on this closet floor, under the shelves, as if it had been rolled there by a careless foot, a button, evidently from a man's clothing. It is an ordinary black enamelled metal trousers-button; it had evidently been worn off and clumsily sewn on again, for a quantity of stout white thread is still clinging to it. This button must have belonged either to a single man or to one with an idle wife.

If one black button had been sewn on with white thread, another is likely to be. I may be wrong, but I regard this button as a clue.

The pantry was thoroughly swept — cleaned, indeed, by Rufus's wife, the day before she left. Neither my father nor Rufus could have dropped it there, and they never had occasion to go to that closet. The murderer dropped the button.

I have a white pasteboard box which I have marked "clues." In it I have put the button.

This afternoon Phœbe Dole came in. She is very kind. She had re-cut the dyed silk, and she fitted it to me. Her great shears clicking in my ears made me nervous. I did not feel like stopping to think about clothes. I hope I did not appear ungrateful, for she is the only soul beside Henry who has treated me as she did before this happened.

Phœbe asked me what I found to busy myself about, and I replied, "I am searching for my father's murderer." She asked me if I thought I should find a clue, and I replied, "I think so." I had found the button then, but I did not speak of it. She said Maria was not very well.

I saw her eyeing the stains on the doors, and I said I had not washed them off, for I thought they might yet serve a purpose in detecting the murderer. She looked closely at those on the entry-door — the brightest ones — and said she did not see how they could help, for there were no plain finger-marks there, and she should think they would make me nervous.

"I'm beyond being nervous," I replied.

Saturday.— To-day I have found something which I cannot understand. I have been at work in the room where my father came to his dreadful end. Of course some of the most startling evidences have been removed. The bed is clean, and the carpet washed, but the worst horror of it all clings to that room. The spirit of murder seemed to haunt it. It seemed to me at first that I could not enter that room, but in it I made a strange discovery.

My father, while he carried little money about his person, was in the habit of keeping considerable sums in the house; there is no bank within ten miles. However he was wary; he had a hiding-place which he had revealed to no one but myself. He had a small stand in his room near the end of his bed. Under this stand, or rather under the top of it, he had tacked a large leather wallet. In this he kept all his spare money. I remember how his eyes twinkled when he showed it to me.

"The average mind thinks things have either got to be in or on," said my father. "They don't consider there's ways of getting around gravitation and calculation."

In searching my father's room I called to mind that saying of his, and his peculiar system of concealment, and then I made my discovery. I have argued that in a search of this kind I ought not only to search for hidden traces of the criminal, but for everything which had been for any reason concealed. Something which my father himself had hidden, something from his past history, may furnish a motive for some one else.

The money in the wallet under the table, some five hundred dollars, had been removed and deposited in the bank. Nothing more was to be found there. I examined the bottom of the bureau, and the undersides of the chair seats. There are two chairs in the room, besides the cushioned rocker — green-painted wooden chairs, with flag seats. I found nothing under the seats.

Then I turned each of the green chairs completely over, and examined the bottoms of the legs. My heart leaped when I found a bit of leather tacked over one. I got the tack-hammer and drew the tacks. The chair-leg had been hollowed out, and for an inch the hole was packed tight with cotton. I began picking out the cotton, and soon I felt something hard. It proved to be an old-fashioned gold band, quite wide and heavy, like a wedding-ring.

I took it over to the window and found this inscription on the inside: "Let love abide for ever." There were two dates — one in August, forty years ago, and the other in August of the present year.

I think the ring had never been worn; while the first part of the inscription is perfectly clear, it looks old, and the last is evidently freshly cut.

This could not have been my mother's ring. She had only her wedding-ring, and that was buried with her. I think my father must have treasured up this ring for years; but why? What does it mean? This can hardly be a clue; this can hardly lead to the discovery of a motive, but I will put it in the box with the rest.

Sunday night. — To-day, of course, I did not pursue my search. I did not go to church. I could not face old friends that could not face me. Sometimes I think that everybody in my native village believes in my guilt. What must I have been in my general appearance and demeanour all my life? I have studied myself in the glass, and tried to discover the possibilities of evil that they must see in my face.

This afternoon about three o'clock, the hour when people here have just finished their Sunday dinner, there was a knock on the north door. I answered it, and a strange young man stood there with a large book under his arm. He was thin and cleanly shaved, with a clerical air.

"I have a work here to which I would like to call your attention," he began; and I stared at him in astonishment, for why should a book agent be peddling his wares upon the Sabbath?

His mouth twitched a little.

"It's a Biblical Cyclopædia," said he.

"I don't think I care to take it," said I.

"You are Miss Sarah Fairbanks, I believe?"

"That is my name," I replied stiffly.

"Mr. Henry Ellis, of Digby, sent me here," he said next. "My name is Dix—Francis Dix."

Then I knew it was Henry's first cousin from Boston—the detective who had come to help me. I felt the tears coming to my eyes.

"You are very kind to come," I managed to say.

"I am selfish, not kind," he returned, "but you had better let me come in, or any chance of success in my book agency is lost, if the neighbours see me trying to sell it on a Sunday. And, Miss Fairbanks, this is a *bonâ fide* agency. I shall canvass the town."

He came in. I showed him all that I have written, and he read it carefully. When he had finished he sat still for a long time, with his face screwed up in a peculiar meditative fashion.

"We'll ferret this out in three days at the most," said he finally, with a sudden clearing of his face and a flash of his eyes at me.

"I had planned for three years, perhaps," said I.

"I tell you, we'll do it in three days," he repeated. "Where can I get board while I canvass for this remarkable and interesting book under my arm? I can't stay here, of course, and there is no hotel. Do you think the two dressmakers next door, Phœbe Dole and the other one, would take me in?"

I said they had never taken boarders.

"Well, I'll go over and enquire," said Mr. Dix; and he had gone, with his book under his arm, almost before I knew it.

Never have I seen any one act with the strange noiseless soft speed that this man does. Can he prove me innocent in three days? He must have succeeded in getting board at Phœbe Dole's, for I saw him go past to meeting with her this evening. I feel sure he will be over very early to-morrow morning.

CHAPTER V. THE EVIDENCE POINTS TO ONE.

Monday night.—The detective came as I expected. I was up as soon as it was light, and he came across the dewy fields, with his Cyclopædia under his arm. He had stolen out from Phœbe Dole's back door.

He had me bring my father's pistol; then he bade me come with him out into the back yard.

"Now, fire it," he said, thrusting the pistol into my hands. As I have said before, the charge was still in the barrel.

"I shall arouse the neighbourhood," I said.

"Fire it," he ordered.

I tried; I pulled the trigger as hard as I could.

"I can't do it," I said.

"And you are a reasonably strong woman, too, aren't you?"

I said I had been considered so. Oh, how much I heard about the strength of my poor woman's arms, and their ability to strike that murderous weapon home!

Mr. Dix took the pistol himself, and drew a little at the trigger.

"I could do it," he said, "but I won't. It would arouse the neighbourhood."

"This is more evidence against me," I said despairingly. "The murderer had tried to fire the pistol and failed."

"It is more evidence against the murderer," said Mr. Dix.

We went into the house, where he examined my box of clues long and carefully. Looking at the ring, he asked whether there was a jeweller in this village, and I said there was not. I told him that my father oftener went on business to Acton, ten miles away, than elsewhere.

He examined very carefully the button which I had found in the closet, and then asked to see my father's wardrobe. That was soon done. Beside the suit in which father was laid away there was one other complete one in the closet in his room. Besides that, there were in this closet two overcoats, an old black frock coat, a pair of pepper-and-salt trousers, and two black vests. Mr. Dix examined all the buttons; not one was missing.

There was still another old suit in the closet off the kitchen. This was examined, and no button found wanting.

"What did your father do for work the day before he died?" he then asked.

I reflected and said that he had unpacked some stores which had come down from Vermont, and done some work out in the garden.

"What did he wear?"

"I think he wore the pepper-and-salt trousers and the black vest. He wore no coat, while at work."

Mr. Dix went quietly back to father's room and his closet, I following. He took out the grey trousers and the black vest, and examined them closely.

"What did he wear to protect these?" he asked.

"Why, he wore overalls!" I said at once. As I spoke I remembered seeing father go around the path to the yard, with those blue overalls drawn up high under his arms.

"Where are they?"

"Weren't they in the kitchen closet?"

"No."

We looked again, however, in the kitchen closet; we searched the shed thoroughly. The cat came in through her little door, as we stood there, and brushed around our feet. Mr. Dix stooped and stroked her. Then he went quickly to the door, beside which her little entrance was arranged, unhooked it, and stepped out. I was following him, but he motioned me back.

"None of my boarding mistress's windows command us," he said, "but she might come to the back door."

I watched him. He passed slowly around the little winding footpath, which skirted the rear of our house and extended faintly through the grassy fields to the rear of Phœbe Dole's. He stopped, searched a clump of sweetbriar, went on to an old well, and stopped there. The well had been dry many a year, and was choked up with stones and rubbish. Some boards are laid over it, and a big stone or two, to keep them in place.

Mr. Dix, glancing across at Phœbe Dole's back door, went down on his knees, rolled the stones away, then removed the boards and peered down the well. He stretched far over the brink, and reached down. He made many efforts; then he got up and came to me, and asked me to get for him an umbrella with a crooked handle, or something that he could hook into clothing.

I brought my own umbrella, the silver handle of which formed an exact hook. He went back to the well, knelt again, thrust in the umbrella and drew up, easily enough, what he had been fishing for. Then he came bringing it to me.

"Don't faint," he said, and took hold of my arm. I gasped when I saw what he had — my father's blue overalls, all stained and splotched with blood!

I looked at them, then at him.

"Don't faint," he said again. "We're on the right track. This is where the button came from — see, see!" He pointed to one of the straps of the overalls, and the button was gone. Some white thread clung to it. Another black metal button was sewed on roughly with the same white thread that I found on the button in my box of clues.

"What does it mean?" I gasped out. My brain reeled.

"You shall know soon," he said. He looked at his watch. Then he laid down the ghastly bundle he carried. "It has puzzled you to know how the murderer went in and out and yet kept the doors locked, has it not?" he said.

"Yes."

"Well, I am going out now. Hook that door after me."

He went out, still carrying my umbrella. I hooked the door. Presently I saw the lid of the cat's door lifted, and his hand and arm thrust through. He curved his arm up towards the hook, but it came short by half a foot. Then he withdrew his arm, and thrust in my silver-handled umbrella. He reached the door-hook easily enough with that.

Then he hooked it again. That was not so easy. He had to work a long time. Finally he accomplished it, unhooked the door again, and came in.

"That was how!" I said.

"No, it was not," he returned. "No human being, fresh from such a deed, could have used such patience as that to fasten the door after him. Please hang your arm down by your side."

I obeyed. He looked at my arm, then at his own.

"Have you a tape measure?" he asked.

I brought one out of my work-basket. He measured his arm, then mine, and then the distance from the cat-door to the hook.

"I have two tasks for you to-day and to-morrow," he said. "I shall come here very little. Find all your father's old letters, and read them. Find a man or woman in this town whose arm is six inches longer than yours. Now I must go home, or my boarding-mistress will get curious."

He went through the house to the front door, looked all ways to be sure no eyes were upon him, made three strides down the yard, and was pacing soberly up the street, with his Cyclopædia under his arm.

I made myself a cup of coffee, then I went about obeying his instructions. I read old letters all the forenoon; I found packages in trunks in the garret; there were quantities in father's desk. I have selected several to submit to Mr. Dix. One of them treats of an old episode in father's youth, which must have years since ceased to interest him. It was concealed after his favourite fashion — tacked under the bottom of his desk. It was written forty years ago, by Maria Woods, two years before my father's marriage — and it was a refusal of an offer of his hand. It was written in the stilted fashion of that day; it might have been copied from a "Complete Letter-writer."

My father must have loved Maria Woods as dearly as I love Henry, to keep that letter so carefully all these years. I thought he cared for my mother. He seemed as fond of her as other men of their wives, although I did use to wonder if Henry and I would ever get to be quite so much accustomed to each other.

Maria Woods must have been as beautiful as an angel when she was a girl. Mother was not pretty; she was stout, too, and awkward, and I suppose people would have called her rather slow and dull. But she was a good woman, and tried to do her duty.

Tuesday night. — This evening was my first opportunity to obey the second of Mr. Dix's orders. It seemed to me the best way to compare the average length of arms was to go to the prayer-meeting. I could not go about the town with my tape measure, and demand of people that they should hold out their arms. Nobody knows how I dreaded to go to the meeting, but I went, and I looked not at my neighbours' cold altered faces, but at their arms.

I discovered what Mr. Dix wished me to, but the discovery can avail nothing, and it is one he could have made himself. Phœbe Dole's arm is fully seven inches longer than mine. I never noticed it before, but she has an almost abnormally long arm. But why should Phœbe Dole have unhooked that door?

She made a prayer — a beautiful prayer. It comforted even me a little. She spoke of the tenderness of God in all the troubles of life, and how it never failed us.

When we were all going out I heard several persons speak of Mr. Dix and his Biblical Cyclopædia. They decided that he was a theological student, book-canvassing to defray the expenses of his education.

Maria Woods was not at the meeting. Several asked Phœbe how she was, and she replied, "Not very well."

It is very late. I thought Mr. Dix might be over to-night, but he has not been here.

Wednesday. — I can scarcely believe what I am about to write. Our investigations seem to point all to one person, and that person — It is incredible! I will not believe it.

Mr. Dix came as before, at dawn. He reported, and I reported. I showed Maria Woods's letter. He said he had driven to Acton, and found that the jeweller there had engraved the last date in the ring about six weeks ago.

"I don't want to seem rough, but your father was going to get married again," said Mr. Dix.

"I never knew him to go near any woman since mother died," I protested.

"Nevertheless, he had made arrangements to be married," persisted Mr. Dix.

"Who was the woman?"

He pointed at the letter in my hand.

"Maria Woods!"

He nodded.

I stood looking at him — dazed. Such a possibility had never entered my head.

He produced an envelope from his pocket, and took out a little card with blue and brown threads neatly wound upon it.

"Let me see those threads you found," he said.

I got the box and we compared them. He had a number of pieces of blue sewing-silk and brown woollen ravellings, and they matched mine exactly.

"Where did you find them?" I asked.

"In my boarding-mistress's piecebag."

I stared at him.

"What does it mean?" I gasped out.

"What do you think?"

"It is impossible!"

CHAPTER VI.
THE REVELATION.

Wednesday, continued.—When Mr. Dix thus suggested to me the absurd possibility that Phœbe Dole had committed the murder, he and I were sitting in the kitchen. He was near the table; he laid a sheet of paper upon it, and began to write. The paper is before me.

"First," said Mr. Dix, and he wrote rapidly as he talked, "Whose arm is of such length that it might unlock a certain door of this house from the outside?—Phœbe Dole's.

"Second, who had in her piece-bag bits of the same threads and ravellings found upon your parlour floor, where she had not by your knowledge entered?—Phœbe Dole.

"Third, who interested herself most strangely in your blood-stained green silk dress, even to dyeing it?—Phœbe Dole.

"Fourth, who was caught in a lie, while trying to force the guilt of the murder upon an innocent man?—Phœbe Dole."

Mr. Dix looked at me. I had gathered myself together. "That proves nothing," I said. "There is no motive in her case."

"There is a motive."

"What is it?"

"Maria Woods shall tell you this afternoon."

He then wrote—

"Fifth, who was seen to throw a bundle down the old well, in the rear of Martin Fairbanks's house, at one o'clock in the morning?—Phœbe Dole."

"Was she—seen?" I gasped.

Mr. Dix nodded. Then he wrote.

"Sixth, who had a strong motive, which had been in existence many years ago?—Phœbe Dole."

Mr. Dix laid down his pen, and looked at me again.

"Well, what have you to say?" he asked.

"It is impossible!"

"Why?"

"She is a woman."

"A man could have fired that pistol, as she tried to do."

"It would have taken a man's strength to kill with the kind of weapon that was used," I said.

"No, it would not. No great strength is required for such a blow."

"But she is a woman!"

"Crime has no sex."

"But she is a good woman — a church member. I heard her pray yesterday afternoon. It is not in character."

"It is not for you, nor for me, nor for any mortal intelligence, to know what is or is not in character," said Mr. Dix.

He arose and went away. I could only stare at him in a half-dazed manner.

Maria Woods came this afternoon, taking advantage of Phœbe's absence on a dressmaking errand. Maria has aged ten years in the last few weeks. Her hair is white, her cheeks are fallen in, her pretty colour is gone.

"May I have the ring he gave me forty years ago?" she faltered.

I gave it to her; she kissed it and sobbed like a child.

"Phœbe took it away from me before," she said; "but she shan't this time."

Maria related with piteous sobs the story of her long subordination to Phœbe Dole. This sweet child-like woman had always been completely under the sway of the other's stronger nature. The subordination went back beyond my father's original proposal to her; she had, before he made love to her as a girl, promised Phœbe she would not marry; and it was Phœbe who, by representing to her that she was bound by this solemn promise, had led her to write a letter to my father declining his offer, and sending back the ring.

"And after all, we were going to get married, if he had not died," she said. "He was going to give me this ring again, and he had had the other date put in. I should have been so happy!"

She stopped and stared at me with horror-stricken enquiry.

"What was Phœbe Dole doing in your backyard at one o'clock that night?" she cried.

"What do you mean?" I returned.

"I saw Phœbe come out of your back shed door at one o'clock that very night. She had a bundle in her arms. She went along the path about as far as the old well, then she stooped down, and seemed to be working at something. When she got up she didn't have the bundle. I was watching at our back door. I thought I heard her go out a little while before, and went downstairs, and found that door unlocked. I went in quick, and up to my chamber, and into my bed, when she started home across the fields. Pretty soon I heard her come in, then I heard the pump going. She slept downstairs; she went on to her bedroom. What was she doing in your backyard that night?"

"You must ask her," said I. I felt my blood running cold.

"I've been afraid to," moaned Maria Woods. "She's been dreadful strange lately. I wish that book agent was going to stay at our house."

Maria Woods went home in about an hour. I got a ribbon for her, and she has my poor father's ring concealed in her withered bosom. Again I cannot believe this.

Thursday.—It is all over, Phœbe Dole has confessed! I do not know now in exactly what way Mr. Dix brought it about—how he accused her of her crime. After breakfast I saw them coming across the fields; Phœbe came first, advancing with rapid strides like a man, Mr. Dix followed, and my father's poor old sweetheart tottered behind, with her handkerchief at her eyes. Just as I noticed them the front door bell rang; I found several people there, headed by the high sheriff. They crowded into the sitting-room just as Phœbe Dole came rushing in, with Mr. Dix and Maria Woods.

"I did it!" Phœbe cried out to me. "I am found out, and I have made up my mind to confess. She was going to marry your father—I found it out. I stopped it once before. This time I knew I couldn't unless I killed him. She's lived with me in that house for over forty years. There are other ties as strong as the marriage one, that are just as sacred. What right had he to take her away from me and break up my home?

"I overheard your father and Rufus Bennett having words. I thought folks would think he did it. I reasoned it all out. I had watched your cat go in that little door, I knew the shed door hooked, I knew how long my arm was; I thought I could undo it. I stole over here a little after midnight. I went all around the house to be sure nobody was awake. Out in the front yard I happened to think my shears were tied on my belt with a ribbon, and I untied them. I thought I put the ribbon in my pocket—it was a piece of yellow ribbon—but I suppose I didn't, because they found it afterwards, and thought it came off your young man's whip.

"I went round to the shed door, unhooked it, and went in. The moon was light enough. I got out your father's overalls from the kitchen closet; I knew where they were. I went through the sitting-room to the parlour.

"In there I slipped off my dress and skirts and put on the overalls. I put a handkerchief over my face, leaving only my eyes exposed. I crept out then into the sitting-room; there I pulled off my shoes and went into the bedroom.

"Your father was fast asleep; it was such a hot night, the clothes were thrown back and his chest was bare. The first thing I saw was that pistol on the stand beside his bed. I suppose he had had some fear of Rufus Bennett coming back, after all. Suddenly I thought I'd better shoot him. It would be surer and quicker; and if you were aroused I knew that I could get away, and everybody would suppose that he had shot himself.

"I took up the pistol and held it close to his head. I had never fired a pistol, but I knew how it was done. I pulled, but it would not go off. Your father stirred a little—I was mad with horror—I struck at his head with the pistol. He opened his eyes and cried out; then I dropped the pistol, and took these"—Phœbe Dole pointed to the great shining shears hanging at her waist—"for I am strong in my wrists. I only struck twice, over his heart.

"Then I went back into the sitting-room. I thought I heard a noise in the kitchen—I was full of terror then—and slipped into the sitting-room closet. I felt as if I were fainting, and clutched the shelf to keep from falling.

"I felt that I must go upstairs to see if you were asleep, to be sure you had not waked up when your father cried out. I thought if you had I should have to do the same by you. I crept upstairs to your chamber. You seemed sound asleep, but, as I watched, you stirred a little; but instead of striking at you I slipped into your closet. I heard nothing more from you. I felt myself wet with blood. I caught something hanging in your closet, and wiped myself over with it. I knew by the feeling it was your green silk. You kept quiet, and I saw you were asleep, so crept out of the closet, and down the stairs, got my clothes and shoes, and, out in the shed, took off the overalls and dressed myself. I rolled up the overalls, and took a board away from the old well and threw them in as I went home. I thought if they were found it would be no clue to me. The handkerchief, which was not much stained, I put to soak that night, and washed it out next morning, before Maria was up. I washed my hands and arms carefully that night, and also my shears.

"I expected Rufus Bennett would be accused of the murder, and, maybe, hung. I was prepared for that, but I did not like to think I had thrown suspicion upon you by staining your dress. I had nothing against you. I made up my mind I'd get hold of that dress — before anybody suspected you — and dye it black. I came in and got it, as you know. I was astonished not to see any more stains on it. I only found two or three little streaks that scarcely anybody would have noticed. I didn't know what to think. I suspected, of course, that you had found the stains and got them off, thinking they might bring suspicion upon you.

"I did not see how you could possibly suspect me in any case. I was glad when your young man was cleared. I had nothing against him. That is all I have to say."

I think I must have fainted away then. I cannot describe the dreadful calmness with which that woman told this — that woman with the good face, whom I had last heard praying like a saint in meeting. I believe in demoniacal possession after this.

When I came to, the neighbours were around me, putting camphor on my head, and saying soothing things to me, and the old friendly faces had returned. But I wish I could forget!

They have taken Phœbe Dole away — I only know that I cannot bear to talk any more about it when I think there must be a trial, and I must go!

Henry has been over this evening. I suppose we shall be happy after all, when I have had a little time to get over this. He says I have nothing more to worry about. Mr. Dix has gone home. I hope Henry and I may be able to repay his kindness some day.

* * * * *

A month later. I have just heard that Phœbe Dole has died in prison. This is my last entry. May God help all other innocent women in hard straights as He has helped me!

Baroness Orczy (1865–1947)

In 1868, less than three years after the birth of Emma Magdalena Rosalia Maria Josepha Barbara Orczy, her aristocratic family fled Hungary, fearing a peasant uprising. Her father, Baron Felix Orczy, was a composer acquainted with Franz Liszt and Richard Wagner, and young "Emmuska" studied music in Paris before the family settled in Great Britain in 1880. There she enrolled in art school and met Montagu Barstow, whom she married in 1894, and together they published four illustrated translations of Hungarian folk tales the following year. Turning to fiction as a means of support, she published two novels and began placing stories, including tales of detection, in magazines at the turn to the twentieth century. In 1903, she reworked one of her short pieces set during the French Revolution into both a play and a novel, each bearing the title *The Scarlet Pimpernel.* It was only after the former was a success on the London stage that she was able to find a publisher for the latter, which would become one of the greatest literary sensations of the era. In the years to come, she would write a prodigious number of novels, including several sequels to *The Scarlet Pimpernel,* and her success as a writer enabled her to return to her aristocratic roots and live in Monte Carlo. Orczy's first book of detective stories, *The Case of Miss Elliot,* featuring her armchair detective known as the Old Man, appeared in 1905. Several other collections would follow, including *The Man on the Corner* in 1909, *Lady Molly of Scotland Yard* in 1910, *Unravelled Knots* in 1926, and *Skin o' My Tooth* in 1928. Like John Watson vis-à-vis Sherlock Holmes, Mary Granard assists Lady Molly in her investigations and keeps a record of her cases, beginning with the story reprinted here, "The Ninescore Mystery." However, Granard asserts the crime-solving abilities of members of her sex, particularly those of Lady Molly, a professional rather than amateur detective who works for the Female Department of Scotland Yard nearly a decade before women were given full police status in England.

The Ninescore Mystery
by Baroness Orczy

(1910)

Well, you know, some say she is the daughter of a duke, others that she was born in the gutter, and that the handle has been soldered on to her name in order to give her style and influence.

I could say a lot, of course, but "my lips are sealed," as the poets say. All through her successful career at the Yard she honoured me with her friendship and confidence, but when she took me in partnership, as it were, she made me promise that I would never breathe a word of her private life, and this I swore on my Bible oath — "wish I may die," and all the rest of it.

Yes, we always called her "my lady," from the moment that she was put at the head of our section; and the chief called her "Lady Molly" in our presence. We of the Female Department are dreadfully snubbed by the men, though don't tell me that women have not ten times as much intuition as the blundering and sterner sex; my firm belief is that we shouldn't have half so many undetected crimes if some of the so-called mysteries were put to the test of feminine investigation.

Do you suppose for a moment, for instance, that the truth about that extraordinary case at Ninescore would ever have come to light if the men alone had had the handling of it? Would any man have taken so bold a risk as Lady Molly did when — But I am anticipating.

Let me go back to that memorable morning when she came into my room in a wild state of agitation.

"The chief says I may go down to Ninescore if I like, Mary," she said in a voice all a-quiver with excitement.

"You!" I ejaculated. "What for?"

"What for — what for?" she repeated eagerly. "Mary, don't you understand? It is the chance I have been waiting for — the chance of a lifetime? They are all desperate about the case up at the Yard; the public is furious, and columns of sarcastic letters appear in the daily press. None of our men know what to do; they are at their wits' end, and so this morning I went to the chief—"

"Yes?" I queried eagerly, for she had suddenly ceased speaking.

"Well, never mind now how I did it — I will tell you all about it on the way, for we have just got time to catch the 11 a.m. down to Canterbury. The chief says I may go, and that I may take whom I like with me. He suggested one of the men, but somehow I feel that this is woman's work, and I'd rather have you, Mary, than anyone. We will go over the preliminaries of the case together in the train, as I don't suppose that you have got them at your fingers' ends yet, and you have only just got time to put a few things together and meet me at Charing Cross booking-office in time for that 11.0 sharp."

She was off before I could ask her any more questions, and anyhow I was too flabbergasted to say much. A murder case in the hands of the Female Department! Such a thing had been unheard of until now. But I was all excitement, too, and you may be sure I was at the station in good time.

Fortunately Lady Molly and I had a carriage to ourselves. It was a non-stop run to Canterbury, so we had plenty of time before us, and I was longing to know all about this case, you bet, since I was to have the honour of helping Lady Molly in it.

The murder of Mary Nicholls had actually been committed at Ash Court, a fine old mansion which stands in the village of Ninescore. The Court is surrounded by magnificently timbered grounds, the most fascinating portion of which is an island in the midst of a small pond, which is spanned by a tiny rustic bridge. The island is called "The Wilderness," and is at the furthermost end of the grounds, out of sight and earshot of the mansion itself. It was in this charming spot, on the edge of the pond, that the body of a girl was found on the 5th of February last.

I will spare you the horrible details of this gruesome discovery. Suffice it to say for the present that the unfortunate woman was lying on her face, with the lower portion of her body on the small grass-covered embankment, and her head, arms, and shoulders sunk in the slime of the stagnant water just below.

It was Timothy Coleman, one of the under-gardeners at Ash Court, who first made this appalling discovery. He had crossed the rustic bridge and traversed the little island in its entirety, when he noticed something blue lying half in and half out of the water beyond. Timothy is a stolid, unemotional kind of yokel, and, once having ascertained that the object was a woman's body in a blue dress with white facings, he quietly stooped and tried to lift it out of the mud.

But here even his stolidity gave way at the terrible sight which was revealed before him. That the woman — whoever she might be — had been brutally murdered was obvious, her dress in front being stained with blood; but what was so awful that it even turned old Timothy sick with horror, was that, owing to the head, arms and shoulders having apparently been in the slime for some time, they were in an advanced state of decomposition.

Well, whatever was necessary was immediately done, of course. Coleman went to get assistance from the lodge, and soon the police were on the scene and had removed the unfortunate victim's remains to the small local police-station.

Ninescore is a sleepy, out-of-the-way village, situated some seven miles from Canterbury and four from Sandwich. Soon everyone in the place had heard that a terrible murder had been committed in the village, and all the details were already freely discussed at the Green Man.

To begin with, everyone said that though the body itself might be practically unrecognisable, the bright blue serge dress with the white facings was unmistakable, as were the pearl and ruby ring and the red leather purse found by Inspector Meisures close to the murdered woman's hand.

Within two hours of Timothy Coleman's gruesome find the identity of the unfortunate victim was firmly established as that of Mary Nicholls, who lived with her sister Susan at 2, Elm Cottages, in Ninescore Lane, almost opposite Ash Court. It was also known that when the police called at that address they found the place locked and apparently uninhabited.

Mrs. Hooker, who lived at No. 1 next door, explained to Inspector Meisures that Susan and Mary Nicholls had left home about a fortnight ago, and that she had not seen them since.

"It'll be a fortnight to-morrow," she said. "I was just inside my own front door a-calling to the cat to come in. It was past seven o'clock, and as dark a night as ever you did see. You could hardly see your 'and afore your eyes, and there was a nasty damp drizzle comin' from everywhere. Susan and Mary come out of their cottage; I couldn't rightly see Susan, but I 'eard Mary's voice quite distinck. She says: 'We'll have to 'urry,' says she. I, thinkin' they might be goin' to do some shoppin' in the village, calls out to them that I'd just 'eard the church clock strike seven, and that bein' Thursday, and early closin,' they'd find all the shops shut at Ninescore. But they took no notice, and walked off towards the village, and that's the last I ever seed o' them two."

Further questioning among the village folk brought forth many curious details. It seems that Mary Nicholls was a very flighty young woman, about whom there had already been quite a good deal of scandal, whilst Susan, on the other hand — who was very sober and steady in her conduct — had chafed considerably under her younger sister's questionable reputation, and, according to Mrs. Hooker, many were the bitter quarrels which occurred between the two girls. These quarrels, it seems, had been especially violent within the last year whenever Mr. Lionel Lydgate called at the cottage. He was a London gentleman, it appears — a young man about town, it afterwards transpired — but he frequently stayed at Canterbury, where he had some friends, and on those occasions he would come over to Ninescore in his smart dogcart[1] and take Mary out for drives.

Mr. Lydgate is brother to Lord Edbrooke, the multi-millionaire, who was the recipient of birthday honours last year. His lordship resides at Edbrooke Castle, but he and his brother Lionel had rented Ash Court once or twice, as both were keen golfers and Sandwich Links are very close by. Lord Edbrooke, I may add, is a married man. Mr. Lionel Lydgate, on the other hand, is just engaged to Miss Marbury, daughter of one of the canons[2] of Canterbury.

No wonder, therefore, that Susan Nicholls strongly objected to her sister's name being still coupled with that of a young man far above her in station, who, moreover, was about to marry a young lady in his own rank of life.

But Mary seemed not to care. She was a young woman who only liked fun and pleasure, and she shrugged her shoulders at public opinion, even though there were ugly rumours anent the parentage of a little baby girl whom she herself had placed under the care of Mrs. Williams, a widow who lived in a somewhat isolated cottage on the Canterbury road. Mary had told Mrs. Williams that the father of the child, who was her own brother, had died very suddenly, leaving the little one on her and Susan's hands; and, as they couldn't look after it properly, they wished Mrs. Williams to have charge of it. To this the latter readily agreed.

The sum for the keep of the infant was decided upon, and thereafter Mary

[1]Open two-wheeled carriage. [2]Ministers.

Nicholls had come every week to see the little girl, and always brought the money with her.

Inspector Meisures called on Mrs. Williams, and certainly the worthy widow had a very startling sequel to relate to the above story.

"A fortnight to-morrow," explained Mrs. Williams to the inspector, "a little after seven o'clock, Mary Nicholls come runnin' into my cottage. It was an awful night, pitch dark and a nasty drizzle. Mary says to me she's in a great hurry; she is goin' up to London by a train from Canterbury and wants to say good-bye to the child. She seemed terribly excited, and her clothes were very wet. I brings baby to her, and she kisses it rather wild-like and says to me: 'You'll take great care of her, Mrs. Williams,' she says; 'I may be gone some time.' Then she puts baby down and gives me £2, the child's keep for eight weeks."

After which, it appears, Mary once more said "good-bye" and ran out of the cottage, Mrs. Williams going as far as the front door with her. The night was very dark, and she couldn't see if Mary was alone or not, until presently she heard her voice saying tearfully: "I had to kiss baby—" then the voice died out in the distance "on the way to Canterbury," Mrs. Williams said most emphatically.

So far, you see, Inspector Meisures was able to fix the departure of the two sisters Nicholls from Ninescore on the night of January 23rd. Obviously they left their cottage about seven, went to Mrs. Williams, where Susan remained outside while Mary went in to say good-bye to the child.

After that all traces of them seem to have vanished. Whether they did go to Canterbury, and caught the last up train, at what station they alighted, or when poor Mary came back, could not at present be discovered.

According to the medical officer, the unfortunate girl must have been dead twelve or thirteen days at the very least, as, though the stagnant water may have accelerated decomposition, the head could not have got into such an advanced state much under a fortnight.

At Canterbury station neither the booking-clerk nor the porters could throw any light upon the subject. Canterbury West is a busy station, and scores of passengers buy tickets and go through the barriers every day. It was impossible, therefore, to give any positive information about two young women who may or may not have travelled by the last up train on Saturday, January 23rd—that is, a fortnight before.

One thing only was certain—whether Susan went to Canterbury and travelled by that up train or not, alone or with her sister—Mary had undoubtedly come back to Ninescore either the same night or the following day, since Timothy Coleman found her half-decomposed remains in the grounds of Ash Court a fortnight later.

Had she come back to meet her lover, or what? And where was Susan now?

From the first, therefore, you see, there was a great element of mystery about the whole case, and it was only natural that the local police should feel that, unless something more definite came out at the inquest, they would like to have the assistance of some of the fellows at the Yard.

So the preliminary notes were sent up to London, and some of them drifted into our hands. Lady Molly was deeply interested in it from the first, and my firm belief is that she simply worried the chief into allowing her to go down to Ninescore and see what she could do.

2

At first it was understood that Lady Molly should only go down to Canterbury after the inquest, if the local police still felt that they were in want of assistance from London. But nothing was further from my lady's intentions than to wait until then.

"I was not going to miss the first act of a romantic drama," she said to me just as our train steamed into Canterbury station. "Pick up your bag, Mary. We're going to tramp it to Ninescore — two lady artists on a sketching tour, remember — and we'll find lodgings in the village, I dare say."

We had some lunch in Canterbury, and then we started to walk the six and a half miles to Ninescore, carrying our bags. We put up at one of the cottages, where the legend "Apartments for single respectable lady or gentleman" had hospitably invited us to enter, and at eight o'clock the next morning we found our way to the local police-station, where the inquest was to take place. Such a funny little place, you know — just a cottage converted for official use — and the small room packed to its utmost holding capacity. The entire able-bodied population of the neighbourhood had, I verily believe, congregated in these ten cubic yards of stuffy atmosphere.

Inspector Meisures, apprised by the chief of our arrival, had reserved two good places for us well in sight of witnesses, coroner and jury. The room was insupportably close, but I assure you that neither Lady Molly nor I thought much about our comfort then. We were terribly interested.

From the outset the case seemed, as it were, to wrap itself more and more in its mantle of impenetrable mystery. There was precious little in the way of clues, only that awful intuition, that dark unspoken suspicion with regard to one particular man's guilt, which one could feel hovering in the minds of all those present.

Neither the police nor Timothy Coleman had anything to add to what was already known. The ring and purse were produced, also the dress worn by the murdered woman. All were sworn to by several witnesses as having been the property of Mary Nicholls.

Timothy, on being closely questioned, said that, in his opinion, the girl's body had been pushed into the mud, as the head was absolutely embedded in it, and he didn't see how she could have fallen like that.

Medical evidence was repeated; it was as uncertain — as vague — as before. Owing to the state of the head and neck it was impossible to ascertain by what means the death blow had been dealt. The doctor repeated his statement that the unfortunate girl must have been dead quite a fortnight. The body was discovered on February 5th — a fortnight before that would have been on or about January 23rd.

The caretaker who lived at the lodge at Ash Court could also throw but little light on the mysterious event. Neither he nor any member of his family had seen or heard anything to arouse their suspicions. Against that he explained that "The Wilderness," where the murder was committed, is situated some 200 yards from the lodge, with the mansion and flower garden lying between. Replying to a question put to him by a juryman, he said that that portion of the grounds is only divided off from Ninescore Lane by a low, brick wall, which has a door in it, opening into the lane almost opposite Elm Cottages. He added that the mansion had been empty for over a year, and that he succeeded the last man, who died, about twelve months ago. Mr. Lydgate had not been down for golf since the witness had been in charge.

It would be useless to recapitulate all that the various witnesses had already told the police, and were now prepared to swear to. The private life of the two sisters Nicholls was gone into at full length, as much, at least, as was publicly known. But you know what village folk are; except when there is a bit of scandal and gossip, they know precious little of one another's inner lives.

The two girls appeared to be very comfortably off. Mary was always smartly dressed; and the baby girl, whom she had placed in Mrs. Williams's charge, had plenty of good and expensive clothes, whilst her keep, 5s. a week, was paid with unfailing regularity. What seemed certain, however, was that they did not get on well together, that Susan violently objected to Mary's association with Mr. Lydgate, and that recently she had spoken to the vicar asking him to try to persuade her sister to go away from Ninescore altogether, so as to break entirely with the past. The Reverend Octavius Ludlow, Vicar of Ninescore, seems thereupon to have had a little talk with Mary on the subject, suggesting that she should accept a good situation in London.

"But," continued the reverend gentleman, "I didn't make much impression on her. All she replied to me was that she certainly need never go into service, as she had a good income of her own, and could obtain £5,000 or more quite easily at any time if she chose."

"Did you mention Mr. Lydgate's name to her at all?" asked the coroner.

"Yes, I did," said the vicar, after a slight hesitation.

"Well, what was her attitude then?"

"I am afraid she laughed," replied the Reverend Octavius, primly, "and said very picturesquely, if somewhat ungrammatically, that 'some folks didn't know what they was talkin' about.'"

All very indefinite, you see. Nothing to get hold of, no motive suggested — beyond a very vague suspicion, perhaps, of blackmail — to account for a brutal crime. I must not, however, forget to tell you the two other facts which came to light in the course of this extraordinary inquest. Though, at the time, these facts seemed of wonderful moment for the elucidation of the mystery, they only helped ultimately to plunge the whole case into darkness still more impenetrable than before.

I am alluding, firstly, to the deposition of James Franklin, a carter in the employ of one of the local farmers. He stated that about half-past six on that same Saturday night, January 23rd, he was walking along Ninescore Lane leading his horse and cart, as the night was indeed pitch dark. Just as he came somewhere near Elm Cottages he heard a man's voice saying in a kind of hoarse whisper:

"Open the door, can't you? It's as dark as blazes!"

Then a pause, after which the same voice added:

"Mary, where the dickens are you?" Whereupon a girl's voice replied: "All right, I'm coming."

James Franklin heard nothing more after that, nor did he see anyone in the gloom.

With the stolidity peculiar to the Kentish peasantry, he thought no more of this until the day when he heard that Mary Nicholls had been murdered; then he voluntarily came forward and told his story to the police. Now, when he was closely questioned, he was quite unable to say whether these voices proceeded from that side of the lane where stand Elm Cottages or from the other side, which is edged by the low, brick wall.

Finally, Inspector Meisures, who really showed an extraordinary sense of what was dramatic, here produced a document which he had reserved for the last. This was a piece of paper which he had found in the red leather purse already mentioned, and which at first had not been thought very important, as the writing was identified by several people as that of the deceased, and consisted merely of a series of dates and hours scribbled in pencil on a scrap of notepaper. But suddenly these dates had assumed a weird and terrible significance: two of them, at least — December 26th and January 1st followed by "10 a.m." — were days on which Mr. Lydgate came over to Ninescore and took Mary for drives. One or two witnesses swore to this positively. Both dates had been local meets of the harriers,[3] to which other folk from the village had gone, and Mary had openly said afterwards how much she had enjoyed these.

The other dates (there were six altogether) were more or less vague. One Mrs. Hooker remembered as being coincident with a day Mary Nicholls had spent away from home; but the last date, scribbled in the same handwriting, was January 23rd, and below it the hour — 6 p.m.

[3]*Runners.*

The coroner now adjourned the inquest. An explanation from Mr. Lionel Lydgate had become imperative.

3

Public excitement had by now reached a very high pitch; it was no longer a case of mere local interest. The country inns all round the immediate neighbourhood were packed with visitors from London, artists, journalists, dramatists, and actor-managers, whilst the hotels and fly-proprietors[4] of Canterbury were doing a roaring trade.

Certain facts and one vivid picture stood out clearly before the thoughtful mind in the midst of a chaos of conflicting and irrelevant evidence: the picture was that of the two women tramping in the wet and pitch dark night towards Canterbury. Beyond that everything was a blur.

When did Mary Nicholls come back to Ninescore, and why?

To keep an appointment made with Lionel Lydgate, it was openly whispered; but that appointment — if the rough notes were interpreted rightly — was for the very day on which she and her sister went away from home. A man's voice called to her at half-past six certainly, and she replied to it. Franklin, the carter, heard her; but half an hour afterwards Mrs. Hooker heard her voice when she left home with her sister, and she visited Mrs. Williams after that.

The only theory compatible with all this was, of course, that Mary merely accompanied Susan part of the way to Canterbury, then went back to meet her lover, who enticed her into the deserted grounds of Ash Court, and there murdered her.

The motive was not far to seek. Mr. Lionel Lydgate, about to marry, wished to silence for ever a voice that threatened to be unpleasantly persistent in its demands for money and in its threats of scandal.

But there was one great argument against that theory — the disappearance of Susan Nicholls. She had been extensively advertised for. The murder of her sister was published broadcast in every newspaper in the United Kingdom — she could not be ignorant of it. And, above all, she hated Mr. Lydgate. Why did she not come and add the weight of her testimony against him if, indeed, he was guilty?

And if Mr. Lydgate was innocent, then where was the criminal? And why had Susan Nicholls disappeared?

Why? Why? Why?

Well, the next day would show. Mr. Lionel Lydgate had been cited by the police to give evidence at the adjourned inquest.

Good-looking, very athletic, and obviously frightfully upset and nervous, he entered the little courtroom, accompanied by his solicitor, just before the coroner and jury took their seats.

[4]*Owners of one-horse hackney carriages.*

He looked keenly at Lady Molly as he sat down, and from the expression on his face I guessed that he was much puzzled to know who she was.

He was the first witness called. Manfully and clearly he gave a concise account of his association with the deceased.

"She was pretty and amusing," he said. "I liked to take her out when I was in the neighbourhood; it was no trouble to me. There was no harm in her, whatever the village gossips might say. I know she had been in trouble, as they say, but that had nothing to do with me. It wasn't for me to be hard on a girl, and I fancy that she has been very badly treated by some scoundrel."

Here he was hard pressed by the coroner, who wished him to explain what he meant. But Mr. Lydgate turned obstinate, and to every leading question he replied stolidly and very emphatically:

"I don't know who it was. It had nothing to do with me, but I was sorry for the girl because of everyone turning against her, including her sister, and I tried to give her a little pleasure when I could."

That was all right. Very sympathetically told. The public quite liked this pleasing specimen of English cricket-, golf- and football-loving manhood. Subsequently Mr. Lydgate admitted meeting Mary on December 26th and January 1st, but he swore most emphatically that that was the last he ever saw of her.

"But the 23rd of January," here insinuated the coroner; "you made an appointment with the deceased then?"

"Certainly not," he replied.

"But you met her on that day?"

"Most emphatically no," he replied quietly. "I went down to Edbrooke Castle, my brother's place in Lincolnshire, on the 20th of last month, and only got back to town about three days ago."

"You swear to that, Mr. Lydgate?" asked the coroner.

"I do, indeed, and there are a score of witnesses to bear me out. The family, the house-party, the servants."

He tried to dominate his own excitement. I suppose, poor man, he had only just realised that certain horrible suspicions had been resting upon him. His solicitor pacified him, and presently he sat down, whilst I must say that everyone there present was relieved at the thought that the handsome young athlete was not a murderer, after all. To look at him it certainly seemed preposterous.

But then, of course, there was the deadlock, and as there were no more witnesses to be heard, no new facts to elucidate, the jury returned the usual verdict against some person or persons unknown; and we, the keenly interested spectators, were left to face the problem — Who murdered Mary Nicholls, and where was her sister Susan?

4

After the verdict we found our way back to our lodgings. Lady Molly tramped along silently, with that deep furrow between her brows which I knew meant that she was deep in thought.

"Now we'll have some tea," I said, with a sigh of relief, as soon as we entered the cottage door.

"No, you won't," replied my lady, dryly. "I am going to write out a telegram, and we'll go straight on to Canterbury and send it from there."

"To Canterbury!" I gasped. "Two hours' walk at least, for I don't suppose we can get a trap,[5] and it is past three o'clock. Why not send your telegram from Ninescore?"

"Mary, you are stupid," was all the reply I got.

She wrote out two telegrams — one of which was at least three dozen words long — and, once more calling to me to come along, we set out for Canterbury.

I was tea-less, cross, and puzzled. Lady Molly was alert, cheerful, and irritatingly active.

We reached the first telegraph office a little before five. My lady sent the telegram without condescending to tell me anything of its destination or contents; then she took me to the Castle Hotel and graciously offered me tea.

"May I be allowed to inquire whether you propose tramping back to Ninescore to-night?" I asked with a slight touch of sarcasm, as I really felt put out.

"No, Mary," she replied, quietly munching a bit of Sally Lunn[6]; "I have engaged a couple of rooms at this hotel and wired the chief that any message will find us here to-morrow morning."

After that there was nothing for it but quietude, patience, and finally supper and bed.

The next morning my lady walked into my room before I had finished dressing. She had a newspaper in her hand, and threw it down on the bed as she said calmly:

"It was in the evening paper all right last night. I think we shall be in time."

No use asking her what "it" meant. It was easier to pick up the paper, which I did. It was a late edition of one of the leading London evening shockers, and at once the front page, with its startling headline, attracted my attention:

THE NINESCORE MYSTERY

MARY NICHOLLS'S BABY DYING

Then, below that, a short paragraph: —

[5] *Light, two-wheeled carriage.*
[6] *Traditional English yeast bread.*

> "We regret to learn that the little baby daughter of the unfortunate girl who was murdered recently at Ash Court, Ninescore, Kent, under such terrible and mysterious circumstances, is very seriously ill at the cottage of Mrs. Williams, in whose charge she is. The local doctor who visited her to-day declares that she cannot last more than a few hours. At the time of going to press the nature of the child's complaint was not known to our special representative at Ninescore."

"What does this mean?" I gasped.

But before she could reply there was a knock at the door.

"A telegram for Miss Granard," said the voice of the hall-porter.

"Quick, Mary," said Lady Molly, eagerly. "I told the chief and also Meisures to wire here and to you."

The telegram turned out to have come from Ninescore, and was signed "Meisures." Lady Molly read it aloud:

"Mary Nicholls arrived here this morning. Detained her at station. Come at once."

"Mary Nicholls! I don't understand," was all I could contrive to say.

But she only replied:

"I knew it! I knew it! Oh, Mary, what a wonderful thing is human nature, and how I thank Heaven that gave me a knowledge of it!"

She made me get dressed all in a hurry, and then we swallowed some breakfast hastily whilst a fly was being got for us. I had, perforce, to satisfy my curiosity from my own inner consciousness. Lady Molly was too absorbed to take any notice of me. Evidently the chief knew what she had done and approved of it: the telegram from Meisures pointed to that.

My lady had suddenly become a personality. Dressed very quietly, and in a smart close-fitting hat, she looked years older than her age, owing also to the seriousness of her mien.

The fly took us to Ninescore fairly quickly. At the little police-station we found Meisures awaiting us. He had Elliot and Pegram from the Yard with him. They had obviously got their orders, for all three of them were mighty deferential.

"The woman is Mary Nicholls, right enough," said Meisures, as Lady Molly brushed quickly past him, "the woman who was supposed to have been murdered. It's that silly bogus paragraph about the infant brought her out of her hiding-place. I wonder how it got in," he added blandly; "the child is well enough."

"I wonder," said Lady Molly, whilst a smile — the first I had seen that morning — lit up her pretty face.

"I suppose the other sister will turn up too, presently," rejoined Elliot. "Pretty lot of trouble we shall have now. If Mary Nicholls is alive and kickin,' who was murdered at Ash Court, say I?"

"I wonder," said Lady Molly, with the same charming smile.

Then she went in to see Mary Nicholls.

The Reverend Octavius Ludlow was sitting beside the girl, who seemed in great distress, for she was crying bitterly.

Lady Molly asked Elliott and the others to remain in the passage whilst she herself went into the room, I following behind her.

When the door was shut, she went up to Mary Nicholls, and assuming a hard and severe manner, she said:

"Well, you have at last made up your mind, have you, Nicholls? I suppose you know that we have applied for a warrant for your arrest?"

The woman gave a shriek which unmistakably was one of fear.

"My arrest?" she gasped. "What for?"

"The murder of your sister Susan."

"'Twasn't me!" she said quickly.

"Then Susan *is* dead?" retorted Lady Molly, quietly.

Mary saw that she had betrayed herself. She gave Lady Molly a look of agonised horror, then turned as white as a sheet and would have fallen had not the Reverend Octavius Ludlow gently led her to a chair.

"It wasn't me," she repeated, with a heart-broken sob.

"That will be for you to prove," said Lady Molly dryly. "The child cannot now, of course remain with Mrs. Williams; she will be removed to the workhouse, and —"

"No, that shan't be," said the mother excitedly. "She shan't be, I tell you. The workhouse, indeed," she added in a paroxysm of hysterical tears, "and her father a lord!"

The reverend gentleman and I gasped in astonishment; but Lady Molly had worked up to this climax so ingeniously that it was obvious she had guessed it all along, and had merely led Mary Nicholls on in order to get this admission from her.

How well she had known human nature in pitting the child against the sweetheart! Mary Nicholls was ready enough to hide herself, to part from her child even for a while, in order to save the man she had once loved from the consequences of his crime; but when she heard that her child was dying, she no longer could bear to leave it among strangers, and when Lady Molly taunted her with the workhouse, she exclaimed in her maternal pride:

"The workhouse! And her father a lord!"

Driven into a corner, she confessed the whole truth.

Lord Edbrooke, then Mr. Lydgate, was the father of her child. Knowing this, her sister Susan had, for over a year now, systematically blackmailed the unfortunate man — not altogether, it seems, without Mary's connivance. In January last she got him to come down to Ninescore under the distinct promise that Mary would meet him and hand over to him the letters she had received from him, as well as the ring he had given her, in exchange for the sum of £5,000.

The meeting-place was arranged, but at the last moment Mary was afraid to go in the dark. Susan, nothing daunted, but anxious about her own reputation in case she should be seen talking to a man so late at night, put on Mary's dress, took the ring and the letters, also her sister's purse, and went to meet Lord Edbrooke.

What happened at that interview no one will ever know. It ended with the murder of the blackmailer. I suppose the fact that Susan had, in measure, begun by impersonating her sister, gave the murderer the first thought of confusing the identity of his victim by the horrible device of burying the body in the slimy mud. Anyway, he almost did succeed in hoodwinking the police, and would have done so entirely but for Lady Molly's strange intuition in the matter.

After his crime he ran instinctively to Mary's cottage. He had to make a clean breast of it to her, as, without her help, he was a doomed man.

So he persuaded her to go away from home and to leave no clue or trace of herself or her sister in Ninescore. With the help of money which he would give her, she could begin life anew somewhere else, and no doubt he deluded the unfortunate girl with promises that her child would be restored to her very soon.

Thus he enticed Mary Nicholls away, who would have been the great and all-important witness against him the moment his crime was discovered. A girl of Mary's type and class instinctively obeys the man she has once loved, the man who is the father of her child. She consented to disappear and to allow all the world to believe that she had been murdered by some unknown miscreant.

Then the murderer quietly returned to his luxurious home at Edbrooke Castle, unsuspected. No one had thought of mentioning his name in connection with that of Mary Nicholls. In the days when he used to come down to Ash Court he was Mr. Lydgate, and, when he became a peer, sleepy, out-of-the-way Ninescore ceased to think of him.

Perhaps Mr. Lionel Lydgate knew all about his brother's association with the village girl. From his attitude at the inquest I should say he did, but of course he would not betray his own brother unless forced to do so.

Now, of course, the whole aspect of the case was changed: the veil of mystery had been torn asunder owing to the insight, the marvellous intuition, of a woman who, in my opinion, is the most wonderful psychologist of her time.

You know the sequel. Our fellows at the Yard, aided by the local police, took their lead from Lady Molly, and began their investigations of Lord Edbrooke's movements on or about the 23rd of January.

Even their preliminary inquiries revealed the fact that his lordship had left Edbrooke Castle on the 21st. He went up to town, saying to his wife and household that he was called away on business, and not even taking his valet with him. He put up at the Langham Hotel.

But here police investigations came to an abrupt ending. Lord Edbrooke evidently got wind of them. Anyway, the day after Lady Molly so cleverly enticed Mary Nicholls out of her hiding-place, and surprised her into an admission of the truth, the unfortunate man threw himself in front of the express train at Grantham railway station, and was instantly killed. Human justice cannot reach him now!

But don't tell me that a man would have thought of that bogus paragraph, or of the taunt which stung the motherly pride of the village girl to the quick, and thus wrung from her an admission which no amount of male ingenuity would ever have obtained.

Anna Katharine Green (1846–1935)

Born in Brooklyn and a graduate of Ripley Female College in Vermont, Anna Katharine Green wrote poems and fiction from an early age. However, because her New York trial attorney father disapproved of novel writing, she composed *The Leavenworth Case: A Lawyer's Story* in secret over a period of a few years. Published in 1878, the book, which introduced Green's series character Ebenezer Gryce, sold over a million copies and became a required text at Yale Law School. Although she was not the first American woman to publish a detective novel, she was the first to do so under her own name. *The Leavenworth Case* marked the auspicious beginning of a forty-five year career in which Green published thirty-five novels and four short story collections. In a trio of books beginning with *That Affair Next Door* in 1897 (and over three decades before the initial appearance of Agatha Christie's Miss Marple), Green teamed the professional detective Gryce with the wealthy amateur spinster Amelia Butterworth, thereby altering the convention of having two men working together to solve crimes pioneered by Poe and refined by Conan Doyle. Critics in the 1980s and early 1990s hailed Butterworth as a feminist detective, an assessment that subsequent observers have questioned. Nevertheless, it is certainly the case, as Catherine Nickerson asserts, that Green "did use her novels, with their mix of domestic and gothic tropes, as a kind of social criticism."

In the 1915 collection of linked short stories, *The Golden Slipper and Other Problems for Violet Strange*, Green introduced another female detective. A young, diminutive socialite, Strange surreptitiously works as a professional investigator, earning money to support her older sister whom her father has disowned because of her decision to pursue a singing career. The eighth of nine problems Strange confronts in *The Golden Slipper*, the deliciously gothic "Missing: Page Thirteen" contains a little bit of everything, being one part stolen document mystery, one part missing person case, and one part historical whodunit. Exceeding everyone's expectations, Violet exhibits uncanny intuition, remarkable courage, and tremendous empathy.

Missing: Page Thirteen
by Anna Katharine Green

(1915)

I

"One more! just one more well paying affair, and I promise to stop; really and truly to stop."

"But, Puss, why one more? You have earned the amount you set for yourself,— or very nearly,— and though my help is not great, in three months I can add enough —"

"No, you cannot, Arthur. You are doing well; I appreciate it; in fact, I am just delighted to have you work for me in the way you do, but you cannot, in your present position, make enough in three months, or in six, to meet the situation as I see it. Enough does not satisfy me. The measure must be full, heaped up, and running over. Possible failure following promise must be provided for. Never must I feel myself called upon to do this kind of thing again. Besides, I have never got over the Zabriskie tragedy.[1] It haunts me continually. Something new may help to put it out of my head. I feel guilty. I was responsible —"

"No, Puss. I will not have it that you were responsible. Some such end was bound to follow a complication like that. Sooner or later he would have been driven to shoot himself—"

"But not her."

"No, not her. But do you think she would have given those few minutes of perfect understanding with her blind husband for a few years more of miserable life?"

Violet made no answer; she was too absorbed in her surprise. Was this Arthur? Had a few weeks' work and a close connection with the really serious things of life made this change in him? Her face beamed at the thought, which seeing, but not understanding what underlay this evidence of joy, he bent and kissed her, saying with some of his old nonchalance:

"Forget it, Violet; only don't let any one or anything lead you to interest yourself in another affair of the kind. If you do, I shall have to consult a certain friend of yours as to the best way of stopping this folly. I mention no names. Oh! you need not look so frightened. Only behave; that's all."

"He's right," she acknowledged to herself, as he sauntered away; "altogether right."

Yet because she wanted the extra money —

[1]*At the start of the story, Violet and her brother Arthur discuss her clandestine work as a private detective, including a previous case involving the Zabriskies.*

* * * *

The scene invited alarm,—that is, for so young a girl as Violet, surveying it from an automobile some time after the stroke of midnight. An unknown house at the end of a heavily shaded walk, in the open doorway of which could be seen the silhouette of a woman's form leaning eagerly forward with arms outstretched in an appeal for help! It vanished while she looked, but the effect remained, holding her to her seat for one startled moment. This seemed strange, for she had anticipated adventure. One is not summoned from a private ball to ride a dozen miles into the country on an errand of investigation, without some expectation of encountering the mysterious and the tragic. But Violet Strange, for all her many experiences, was of a most susceptible nature, and for the instant in which that door stood open, with only the memory of that expectant figure to disturb the faintly lit vista of the hall beyond, she felt that grip upon the throat which comes from an indefinable fear which no words can explain and no plummet sound.

But this soon passed. With the setting of her foot to ground, conditions changed and her emotions took on a more normal character. The figure of a man now stood in the place held by the vanished woman, and it was not only that of one she knew but that of one whom she trusted—a friend whose very presence gave her courage. With this recognition came a better understanding of the situation, and it was with a beaming eye and unclouded features that she tripped up the walk to meet the expectant figure and outstretched hand of Roger Upjohn.

"You here!" she exclaimed, amid smiles and blushes, as he drew her into the hall.

He at once launched forth into explanations mingled with apologies for the presumption he had shown in putting her to this inconvenience. There was trouble in the house—great trouble. Something had occurred for which an explanation must be found before morning, or the happiness and honour of more than one person now under this unhappy roof would be wrecked. He knew it was late—that she had been obliged to take a long and dreary ride alone, but her success with the problem which had once come near wrecking his own life had emboldened him to telephone to the office and—"But you are in ball-dress," he cried in amazement. "Did you think—"

"I came from a ball. Word reached me between the dances. I did not go home. I had been bidden to hurry."

He looked his appreciation, but when he spoke it was to say:

"This is the situation. Miss Digby—"

"The lady who is to be married to-morrow?"

"Who *hopes* to be married to-morrow."

"How, *hopes*?"

"Who will be married to-morrow, if a certain article lost in this house to-night can be found before any of the persons who have been dining here leave for their homes."

Violet uttered an exclamation.

"Then, Mr. Cornell," she began—

"Mr. Cornell has our utmost confidence," Roger hastened to interpose. "But the article missing is one which he might reasonably desire to possess and which he alone of all present had the opportunity of securing. You can therefore see why he, with his pride—the pride off a man not rich, engaged to marry a woman who is—should declare that unless his innocence is established before daybreak, the doors of St. Bartholomew will remain shut to-morrow."

"But the article lost—what is it?"

"Miss Digby will give you the particulars. She is waiting to receive you," he added with a gesture towards a half-open door at their right.

Violet glanced that way, then cast her looks up and down the hall in which they stood.

"Do you know that you have not told me in whose house I am? Not hers, I know. She lives in the city."

"And you are twelve miles from Harlem. Miss Strange, you are in the Van Broecklyn mansion, famous enough you will acknowledge. Have you never been here before?"

"I have been by here, but I recognized nothing in the dark. What an exciting place for an investigation!"

"And Mr. Van Broecklyn? Have you never met him?"

"Once, when a child. He frightened me *then*."

"And may frighten you now; though I doubt it. Time has mellowed him. Besides, I have prepared him for what might otherwise occasion him some astonishment. Naturally he would not look for just the sort of lady investigator I am about to introduce to him."

She smiled. Violet Strange was a very charming young woman, as well as a keen prober of odd mysteries.

The meeting between herself and Miss Digby was a sympathetic one. After the first inevitable shock which the latter felt at sight of the beauty and fashionable appearance of the mysterious little being who was to solve her difficulties, her glance, which, under other circumstances, might have lingered unduly upon the piquant features and exquisite dressing of the fairy-like figure before her, passed at once to Violet's eyes, in whose steady depths beamed an intelligence quite at odds with the coquettish dimples which so often misled the casual observer in his estimation of a character singularly subtle and well-poised.

As for the impression she herself made upon Violet, it was the same she made upon everyone. No one could look long at Florence Digby and not recognize the loftiness of her spirit and the generous nature of her impulses. In person she was tall and as she leaned to take Violet's hand, the difference between them brought out the salient points in each, to the great admiration of the one onlooker.

Meantime, for all her interest in the case in hand, Violet could not help casting a hurried look about her, in gratification of the curiosity incited by her entrance into a house signalized from its foundation by such a series of tragic events. The result was disappointing. The walls were plain, the furniture simple. Nothing suggestive in either, unless it was the fact that nothing was new, nothing modern. As it looked in the days of Burr and Hamilton[2] so it looked to-day, even to the rather startling detail of candles which did duty on every side in place of gas.

As Violet recalled the reason for this, the fascination of the past seized upon her imagination. There was no knowing where this might have carried her, had not the feverish gleam in Miss Digby's eyes warned her that the present held its own excitement. Instantly, she was all attention and listening with undivided mind to that lady's disclosures.

They were brief and to the following effect:

The dinner which had brought some half-dozen people together in this house had been given in celebration of her impending marriage. But it was also in a way meant as a compliment to one of the other guests, a Mr. Spielhagen, who, during the week, had succeeded in demonstrating to a few experts the value of a discovery he had made which would transform a great industry.

In speaking of this discovery, Miss Digby did not go into particulars, the whole matter being far beyond her understanding; but in stating its value she openly acknowledged that it was in the line of Mr. Cornell's own work, and one which involved calculations and a formula which, if prematurely disclosed, would invalidate the contract Mr. Spielhagen hoped to make, and thus destroy his present hopes.

Of this formula but two copies existed. One was locked up in a safe deposit vault in Boston, the other he had brought into the house on his person, and it was the latter which was now missing, having been abstracted during the evening from a manuscript of sixteen or more sheets, under circumstances which she would now endeavour to relate.

Mr. Van Broecklyn, their host, had in his melancholy life but one interest which could be called at all absorbing. This was for explosives. As a consequence, much of the talk at the dinner-table had been on Mr. Spielhagen's discovery, and possible changes it might introduce into this especial industry. As these, worked out from a formula kept secret from the trade, could not but affect greatly Mr. Cornell's interests, she found herself listening intently, when Mr. Van Broecklyn, with an apology for his interference, ventured to remark that if Mr. Spielhagen had made a valuable discovery in this line, so had he, and one which he had substantiated by many experiments. It was not a marketable one, such as Mr. Spielhagen's was, but in his work upon the same, and in the tests which he had been led to make, he had discovered certain instances he would gladly name, which demanded exceptional procedure to be successful. If Mr. Spielhagen's method did not allow for these exceptions, nor

[2]*In 1804 American politicians Aaron Burr and Alexander Hamilton engaged in a duel that cost Hamilton his life.*

make suitable provision for them, then Mr. Spielhagen's method would fail more times than it would succeed. Did it so allow and so provide? It would relieve him greatly to learn that it did.

The answer came quickly. Yes, it did. But later and after some further conversation, Mr. Spielhagen's confidence seemed to wane, and before they left the dinner-table, he openly declared his intention of looking over his manuscript again that very night, in order to be sure that the formula therein contained duly covered all the exceptions mentioned by Mr. Van Broecklyn.

If Mr. Cornell's countenance showed any change at this moment, she for one had not noticed it; but the bitterness with which he remarked upon the other's good fortune in having discovered this formula of whose entire success he had no doubt, was apparent to everybody, and naturally gave point to the circumstances which a short time afterward associated him with the disappearance of the same.

The ladies (there were two others besides herself) having withdrawn in a body to the music-room, the gentlemen all proceeded to the library to smoke. Here, conversation loosed from the one topic which had hitherto engrossed it, was proceeding briskly, when Mr. Spielhagen, with nervous gesture, impulsively looked about him and said:

"I cannot rest till I have run through my thesis again. Where can I find a quiet spot? I won't be long; I read very rapidly."

It was for Mr. Van Broecklyn to answer, but no word coming from him, every eye turned his way, only to find him sunk in one of those fits of abstraction so well known to his friends, and from which no one who has this strange man's peace of mind at heart ever presumes to rouse him.

What was to be done? These moods of their singular host sometimes lasted half an hour, and Mr. Spielhagen had not the appearance of a man of patience. Indeed he presently gave proof of the great uneasiness he was labouring under, for noticing a door standing ajar on the other side of the room, he remarked to those around him:

"A den! and lighted! Do you see any objection to my shutting myself in there for a few minutes?"

No one venturing to reply, he rose, and giving a slight push to the door, disclosed a small room exquisitely panelled and brightly lighted, but without one article of furniture in it, not even a chair.

"The very place," quoth Mr. Spielhagen, and lifting a light cane-bottomed chair from the many standing about, he carried it inside and shut the door behind him.

Several minutes passed during which the man who had served at table entered with a tray on which were several small glasses evidently containing some choice liqueur. Finding his master fixed in one of his strange moods, he set the tray down and, pointing to one of the glasses, said:

"That is for Mr. Van Broecklyn. It contains his usual quieting powder." And urging the gentlemen to help themselves, he quietly left the room.

Mr. Upjohn lifted the glass nearest him, and Mr. Cornell seemed about to do the same when he suddenly reached forward and catching up one farther off started for the room in which Mr. Spielhagen had so deliberately secluded himself.

Why he did all this — why, above all things, he should reach across the tray for a glass instead of taking the one under his hand, he can no more explain than why he has followed many another unhappy impulse. Nor did he understand the nervous start given by Mr. Spielhagen at his entrance, or the stare with which that gentleman took the glass from his hand and mechanically drank its contents, till he saw how his hand had stretched itself across the sheet of paper he was reading, in an open attempt to hide the lines visible between his fingers. Then indeed the intruder flushed and withdrew in great embarrassment, fully conscious of his indiscretion but not deeply disturbed till Mr. Van Broecklyn, suddenly arousing and glancing down at the tray placed very near his hand remarked in some surprise: "Dobbs seems to have forgotten me." Then indeed, the unfortunate Mr. Cornell realized what he had done. It was the glass intended for his host which he had caught up and carried into the other room — the glass which he had been told contained a drug. Of what folly he had been guilty, and how tame would be any effort at excuse!

Attempting none, he rose and with a hurried glance at Mr. Upjohn who flushed in sympathy at his distress, he crossed to the door he had lately closed upon Mr. Spielhagen. But feeling his shoulder touched as his hand pressed the knob, he turned to meet the eye of Mr. Van Broecklyn fixed upon him with an expression which utterly confounded him.

"Where are you going?" that gentleman asked.

The questioning tone, the severe look, expressive at once of displeasure and astonishment, were most disconcerting, but Mr. Cornell managed to stammer forth:

"Mr. Spielhagen is in here consulting his thesis. When your man brought in the cordial, I was awkward enough to catch up your glass and carry it in to Mr. Spielhagen. He drank it and I — I am anxious to see if it did him any harm."

As he uttered the last word he felt Mr. Van Broecklyn's hand slip from his shoulder, but no word accompanied the action, nor did his host make the least move to follow him into the room.

This was a matter of great regret to him later, as it left him for a moment out of the range of every eye, during which he says he simply stood in a state of shock at seeing Mr. Spielhagen still sitting there, manuscript in hand, but with head fallen forward and eyes closed; dead, asleep or — he hardly knew what; the sight so paralysed him.

Whether or not this was the exact truth and the whole truth, Mr. Cornell certainly looked very unlike himself as he stepped back into Mr. Van Broecklyn's presence; and he was only partially reassured when that gentleman protested that there was no real harm in the drug, and that Mr. Spielhagen would be all right if left to wake naturally and without shock. However, as his present attitude was one of great discomfort, they decided to carry him back and lay him on the library lounge. But before doing this, Mr. Upjohn drew from his flaccid grasp, the precious manuscript, and carrying it into the larger room placed it on a remote table, where it remained undisturbed till Mr. Spielhagen, suddenly coming to himself at the end of some fifteen minutes, missed the sheets from his hand, and bounding up, crossed the room to repossess himself of them.

His face, as he lifted them up and rapidly ran through them with ever-accumulating anxiety, told them what they had to expect.

The page containing the formula was gone!

Violet now saw her problem.

II

There was no doubt about the loss I have mentioned; all could see that page 13 was not there. In vain a second handling of every sheet, the one so numbered was not to be found. Page 14 met the eye on the top of the pile, and page 12 finished it off at the bottom, but no page 13 in between, or anywhere else.

Where had it vanished, and through whose agency had this misadventure occurred? No one could say, or, at least, no one there made any attempt to do so, though everybody started to look for it.

But where look? The adjoining small room offered no facilities for hiding a cigar-end, much less a square of shining white paper. Bare walls, a bare floor, and a single chair for furniture, comprised all that was to be seen in this direction. Nor could the room in which they then stood be thought to hold it, unless it was on the person of some one of them. Could this be the explanation of the mystery? No man looked his doubts; but Mr. Cornell, possibly divining the general feeling, stepped up to Mr. Van Broecklyn and in a cool voice, but with the red burning hotly on either cheek, said, so as to be heard by everyone present:

"I demand to be searched — at once and thoroughly."

A moment's silence, then the common cry:

"We will all be searched."

"Is Mr. Spielhagen sure that the missing page was with the others when he sat down in the adjoining room to read his thesis?" asked their perturbed host.

"Very sure," came the emphatic reply. "Indeed, I was just going through the formula itself when I fell asleep."

"You are ready to assert this?"

"I am ready to swear it."

Mr. Cornell repeated his request.

"I demand that you make a thorough search of my person. I must be cleared, and instantly, of every suspicion," he gravely asserted, "or how can I marry Miss Digby to-morrow."

After that there was no further hesitation. One and all subjected themselves to the ordeal suggested; even Mr. Spielhagen. But this effort was as futile as the rest. The lost page was not found.

What were they to think? What were they to do?

There seemed to be nothing left to do, and yet some further attempt must be made towards the recovery of this important formula. Mr. Cornell's marriage and Mr. Spielhagen's business success both depended upon its being in the latter's hands before six in the morning, when he was engaged to hand it over to a certain manufacturer sailing for Europe on an early steamer.

Five hours!

Had Mr. Van Broecklyn a suggestion to offer? No, he was as much at sea as the rest.

Simultaneously look crossed look. Blankness was on every face.

"Let us call the ladies," suggested one.

It was done, and however great the tension had been before, it was even greater when Miss Digby stepped upon the scene. But she was not a woman to be shaken from her poise even by a crisis of this importance. When the dilemma had been presented to her and the full situation grasped, she looked first at Mr. Cornell and then at Mr. Spielhagen, and quietly said:

"There is but one explanation possible of this matter. Mr. Spielhagen will excuse me, but he is evidently mistaken in thinking that he saw the lost page among the rest. The condition into which he was thrown by the unaccustomed drug he had drank, made him liable to hallucinations. I have not the least doubt he thought he had been studying the formula at the time he dropped off to sleep. I have every confidence in the gentleman's candour. But so have I in that of Mr. Cornell," she supplemented, with a smile.

An exclamation from Mr. Van Broecklyn and a subdued murmur from all but Mr. Spielhagen testified to the effect of this suggestion, and there is no saying what might have been the result if Mr. Cornell had not hurriedly put in this extraordinary and most unexpected protest:

"Miss Digby has my gratitude," said he, "for a confidence which I hope to prove to be deserved. But I must say this for Mr. Spielhagen. He was correct in stating that he was engaged in looking over his formula when I stepped into his presence with the glass of cordial. If you were not in a position to see the hurried way in which his hand instinctively spread itself over the page he was reading, I was; and if that does not seem conclusive to you, then I feel bound to state that in unconsciously following this movement of his, I plainly saw the number written on the top of the page, and that number was —13."

A loud exclamation, this time from Spielhagen himself, announced his gratitude and corresponding change of attitude toward the speaker.

"Wherever that damned page has gone," he protested, advancing towards Cornell with outstretched hand, "you have nothing to do with its disappearance."

Instantly all constraint fled, and every countenance took on a relieved expression. *But the problem remained.*

Suddenly those very words passed some one's lips, and with their utterance Mr. Upjohn remembered how at an extraordinary crisis in his own life he had been helped and an equally difficult problem settled, by a little lady secretly attached to a private detective agency. If she could only be found and hurried here before morning, all might yet be well. He would make the effort. Such wild schemes sometimes work. He telephoned to the office and—

Was there anything else Miss Strange would like to know?

III

Miss Strange, thus appealed to, asked where the gentlemen were now.

She was told that they were still all together in the library; the ladies had been sent home.

"Then let us go to them," said Violet, hiding under a smile her great fear that here was an affair which might very easily spell for her that dismal word, *failure.*

So great was that fear that under all ordinary circumstances she would have had no thought for anything else in the short interim between this stating of the problem and her speedy entrance among the persons involved. But the circumstances of this case were so far from ordinary, or rather let me put it in this way, the setting of the case was so very extraordinary, that she scarcely thought of the problem before her, in her great interest in the house through whose rambling halls she was being so carefully guided. So much that was tragic and heartrending had occurred here. The Van Broecklyn name, the Van Broecklyn history, above all the Van Broecklyn tradition, which made the house unique in the country's annals (of which more hereafter), all made an appeal to her imagination, and centred her thoughts on what she saw about her. There was door which no man ever opened—had never opened since Revolutionary times—should she see it? Should she know it if she did see it? Then Mr. Van Broecklyn himself! Just to meet him, under any conditions and in any place, was an event. But to meet him here, under the pall of his own mystery! No wonder she had no words for her companions, or that her thoughts clung to this anticipation in wonder and almost fearsome delight.

His story was a well-known one. A bachelor and a misanthrope, he lived absolutely alone save for a large entourage of servants, all men and elderly ones at that. He never visited. Though he now and then, as on this occasion, entertained certain persons under his roof, he declined every invitation for himself, avoiding even, with equal strictness, all evening amusements of whatever kind, which would detain him in the city after ten at night. Perhaps this was to ensure no break in his rule of life never to sleep out of his own bed. Though he was a man well over fifty he had not spent, according to his own statement, but two nights out of his own bed since his return from Europe in early boyhood, and those were in obedience to a judicial summons which took him to Boston.

This was his main eccentricity, but he had another which is apparent enough from what has already been said. He avoided women. If thrown in with them during his short visits into town, he was invariably polite and at times companionable, but he never sought them out, nor had gossip, contrary to its usual habit, ever linked his name with one of the sex.

Yet he was a man of more than ordinary attraction. His features were fine and his figure impressive. He might have been the cynosure of all eyes had he chosen to enter crowded drawing-rooms, or even to frequent public assemblages, but having turned his back upon everything of the kind in his youth, he had found it impossible to alter his habits with advancing years; nor was he now expected to. The position he had taken was respected. Leonard Van Broecklyn was no longer criticized.

Was there any explanation for this strangely self-centred life? Those who knew him best seemed to think so. In the first place he had sprung from an unfortunate stock. Events of unusual and tragic nature had marked the family of both parents. Nor had his parents themselves been exempt from this seeming fatality. Antagonistic in tastes and temperament, they had dragged on an unhappy existence in the old home, till both natures rebelled, and a separation ensued which not only disunited their lives but sent them to opposite sides of the globe never to return again, at least, that was the inference drawn from the peculiar circumstances attending the event. On the morning of one never-to-be-forgotten day, John Van Broecklyn, the grandfather of the present representative of the family, found the following note from his son lying on the library table:

"FATHER:

"Life in this house, or any house, with *her* is no longer endurable. One of us must go. The mother should not be separated from her child. Therefore it is I whom you will never see again. Forget me, but be considerate of her and the boy.

"WILLIAM."

Six hours later another note was found, this time from the wife:

"FATHER:

"Tied to a rotting corpse what does one do? Lop off one's arm if necessary to rid one of the contact. As all love between your son and myself is dead, I can no longer live within the sound of his voice. As this is his home, he is the one to remain in it. May our child reap the benefit of his mother's loss and his father's affection.

"RHODA."

Both were gone, and gone forever. Simultaneous in their departure, they preserved each his own silence and sent no word back. If the one went east and the other west, they may have met on the other side of the globe, but never again in the home which sheltered their boy. For him and for his grandfather they had sunk from sight in the great sea of humanity, leaving them stranded on an isolated and mournful shore. The grandfather steeled himself to the double loss, for the child's sake; but the boy of eleven succumbed. Few of the world's great sufferers, of whatever age or condition, have mourned as this child mourned, or shown the effects of his grief so deeply or so long. Not till he had passed his majority[3] did the line, carved in one day in his baby forehead, lose any of its intensity; and there are those who declare that even later than that, the midnight stillness of the house was disturbed from time to time by his muffled shriek of "Mother! Mother!" sending the servants from the house, and adding one more horror to the many which clung about this accursed mansion.

Of this cry Violet had heard, and it was that and the door — But I have already told you about the door which she was still looking for, when her two companions suddenly halted, and she found herself on the threshold of the library, in full view of Mr. Van Broecklyn and his two guests.

Slight and fairy-like in figure, with an air of modest reserve more in keeping with her youth and dainty dimpling beauty than with her errand, her appearance produced an astonishment none of which the gentlemen were able to disguise. This the clever detective, with a genius for social problems and odd elusive cases! This darling of the ball-room in satin and pearls! Mr. Spielhagen glanced at Mr. Cornell, and Mr. Cornell at Mr. Spielhagen, and both at Mr. Upjohn, in very evident distrust. As for Violet, she had eyes only for Mr. Van Broecklyn, who stood before her in a surprise equal to that of the others but with more restraint in its expression.

She was not disappointed in him. She had expected to see a man, reserved almost to the point of austerity. And she found his first look even more awe-compelling than her imagination had pictured; so much so indeed, that her resolution faltered, and she took a quick step backward; which seeing, he smiled and her heart and hopes grew warm again. That he could smile, and smile with absolute sweetness, was her great comfort when later — But I am introducing you too hurriedly to the catastrophe. There is much to be told first.

I pass over the preliminaries, and come at once to the moment when Violet, having listened to a repetition of the full facts, stood with downcast eyes before these gentlemen, complaining in some alarm to herself:

"They expect me to tell them now and without further search or parley just where this missing page is. I shall have to balk that expectation without losing their confidence. But how?"

Summoning up her courage and meeting each inquiring eye with a look which seemed to carry a different message to each, she remarked very quietly:

"This is not a matter to guess at. I must have time and I must look a little deeper

[3]*Attained full legal age.*

into the facts just given me. I presume that the table I see over there is the one upon which Mr. Upjohn laid the manuscript during Mr. Spielhagen's unconsciousness."

All nodded.

"Is it — I mean the table — in the same condition it was then? Has nothing been taken from it except the manuscript?"

"Nothing."

"Then the missing page is not there," she smiled, pointing to its bare top. A pause, during which she stood with her gaze fixed on the floor before her. She was thinking and thinking hard.

Suddenly she came to a decision. Addressing Mr. Upjohn she asked if he were quite sure that in taking the manuscript from Mr. Spielhagen's hand he had neither disarranged nor dropped one of its pages.

The answer was unequivocal.

"Then," she declared, with quiet assurance and a steady meeting with her own of every eye, "as the thirteenth page was not found among the others when they were taken from this table, nor on the persons of either Mr. Cornell or Mr. Spielhagen, it is still in that inner room."

"Impossible!" came from every lip, each in a different tone. "That room is absolutely empty."

"May I have a look at its emptiness?" she asked, with a naïve glance at Mr. Van Broecklyn.

"There is positively nothing in the room but the chair Mr. Spielhagen sat on," objected that gentleman with a noticeable air of reluctance.

"Still, may I not have a look at it?" she persisted, with that disarming smile she kept for great occasions.

Mr. Van Broecklyn bowed. He could not refuse a request so urged, but his step was slow and his manner next to ungracious as he led the way to the door of the adjoining room and threw it open.

Just what she had been told to expect! Bare walls and floors and an empty chair! Yet she did not instantly withdraw, but stood silently contemplating the panelled wainscoting surrounding her, as though she suspected it of containing some secret hiding-place not apparent to the eye.

Mr. Van Broecklyn, noting this, hastened to say:

"The walls are sound, Miss Strange. They contain no hidden cupboards."

"And that door?" she asked, pointing to a portion of the wainscoting so exactly like the rest that only the most experienced eye could detect the line of deeper colour which marked an opening.

For an instant Mr. Van Broecklyn stood rigid, then the immovable pallor, which was one of his chief characteristics, gave way to a deep flush as he explained:

"There was a door there once; but it has been permanently closed. With cement," he forced himself to add, his countenance losing its evanescent colour till it shone ghastly again in the strong light.

With difficulty Violet preserved her show of composure. "*The* door!" she murmured to herself. "I have found it. The great historic door!" But her tone was light as she ventured to say:

"Then it can no longer be opened by your hand or any other?"

"It could not be opened with an axe."

Violet sighed in the midst of her triumph. Her curiosity had been satisfied, but the problem she had been set to solve looked inexplicable. But she was not one to yield easily to discouragement. Marking the disappointment approaching to disdain in every eye but Mr. Upjohn's, she drew herself up—(she had not far to draw) and made this final proposal.

"A sheet of paper," she remarked, "of the size of this one cannot be spirited away, or dissolved into thin air. It exists; it is here; and all we want is some happy thought in order to find it. I acknowledge that that happy thought has not come to me yet, but sometimes I get it in what may seem to you a very odd way. Forgetting myself, I try to assume the individuality of the person who has worked the mystery. If I can think with his thoughts, I possibly may follow him in his actions. In this case I should like to make believe for a few moments that I am Mr. Spielhagen" (with what a delicious smile she said this) "I should like to hold his thesis in my hand and be interrupted in my reading by Mr. Cornell offering his glass of cordial; then I should like to nod and slip off mentally into a deep sleep. Possibly in that sleep the dream may come which will clarify the whole situation. Will you humour me so far?"

A ridiculous concession, but finally she had her way; the farce was enacted and they left her as she had requested them to do, alone with her dreams in the small room.

Suddenly they heard her cry out, and in another moment she appeared before them, the picture of excitement.

"Is this chair standing exactly as it did when Mr. Spielhagen occupied it?" she asked.

"No," said Mr. Upjohn, "it faced the other way."

She stepped back and twirled the chair about with her disengaged hand.

"So?"

Mr. Upjohn and Mr. Spielhagen both nodded, so did the others when she glanced at them.

With a sign of ill-concealed satisfaction, she drew their attention to herself; then eagerly cried:

"Gentlemen, look here!"

Seating herself, she allowed her whole body to relax till she presented the picture of one calmly asleep. Then, as they continued to gaze at with fascinated eyes, not knowing what to expect, they saw something white escape from her lap and slide across the floor till it touched and was stayed by the wainscot. It was the top page of the manuscript she held, and as some inkling of the truth reached their astonished minds, she sprang impetuously to her feet and, pointing to the fallen sheet, cried:

"Do you understand now? Look where it lies and then look here!"

She had bounded towards the wall and was now on her knees pointing to the bottom of the wainscot, just a few inches to the left of the fallen page.

"A crack!" she cried, "under what was once the door. It's a very thin one, hardly perceptible to the eye. But see!" Here she laid her finger on the fallen paper and drawing it towards her, pushed it carefully against the lower edge of the wainscot. Half of it at once disappeared.

"I could easily slip it all through," she assured them, withdrawing the sheet and leaping to her feet in triumph. "You know now where the missing page lies, Mr. Spielhagen. All that remains is for Mr. Van Broecklyn to get it for you."

IV

The cries of mingled astonishment and relief which greeted this simple elucidation of the mystery were broken by a curiously choked, almost unintelligible, cry. It came from the man thus appealed to, who, unnoticed by them all, had started at her first word and gradually, as action followed action, withdrawn himself till he now stood alone and in an attitude almost of defiance behind the large table in the centre of the library.

"I am sorry," he began, with a brusqueness which gradually toned down into a forced urbanity as he beheld every eye fixed upon him in amazement, "that circumstances forbid my being of assistance to you in this unfortunate matter. If the paper lies where you say, and I see no other explanation of its loss, I am afraid it will have to remain there for this night at least. The cement in which that door is embedded is thick as any wall; it would take men with pickaxes, possibly with dynamite, to make a breach there wide enough for any one to reach in. And we are far from any such help."

In the midst of the consternation caused by these words, the clock on the mantel behind his back rang out the hour. It was but a double stroke, but that meant two hours after midnight and had the effect of a knell[4] in the hearts of those most interested.

"But I am expected to give that formula into the hands of our manager before six o'clock in the morning. The steamer sails at a quarter after."

"Can't you reproduce a copy of it from memory?" some one asked; "and insert it in its proper place among the pages you hold there?"

"The paper would not be the same. That would lead to questions and the truth

[4] *The sound of a bell announcing a death or funeral.*

would come out. As the chief value of the process contained in that formula lies in its secrecy, no explanation I could give would relieve me from the suspicions which an acknowledgment of the existence of a third copy, however well hidden, would entail. I should lose my great opportunity."

Mr. Cornell's state of mind can be imagined. In an access of mingled regret and despair, he cast a glance at Violet, who, with a nod of understanding, left the little room in which they still stood, and approached Mr. Van Broecklyn.

Lifting up her head,—for he was very tall,—and instinctively rising on her toes the nearer to reach his ear, she asked in a cautious whisper:

"Is there no other way of reaching that place?"

She acknowledged afterwards, that for one moment her heart stood still from fear, such a change took place in his face, though she says he did not move a muscle.

Then, just when she was expecting from him some harsh or forbidding word, he wheeled abruptly away from her and crossing to a window at his side, lifted the shade and looked out. When he returned, he was his usual self so far as she could see.

"There is a way," he now confided to her in a tone as low as her own, "but it can only be taken by a child."

"Not by me?" she asked, smiling down at her own childish proportions.

For an instant he seemed taken aback, then she saw his hand begin to tremble and his lips twitch. Somehow—she knew not why—she began to pity him, and asked herself as she felt rather than saw the struggle in his mind, that here was a trouble which if once understood would greatly dwarf that of the two men in the room behind them.

"I am discreet," she whisperingly declared. "I have heard the history of that door—how it was against the tradition of the family to have it opened. There must have been some very dreadful reason. But old superstitions do not affect me, and if you will allow me to take the way you mention, I will follow your bidding exactly, and will not trouble myself about anything but the recovery of this paper, which must lie only a little way inside that blocked-up door."

Was his look one of rebuke at her presumption, or just the constrained expression of a perturbed mind? Probably, the latter, for while she watched him for some understanding of his mood, he reached out his hand and touched one of the satin folds crossing her shoulder.

"You would soil this irretrievably," said he.

"There is stuff in the stores for another," she smiled. Slowly his touch deepened into pressure. Watching him she saw the crust of some old fear or dominant superstition melt under her eyes, and was quite prepared, when he remarked, with what for him was a lightsome air:

"I will buy the stuff, if you will dare the darkness and intricacies of our old cellar. I can give you no light. You will have to feel your way according to my direction."

"I am ready to dare anything."

He left her abruptly.

"I will warn Miss Digby," he called back. "She shall go with you as far as the cellar."

V

Violet in her short career as an investigator of mysteries had been in many a situation calling for more than womanly nerve and courage. But never — or so it seemed to her at the time — had she experienced a greater depression of spirit than when she stood with Miss Digby before a small door at the extreme end of the cellar, and understood that here was her road — a road which once entered, she must take alone.

First, it was such a small door! No child older than eleven could possibly squeeze through it. But she was of the size of a child of eleven and might possibly manage that difficulty.

Secondly: there are always some unforeseen possibilities in every situation, and though she had listened carefully to Mr. Van Broecklyn's directions and was sure that she knew them by heart, she wished she had kissed her father more tenderly in leaving him that night for the ball, and that she had not pouted so undutifully at some harsh stricture he had made. Did this mean fear? She despised the feeling if it did.

Thirdly: she hated darkness. She knew this when she offered herself for this undertaking; but she was in a bright room at the moment and only imagined what she must now face as a reality. But one jet had been lit in the cellar and that near the entrance. Mr. Van Broecklyn seemed not to need light, even in his unfastening of the small door which Violet was sure had been protected by more than one lock.

Doubt, shadow, and a solitary climb between unknown walls, with only a streak of light for her goal, and the clinging pressure of Florence Digby's hand on her own for solace — surely the prospect was one to tax the courage of her young heart to its limit. But she had promised, and she would fulfill. So with a brave smile she stooped to the little door, and in another moment had started her journey.

For journey the shortest distance may seem when every inch means a heart-throb and one grows old in traversing a foot. At first the way was easy; she had but to crawl up a slight incline with the comforting consciousness that two people were within reach of her voice, almost within sound of her beating heart. But presently she came to a turn, beyond which her fingers failed to reach any wall on her left. Then came a step up which she stumbled, and farther on a short flight, each tread of which she had been told to test before she ventured to climb it, lest the decay of innumerable years should have weakened the wood too much to bear her weight. One, two, three, four, five steps! Then a landing with an open space beyond. Half of her journey was done. Here she felt she could give a minute to drawing her breath naturally, if the air, unchanged in years, would allow her to do so. Besides, here she had been enjoined to do a certain thing and to do it according to instructions. Three matches had been given her and a little night candle. Denied all light up to now, it was at this point she was to light her candle and place it on the floor, so that in returning she should not miss the staircase and get a fall. She had promised to do this, and was only too happy to see a spark of light scintillate into life in the immeasurable darkness.

She was now in a great room long closed to the world, where once officers in Colonial wars had feasted, and more than one council had been held. A room, too, which had seen more than one tragic happening, as its almost unparalleled isolation proclaimed. So much Mr. Van Broecklyn had told her; but she was warned to be careful in traversing it and not upon any pretext to swerve aside from the right-hand wall till she came to a huge mantelpiece. This passed, and a sharp corner turned, she ought to see somewhere in the dim spaces before her a streak of vivid light shining through the crack at the bottom of the blocked-up door. The paper should be somewhere near this streak.

All simple, all easy of accomplishment, if only that streak of light were all she was likely to see or think of. If the horror which was gripping her throat should not take shape! If things would remain shrouded in impenetrable darkness, and not force themselves in shadowy suggestion upon her excited fancy! But the blackness of the passage-way through which she had just struggled was not to be found here. Whether it was the effect of that small flame flickering at the top of the staircase behind her, or of some change in her own powers of seeing, surely there was a difference in her present outlook. Tall shapes were becoming visible — the air was no longer blank — she could see — Then suddenly she saw why. In the wall high up on her right was a window. It was small and all but invisible, being covered on the outside with vines, and on the inside with the cobwebs of a century. But some small gleams from the starlight night came through, making phantasms out of ordinary things, which unseen were horrible enough, and half seen choked her heart with terror.

"I cannot bear it," she whispered to herself even while creeping forward, her hand upon the wall. "I will close my eyes" was her next thought. "I will make my own darkness," and with a spasmodic forcing of her lids together, she continued to creep on, passing the mantelpiece, where she knocked against something which fell with an awful clatter.

This sound, followed as it was by that of smothered voices from the excited group awaiting the result of her experiment from behind the impenetrable wall she should be nearing now if she had followed her instructions aright, freed her instantly from her fancies; and opening her eyes once more, she cast a look ahead, and to her delight, saw but a few steps away, the thin streak of bright light which marked the end of her journey.

It took her but a moment after that to find the missing page, and picking it up in haste from the dusty floor, she turned herself quickly about and joyfully began to retrace her steps. Why then, was it that in the course of a few minutes more her voice suddenly broke into a wild, unearthly shriek, which ringing with terror burst the bounds of that dungeon-like room, and sank, a barbed shaft, into the breasts of those awaiting the result of her doubtful adventure, at either end of this dread no-thoroughfare.

What had happened?

If they had thought to look out, they would have seen that the moon — held in check by a bank of cloud occupying half the heavens — had suddenly burst its bounds and was sending long bars of revealing light into every uncurtained window.

VI

Florence Digby, in her short and sheltered life, had possibly never known any very great or deep emotion. But she touched the bottom of extreme terror at that moment, as with her ears still thrilling with Violet's piercing cry, she turned to look at Mr. Van Broecklyn, and beheld the instantaneous wreck it had made of this seemingly strong man. Not till he came to lie in his coffin would he show a more ghastly countenance; and trembling herself almost to the point of falling, caught him by the arm and sought to read in his face what had happened. Something disastrous she was sure; something which he had feared and was partially prepared for, yet which in happening had crushed him. Was it a pitfall into which the poor little lady had fallen? If so — But he is speaking — mumbling low words to himself. Some of them she can hear. He is reproaching himself— repeating over and over that he should never have taken such a chance; that he should have remembered her youth — the weakness of a young girl's nerve. He had been mad, and now — and now —

With the repetition of this word his murmuring ceased. All his energies were now absorbed in listening at the low door separating him from what he was agonizing to know — a door impossible to enter, impossible to enlarge — a barrier to all help — an opening whereby sound might pass but nothing else, save her own small body, now lying — where?

"Is she hurt?" faltered Florence, stooping, herself, to listen. "Can you hear anything — anything?"

For an instant he did not answer; every faculty was absorbed in the one sense; then slowly and in gasps he began to mutter:

"I think — I hear —*something*. Her step — no, no, no step. All is as quiet as death; not a sound,— not a breath — she has fainted. O God! O God! Why this calamity on top of all!"

He had sprung to his feet at the utterance this invocation, but next moment was down on knees again, listening—listening.

Never was silence more profound; they were hearkening for murmurs from a tomb. Florence began to sense the full horror of it all, and was swaying helplessly when Mr. Van Broecklyn impulsively lifted his hand in an admonitory Hush! and through the daze of her faculties a small far sound began to make itself heard, growing louder as she waited, then becoming faint again, then altogether ceasing only to renew itself once more, till it resolved into an approaching step, faltering in its course, but coming ever nearer and nearer.

"She's safe! She's not hurt!" sprang from Florence's lips in inexpressible relief; and expecting Mr. Van Broecklyn to show an equal joy, she turned towards him, with the cheerful cry,

"Now if she has been so fortunate as to find that missing page, we shall all be repaid for our fright."

A movement on his part, a shifting of position which brought him finally to his feet, but he gave no other proof of having heard her, nor did his countenance mirror her relief. "It is as if he dreaded, instead of hailed, her return," was Florence's inward comment as she watched him involuntarily recoil at each fresh token of Violet's advance.

Yet because this seemed so very unnatural, she persisted in her efforts to lighten the situation, and when he made no attempt to encourage Violet in her approach, she herself stooped and called out a cheerful welcome which must have rung sweetly in the poor little detective's ears.

A sorry sight was Violet, when, helped by Florence, she finally crawled into view through the narrow opening and stood once again on the cellar floor. Pale, trembling, and soiled with the dust of years, she presented a helpless figure enough, till the joy in Florence's face recalled some of her spirit, and, glancing down at her hand in which a sheet of paper was visible, she asked for Mr. Spielhagen.

"I've got the formula," she said. "If you will bring him, I will hand it over to him here."

Not a word of her adventure; nor so much as one glance at Mr. Van Broecklyn, standing far back in the shadows.

Nor was she more communicative, when, the formula restored and everything made right with Mr. Spielhagen, they all came together again in the library for a final word. "I was frightened by the silence and the darkness, and so cried out," she explained in answer to their questions. "Any one would have done so who found himself alone in so musty a place," she added, with an attempt at lightsomeness which deepened the pallor on Mr. Van Broecklyn's cheek, already sufficiently noticeable to have been remarked upon by more than one.

"No ghosts?" laughed Mr. Cornell, too happy in the return of his hopes to be fully sensible of the feelings of those about him. "No whispers from impalpable lips or touches from spectre hands? Nothing to explain the mystery of that room so long shut up that even Mr. Van Broecklyn declares himself ignorant of its secret?"

"Nothing," returned Violet, showing her dimples in full force now.

"If Miss Strange had any such experiences — if she has anything to tell worthy of so marked a curiosity, she will tell it now," came from the gentleman just alluded to, in tones so stern and strange that all show of frivolity ceased on the instant. "Have you anything to tell, Miss Strange?"

Greatly startled, she regarded him with widening eyes for a moment, then with a move towards the door, remarked, with a general look about her:

"Mr. Van Broecklyn knows his own house, and doubtless can relate its histories if he will. I am a busy little body who having finished my work am now ready to return home, there to wait for the next problem which an indulgent fate may offer me."

She was near the threshold — she was about to take her leave, when suddenly she felt two hands fall on her shoulder, and turning, met the eyes of Mr. Van Broecklyn burning into her own.

"*You saw!*" dropped in an almost inaudible whisper from his lips.

The shiver which shook her answered him better than any word.

With an exclamation of despair, he withdrew his hands, and facing the others now standing together in a startled group, he said, as soon as he could recover some of his self-possession:

"I must ask for another hour of your company. I can no longer keep my sorrow to myself. A dividing line has just been drawn across my life, and I must have the sympathy of someone who knows my past, or I shall go mad in my self-imposed solitude. Come back, Miss Strange. You of all others have the prior right to hear."

VII

"I shall have to begin," said he, when they were all seated and ready to listen, "by giving you some idea, not so much of the family tradition, as of the effect of this tradition upon all who bore the name of Van Broecklyn. This is not the only house, even in America, which contains a room shut away from intrusion. In England there are many. But there is this difference between most of them and ours. No bars or locks forcibly held shut the door we were forbidden to open. The command was enough; that and the superstitious fear which such a command, attended by a long and unquestioning obedience, was likely to engender.

"I know no more than you do why some early ancestor laid his ban upon this room. But from my earliest years I was given to understand that there was one latch in the house which was never to be lifted; that any fault would be forgiven sooner than that; that the honour of the whole family stood in the way of disobedience, and that I was to preserve that honour to my dying day. You will say that all this is fantastic, and wonder that sane people in these modern times should subject themselves to such a ridiculous restriction, especially when no good reason was alleged, and the very source of the tradition from which it sprung forgotten. You are right; but if you look long into human nature, you will see that the bonds which hold the firmest are not material ones—that an idea will make a man and mould a character—that it lies at the source of all heroisms and is to be courted or feared as the case may be.

"For me it possessed a power proportionate to my loneliness. I don't think there was ever a more lonely child. My father and mother were so unhappy in each other's companionship that one or other of them was almost always away. But I saw little of either even when they were at home. The constraint in their attitude towards each other affected their conduct towards me. I have asked myself more than once if either of them had any real affection for me. To my father I spoke of her; to her of him; and never pleasurably. This I am forced to say, or you cannot understand my story. Would to God I could tell another tale! Would to God I had such memories as other men have of a father's clasp, a mother's kiss—but no! my grief, already profound, might have become abysmal. Perhaps it is best as it is; only, I might have been a different child, and made for myself a different fate—who knows.

"As it was, I was thrown almost entirely upon my own resources for any amusement. This led me to a discovery I made one day. In a far part of the cellar behind some heavy casks, I found a little door. It was so low—so exactly fitted to my small body, that I had the greatest desire to enter it. But I could not get around the casks. At last an expedient occurred to me. We had an old servant who came nearer loving me than any one else. One day when I chanced to be alone in the cellar, I took out my ball and began throwing it about. Finally it landed behind the casks, and I ran with a beseeching cry to Michael, to move them.

"It was a task requiring no little strength and address, but he managed, after a few herculean efforts, to shift them aside and I saw with delight, my way opened to that mysterious little door. But I did not approach it then; some instinct deterred me. But when the opportunity came for me to venture there alone, I did so, in the most adventurous spirit, and began my operations by sliding behind the casks and testing the handle of the little door. It turned, and after a pull or two the door yielded. With my heart in my mouth, I stooped and peered in. I could see nothing—a black hole and nothing more. This caused me a moment's hesitation. I was afraid of the dark—had always been. But curiosity and the spirit of adventure triumphed. Saying to myself that I was Robinson Crusoe exploring the cave, I crawled in, only to find that I had gained nothing. It was as dark inside as it had looked to be from without.

"There was no fun in this, so I crawled back, and when I tried the experiment again, it was with a bit of candle in my hand, and a surreptitious match or two. What I saw, when with a very trembling little hand I had lighted one of the matches, would have been disappointing to most boys, but not to me. The litter and old boards I saw in odd corners about me were full of possibilities, while in the dimness beyond I seemed to perceive a sort of staircase which might lead — I do not think I made any attempt to answer that question even in my own mind, but when, after some hesitation and a sense of great daring, I finally crept up those steps, I remember very well my sensation at finding myself in front of a narrow closed door. It suggested too vividly the one in Grandfather's little room — the door in the wainscot which we were never to open. I had my first real trembling fit here, and at once fascinated and repelled by this obstruction I stumbled and lost my candle, which, going out in the fall, left me in total darkness and a very frightened state of mind. For my imagination which had been greatly stirred by my own vague thoughts of the forbidden room, immediately began to people the space about me with ghoulish figures. How should I escape them, how ever reach my own little room again undetected and in safety?

"But these terrors, deep as they were, were nothing to the real fright which seized me when, the darkness finally braved, and the way found back into the bright, wide-open halls of the house, I became conscious of having dropped something besides the candle. My match-box was gone — not *my* match-box, but my grandfather's which I had found lying on his table and carried off on this adventure, in all the confidence of irresponsible youth. To make use of it for a little while, trusting to his not missing it in the confusion I had noticed about the house that morning, was one thing; to lose it was another. It was no common box. Made of gold and cherished for some special reason well known to himself, I had often hear him say that some day I would appreciate its value, and be glad to own it. And I had left it in that hole and at any minute he might miss it — possibly ask for it! The day was one of torment. My mother was away or shut up in her room. My father — I don't know just what thoughts I had about him. He was not to be seen either, and the servants cast strange looks at me when I spoke his name. But I little realized the blow which had just fallen upon the house in his definite departure, and only thought of my own trouble, and of how I should meet my grandfather's eye when the hour came for him to draw me to his knee for his usual good-night.

"That I was spared this ordeal for the first time this very night first comforted me, then added to my distress. He had discovered his loss and was angry. On the morrow he would ask me for the box and I would have to lie, for never could I find the courage to tell him where I had been. Such an act of presumption he would never forgive, or so I thought as I lay and shivered in my little bed. That his coldness, his neglect, sprang from the discovery just made that my mother as well as my father had just fled the house forever was as little known to me as the morning calamity. I had been given my usual tendance and was tucked safely into bed; but the gloom, the silence which presently settled upon the house had a very different explanation in my mind from the real one. My sin (for such it loomed large in my mind by this time) coloured the whole situation and accounted for every event.

"At what hour I slipped from my bed on to the cold floor, I shall never know. To me it seemed to be in the dead of night; but I doubt if it were more than ten. So slowly creep away the moments to a wakeful child. I had made a great resolve. Awful as the prospect seemed to me,—frightened as I was by the very thought,—I had determined in my small mind to go down into the cellar, and into that midnight hole again, in search of the lost box. I would take a candle and matches, this time from my own mantel-shelf, and if everyone was asleep, as appeared from the deathly quiet of the house, I would be able to go and come without anybody ever being the wiser.

"Dressing in the dark, I found my matches and my candle and, putting them in one of my pockets, softly opened my door and looked out. Nobody was stirring; every light was out except a solitary one in the lower hall. That this still burned conveyed no meaning to my mind. How could I know that the house was so still and the rooms dark because everyone was out searching for some clue to my mother's flight? If I had looked at the clock—but I did not; I was too intent upon my errand, too filled with the fever of my desperate undertaking, to be affected by anything not bearing directly upon it.

"Of the terror caused by my own shadow on the wall as I made the turn in the hall below, I have as keen a recollection to-day as though it happened yesterday. But that did not deter me; nothing deterred me, till safe in the cellar I crouched down behind the casks to get my breath again before entering the hole beyond.

"I had made some noise in feeling my way around these casks, and I trembled lest these sounds had been heard upstairs! But this fear soon gave place to one far greater. Other sounds were making themselves heard. A din of small skurrying feet above, below, on every side of me! Rats! rats in the wall! rats on the cellar bottom! How I ever stirred from the spot I do not know, but when I did stir, it was to go forward, and enter the uncanny hole.

"I had intended to light my candle when I got inside; but for some reason I went stumbling along in the dark, following the wall till I got to the steps where I had dropped the box. Here a light was necessary, but my hand did not go to my pocket. I thought it better to climb the steps first, and softly one foot found the tread and then another. I had only three more to climb and then my right hand, now feeling its way along the wall, would be free to strike a match. I climbed the three steps and was steadying myself against the door for a final plunge, when something happened—something so strange, so unexpected, and so incredible that I wonder I did not shriek aloud in my terror. The door was moving under my hand. It was slowly opening inward. I could feel the chill made by the widening crack. Moment by moment this chill increased; the gap was growing—a presence was there—a presence before which I sank in a small heap upon the landing. Would it advance? Had it feet—hands? Was it a presence which could be felt?

"Whatever it was, it made no attempt to pass, and presently I lifted my head only to quake anew at the sound of a voice — a human voice — my mother's voice — so near me that by putting out my arms I might have touched her.

"She was speaking to my father. I knew from the tone. She was saying words which, little understood as they were, made such a havoc in my youthful mind that I have never forgotten the effect.

"'I have come!' she said. 'They think I have fled the house and are looking far and wide for me. We shall not be disturbed. Who would think of looking here for either you or me.'

"*Here*! The word sank like a plummet in my breast. I had known for some few minutes that I was on the threshold of the forbidden room; but they were *in* it. I can scarcely make you understand the tumult which this awoke in my brain. Somehow, I had never thought that any such braving of the house's law would be possible.

"I heard my father's answer, but it conveyed no meaning to me. I also realized that he spoke from a distance,— that he was at one end of the room while we were at the other. I was presently to have this idea confirmed, for while I was striving with all my might and main to subdue my very heart-throbs so that she would not hear me or suspect my presence, the darkness — I should rather say the blackness of the place yielded to a flash of lightning — heat lightning, all glare and no sound — and I caught an instantaneous vision of my father's figure standing with gleaming things about him, which affected me at the moment as supernatural, but which, in later years, I decided to have been weapons hanging on a wall.

"She saw him too, for she gave a quick laugh and said they would not need any candles; and then, there was another flash and I saw something in his hand and something in hers, and though I did not yet understand, I felt myself turning deathly sick and gave a choking gasp which was lost in the rush she made into the centre of the room, and the keenness of her swift low cry.

"'*Garde-toi!*[5] for only one of us will ever leave this room alive!'

"A duel! a duel to the death between this husband and wife — this father and mother — in this hole of dead tragedies and within the sight and hearing of their child! Has Satan ever devised a scheme more hideous for ruining the life of an eleven-year-old boy!

"Not that I took it all in at once. I was too innocent and much too dazed to comprehend such hatred, much less the passions which engender it. I only knew that something horrible — something beyond the conception of my childish mind — was going to take place in the darkness before me; and the terror of it made me speechless; would to God it had made me deaf and blind and dead!

"She had dashed from her corner and he had slid away from his, as the next fantastic glare which lit up the room showed me. It also showed the weapons in their hands, and for a moment I felt reassured when I saw that these were swords, for I had

[5]*Guard yourself (a fencing term).*

seen them before with foils in their hands practising for exercise, as they said, in the great garret. But the swords had buttons on them, and this time the tips were sharp and shone in the keen light.

"An exclamation from her and a growl of rage from him were followed by movements I could scarcely hear, but which were terrifying from their very quiet. Then the sound of a clash. The swords had crossed.

"Had the lightning flashed forth then, the end of one of them might have occurred. But the darkness remained undisturbed, and when the glare relit the great room again, they were already far apart. This called out a word from him; the one sentence he spoke — I can never forget it:

"'Rhoda, there is blood on your sleeve; I have wounded you. Shall we call it off and fly, as the poor creatures in there think we have, to the opposite ends of the earth?'

"I almost spoke; I almost added my childish plea to his for them to stop — to remember me and stop. But not a muscle in my throat responded to my agonized effort. Her cold, clear 'No!' fell before my tongue was loosed or my heart freed from the ponderous weight crushing it.

"'I have vowed and *I* keep my promises,' she went on in a tone quite strange to me. 'What would either's life be worth with the other alive and happy in this world.'

"He made no answer; and those subtle movements — shadows of movements I might almost call them — recommenced. Then there came a sudden cry, shrill and poignant — had Grandfather been in his room he would surely have heard it — and the flash coming almost simultaneously with its utterance, I saw what has haunted my sleep from that day to this, my father pinned against the wall, sword still in hand, and before him my mother, fiercely triumphant, her staring eyes fixed on his and —

"Nature could bear no more; the band loosened from my throat; the oppression lifted from my breast long enough for me to give one wild wail and she turned, saw (heaven sent its flashes quickly at this moment) and recognizing my childish form, all the horror of her deed (or so I have fondly hoped) rose within her, and she gave a start and fell full upon the point upturned to receive her.

"A groan; then a gasping sigh from him, and silence settled upon the room and upon my heart, and so far as I knew upon the whole created world.

"That is my story, friends. Do you wonder that I have never been or lived like other men?"

After a few moments of sympathetic silence, Mr. Van Broecklyn went on, to say:

"I don't think I ever had a moment's doubt that my parents both lay dead on the floor of that great room. When I came to myself — which may have been soon, and may not have been for a long while — the lightning had ceased to flash, leaving the darkness stretching like a blank pall between me and that spot in which were concentrated all the terrors of which my imagination was capable. I dared not enter it.

I dared not take one step that way. My instinct was to fly and hide my trembling body again in my own bed; and associated with this, in fact dominating it and making me old before my time, was another — never to tell; never to let any one, least of all my grandfather — know what that forbidden room now contained. I felt in an irresistible sort of way that my father's and mother's honour was at stake. Besides, terror held me back; I felt that I should die if I spoke. Childhood has such terrors and such heroisms. Silence often covers in such, abysses of thought and feeling which astonish us in later years. There is no suffering like a child's, terrified by a secret which it dare not for some reason disclose.

"Events aided me. When, in desperation to see once more the light and all the things which linked me to life — my little bed, the toys on the window-sill, my squirrel in its cage — I forced myself to retraverse the empty house, expecting at every turn to hear my father's voice or come upon the image of my mother — yes, such was the confusion of my mind, though I knew well enough even then that they were dead and that I should never hear the one or see the other. I was so benumbed with the cold in my half-dressed condition, that I woke in a fever next morning after a terrible dream which forced from my lips the cry of 'Mother! Mother!' — only that.

"I was cautious even in delirium. This delirium and my flushed cheeks and shining eyes led them to be very careful of me. I was told that my mother was away from home; and when after two days of search they were quite sure that all effort to find either her or my father were likely to prove fruitless, that she had gone to Europe where we would follow her as soon as I was well. This promise, offering as it did, a prospect of immediate release from the terrors which were consuming me, had an extraordinary effect upon me. I got up out of my bed saying that I was well now and ready to start on the instant. The doctor, finding my pulse equable, and my whole condition wonderfully improved, and attributing it, as was natural, to my hope of soon joining my mother, advised my whim to be humoured and this hope kept active till travel and intercourse with children should give me strength and prepare me for the bitter truth ultimately awaiting me. They listened to him and in twenty-four hours our preparations were made. We saw the house closed — with what emotions surging in one small breast, I leave you to imagine — and then started on our long tour. For five years we wandered over the continent of Europe, my grandfather finding distraction, as well as myself, in foreign scenes and associations.

"But return was inevitable. What I suffered on re-entering this house, God and my sleepless pillow alone know. Had any discovery been made in our absence; or would it be made now that renovation and repairs of all kinds were necessary? Time finally answered me. My secret was safe and likely to continue so, and this fact once settled, life became endurable, if not cheerful. Since then I have spent only two nights out of this house, and they were unavoidable. When my grandfather died I had the wainscot door cemented in. It was done from this side and the cement painted to match the wood. No one opened the door nor have I ever crossed its threshold. Sometimes I think I have been foolish; and sometimes I know that I have been very wise. My reason has stood firm; how do I know that it would have done so if I had subjected myself to the possible discovery that one of both of them might have been saved if I had disclosed instead of concealed my adventure."

A pause during which white horror had shone on every face; then with a final glance at Violet, he said:

"What sequel do you see to this story, Miss Strange? I can tell the past, I leave you to picture the future."

Rising, she let her eye travel from face to face till it rested on the one awaiting it, when she answered dreamily:

"If some morning in the news column there should appear an account of the ancient and historic home of the Van Broecklyns having burned to the ground in the night, the whole country would mourn, and the city feel defrauded of one of its treasures. But there are five persons who would see in it the sequel which you ask for."

When this happened, as it did happen, some few weeks later, the astonishing discovery was made that no insurance had been put upon this house. Why was it that after such a loss Mr. Van Broecklyn seemed to renew his youth? It was a constant source of comment among his friends.

SUSAN GLASPELL (1876–1948)

Journalist, novelist, short story writer, and playwright Susan Glaspell was born and raised in Davenport, Iowa. She began working for local newspapers in 1894, enrolled at Drake College in 1897, and graduated with a degree in Philosophy in 1899. For the next two years, she worked as a reporter for the *Des Moines Daily News* and in 1901 covered the Hossack murder trial. While he was sleeping, John Hossack, a farmer, was struck by two blows from an ax, and, in the absence of other suspects, his wife Margaret was tried and found guilty of the crime. She insisted on her innocence, however, asserting that she had slept through the attack, and a second trial overturned her conviction.

Abandoning newspaper work, Glaspell moved to Chicago and embarked on a career as a writer, placing stories in *Good Housekeeping* and *Women's Home Companion*, winning prizes of $150 and $500 for her submissions to *Black Cat* magazine, and publishing her first novel in 1909. Beginning in 1913 she divided her time between the New York literary world and Cape Cod, where, in 1915, she co-founded the Provincetown Players. Along with Eugene O'Neill, she wrote one-act plays for the troupe, including *Trifles* in 1916, and served as a member of the board of the Players until 1922. In 1917, *Every Week* magazine published "A Jury of Her Peers," which is closely based on *Trifles*. Glaspell continued to publish novels and write for the theatre during the 1920s and 1930s, receiving the Pulitzer Prize in 1931 for *Alison's House*, a play inspired by the life of Emily Dickinson.

She served as the director of the Midwest Play Bureau of the Federal Writers Project from 1936 to 1938 and published three novels in the last decade of her life. Critics have read "A Jury of Her Peers" as not only a riveting work of detection but also as well-crafted short story, a powerful example of local color writing, and a path-breaking feminist text. Unlike male detectives of the late nineteenth and early twentieth century, who often tend to be stoic thinking machines, the housewives turned sleuths in Glaspell's story are sympathetic, intuitive, and knowledgeable about the lives of women. Not so much a whodunit as a why-did-she-do-it, "A Jury of Her Peers" uses unaccepted and unexpected female behavior to examine, question, and overturn the roles assigned to women in patriarchal society.

A Jury of Her Peers
by Susan Glaspell

(1917)

When Martha Hale opened the storm-door and got a cut of the north wind, she ran back for her big woolen scarf. As she hurriedly wound that round her head her eye made a scandalized sweep of her kitchen. It was no ordinary thing that called her away — it was probably further from ordinary than anything that had ever happened in Dickson County. But what her eye took in was that her kitchen was in no shape for leaving: her bread all ready for mixing, half the flour sifted and half unsifted.

She hated to see things half done; but she had been at that when the team from town stopped to get Mr. Hale, and then the sheriff came running in to say his wife wished Mrs. Hale would come too — adding, with a grin, that he guessed she was getting scarey and wanted another woman along. So she had dropped everything right where it was.

"Martha!" now came her husband's impatient voice. "Don't keep folks waiting out here in the cold."

She again opened the storm-door, and this time joined the three men and the one woman waiting for her in the big two-seated buggy.

After she had the robes tucked around her she took another look at the woman who sat beside her on the back seat. She had met Mrs. Peters the year before at the county fair, and the thing she remembered about her was that she didn't seem like a sheriff's wife. She was small and thin and didn't have a strong voice. Mrs. Gorman, sheriff's wife before Gorman went out and Peters came in, had a voice that somehow seemed to be backing up the law with every word. But if Mrs. Peters didn't look like a sheriff's wife, Peters made it up in looking like a sheriff. He was to a dot the kind of man who could get himself elected sheriff— a heavy man with a big voice, who was particularly genial with the law-abiding, as if to make it plain that he knew the difference between criminals and non-criminals. And right there it came into Mrs. Hale's mind, with a stab, that this man who was so pleasant and lively with all of them was going to the Wrights' now as a sheriff.

"The country's not very pleasant this time of year," Mrs. Peters at last ventured, as if she felt they ought to be talking as well as the men.

Mrs. Hale scarcely finished her reply, for they had gone up a little hill and could see the Wright place now, and seeing it did not make her feel like talking. It looked very lonesome this cold March morning. It had always been a lonesome-looking place. It was down in a hollow, and the poplar trees around it were lonesome-looking trees. The men were looking at it and talking about what had happened. The county attorney was bending to one side of the buggy, and kept looking steadily at the place as they drew up to it.

"I'm glad you came with me," Mrs. Peters said nervously, as the two women were about to follow the men in through the kitchen door.

Even after she had her foot on the door-step, her hand on the knob, Martha Hale had a moment of feeling she could not cross that threshold. And the reason it seemed she couldn't cross it now was simply because she hadn't crossed it before. Time and time again it had been in her mind, "I ought to go over and see Minnie Foster"—she still thought of her as Minnie Foster, though for twenty years she had been Mrs. Wright. And then there was always something to do and Minnie Foster would go from her mind. But *now* she could come.

The men went over to the stove. The women stood close together by the door. Young Henderson, the county attorney, turned around and said, "Come up to the fire, ladies."

Mrs. Peters took a step forward, then stopped. "I'm not—cold," she said.

And so the two women stood by the door, at first not even so much as looking around the kitchen.

The men talked for a minute about what a good thing it was the sheriff had sent his deputy out that morning to make a fire for them, and then Sheriff Peters stepped back from the stove, unbuttoned his outer coat, and leaned his hands on the kitchen table in a way that seemed to mark the beginning of official business. "Now, Mr. Hale," he said in a sort of semi-official voice, "before we move things about, you tell Mr. Henderson just what it was you saw when you came here yesterday morning."

The county attorney was looking around the kitchen.

"By the way," he said, "has anything been moved?" He turned to the sheriff. "Are things just as you left them yesterday?"

Peters looked from cupboard to sink; from that to a small worn rocker a little to one side of the kitchen table.

"It's just the same."

"Somebody should have been left here yesterday," said the county attorney.

"Oh—yesterday," returned the sheriff, with a little gesture as of yesterday having been more than he could bear to think of. "When I had to send Frank to Morris Center for that man who went crazy—let me tell you, I had my hands full *yesterday*. I knew you could get back from Omaha by to-day, George, and as long as I went over everything here myself—"

"Well, Mr. Hale," said the county attorney, in a way of letting what was past and gone go, "tell just what happened when you came here yesterday morning."

Mrs. Hale, still leaning against the door, had that sinking feeling of the mother whose child is about to speak a piece. Lewis often wandered along and got things mixed up in a story. She hoped he would tell this straight and plain, and not say unnecessary things that would just make things harder for Minnie Foster. He didn't begin at once, and she noticed that he looked queer — as if standing in that kitchen and having to tell what he had seen there yesterday morning made him almost sick.

"Yes, Mr. Hale?" the county attorney reminded.

"Harry and I had started to town with a load of potatoes," Mrs. Hale's husband began.

Harry was Mrs. Hale's oldest boy. He wasn't with them now, for the very good reason that those potatoes never got to town yesterday and he was taking them this morning, so he hadn't been home when the sheriff stopped to say he wanted Mr. Hale to come over to the Wright place and tell the county attorney his story there, where he could point it all out. With all Mrs. Hale's other emotions came the fear now that maybe Harry wasn't dressed warm enough — they hadn't any of them realized how that north wind did bite.

"We come along this road," Hale was going on, with a motion of his hand to the road over which they had just come, "and as we got in sight of the house I says to Harry, 'I'm goin' to see if I can't get John Wright to take a telephone.' You see," he explained to Henderson, "unless I can get somebody to go in with me they won't come out this branch road except for a price *I* can't pay. I'd spoke to Wright about it once before; but he put me off, saying folks talked too much anyway, and all he asked was peace and quiet — guess you know about how much he talked himself. But I thought maybe if I went to the house and talked about it before his wife, and said all the women-folks liked the telephones, and that in this lonesome stretch of road it would be a good thing — well, I said to Harry that that was what I was going to say — though I said at the same time that I didn't know as what his wife wanted made much difference to John — "

Now there he was! — saying things he didn't need to say. Mrs. Hale tried to catch her husband's eye, but fortunately the county attorney interrupted with:

"Let's talk about that a little later, Mr. Hale. I do want to talk about that, but I'm anxious now to get along to just what happened when you got here."

When he began this time, it was very deliberately and carefully:

"I didn't see or hear anything. I knocked at the door. And still it was all quiet inside. I knew they must be up — it was past eight o'clock. So I knocked again, louder, and I thought I heard somebody say, 'Come in.' I wasn't sure — I'm not sure yet. But I opened the door — this door," jerking a hand toward the door by which the two women stood, "and there, in that rocker" — pointing to it — "sat Mrs. Wright."

Every one in the kitchen looked at the rocker. It came into Mrs. Hale's mind that that rocker didn't look in the least like Minnie Foster — the Minnie Foster of twenty years before. It was a dingy red, with wooden rungs up the back, and the middle rung was gone, and the chair sagged to one side.

"How did she — look?" the county attorney was inquiring.

"Well," said Hale, "she looked — queer."

"How do you mean — queer?"

As he asked it he took out a note-book and pencil. Mrs. Hale did not like the sight of that pencil. She kept her eye fixed on her husband, as if to keep him from saying unnecessary things that would go into that note-book and make trouble.

Hale did speak guardedly, as if the pencil had affected him too.

"Well, as if she didn't know what she was going to do next. And kind of— done up."

"How did she seem to feel about your coming?"

"Why, I don't think she minded — one way or other. She didn't pay much attention. I said, 'Ho' do, Mrs. Wright? It's cold, ain't it?' And she said. 'Is it?' — and went on pleatin' at her apron.

"Well, I was surprised. She didn't ask me to come up to the stove, or to sit down, but just set there, not even lookin' at me. And so I said: 'I want to see John.'

"And then she — laughed. I guess you would call it a laugh.

"I thought of Harry and the team outside, so I said, a little sharp, 'Can I see John?' 'No,' says she — kind of dull like. 'Ain't he home?' says I. Then she looked at me. 'Yes,' says she, 'he's home.' 'Then why can't I see him?' I asked her, out of patience with her now. ''Cause he's dead,' says she, just as quiet and dull — and fell to pleatin' her apron. 'Dead?' says I, like you do when you can't take in what you've heard.

"She just nodded her head, not getting a bit excited, but rockin' back and forth.

"'Why — where is he?' says I, not knowing *what* to say.

"She just pointed upstairs — like this" — pointing to the room above.

"I got up, with the idea of going up there myself. By this time I — didn't know what to do. I walked from there to here; then I says: 'Why, what did he die of?'

"'He died of a rope around his neck,' says she; and just went on pleatin' at her apron."

Hale stopped speaking, and stood staring at the rocker, as if he were still seeing the woman who had sat there the morning before. Nobody spoke; it was as if every one were seeing the woman who had sat there the morning before.

"And what did you do then?" the county attorney at last broke the silence.

"I went out and called Harry. I thought I might — need help. I got Harry in, and we went upstairs." His voice fell almost to a whisper. "There he was — lying over the —"

"I think I'd rather have you go into that upstairs," the county attorney interrupted, "where you can point it all out. Just go on now with the rest of the story."

"Well, my first thought was to get that rope off. It looked —"

He stopped, his face twitching.

"But Harry, he went up to him, and he said. 'No, he's dead all right, and we'd better not touch anything.' So we went downstairs.

"She was still sitting that same way. 'Has anybody been notified?' I asked. 'No,' says she, unconcerned.

'Who did this, Mrs. Wright?' said Harry. He said it businesslike, and she stopped pleatin' at her apron. 'I don't know,' she says. 'You don't *know*?' says Harry. 'Weren't you sleepin' in the bed with him?' 'Yes,' says she, 'but I was on the inside.' 'Somebody slipped a rope round his neck and strangled him, and you didn't wake up?' says Harry. 'I didn't wake up,' she said after him.

"We may have looked as if we didn't see how that could be, for after a minute she said, 'I sleep sound.'

"Harry was going to ask her more questions, but I said maybe that weren't our business; maybe we ought to let her tell her story first to the coroner or the sheriff. So Harry went fast as he could over to High Road — the Rivers' place, where there's a telephone."

"And what did she do when she knew you had gone for the coroner?" The attorney got his pencil in his hand all ready for writing.

"She moved from that chair to this one over here"— Hale pointed to a small chair in the corner —"and just sat there with her hands held together and looking down. I got a feeling that I ought to make some conversation, so I said I had come in to see if John wanted to put in a telephone; and at that she started to laugh, and then she stopped and looked at me — scared."

At the sound of a moving pencil the man who was telling the story looked up.

"I dunno — maybe it wasn't scared," he hastened; "I wouldn't like to say it was. Soon Harry got back, and then Dr. Lloyd came, and you, Mr. Peters, and so I guess that's all I know that you don't."

He said that last with relief, and moved a little, as if relaxing. Every one moved a little. The county attorney walked toward the stair door.

"I guess we'll go upstairs first — then out to the barn and around there."

He paused and looked around the kitchen.

"You're convinced there was nothing important here?" he asked the sheriff. "Nothing that would — point to any motive?"

The sheriff too looked all around, as if to re-convince himself.

"Nothing here but kitchen things," he said, with a little laugh for the insignificance of kitchen things.

The county attorney was looking at the cupboard — a peculiar, ungainly structure, half closet and half cupboard, the upper part of it being built in the wall, and the lower part just the old-fashioned kitchen cupboard. As if its queerness attracted him, he got a chair and opened the upper part and looked in. After a moment he drew his hand away sticky.

"Here's a nice mess," he said resentfully.

The two women had drawn nearer, and now the sheriff's wife spoke.

"Oh—her fruit," she said, looking to Mrs. Hale for sympathetic understanding.

She turned back to the county attorney and explained: "She worried about that when it turned so cold last night. She said the fire would go out and her jars might burst."

Mrs. Peters' husband broke into a laugh.

"Well, can you beat the women! Held for murder, and worrying about her preserves!"

The young attorney set his lips.

"I guess before we're through with her she may have something more serious than preserves to worry about."

"Oh, well," said Mrs. Hale's husband, with good-natured superiority, "women are used to worrying over trifles."

The two women moved a little closer together. Neither of them spoke. The county attorney seemed suddenly to remember his manners—and think of his future.

"And yet," said he, with the gallantry of a young politician, "for all their worries, what would we do without the ladies?"

The women did not speak, did not unbend. He went to the sink and began washing his hands. He turned to wipe them on the roller towel—whirled it for a cleaner place.

"Dirty towels! Not much of a housekeeper, would you say, ladies?"

He kicked his foot against some dirty pans under the sink.

"There's a great deal of work to be done on a farm," said Mrs. Hale stiffly.

"To be sure. And yet"—with a little bow to her—"I know there are some Dickson County farm-houses that do not have such roller towels." He gave it a pull to expose its full length again.

"Those towels get dirty awful quick. Men's hands aren't always as clean as they might be."

"Ah, loyal to your sex, I see," he laughed. He stopped and gave her a keen look, "But you and Mrs. Wright were neighbors. I suppose you were friends, too."

Martha Hale shook her head.

"I've seen little enough of her of late years. I've not been in this house—it's more than a year."

"And why was that? You didn't like her?"

"I liked her well enough," she replied with spirit. "Farmers' wives have their hands full, Mr. Henderson. And then"—She looked around the kitchen.

"Yes?" he encouraged.

"It never seemed a very cheerful place," said she, more to herself than to him.

"No," he agreed; "I don't think any one would call it cheerful. I shouldn't say she had the home-making instinct."

"Well, I don't know as Wright had, either," she muttered.

"You mean they didn't get on very well?" he was quick to ask.

"No; I don't mean anything," she answered, with decision. As she turned a little away from him, she added: "But I don't think a place would be any the cheerfuler for John Wright's bein' in it."

"I'd like to talk to you about that a little later, Mrs. Hale," he said. "I'm anxious to get the lay of things upstairs now."

He moved toward the stair door, followed by the two men.

"I suppose anything Mrs. Peters does'll be all right?" the sheriff inquired. "She was to take in some clothes for her, you know — and a few little things. We left in such a hurry yesterday."

The county attorney looked at the two women they were leaving alone there among the kitchen things.

"Yes — Mrs. Peters," he said, his glance resting on the woman who was not Mrs. Peters, the big farmer woman who stood behind the sheriff's wife. "Of course Mrs. Peters is one of us," he said, in a manner of entrusting responsibility. "And keep your eye out, Mrs. Peters, for anything that might be of use. No telling; you women might come upon a clue to the motive — and that's the thing we need."

Mr. Hale rubbed his face after the fashion of a showman getting ready for a pleasantry.

"But would the women know a clue if they did come upon it?" he said; and, having delivered himself of this, he followed the others through the stair door.

The women stood motionless and silent, listening to the footsteps, first upon the stairs, then in the room above them.

Then, as if releasing herself from something strange, Mrs. Hale began to arrange the dirty pans under the sink, which the county attorney's disdainful push of the foot had deranged.

"I'd hate to have men comin' into my kitchen," she said testily — "snoopin' round and criticizin.'"

"Of course it's no more than their duty," said the sheriff's wife, in her manner of timid acquiescence.

"Duty's all right," replied Mrs. Hale bluffly; "but I guess that deputy sheriff that come out to make the fire might have got a little of this on." She gave the roller towel a pull. "Wish I'd thought of that sooner! Seems mean to talk about her for not having things slicked up, when she had to come away in such a hurry."

She looked around the kitchen. Certainly it was not "slicked up." Her eye was held by a bucket of sugar on a low shelf. The cover was off the wooden bucket, and beside it was a paper bag — half full.

Mrs. Hale moved toward it.

"She was putting this in there," she said to herself— slowly.

She thought of the flour in her kitchen at home — half sifted, half not sifted. She had been interrupted, and had left things half done. What had interrupted Minnie

Foster? Why had that work been left half done? She made a move as if to finish it,—unfinished things always bothered her,—and then she glanced around and saw that Mrs. Peters was watching her—and she didn't want Mrs. Peters to get that feeling she had got of work begun and then—for some reason—not finished.

"It's a shame about her fruit," she said, and walked toward the cupboard that the county attorney had opened, and got on the chair, murmuring: "I wonder if it's all gone."

It was a sorry enough looking sight, but "Here's one that's all right," she said at last. She held it toward the light. "This is cherries, too." She looked again. "I declare I believe that's the only one."

With a sigh, she got down from the chair, went to the sink, and wiped off the bottle.

"She'll feel awful bad, after all her hard work in the hot weather. I remember the afternoon I put up my cherries last summer."

She set the bottle on the table, and, with another sigh, started to sit down in the rocker. But she did not sit down. Something kept her from sitting down in that chair. She straightened—stepped back, and, half turned away, stood looking at it, seeing the woman who had sat there "pleatin' at her apron."

The thin voice of the sheriff's wife broke in upon her: "I must be getting those things from the front room closet." She opened the door into the other room, started in, stepped back. "You coming with me, Mrs. Hale?" she asked nervously. "You—you could help me get them."

They were soon back—the stark coldness of that shut-up room was not a thing to linger in.

"My!" said Mrs. Peters, dropping the things on the table and hurrying to the stove.

Mrs. Hale stood examining the clothes the woman who was being detained in town had said she wanted.

"Wright was close!" she exclaimed, holding up a shabby black skirt that bore the marks of much making over. "I think maybe that's why she kept so much to herself. I s'pose she felt she couldn't do her part; and then, you don't enjoy things when you feel shabby. She used to wear pretty clothes and be lively—when she was Minnie Foster, one of the town girls, singing in the choir. But that—oh, that was twenty years ago."

With a carefulness in which there was something tender, she folded the shabby clothes and piled them at one corner of the table. She looked up at Mrs. Peters, and there was something in the other woman's look that irritated her.

"She don't care," she said to herself. "Much difference it makes to her whether Minnie Foster had pretty clothes when she was a girl."

Then she looked again, and she wasn't so sure; in fact, she hadn't at any time been perfectly sure about Mrs. Peters. She had that shrinking manner, and yet her eyes looked as if they could see a long way into things.

"This all you was to take in?" asked Mrs. Hale.

"No," said the sheriff's wife; "she said she wanted an apron. Funny thing to want," she ventured in her nervous little way, "for there's not much to get you dirty in jail, goodness knows. But I suppose just to make her feel more natural. If you're used to wearing an apron —. She said they were in the bottom drawer of this cupboard. Yes — here they are. And then her little shawl that always hung on the stair door."

She took the small gray shawl from behind the door leading upstairs, and stood a minute looking at it.

Suddenly Mrs. Hale took a quick step toward the other woman, "Mrs. Peters!"

"Yes, Mrs. Hale?"

"Do you think she — did it?'

A frightened look blurred the other things in Mrs. Peters' eyes.

"Oh, I don't know," she said, in a voice that seemed to shrink away from the subject.

"Well, I don't think she did," affirmed Mrs. Hale stoutly. "Asking for an apron, and her little shawl. Worryin' about her fruit."

"Mr. Peters says —." Footsteps were heard in the room above; she stopped, looked up, then went on in a lowered voice: "Mr. Peters says — it looks bad for her. Mr. Henderson is awful sarcastic in a speech, and he's going to make fun of her saying she didn't — wake up."

For a moment Mrs. Hale had no answer. Then, "Well, I guess John Wright didn't wake up — when they was slippin' that rope under his neck," she muttered.

"No, it's *strange,*" breathed Mrs. Peters. "They think it was such a — funny way to kill a man."

She began to laugh; at sound of the laugh, abruptly stopped.

"That's just what Mr. Hale said," said Mrs. Hale, in a resolutely natural voice. "There was a gun in the house. He says that's what he can't understand."

"Mr. Henderson said, coming out, that what was needed for the case was a motive. Something to show anger — or sudden feeling."

"Well, I don't see any signs of anger around here," said Mrs. Hale, "I don't —"

She stopped. It was as if her mind tripped on something. Her eye was caught by a dish-towel in the middle of the kitchen table. Slowly she moved toward the table. One half of it was wiped clean, the other half messy. Her eyes made a slow, almost unwilling turn to the bucket of sugar and the half empty bag beside it. Things begun — and not finished.

After a moment she stepped back, and said, in that manner of releasing herself:

"Wonder how they're finding things upstairs? I hope she had it a little more red up[1] up there. You know," — she paused, and feeling gathered, — "it seems kind of *sneak-*

[1]*Tidy.*

ing; locking her up in town and coming out here to get her own house to turn against her!"

"But, Mrs. Hale," said the sheriff's wife, "the law is the law."

"I s'pose 'tis," answered Mrs. Hale shortly.

She turned to the stove, saying something about that fire not being much to brag of. She worked with it a minute, and when she straightened up she said aggressively:

"The law is the law — and a bad stove is a bad stove. How'd you like to cook on this?" — pointing with the poker to the broken lining. She opened the oven door and started to express her opinion of the oven; but she was swept into her own thoughts, thinking of what it would mean, year after year, to have that stove to wrestle with. The thought of Minnie Foster trying to bake in that oven — and the thought of her never going over to see Minnie Foster — .

She was startled by hearing Mrs. Peters say: "A person gets discouraged — and loses heart."

The sheriff's wife had looked from the stove to the sink — to the pail of water which had been carried in from outside. The two women stood there silent, above them the footsteps of the men who were looking for evidence against the woman who had worked in that kitchen. That look of seeing into things, of seeing through a thing to something else, was in the eyes of the sheriff's wife now. When Mrs. Hale next spoke to her, it was gently:

"Better loosen up your things, Mrs. Peters. We'll not feel them when we go out."

Mrs. Peters went to the back of the room to hang up the fur tippet she was wearing. A moment later she exclaimed, "Why, she was piecing a quilt," and held up a large sewing basket piled high with quilt pieces.

Mrs. Hale spread some of the blocks on the table.

"It's log-cabin pattern," she said, putting several of them together, "Pretty, isn't it?"

They were so engaged with the quilt that they did not hear the footsteps on the stairs. Just as the stair door opened Mrs. Hale was saying:

"Do you suppose she was going to quilt it or just knot it?"[2]

The sheriff threw up his hands.

"They wonder whether she was going to quilt it or just knot it!"

There was a laugh for the ways of women, a warming of hands over the stove, and then the county attorney said briskly:

"Well, let's go right out to the barn and get that cleared up."

"I don't see as there's anything so strange," Mrs. Hale said resentfully, after the outside door had closed on the three men — "our taking up our time with little things while we're waiting for them to get the evidence. I don't see as it's anything to laugh about."

[2]*Knotting refers to tying the layers of a quilt together while quilting involves sewing designs on the fabric.*

"Of course they've got awful important things on their minds," said the sheriff's wife apologetically.

They returned to an inspection of the block for the quilt. Mrs. Hale was looking at the fine, even sewing, and preoccupied with thoughts of the woman who had done that sewing, when she heard the sheriff's wife say, in a queer tone:

"Why, look at this one."

She turned to take the block held out to her.

"The sewing," said Mrs. Peters, in a troubled way, "All the rest of them have been so nice and even — but — this one. Why, it looks as if she didn't know what she was about!"

Their eyes met — something flashed to life, passed between them; then, as if with an effort, they seemed to pull away from each other. A moment Mrs. Hale sat there, her hands folded over that sewing which was so unlike all the rest of the sewing. Then she had pulled a knot and drawn the threads.

"Oh, what are you doing, Mrs. Hale?" asked the sheriff's wife, startled.

"Just pulling out a stitch or two that's not sewed very good," said Mrs. Hale mildly.

"I don't think we ought to touch things," Mrs. Peters said, a little helplessly.

"I'll just finish up this end," answered Mrs. Hale, still in that mild, matter-of-fact fashion.

She threaded a needle and started to replace bad sewing with good. For a little while she sewed in silence. Then, in that thin, timid voice, she heard:

"Mrs. Hale!"

"Yes, Mrs. Peters?"

"What do you suppose she was so — nervous about?"

"Oh, *I* don't know," said Mrs. Hale, as if dismissing a thing not important enough to spend much time on. "I don't know as she was — nervous. I sew awful queer sometimes when I'm just tired."

She cut a thread, and out of the corner of her eye looked up at Mrs. Peters. The small, lean face of the sheriff's wife seemed to have tightened up. Her eyes had that look of peering into something. But next moment she moved, and said in her thin, indecisive way:

"Well, I must get those clothes wrapped. They may be through sooner than we think. I wonder where I could find a piece of paper — and string."

"In that cupboard, maybe," suggested to Mrs. Hale, after a glance around.

One piece of the crazy sewing remained unripped. Mrs. Peters' back turned, Martha Hale now scrutinized that piece, compared it with the dainty, accurate sewing of the other blocks. The difference was startling. Holding this block made her feel queer, as if the distracted thoughts of the woman who had perhaps turned to it to try and quiet herself were communicating themselves to her.

Mrs. Peters' voice roused her.

"Here's a bird-cage," she said. "Did she have a bird, Mrs. Hale?"

"Why, I don't know whether she did or not." She turned to look at the cage Mrs. Peters was holding up. "I've not been here in so long." She sighed. "There was a man round last year selling canaries cheap — but I don't know as she took one. Maybe she did. She used to sing real pretty herself."

Mrs. Peters looked around the kitchen.

"Seems kind of funny to think of a bird here." She half laughed — an attempt to put up a barrier. "But she must have had one — or why would she have a cage? I wonder what happened to it."

"I suppose maybe the cat got it," suggested Mrs. Hale, resuming her sewing.

"No; she didn't have a cat. She's got that feeling some people have about cats — being afraid of them. When they brought her to our house yesterday, my cat got in the room, and she was real upset and asked me to take it out."

"My sister Bessie was like that," laughed Mrs. Hale.

The sheriff's wife did not reply. The silence made Mrs. Hale turn round. Mrs. Peters was examining the bird-cage.

"Look at this door," she said slowly. "It's broke. One hinge has been pulled apart."

Mrs. Hale came nearer.

"Looks as if someone must have been — rough with it."

Again their eyes met — startled, questioning, apprehensive. For a moment neither spoke nor stirred. Then Mrs. Hale, turning away, said brusquely:

"If they're going to find any evidence, I wish they'd be about it. I don't like this place."

"But I'm awful glad you came with me, Mrs. Hale." Mrs. Peters put the bird-cage on the table and sat down. "It would be lonesome for me — sitting here alone."

"Yes, it would, wouldn't it?" agreed Mrs. Hale, a certain determined naturalness in her voice. She had picked up the sewing, but now it dropped in her lap, and she murmured in a different voice: "But I tell you what I *do* wish, Mrs. Peters. I wish I had come over sometimes when she was here. I wish — I had."

"But of course you were awful busy, Mrs. Hale. Your house — and your children."

"I could've come," retorted Mrs. Hale shortly. "I stayed away because it weren't cheerful — and that's why I ought to have come. I" — she looked around — "I've never liked this place. Maybe because it's down in a hollow and you don't see the road. I don't know what it is, but it's a lonesome place, and always was. I wish I had come over to see Minnie Foster sometimes. I can see now —" She did not put it into words.

"Well, you mustn't reproach yourself," counseled Mrs. Peters. "Somehow, we just don't see how it is with other folks till — something comes up."

"Not having children makes less work," mused Mrs. Hale, after a silence, "but it makes a quiet house — and Wright out to work all day — and no company when he did come in. Did you know John Wright, Mrs. Peters?"

"Not to know him. I've seen him in town. They say he was a good man."

"Yes — good," conceded John Wright's neighbor grimly. "He didn't drink, and kept his word as well as most, I guess, and paid his debts. But he was a hard man, Mrs. Peters. Just to pass the time of day with him —." She stopped, shivered a little. "Like a raw wind that gets to the bone." Her eye fell upon the cage on the table before her, and she added, almost bitterly: "I should think she would've wanted a bird!"

Suddenly she leaned forward, looking intently at the cage. "But what do you s'pose went wrong with it?"

"I don't know," returned Mrs. Peters; "unless it got sick and died."

But after she said it she reached over and swung the broken door. Both women watched it as if somehow held by it.

"You didn't know — her?" Mrs. Hale asked, a gentler note in her voice.

"Not till they brought her yesterday," said the sheriff's wife.

"She — come to think of it, she was kind of like a bird herself. Real sweet and pretty, but kind of timid and — fluttery. How — she — did — change."

That held her for a long time. Finally, as if struck with a happy thought and relieved to get back to everyday things, she exclaimed:

"Tell you what, Mrs. Peters, why don't you take the quilt in with you? It might take up her mind."

"Why, I think that's a real nice idea, Mrs. Hale," agreed the sheriff's wife, as if she too were glad to come into the atmosphere of a simple kindness. "There couldn't possibly be any objection to that, could there? Now, just what will I take? I wonder if her patches are in here — and her things?"

They turned to the sewing basket.

"Here's some red," said Mrs. Hale, bringing out a roll of cloth. Underneath that was a box. "Here, maybe her scissors are in here — and her things." She held it up. "What a pretty box! I'll warrant that was something she had a long time ago — when she was a girl."

She held it in her hand a moment; then, with a little sigh, opened it.

Instantly her hand went to her nose.

"Why —!"

Mrs. Peters drew nearer — then turned away.

"There's something wrapped up in this piece of silk," faltered Mrs. Hale.

"This isn't her scissors," said Mrs. Peters, in a shrinking voice.

Her hand not steady, Mrs. Hale raised the piece of silk. "Oh, Mrs. Peters!" she cried. "It's —"

Mrs. Peters bent closer.

"It's the bird," she whispered.

"But, Mrs. Peters!" cried Mrs. Hale. "*Look* at it! Its *neck*— look at its neck! It's all — other side *to*."

She held the box away from her.

The sheriff's wife again bent closer.

"Somebody wrung its neck," said she, in a voice that was slow and deep.

And then again the eyes of the two women met — this time clung together in a look of dawning comprehension, of growing horror. Mrs. Peters looked from the dead bird to the broken door of the cage. Again their eyes met. And just then there was a sound at the outside door.

Mrs. Hale slipped the box under the quilt pieces in the basket, and sank into the chair before it. Mrs. Peters stood holding to the table. The county attorney and the sheriff came in from outside.

"Well, ladies," said the county attorney, as one turning from serious things to little pleasantries, "have you decided whether she was going to quilt it or knot it?"

"We think," began the sheriff's wife in a flurried voice, "that she was going to — knot it."

He was too preoccupied to notice the change that came in her voice on that last.

"Well, that's very interesting, I'm sure," he said tolerantly. He caught sight of the bird-cage.

"Has the bird flown?"

"We think the cat got it," said Mrs. Hale in a voice curiously even.

He was walking up and down, as if thinking something out.

"Is there a cat?" he asked absently.

Mrs. Hale shot a look up at the sheriff's wife.

"Well, not *now,*" said Mrs. Peters. "They're superstitious, you know; they leave." She sank into her chair.

The county attorney did not heed her. "No sign at all of anyone having come in from the outside," he said to Peters, in the manner of continuing an interrupted conversation. "Their own rope. Now let's go upstairs again and go over it, piece by piece. It would have to have been someone who knew just the —"

The stair door closed behind them and their voices were lost.

The two women sat motionless, not looking at each other, but as if peering into something and at the same time holding back. When they spoke now it was as if they were afraid of what they were saying, but as if they could not help saying it.

"She liked the bird," said Martha Hale, low and slowly. "She was going to bury it in that pretty box."

"When I was a girl," said Mrs. Peters, under her breath, "my kitten — there was a boy took a hatchet, and before my eyes — before I could get there —" She covered her face an instant. "If they hadn't held me back I would have"— she caught herself, looked upstairs where footsteps were heard, and finished weakly —"hurt him."

Then they sat without speaking or moving.

"I wonder how it would seem," Mrs. Hale at last began, as if feeling her way over strange ground—"never to have had any children around?" Her eyes made a slow sweep of the kitchen, as if seeing what that kitchen had meant through all the years. "No, Wright wouldn't like the bird," she said after that—"a thing that sang. She used to sing. He killed that too." Her voice tightened.

Mrs. Peters moved uneasily.

"Of course we don't know who killed the bird."

"I knew John Wright," was Mrs. Hale's answer.

"It was an awful thing was done in this house that night, Mrs. Hale," said the sheriff's wife. "Killing a man while he slept—slipping a thing round his neck that choked the life out of him."

Mrs. Hale's hand went out to the bird-cage.

"His neck. Choked the life out of him."

"We don't *know* who killed him," whispered Mrs. Peters wildly. "We don't *know*."

Mrs. Hale had not moved. "If there had been years and years of—nothing, then a bird to sing to you, it would be awful—still—after the bird was still."

It was as if something within her not herself had spoken, and it found in Mrs. Peters something she did not know as herself.

"I know what stillness is," she said, in a queer, monotonous voice. "When we homesteaded in Dakota, and my first baby died—after he was two years old—and me with no other then—"

Mrs. Hale stirred.

"How soon do you suppose they'll be through looking for the evidence?"

"I know what stillness is," repeated Mrs. Peters, in just that same way. Then she too pulled back. "The law has got to punish crime, Mrs. Hale," she said in her tight little way.

"I wish you'd seen Minnie Foster," was the answer, "when she wore a white dress with blue ribbons, and stood up there in the choir and sang."

The picture of that girl, the fact that she had lived neighbor to that girl for twenty years, and had let her die for lack of life, was suddenly more than she could bear.

"Oh, I *wish* I'd come over here once in a while!" she cried. "That was a crime! Who's going to punish that?"

"We mustn't take on," said Mrs. Peters, with a frightened look toward the stairs.

"I might 'a' *known* she needed help! I tell you, it's *queer*, Mrs. Peters. We live close together, and we live far apart. We all go through the same things—it's all just a different kind of the same thing! If it weren't—why do you and I *understand*? Why do we *know*—what we know this minute?"

She dashed her hand across her eyes. Then, seeing the jar of fruit on the table, she reached for it and choked out:

"If I was you I wouldn't *tell* her her fruit was gone! Tell her it *ain't*. Tell her it's all right — all of it. Here — take this in to prove it to her! She — she may never know whether it was broke or not."

She turned away.

Mrs. Peters reached out for the bottle of fruit as if she were glad to take it — as if touching a familiar thing, having something to do, could keep her from something else. She got up, looked about for something to wrap the fruit in, took a petticoat from the pile of clothes she had brought from the front room, and nervously started winding that round the bottle.

"My!" she began, in a high, false voice, "it's a good thing the men couldn't hear us! Getting all stirred up over a little thing like a — dead canary." She hurried over that. "As if that could have anything to do with — with — My, wouldn't they *laugh*?"

Footsteps were heard on the stairs.

"Maybe they would," muttered Mrs. Hale — "maybe they wouldn't."

"No, Peters," said the county attorney incisively; "it's all perfectly clear, except the reason for doing it. But you know juries when it comes to women. If there was some definite thing — something to show. Something to make a story about. A thing that would connect up with this clumsy way of doing it."

In a covert way Mrs. Hale looked at Mrs. Peters. Mrs. Peters was looking at her. Quickly they looked away from each other. The outer door opened and Mr. Hale came in.

"I've got the team round now," he said. "Pretty cold out there."

"I'm going to stay here awhile by myself," the county attorney suddenly announced. "You can send Frank out for me, can't you?" he asked the sheriff. "I want to go over everything. I'm not satisfied we can't do better."

Again, for one brief moment, the two women's eyes found one another.

The sheriff came up to the table.

"Did you want to see what Mrs. Peters was going to take in?"

The county attorney picked up the apron. He laughed.

"Oh, I guess they're not very dangerous things the ladies have picked out."

Mrs. Hale's hand was on the sewing basket in which the box was concealed. She felt that she ought to take her hand off the basket. She did not seem able to. He picked up one of the quilt blocks which she had piled on to cover the box. Her eyes felt like fire. She had a feeling that if he took up the basket she would snatch it from him.

But he did not take it up. With another little laugh, he turned away, saying:

"No; Mrs. Peters doesn't need supervising. For that matter, a sheriff's wife is married to the law. Ever think of it that way, Mrs. Peters?"

Mrs. Peters was standing beside the table. Mrs. Hale shot a look up at her; but she could not see her face. Mrs. Peters had turned away. When she spoke, her voice was muffled.

"Not — just that way," she said.

"Married to the law!" chuckled Mrs. Peters' husband. He moved toward the door into the front room, and said to the county attorney:

"I just want you to come in here a minute, George. We ought to take a look at these windows."

"Oh — windows," said the county attorney scoffingly.

"We'll be right out, Mr. Hale," said the sheriff to the farmer, who was still waiting by the door.

Hale went to look after the horses. The sheriff followed the county attorney into the other room. Again — for one final moment — the two women were alone in that kitchen.

Martha Hale sprang up, her hands tight together, looking at that other woman, with whom it rested. At first she could not see her eyes, for the sheriff's wife had not turned back since she turned away at that suggestion of being married to the law. But now Mrs. Hale made her turn back. Her eyes made her turn back. Slowly, unwillingly, Mrs. Peters turned her head until her eyes met the eyes of the other woman. There was a moment when they held each other in a steady, burning look in which there was no evasion or flinching. Then Martha Hale's eyes pointed the way to the basket in which was hidden the thing that would make certain the conviction of the other woman — that woman who was not there and yet who had been there with them all through the hour.

For a moment Mrs. Peters did not move. And then she did it. With a rush forward, she threw back the quilt pieces, got the box, tried to put it in her handbag. It was too big. Desperately she opened it, started to take the bird out. But there she broke — she could not touch the bird. She stood there helpless, foolish.

There was the sound of a knob turning in the inner door. Martha Hale snatched the box from the sheriff's wife, and got it in the pocket of her big coat just as the sheriff and the county attorney came back into the kitchen.

"Well, Henry," said the county attorney facetiously, "at least we found out that she was not going to quilt it. She was going to — what is it you call it, ladies?"

Mrs. Hale's hand was against the pocket of her coat.

"We call it — knot it, Mr. Henderson."

Tough Guys

CARROLL JOHN DALY (1889–1958)

A New York native who studied acting and owned movie theatres before he turned to writing, Carroll John Daly published over fifty short stories and eight novels featuring the private eye Race Williams, as well as several narratives about the police detective Satan Hall. Critics sometimes identify Williams or another of Daly's protagonists, Terry Mack (aka Three Gun Terry), as the prototype for the hard-boiled persona; however, an earlier creation, the unnamed narrator of "The False Burton Combs," published in *Black Mask* in December 1922, possesses many of the characteristics associated with this figure. *Black Mask* originally billed itself as *An Illustrated Magazine of Detective Mystery, Adventure, Romance and Spiritualism*; however, the subtitle would change frequently. Although "The False Burton Combs" lacks a mystery per se, the narrator reveals that he has worked as a kind of private detective in the past and has carved out a middle position for himself, operating as a "gentleman adventurer" between the criminals and the police. He exhibits no fear in taking on a vengeful gang of bootleggers, believing that he will prove to be the better man. Anticipating Hemingway's heroes, he vows to face death "as gracefully as possible" when it looks like his fate has been sealed.

In creating the persona of the false Burton Combs, especially his distinctive turn of phrase and his references to a personal "code" of behavior, Daly initiates the hard-boiled tradition, yet the emphasis on competition in the story also links it to Poe and classical detection. Viewing his career as a series of tests of his manhood, the narrator has to play his clients correctly in order to be paid what he's worth, stay one step ahead of the police (who take a dim view of his activities), and know how to outwit criminals so as to relieve them of their ill-gotten gains or help his employers. Because his "game" is strictly one in which he competes as a man against other men, the protagonist's developing relationship with a woman complicates things for him but leads directly to the story's memorable conclusion.

The False Burton Combs
by Carroll John Daly
(1922)

I had an outside stateroom on the upper deck of the Fall River boat[1] and ten minutes after I parked my bag there I knew that I was being watched. The boat had already cleared and was slowly making its way toward the Battery.

I didn't take the shadowing too seriously. There was nothing to be nervous about — my little trip was purely a pleasure one this time. But then a dick getting your smoke is not pleasant under the best of circumstances! And yet I was sure I had come aboard unobserved.

This chap was a new one on me and I thought he must have just picked me up on suspicion — trailed along in the hope of getting something. But I checked up my past offences and there was really nothing they could hold me on.

I ain't a crook; just a gentleman adventurer and make my living working against the law breakers. Not that I work with the police — no — not me. I'm no knight errant, either. It just came to me that the simplest people in the world are crooks. They are so set on their own plans to fleece others that they never imagine that they are the simplest sort to do. Why, the best safe cracker in the country — the dread of the police of seven States — will drop all his hard-earned money in three weeks on the race track and many a well-thought-of stick-up man will turn out his wad in one evening's crap game. Get the game? I guess I'm just one of the few that see how soft the lay is.

There's a lot of little stunts to tell about if I wanted to give away professional secrets but the game's too good to spread broadcast. It's enough to say that I've been in card games with four sharpers and did the quartet. At that I don't know a thing about cards and couldn't stack a deck if I was given half the night.

But as I say, I'm an adventurer. Not the kind the name generally means; those that sit around waiting for a sucker or spend their time helping governments out of trouble. Not that I ain't willing to help governments at a certain price but none have asked me. Those kind of chaps are found between the pages of a book, I guess. I know. I tried the game just once and nearly starved to death. There ain't nothing in governments unless you're a politician. And as I said before, I ain't a crook.

I've done a lot of business in blackmail cases. I find out a lad that's being blackmailed and then I visit him. He pays me for my services and like as not we do the

[1]*From the mid-nineteenth century through 1937, the Fall River Line was a popular means of traveling between New York and Boston.*

blackmailers every time. You see I'm a kind of a fellow in the center—not a crook and not a policeman. Both of them look on me with suspicion, though the crooks don't often know I'm out after their hides. And the police—well they run me pretty close at times but I got to take the chances.

But it ain't a nice feeling to be trailed when you're out for pleasure so I trot about the deck a few times whistling just to be sure there wasn't any mistake. And that bird come a-tramping after me as innocent as if it was his first job.

Then I had dinner and he sits at the next table and eyes me with a wistful longing like he hadn't made a pinch in a long time and is just dying to lock somebody up. But I study him, too, and he strikes me queer. He ain't got none of the earmarks of a dick. He acts like a lad with money and orders without even looking at the prices and it comes to me that I may have him wrong and that he might be one of these fellows that wanted to sell me oil stock. I always fall hard for the oil stock game. There ain't much in it but it passes the time and lets you eat well without paying for it.

Along about nine o'clock I am leaning over the rail just thinking and figuring how far the swim to shore is if a fellow had to do it.

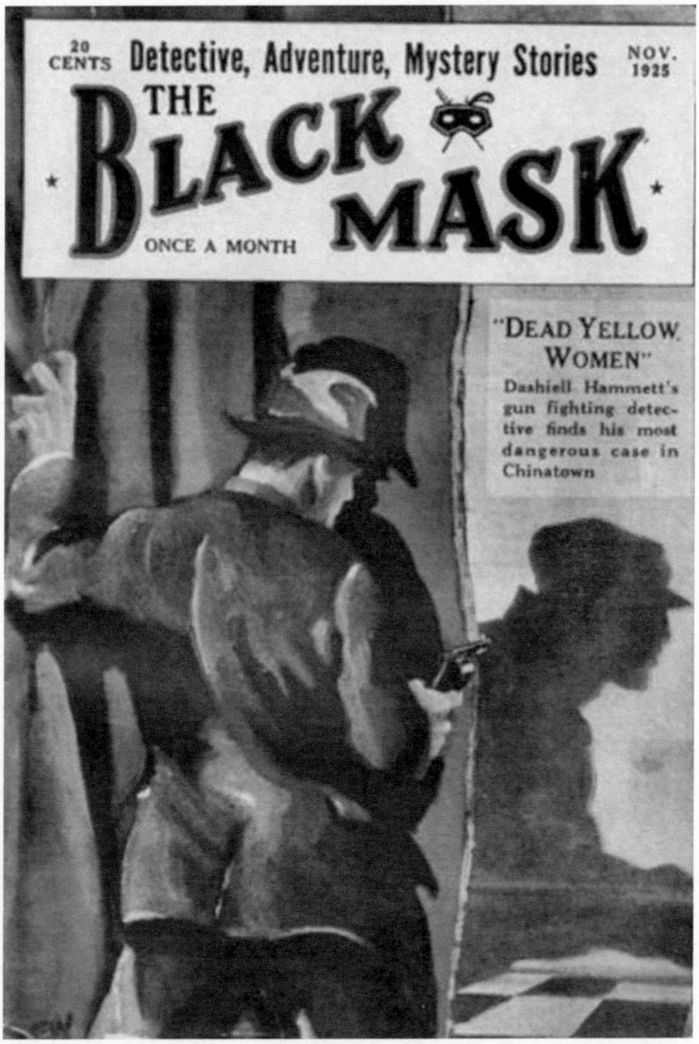

Cover from *Black Mask* magazine, November 1925, copyright © 1925 by Pro-Distributors Publishing Company, Inc.; © renewed 1953 by Popular Publications, Inc., and assigned to Keith Alan Deutsch, successor-in-interest to Popular Publications. Used by permission.

Not that I had any thought of taking to the water — no, not me — but I always like to figure what the chances are. You never can tell. Well, that bird with the longing eyes cuddles right up and leans over the rail alongside of me.

"It's a nice night," he says.

"A first rate night for a swim."

I looked him over carefully out of the comer of my eyes.

He sort of straightens up and looks out toward the flickering shore lights.

"It *is* a long swim," he says, just like he had the idea in mind.

Then he asks me to have a cigar and it's a quarter one and I take it.

"I wonder would you do me a favor," he says, after a bit.

This was about what I expected. Con men are full of that kind of gush.

"Hmmm," is all I get off. My game is a waiting one.

"I came aboard a bit late," he goes right on. "I couldn't get a room — now I wonder would you let me take the upper berth in yours. I have been kind of watching you and saw that you were all alone."

Kind of watching me was right. And now he wanted to share my room. Well, that don't exactly appeal to me, for I'm banking on a good night's sleep. Besides I know that the story is fishy for I bought my room aboard and got an outsider. But I don't tell him that right off. I think I'll work him out a bit first.

"I'm a friend of the purser," I tell him. "I'll get you a room." And I make to pass him.

"No — don't do that," he takes me by the arm. "It isn't that."

"Isn't what?"

I look him straight in the eyes and there's a look there that I have seen before and comes in my line of business. As he half turned and I caught the reflection of his eyes under the tiny deck light I read fear in his face — a real fear — almost a terror. Then I give it to him straight.

"Out with what you want," I says. "Maybe I can help you but let me tell you first that there are plenty of rooms aboard the boat. Now, you don't look like a crook — you don't look sharp enough. What's the big idea of wanting to bunk with me?"

He thought a moment and then leaned far over the rail and started to talk, keeping his eyes on the water.

"I'm in some kind of trouble. I don't know if I have been followed aboard this boat or not. I don't think so but I can't chance it. I haven't had any sleep in two nights and while I don't expect to sleep tonight I'm afraid I may drop off. I don't want to be alone and — and you struck me as an easy-going fellow who might — might — "

"Like to take a chance on getting bumped off," I cut in. He kind of drew away when I said this but I let him see right away that perhaps he didn't have me wrong. "And you would like me to sit up and protect you, eh?"

"I didn't exactly mean that but I — I don't want to be alone. Now, if you were a man I could offer money to — "

He paused and waited. I give him credit for putting the thing delicately and leaving the next move to me.

I didn't want to scare him off by putting him wise that he had come within my line of business. It might look suspicious to him. And I didn't want him to get the impression that I was a novice. There might be some future money in a job like this and it wouldn't do to be underrated.

"I'll tell you what I'll do," I says. "I've been all over the world and done some odd jobs for different South American governments"— that always has its appeal— "and I'll sit up and keep an eye on you for a hundred bucks."

Crude?— maybe — but then I know my game and you don't.

"And I can sleep?" he chirps, and his eyes sort of brighten up.

"Like a baby," I tells him.

"Good," he says, and "Come to my cabin."

So I take the number of his cabin and tell him that I'll meet him there as soon as I get my bag. Then I leave him and fetch my bag and put what money I have in the purser's office, for, although I can size up a game right away, a fellow can't afford to take chances. I have run across queerer ducks than this in my time.

Twenty minutes later he's in bed and we've turned the sign about smoking to the wall and are puffing away on a couple of good cigars. All content — he's paid me the hundred like a man; two nice new fifties.

He just lay there and smoked and didn't talk much and didn't seem as sleepy as I had thought he was. But I guess he was too tired to sleep, which is a queer thing but I've had it lots of times myself.

He seemed to be thinking, too. Like he was planning something and I was concerned in it. But I didn't bother him none. I saw what was on his chest and he didn't seem in a condition to keep things to himself. I thought he'd out with some proposition for me. But I didn't know. I wasn't anxious to travel about and be a nurse to him. That's more of a job for a private detective but they ain't used over much because they want to know all about your business and then you're worse off than you were before.

At last he opens up.

"What's your business?" he says.

And seeing I got his hundred there ain't no reason to dodge the question. I up and tells him.

"I'm a soldier of fortune."

He kind of blinks at this and then asks.

"That means a chap who takes chances for — for a consideration."

"Certain kind of chances." I qualify his statement.

"Like this for instance?"

"Sometimes; but I don't reckon to travel around as a body guard if that's what you're thinking."

He laughs like he was more at ease. But I often see them laugh when they are getting ready to send me into the danger that they fear. It's not downright meanness like I used to think when I was younger. It's relief, I guess.

"I think I can use you," he said slowly. "And pay you well and you won't need to see me again."

"Oh, I ain't got any particular dislike to you," I tell him. "It's only that I like to work alone. Let me hear what you have to offer and then — well, you can get some sleep tonight anyways."

He thought a moment.

"How much do I have to tell you?" he asked.

"As much or as little as you like. The less the better — but all I ought to know to make things go right for you."

"Well, then, there isn't much to tell. In the first place I want you to impersonate me for the summer or a greater part of it."

"That's not so easy." I shook my head.

"It's easy enough," he went on eagerly. "I am supposed to go to my father's hotel on Nantucket Island —"

Then he leaned out of the bed and talked quickly. He spoke very low and was very much in earnest. They could not possibly know me there. His father was abroad and he had not been to Nantucket since he was ten.

"How old are you?" he asked me suddenly.

"Thirty," I told him.

"You don't look more than I do. We are much alike — about the same size — the same features. And you won't meet anyone I know. If things should go wrong I'll be in touch with you."

"And your trouble?" I questioned. "What should I know about that?"

"That my life is threatened. I have been mixed up with some people whom I am not proud of."

"And they threaten to kill you."

I stroked my chin. Not that I minded taking the chances but somewheres I had learned that a laborer is worthy of his hire. It looked like he was hiring me to get bumped off in his place. Which was all right if I was paid enough. I had taken such chances before and nothing had come of it. That is nothing to me.

"Yes, they threaten my life — but I think it's all bluff."

I nodded. I could plainly see it was that, so I handed out a little talk.

"And that's why you paid me a hundred to sit up with you all night. Mind you, I don't mind the risk, but I must be paid accordingly."

When he saw that it was only a question of money he opens up considerable. He didn't exactly give me the facts in the case but he tells me enough and I learned that he had never seen the parties.

The end of it was that he draws up a paper which asks me to impersonate him and lets me out of all trouble. Of course, the paper wouldn't be much good in a bad jam but it would help if his old man should return suddenly from Europe. But I don't aim to produce that paper. I play the game fair and the figure he names was a good one — not what I would have liked perhaps but all he could afford to pay without bringing his old man into the case, which could not be done.

Somehow, when we finished talking, I got the idea that he had been mixed up in a shady deal — bootlegging or something — and a couple of friends had gone to jail on his evidence. There were three others from Canada who were coming on to get him — the three he had never seen. But it didn't matter much to me. I was just to show them that he wasn't afraid and then when they called things off or got me all was over.

Personally I did think that there was a lot of bluff in the whole business but he didn't and it wasn't my game to wise him up.

It was a big hotel I was going to for the summer and if things got melodramatic why I guess I could shoot as good as any bootlegger that ever robbed a church. They're hard guys, yes, but then I ain't exactly a cake-eater myself.

An hour or more talk in which I learn all about his family and the hotel and Burton Combs drops off for his first real sleep in months.

The next morning we part company in his stateroom and I taxied over to New Bedford. He thinks that's better than taking the train because there is a change of cars in the open country and he don't want me to drop too soon.

There are only about ten staterooms on the little tub that makes the trip from New Bedford to Nantucket and I have one of them which is already reserved in Burton Combs's name. After taking a walk about the ship I figure that there ain't no Desperate Desmonds aboard, and having earned my hundred the night before I just curl up in that little cabin and hit the hay.

Five hours and not a dream disturbed me and when I come on deck there's Nantucket right under our nose and we are rounding the little lighthouse that stands on the point leading into the bay.

There's a pile of people on the dock and they sure did look innocent enough and I take a stretch and feel mighty good. From some of the outfits I see I know that I'm going to travel in class and I hope that Burton Combs's clothes fit me for I didn't come away prepared for any social gayety. But it's early in the season yet and I'll get a chance to look around before the big rush begins.

There is a bus at the dock which is labeled "Sea Breeze Inn" and that's my meat. I climb in with about five others and we are off. Up one shady street and down another; up a bit of a hill and a short straightaway and we are at the hotel. It's a peach, too, with a view of the ocean that would knock your eye out.

The manager spots me at once and says that he'd know me among a thousand as a Combs. Which was real sweet of him seeing that he was expecting me, and the others in the bus were an old man, three old women and a young girl about nineteen.

But it wasn't my part to enlighten him and tell him that I was on to his flattery. Besides he was an old bird and probably believed what he said.

He was right glad to see me and tried to look like he meant it and wondered why I hadn't come up there again in all these years but guessed it was because it was kind of slow with my father having a hotel at Atlantic City and at Ostend. And he wanted to know if I was going to study the business. Said my father wrote him that he would like to see me interested in the hotel line.

I didn't say much. There wasn't no need. Mr. Rowlands, the manager, was one of those fussy old parties and he talked all the way up in the elevator and right into the room.

There were about fifty people there all told on the first of July but they kept coming in all the time and after I was there about two weeks the place was fairly well crowded. But I didn't make any effort to learn the business, thinking it might hurt young Combs who didn't strike me as a chap who would like any kind of work.

There was one young girl there — the one that came up in the bus with me — Marion St. James, and we had quite some times together. She was young and full of life and wanted to be up and doing all the time and we did a great deal of golf together.

Then there was another who took an interest in me. She was a widow and a fine looker and it was her first season there. I thought that she was more used to playing Atlantic City for she didn't look like the usual run of staunch New England dames. Sort of out of place and she looked to me to trot her around.

But I didn't have the time; there was Marion to be taken about. She was what you'd call a flapper and talked of the moonlight and such rot but she was real and had a big heart and after all a sensible little head on her shoulders. And she couldn't see the widow a mile and looked upon me as her own special property and blew the widow up every chance she got.

But the widow, I guess, was bent on making a match, and she was finding the Island pretty dead though the son of John B. Combs, the hotel magnate, looked like a big catch. So you see my time was fairly well taken up and I grabbed many a good laugh. I never took women seriously. My game and women don't go well together.

Yet that widow was persistent and curious and wanted to know every place Marion and me went and used to keep asking me where we drove to nights. For the kid and me did a pile of motoring. Yes, I had a car. A nice little touring car came with the Burton Combs moniker.

Marion was different. She was just a slip of a kid stuck up in a place like that and it was up to me to show her a good time. I kind of felt sorry for her and then she was pretty and a fellow felt proud to be seen with her.

All the time I kept an eye peeled for the bad men. I wondered if they'd come at all and if they did I thought that they would come in the busy season when they wouldn't be noticed much. But that they'd come at all I very much doubted.

And then they came — the three of them. I knew them the very second they entered the door. They were dolled right up to the height of fashion — just what the others were wearing. But I knew them. They just didn't belong. Maybe the others didn't spot them as outsiders but I did.

They were no bluff, either. I have met all kinds of men in my day; bad and worse and these three were the real thing. It came to me that if these gents were bent on murder I had better be up and doing.

And that Island boasted that it had never had a real murder. Yes, it sure did look like all records were going to be broken.

One of them was a tall skinny fellow and he looked more like a real summer visitor than the others. But his mouth gave him away. When he thought he was alone with the others he'd talk through the side of it, a trick which is only found in the underworld or on the track.

One of the others was fat and looked like an ex-bartender and the third I should say was just a common jailbird that could cut a man's throat with a smile.

The tall skinny one was the leader and he was booked as Mr. James Farrow. He made friends with me right off the bat. Didn't overdo it, you know; just gave me the usual amount of attention that most of the guests showed toward the owner's son. He must-a read a book about the Island for he tried to tell me things about the different points of interest like he'd been there before. But he had a bad memory like on dates and things. Marion gave me the dope on that. She knew that Island like a book.

I didn't have much doubt as to who they were but I checked them up, liking to make sure. I didn't know just what their game was and I didn't see the big idea of wanting to bump me off. If they wanted money I could catch their point but they seemed well supplied with the ready. Yes, sir, I looked this Farrow over and he's a tough bird and no mistake. But then I've seen them just as tough before and pulled through it. Besides, I hold a few tricks myself. They don't know I'm on and they don't know that I'm mighty quick with the artillery myself.

And that gun is always with me. It ain't like I only carry it when I think there's trouble coming. I always have it. You see, a chap in my line of work makes a lot of bad friends and he can't tell when one of them is going to bob up and demand an explanation. But they all find out that I ain't a bird to fool with and am just as likely to start the fireworks as they are.

Nearly every night after dinner I'd take the car and Marion and me would go for a little spin about the Island. I don't know when I ever enjoyed anything so much and sometimes I'd forget the game I was playing and think that things were different. I've met a pile of women in my time but none like Marion nor near like her. Not since the days when I went to school — and that's a memory only.

Well, we'd just drive about and talk and she'd ask me about the different places I had been to. And I could hold my own there, for I've been all over the world.

Then one night — about ten days after the troupe arrived — I get a real scare.

We've been over 'Sconset way and are driving home along about nine-thirty when—*zip*—there's a whiz in the air and a hole in the windshield. Then there's another *zip* and I see Marion jump.

It's nothing new to me. I knew that sound right away. It's a noiseless gun and someone has taken a couple of plugs at us from the distance. Well, it ain't my cue to stop, so I speed up and it's pretty near town before I slow down beneath a lamp and turn to Marion. There is a little trickle of blood running down her cheek and she's pretty white. But she ain't hurt any. It's just a scratch and I stop in the drug store and get some stuff and bathe it off.

She is a mighty game little kid and don't shake a bit and act nervous. But I'm unsteady for the first time in my life and my hand shook. I wouldn't of been much good on a quick draw then. But later I would, for I was mad—bad mad—if you know what that is. I see that all the danger ain't mine. Not that I think they meant to get Marion. But I had brought that Kid into something, and all because she kind of liked me a bit and I took her around.

On the way back to the hotel I buck up and tell her that it must have been some of the natives hunting the hares and not to say anything about it but that I would speak to the authorities in the morning.

She just looked at me funny and I knew that she did not believe me but she let it go at that.

"If that's all you want to tell me, Burt—why—all right—I shan't say a word to anyone. You can trust me."

That was all. Neither of us spoke again until we reached the hotel and I had parked the car under the shed at the side and we were standing at the bottom of the steps by the little side entrance. Then she turned and put her two tiny hands up on my shoulders and the paleness had gone from her face but just across her cheek where the bullet had passed was the smallest streak of vivid red.

"You can trust me, Burt," she said again and there seemed to be a question in her voice.

"Of course I trust you, Marion," I answered and my voice was husky and seemed to come from a distance.

It all happened very suddenly after that. Her head was very close. I know, for her soft hair brushed my cheek. I think that she leaned forward but I know that she looked up into my eyes and that the next moment I had leaned down and kissed and held her so a moment. So we stood and she did not draw away and I made no movement to release her. We were alone there, very much alone.

Then there was the sudden chug of a motor, a second's flash of light and I had opened my arms and Marion was gone and I stood alone in the blackness.

So the spell of Marion's presence was broken and I stood silently in the shadow as Farrow and his two companions passed and entered the hotel lobby.

Had they seen us? Yes—I knew that they had. For they smiled as they passed.

Smiled and never knew that they had passed close to death. For at that moment it was only the press of a trigger that lay between them and eternity.

The curtain had been rung up on the first act and the show was on. Before, I could sleep easy at night for the danger was mine and I had thought little of it. But now I felt that it was another's — and — well, I resolved to bring things to a head that night.

Ten minutes later I went to my room but not to bed. I put my light out and sat in the room until about twelve o'clock. At that time the hotel was as quiet as death.

Then I stepped out of my window and climbed down the fire escape which led to the little terrace which overlooked the ocean. I knew just where Farrow's room was and I walked along the terrace until I was under it and then swung myself up the fire escape and climbed to the third story. His window was open and thirty seconds later I had dropped into the room and was seated on the end of Farrow's bed.

Then I switched on the light and waited till he woke up. Guess he didn't have much fear of me for he slept right on for another five minutes and then he kind of turned over and blinked and — opened his eyes. He was awake fast enough then for he was looking in the mean end of my automatic.

He was quick witted, too, for he rubbed his eyes with one hand while he let the other slip under his pillow. Then I laughed and he drew it out empty and sat bolt upright in bed and faced the gun.

"Farrow," I says. "You were mighty near to going out tonight. And if I hadn't already lifted that gun of yours I'd a popped you then."

And I half wished that I had let his gun stay there for then there would have been an excuse to let him have it. A poor excuse but still an excuse. It's hard to shoot a man when he ain't armed and prepared but it's another thing to shoot when he's reaching for a gun and it's your life or his. Then you can let him have it with your mind easy.

He was a game bird, was Farrow, for he must have had plenty to think about at that moment. You see he couldn't tell just what was coming to him and from his point of view it must have looked mighty bad but he started right in to talk. Told me the chances I was taking and that I couldn't possibly get away with it. He didn't waste any time in bluffing and pretending surprise at seeing me sitting there with the gun. I give him credit — now — for understanding the situation.

But I stopped his wind.

"Shut up," I says.

And he caught the anger in my eyes and in my voice and he shut — which was good for him, for a chap can't tell for sure what he's going to do when he's seeing red and has the drop on a lad that he figures needs killing.

Then I did a bit of talking. I told him what had taken place that night and I knew it was his doing. And he nodded and never tried to deny it.

"You killed my brother," he says, "for he died in trying to break jail a few months ago — the jail where you sent him."

"So — I killed your brother, eh? Well every man is entitled to his own opinion. Now, I don't know about the killing of your brother but I'll tell you this, my friend, I come mighty near to killing you and I don't miss either and I don't crack windshields and I don't go for to hit innocent parties."

I could see that he was kind of surprised at the way I talked for I wasn't specially careful about my language like I had been about the hotel and like what he would expect from the real Burton Combs. But I could see that he kind of smacked his lips at the mention of the girl and he knew that he had a hold on me there. But I didn't care what was on his chest. I knew that the morning would see the end of the thing one way or the other.

"I am going to give you until the six-thirty boat tomorrow morning to leave the Island," I told him.

And I was not bluffing, either. After a man has had his warning it's good ethics to shoot him down — at least I see it that way. That is, if he needs it bad and you happen to have my code of morals. Also if you want to live to a ripe old age.

"What then?" he sort of sneers.

Seeing as how he wasn't going over the hurdles right away he thinks I'm a bit soft. In the same position his own doubt about shooting me would be the chances of a getaway. And the chances were not good on that Island unless you had made plans in advance. Perhaps he had — I didn't know then for I hadn't seen any boat hanging about the harbor.

"What then?" he sneers again.

"Then —" I says very slowly and thinking of Marion. "Then I'll cop you off at breakfast tomorrow morning. Yes — as soon as that boat leaves the dock I'll be gunning for you, Mr. James Farrow. And as sure as you're not a better shot than you were tonight out on the moors you'll go join your brother."

With that I turned from the bed and, unlocking his door, walked out of his room. The temptation to shoot was too great.

But I didn't go to bed that night. I just put out my light and sat smoking in my room — smoking and thinking. So I spent the second night that summer awake. I knew that the three would meet and talk it over and no doubt — get. But I just sat there; half facing the door and half facing the window with my gun on my knees waiting.

How nice it would be if they would only come by the window. It would be sweet then — and what a lot of credit I'd get as Burton Combs protecting his father's property. They meant real business all right for I see now that there was sentiment behind the whole thing — sentiment and honor. That peculiar honor of the underworld which goes and gets a squealer. Combs had evidently squealed and Farrow's brother had paid the price. And Combs went free. Position and evidence and politics had done the trick, I guess.

I heard the clock strike two and then two-thirty and then there was a footstep in the hall and I turned and faced the door and then there come a light tap on the door. This sure was a surprise.

I didn't turn on the electric light but just went to the door and swung it open suddenly and stepped back. But no one came in.

Then I heard a kind of a gasp — a woman's voice. The first thing I thought of was Marion and then I see the widow in the dim hall light. Her hat was all down and she had thrown a light robe about her and she was excited and her eyes were wide open and she looked frightened.

"It's Marion — little Miss St. James," she sobbed, "and she's in my room now — and it was terrible and I think — I think she fainted."

Then she stopped and kind of choked a bit.

Right away it came to me that this gang had done something to her and I wished that I had settled the whole thing earlier in the evening when I had the chance but —

"Come," I said to the widow and took her by the arm and led her down the hall to her room. The door was open and gun in hand I rushed into the room ahead of her.

"There on the bed," she gasped behind me.

I turned to the bed — and it was empty and then I knew. But it was too late, for I was trapped. There was a muzzle of a gun shoved into the middle of my back and a hard laugh. Then Farrow spoke.

"Throw that gun on the bed and throw it quick."

And — and I threw it and threw it quick. I was done. I should have suspected the widow from the first day I laid eyes on her, for she didn't belong. Yes, she was this gang's come on. And me, who had never fallen for women, was now caught by women. A good one and a bad one. One whom I wanted to protect and one who knew it. Now you see how the game is played. Neither a good nor a bad woman can help you in my sort of life. And yet I would take any chance for that little Marion who used to stand out on the moor at the — but Farrow was talking.

"And now, Mr. Combs, we meet again — and you're the one to do the listening. We are going to take you for a little motor ride — that is, you are going out with me to meet my friends. We don't intend to kill you. That is, if you have proved yourself a man and come along quietly. There is some information I want from you. And thanks for the return of my gun," he finished as he picked the gun off the bed.

Yes, it was his gun and mine was still in my pocket and I'd-a shot him then only I saw that the widow was covering me.

"Come."

Farrow turned and, poking the gun close to my ribs, he induced me to leave the room with him.

"If you make a noise you go," he told me as we walked down the long narrow hall to the servants' stairs. But I didn't intend to cry out. If he would just move that gun of his the least little bit I could draw and shoot. I almost laughed, the thing was so easy.

"The *Elsie* is lying right off the point," he went on, as we approached the little shed where my car was kept. "You remember the *Elsie*—it used to be your boat. The government remembers it, too. But they don't know it now nor would you. But enough of that. Climb into your car—we'll use that for our little jaunt."

We had reached the little shed now and I climbed into the car, always waiting for a chance to use my gun, but he watched me like a hawk. Then he laughed—a queer, weird laugh which had the ring of death in it.

I drove as he said and we turned from the hotel and out onto the moors—that long stretch of desolate road that leads across the Island. And then he made me stop the car and stand up.

"I'll take your gun," he said and he lifted it from my hip. "We won't need more than one gun between us tonight. For if it comes to shooting I'll take care of that end of it."

He threw the gun into the back of the car where I heard it strike the cushion of the rear seat and bounce to the floor.

We drove on in silence. He never said a word but I felt as clearly as if he had told me so that he was driving me to my death. The gun, he had let me carry until we were safe away. Perhaps he had thought that without it I might have cried out in the hotel but this I shall never know. That he knew all along I had it I have no doubt.

More than once I was on the edge of telling him that I was not the man he thought I was, for it looked as though the game was up. But he would not have believed me and besides my little agreement with Combs was back in my hotel room.

Not a soul did we pass as we sped over the deserted road. No light but the dulled rays of the moon broke the darkness all around us. Half hour or more and then suddenly I see a car in the road as the moon pops out from behind the clouds.

Then Farrow spoke and there was the snarl of an animal in his voice.

"Here's where you stop," he growled, "and here's where you get yours. They'll find you out here in the morning and they can think what they want; we'll be gone. And the killing of a rat like you is the only business I've got on the moors this night."

I had pulled up short in the center of the road now for a big touring car which I recognized as Farrow's was stretched across our path blocking the passage. In it I clearly saw his two friends.

It was death now sure but I made up my mind to go out as gracefully as possible and when he ordered me to open the door I leaned over and placed my hand upon the seat. And it fell on the cool muzzle of a revolver. Yes, my fingers closed over a gun and I knew that that gun was mine.

Thrills in life — yes — there are many but I guess that that moment was my biggest. I didn't stop to think how that gun got there. I didn't care. I just tightened on it and felt the blood of life pass quickly through my body — if you know what I mean.

I couldn't turn and shoot him for he had his pistol pressed close against my side. What he feared I don't know but I guess he was just one of these overcareful fellows who didn't take any chances.

"Open that door and get out," he ordered again as he gave me a dig in the ribs.

I leaned over again and placed my hand upon the handle of the door and then I got a happy thought.

"I can't open it," I said and I let my voice tremble and my hand shake. But in my left hand I now held my gun and thanked my lucky stars that I was left-handed, for I knew if I got the one chance that I hoped for it would have to be a perfect shot.

"White livered after all," he muttered and he stooped over and placed his left hand upon the handle of the door.

His right hand still held the gun close to my side and his eyes were watching my every movement. I never seen a man so careful before. I couldn't pull the gun up and shoot for he would get me at the very first movement — and although I was tempted I waited. The other two sat in the car ahead and were smoking and laughing. Of course I knew that if I once stepped out in the moonlight with the gun in my hand that it was all up but I waited and then —

The door really stuck a bit, for the nights are mighty damp on that island and it was that dampness which saved my life. For just the fraction of a second he took his eyes off me — just a glance down at the door with a curse on his lips.

And with that curse on his lips he died.

For as he turned the handle I give it to him right through the heart. I don't miss at that range — no — not me. The door flew open and he tumbled out on the road — dead.

I don't offer no apologies, for it was his life or mine and — as I said — he tumbled out on the road — dead.

Another fellow writing might say that things weren't clear after that. But they were clear enough to me because I never lose my head. That's why I have lived to be thirty and expect to die in bed. Yes, things are always clear when clearness means a little matter of life or death.

Those other chaps were so surprised at the turn things had taken that I had jumped to the road and winged one of them before they knew what had happened. But the other fellow was quick and had started shooting and I felt a sharp pain in my right shoulder. But one shot was all that he fired and then I had him — one good shot was all I needed and — he went out. I don't go for to miss.

I didn't take the time to examine them to see if they were dead. I'm not an undertaker and it wasn't my business. I guessed they were but if they wasn't I didn't intend to finish the job. I'm not a murderer, either. Then there were a couple of houses not so far off and I could see lights — lights that weren't there before — in both of them. Even on a quiet island like that you can't start a gun party without disturbing some of the people.

I just turned my car around and started back to the hotel. Twenty minutes later I had parked it in the shed and gone to my room. As far as I knew no one could know what had taken place on the lonely moor that night. I played doctor to my shoulder. It wasn't so very bad, either, though it pained a lot, but the bullet had gone through the flesh and passed out. I guess a little home treatment was as good as any doctor could do.

Then the morning came and my arm was not so good but I dressed and went down to breakfast and saw the manager and he told me that the widow had gone on the early boat. I don't think that she was a real widow but that she was the wife of one of those chaps. Farrow, I guess. But that didn't bother me none. She was a widow now all right.

And then about nine o'clock news of the three dead men being found away off on the road came in. And I know I got all three of them.

There was a lot of talk and newspaper men from the city came over and detectives and one thing and another. The morning papers of the following day had it all in and wild guesses as to how it happened. The three were recognized by the police as notorious characters and then it got about that a rum-runner[2] had been seen off the east shore that very morning. The general opinion seemed to be that there had been a fight among the pirates and that these three men got theirs — which suited me to a T.

I would-a beat it only that would have looked mighty queer and honestly I didn't see where they had a thing on me. I thought the best thing to do was to sit tight and for nearly a week I sat.

And then the unexpected — unexpected by me at least — happened.

The widow sent a telegram to the Boston police and they came down and nailed me. You see the writing on the wall? Keep clear of the women.

A dick from Boston dropped in one morning and I knew him the minute he stepped foot in the hotel. And I also knew that he was after me though at the time I didn't wise up as to how he was on. But he wasn't sure of himself and he had the manager introduce him to me. Then he talked about everything but the killing and of course he was the only one at the hotel that left that topic out of his conversation. And that was his idea of hiding his identity!

But he was sharp enough at that and hadn't gone about the Island more than a

[2]*A boat used to transport alcohol during Prohibition. Also, a person who transports alcohol illegally.*

couple of days, before he stuck this and that together and had enough on me to make the charge. But he was a decent sort of chap and came up to my room late at night with the manager and put the whole thing straight up to me and told me about the widow's telegram and that I was under arrest and that I had better get a hold of the best lawyer that money could buy for I was in for a tough time.

He was right and I knew that I was in a mighty bad hole. But I also knew that there would be plenty of money behind me when the whole thing came out and money is a mighty good thing to get out of a hole with.

So I played the game and never let on that I wasn't the real Burton Combs. They locked me up and notified my adopted father and the next morning the news was shouted all over the world, for John B. Combs cut a big figure and his son's arrest made some music.

And then the Combs lawyer, Harvey Benton, came up to see me and the minute he set eyes on me the cat was out of the bag and I up and tells him the whole story though I didn't give him the reason for Combs being frightened but just said that he was threatened by these three rum-runners. I felt that my playing the game fair would give me a better standing with the Combses and help loosen up the old purse strings.

Young Combs wasn't such a bad fellow either, for the next day he was down to see me and ready to tell the whole story and stand up for me.

Then we moved over to the mainland and I couldn't get out on bail and the prosecuting attorney started to have my record looked up and I can tell you that after that things didn't look so rosy. It all goes to prove that a clean sheet helps a man though mine wasn't nothing to be ashamed of. But I will admit that it looked pretty sick on the front pages of the newspapers.

Then John B. Combs himself arrives and comes up to see me. He listens to my story at first with a hard, cold face but when I come to the part where I have to shoot quick or die his eyes kind of fill and I see he's thinking of his son and the chances he would of had in the same place — and how if I hadn't got them they would-a got Burton.

Then he stretches forth his hand and grasps mine and I see it would have been better if Burton had taken his father into his confidence in the first place.

Yes, the old boy was a good scout and he told me that he loved his son and that I had saved his son's life and he didn't care what my past had been. And he would see me through this thing that his son had gotten me into if it cost a fortune.

It was a funny thing all around. Here was me, the sufferer, comforting the old boy and telling him that it was nothing. Just like the chair looking me in the face was an everyday affair. But I didn't much like the idea of his being so sad, for it gives me the impression that my chances are not so good and that I am going to pay the price for his son. Which ain't nothing to sing about. But it was my word against the word of the gang, and they being dead wouldn't have much to say.

Yes, I was indicted all right and held for the grand jury—first degree murder was the charge. Then come a wait with my lawyers trying to get a hold of some farmer who might of seen something of the shooting and would corroborate my story.

Then comes the trial and you would-a thought that the District Attorney had a personal grudge against me all his life and that all the politicians and one-horse newspapers were after his job. He paints up those three crooks like they were innocent young country girls that had been trapped by a couple of designing men. And he tells how Burton Combs done them in a shady deal and when he feared they was going to tell the authorities he up and hires a professional murderer to kill them.

I tell you it made a mighty good story and he told it well. One could almost see those three cherubs going forth in child-like innocence to be slaughtered by the butcher — which is me.

And he punched holes in my story. Especially that part about how I put down my hand and found the gun on the seat. And he said that I took them out on some pretense and shot them down in cold blood — quick shooting being my business and shady deals my living.

When he got through with my story it was as full of holes as a sieve and I had a funny feeling around the chest because I thought anyone could see what a rotten gang this was and what a clean-living young fellow I was. For my lawyer painted me up as a young gentleman what went around the world trying to help others.

Just when I think that things are all up and the jury are eyeing me with hard, stern faces comes the surprise. You see, I had never told a soul about Marion being in the car with me when that gang first started the gun play out on the 'Sconset road. You see, I didn't see the need of it and — and — well, somehow I just couldn't drag her into it. Weakness, I'll admit, for a fellow facing death should fight with every weapon he can grab. And there's that thing about women cropping up again.

But somehow there in that stuffy courtroom her innocent face and those soft, child-like eyes come up before me and I see she might of helped me a lot with the simple truth about the bullet that crossed her cheek. And while I was thinking about Marion and telling myself that my goose was cooked comes that big surprise.

My lawyer calls a witness, and it's Marion St. James. Gad! my heart just stops beating for the moment.

She was very quiet and very calm but her voice was low and the jury had to lean forward to catch what she said. She told about the ride that night and how the bullet broke the windshield and scratched her cheek.

And then came the shock. I was just dreaming there and thinking of the trouble I had caused her when I heard what she was saying and I woke up — quick.

"— after I left Mr. Combs — I called him Burton," and she pointed down at me. "I went upstairs but I couldn't sleep. I was thinking about what had happened out on the moor that night. Of course, I didn't believe what Burton had told me — about the hares. And then I remembered the look on his face as he bathed off my cheek — and it was terrible to see and —"

Then she paused a moment and wiped her eyes and went on.

"After a bit I looked out the window and I could see the little shed, where Burt kept his car, and I just caught the glimpse of a man going into it. I thought it was Burt and that he was going to drive out on the moor and—Oh, I didn't know what I thought, but I was frightened and didn't want him to go and I just rushed out of my room and down the back stairs and out toward the shed.

"I was just in time to see a big touring car pull out and two men were in it. And then I waited a minute and went and looked into the shed and Burt's car was still there. I don't know why but I was frightened and I climbed into the little touring car and sat down in the back and kind of rested.

"Then I heard someone coming and I hid down in the back of the car and pulled some rugs up over me and waited."

"And why did you wait?" my lawyer asked her kindly.

"I just thought that I would be able to help Mr.—Burt—and I wanted to help him."

"Was there any other reason?"

"Yes—I thought that he was going into trouble for me and—and—" she paused a moment.

"Yes," the lawyer encouraged.

"And I wanted to help him."

She said the words so low that you could hardly catch them. But the lawyer didn't ask her to repeat them. I guess he thought it went over better that way and it sure did—at least with me. For I knew what she meant.

Then she went on.

"Pretty soon Mr. Combs came along" (for she kept calling me Burton Combs) "and that big man was with him. The one they called Mr. Farrow. I looked carefully up over the door, for it was very dark where I was, and I saw that Mr. Farrow had a gun in his hand and that he held it close up against Mr. Combs's back. And he talked rough but too low to understand and then they both climbed into the front of the machine. I did not know just what I could do, but I thought—oh—I don't know what I thought, but I did so want to help him and I was just too scared to cry out.

"And then they started off and after they were a little way out in the country Mr. Farrow made Burton stop the car and stand up while he searched him. And he found his revolver and took it from him and threw it into the back of the car. It landed on the seat and bounced off and I stretched out my hand and took hold of it and held it there under the rugs. I didn't know what to do with it at first for I had never fired a gun.

"Then I heard Mr. Farrow say that he was going to kill Mr. Combs and I was terribly frightened but I leaned up and stretched my hand over the seat and tried to give the pistol to Mr. Combs. But Mr. Farrow turned suddenly and I became frightened and dropped the pistol. Then I dropped back in the car again but I was half out of the covers and afraid to pull them over me for the car had stopped again and I had a feeling that someone was looking down at me. Then I heard them moving in front of the car and I looked up and I saw that Mr. Farrow had his gun pressed close against Mr. Combs's side and that Mr. Combs was trying to open the door.

"Then came the sudden report and I think that I cried out, for I thought that Burt was shot. Then came several more shots, one right after another, and I looked out and saw Mr. Combs standing in the moonlight and a man beside another big car firing at him — and then the man fell and —"

She broke off suddenly and started to cry.

"And after that?" my lawyer smiled at her.

"I climbed" back under the robes and — Mr. Combs drove me back to the hotel — but he never knew I was there."

Well, that just about settled it, I guess. The room was in more or less of an uproar. And you ought to have heard my lawyer! Now I know why good lawyers get so much money. He started in and he sure did paint that gang up mighty black, and now I was the innocent boy led into danger by these hardened criminals. And he showed how the gun was held close to my side when I fired.

"And if that isn't self-defense and good American pluck I'd like to ask you what in heaven's name is?"

And that's the whole show. One hour later I was a free man. Everybody was shaking hands with me, and from a desperate criminal I had suddenly become a hero. And I guess that Marion had done it.

Then Old Combs came up to me and shook me by the hand and told me how glad he was that I was free and what a plucky little thing Marion was, and how I owed my life twice over to her.

Then he offered me a job. Imagine! Another job for the Combs family. But this was different.

"There is too much good in you to lead the life you have been leading. You may think that it is all right, but there will be others that won't. I can offer you something that will be mighty good."

But I shook my head.

"I guess I'll stick to my trade," I said. "I've had good offers before, and in my line — this little notoriety won't hurt none."

"It's a good position," he says, not paying much attention to what I was getting off. "The right people will be glad to know you — and there will be enough money in it to get married."

I started to shake my head again when he handed me a note.

"Read this note and then let me know. Not another word until you have read it."

He smiles.

I took the little blue envelope and tore it open, and it was from Marion:

I would like to see you again when you take that position of Mr. Combs.

I guess I read that simple sentence over a couple of dozen times before I again turned to Mr. Combs.

"I guess I'll take that job—if it pays enough to get married on," was all that I said.

There ain't no explanation unless—unless I wanted to see Marion again myself.

That's all, unless to warn you that it would be kind of foolish to take too seriously anything I said about keeping clear of the women.

Dashiell Hammett (1894–1961)

Samuel Dashiell Hammett had a difficult childhood growing up in St. Mary's County and Baltimore, Maryland. At the age of fourteen he quit school to help support his family. Between 1915 and 1922, he worked as an operative for the Pinkerton Detective Agency, a job that gave him considerable experience with criminals from which to draw upon when poor health forced him to turn to writing. Thus, when Hammett published his first detective story "The Road Home" under the name Peter Collinson in the December 1922 issue of *Black Mask*, he was, as Joe Gores puts it, "not a writer learning about private detectives, he was a private detective learning about writing." With his third story for *Black Mask*, "Arson Plus," Hammett introduced his unnamed detective known as the Continental Op, who would appear twenty more times in the pages of the magazine between 1923 and 1926.

Hammett briefly took a job in advertising, but when his health faltered again he resumed writing, publishing four novels between 1927 and 1931. Among these was *The Maltese Falcon*, probably the best-known hard-boiled novel, which has sold over four and a half million copies in the United States alone and has been made into three films, including the famous 1941 John Huston version starring Humphrey Bogart as Sam Spade. In the early 1930s, Hammett came to Hollywood to write for the movies and in 1934 published *The Thin Man*, immortalized in the film of the same name and its sequels, starring William Powell and Myrna Loy. Hammett became involved in radical politics during the Depression, served in World War II from 1942 to 1945, and published next to nothing in his later years.

Despite the relative brevity of his career as a crime writer and his somewhat modest output of five novels and fifty-odd stories, it would be hard to overestimate his impact on detection. In the words of William Nolan, "The crime story would never be the same" because Hammett "had altered the basic form of the genre. No writer since Edgar Allan Poe had exerted a greater influence on mystery fiction." Although brief and inconclusive, the apprenticeship piece "The Road Home" adumbrates Hammett's best-known fiction. Like the Continental Op and Sam Spade, Hagedorn identifies himself as a detective, follows his own code of behavior, and resists the temptations to abandon his mission.

The Road Home
by Dashiell Hammett

(1922)

"You're a fool to pass it up! You'll get just as much credit and reward for taking back proof of my death as you will for taking me back. And I got papers and stuff buried back near the Yunnan[1] border that you can have to back up your story; and you needn't be afraid that I'll ever show up to spoil your play."

The gaunt man in faded khaki frowned with patient annoyance and looked away from the blood-shot brown eyes in front of him, over the teak side of the *jahaz* to where the wrinkled snout of a *muggar* broke the surface of the river. When the small crocodile submerged again, Hagedorn's gray eyes came back to the pleading ones before him, and he spoke wearily, as one who has been answering the same arguments again and again.

"I can't do it, Barnes. I left New York two years ago to get you, and for two years I've been in this damned country — here and in Yunnan — hunting you. I promised my people I'd stay until I found you, and I kept my word. Lord! man," with a touch of exasperation, "after all I've gone through you don't expect me to throw them down now — now that the job's as good as done!"

The dark man in the garb of a native smiled an oily, ingratiating smile and brushed away his captor's words with a wave of his hand.

"I ain't offering you a dinky coupla thousand dollars; I'm offering you your pick out of one of the richest gem beds in Asia — a bed that was hidden by the *Mran-ma*[2] when the British jumped the country. Come back up there with me and I'll show you rubies and sapphires and topazes that'll knock your eye out. All I'm asking you is to go back up there with me and take a look at 'em. If you don't like 'em you'll still have me to take back to New York."

Hagedorn shook his head slowly.

"You're going back to New York with me. Maybe man-hunting isn't the nicest trade in the world but it's all the trade I've got, and this jewel bed of yours sounds phony to me. I can't blame you for not wanting to go back — but just the same I'm taking you."

Barnes glared at the detective disgustedly.

"You're a fine chump! And it's costing me and you thousands of dollars! Hell!"

He spat over the side insultingly — native-like — and settled himself back on his corner of the split-bamboo mat.

[1]*Province in Southern China bordering Myanmar (Burma), Laos, and Vietnam.*
[2]*Ancient name for the people of Myanmar.*

Hagedorn was looking past the lateen sail, down the river — the beginning of the route to New York — along which a miasmal breeze was carrying the fifty-foot boat with surprising speed. Four more days and they would be aboard a steamer for Rangoon; then another steamer to Calcutta, and in the end, one to New York — home, after two years!

Two years through unknown country, pursuing what until the very day of the capture had never been more than a vague shadow. Through Yunnan and Burma, combing wilderness with microscopic thoroughness — a game of hide-and-seek up the rivers, over the hills and through the jungles — sometimes a year, sometimes two months and then six behind his quarry. And now successfully home! Betty would be fifteen — quite a lady.

Barnes edged forward and resumed his pleading, with a whine creeping into his voice.

"Say, Hagedorn, why don't you listen to reason? There ain't no sense in us losing all that money just for something that happened over two years ago. I didn't mean to kill that guy, anyway. You know how it is; I was a kid and wild and foolish — but I wasn't mean — and I got in with a bad bunch. Why, I thought of that hold-up as a lark when we planned it! And then that messenger yelled and I guess I was excited, and my gun went off the first thing I knew. I didn't go to kill him; and it won't do him no good to take me back and hang me for it. The express company didn't lose no money. What do they want to hound me like this for? I been trying to live it down."

The gaunt detective answered quietly enough but what kindness there had been in his dry voice before was gone now.

"I know — the old story! And the bruises on the Burmese woman you were living with sure show that there's nothing mean about you. Cut it, Barnes, and make up your mind to face it — you and I are going back to New York."

"The hell we are!"

Barnes got slowly to his feet and backed away a step.

"I'd just as leave —"

Hagedorn's automatic came out a split second too late; his prisoner was over the side and swimming toward the bank. The detective caught up his rifle from the deck behind him and sprang to the rail. Barnes' head showed for a moment and then went down again, to appear again twenty feet nearer shore. Upstream the man in the boat saw the blunt, wrinkled noses of three *muggars,* moving toward the shore at a tangent that would intercept the fugitive. He leaned against the teak rail and summed up the situation.

"Looks like I'm not going to take him back alive after all — but my job's done. I can shoot him when he shows again, or I can let him alone and the *muggars* will get him."

Then the sudden but logical instinct to side with the member of his own species against enemies from another wiped out all other considerations, and sent his rifle to his shoulder to throw a shower of bullets into the *muggars.*

Barnes clambered up the bank of the river, waved his hand over his head without looking back, and plunged into the jungle.

Hagedorn turned to the bearded owner of the *jahaz,* who had come to his side, and addressed him in his broke Burmese.

"Put me ashore —*yu nga apau mye*— and wait —*thaing*— until I bring him back — *thu yughe.*"

The captain wagged his black beard protestingly.

"*Mahok!* In the jungle here, *sahib* a man is as a leaf. Twenty men might find him in a week, or a month, it may take five years. I cannot wait that long."

The gaunt white man gnawed at his lower lip and looked down the river — the road to New York.

"Two years," he said aloud to himself, "it took to find him when he didn't know I was hunting for him. Now — Oh, hell! It may take five years. I wonder about them jewels of his."

He turned to the boatman.

"I go after him. You wait three hours," pointing over head, "until noon —*ne apomha.* If I am not back then do not wait —*malotu thaing, thwa. Thi?*"

The captain nodded.

"*Hokhe!*"

For five hours the captain kept the *jahaz* at anchor, and then, when the shadows of the trees on the west bank were creeping out into the river, he ordered the latten sail hoisted, and the teak craft vanished around a bend in the river.

Cornell Woolrich (1903–1968)

Richard Corliss aptly describes Cornell Woolrich's life as being "as twisted and compelling as his work." He lived with his mother for most of his adult life (except for a brief marriage he entered into as a sick joke); wrote stories and novels that were adapted by such famous film directors as Alfred Hitchcock, François Truffaut, and Rainer Maria Fassbender; and, in a bizarre incident that eerily parallels the mishaps of some of his own characters, lost a leg to gangrene after failing to treat an infection. Born Cornell George Hopley Woolrich in New York City, he left Columbia University in 1926 when he published his first novel, *Cover Charge*, which earned comparisons to the work of F. Scott Fitzgerald. A second novel, *Children of the Ritz*, was made into a movie and brought Woolrich to Hollywood as a screenwriter, eventually leading to his ill-fated marriage to the daughter of the movie mogul J. Stuart Blackton in 1930.

Writing under two pseudonyms, William Irish and George Hopley, as well as his own name, Woolrich published sixteen novels and countless stories in a variety of magazines, including the pulps *Black Mask*, *Detective Fiction Weekly*, and *Dime Detective*, during the 1930s and 1940s. The death of his mother in 1957 intensified his problem with alcohol, effectively putting an end to his writing career. Notoriously reclusive, he refused to divulge facts about his personal life and often made up information about himself. Unlike Poe, Doyle, Christie, Hammett, and Chandler, Woolrich had no recurring series character. What links many of his stories are their gritty urban cityscapes and menacing noirish elements. In "Murder at the Automat," Woolrich chooses as his crime scene the quintessential impersonal urban setting: a self-service restaurant where people purchase their food from a machine rather than a human being and often eat side by side with perfect strangers. Although the personal code of the police detective protagonist, the emphasis on violence, and the street lingo of characters clearly link the story to the hard-boiled school, the confrontation at the end recalls Conan Doyle's "The Adventure of the Speckled Band" and the solution to the mystery harkens back to Poe's "The Purloined Letter."

Murder at the Automat

by Cornell Woolrich

(1937)

Nelson pushed through the revolving-door at twenty to one in the morning, his squadmate, Sarecky, in the compartment behind him. They stepped clear and looked around. The place looked funny. Almost all the little white tables had helpings of food on them, but no one was at them eating. There was a big black crowd ganged up over in one corner, thick as bees and sending up a buzz. One or two were standing up on chairs, trying to see over the heads of the ones in front, rubbering like a flock of cranes.

The crowd burst apart, and a cop came through. "Now, stand back. Get away from this table, all of you," he was saying. "There's nothing to see. The man's dead—that's all."

He met the two dicks halfway between the crowd and the door. "Over there in the corner," he said unnecessarily. "Indigestion, I guess." He went back with them.

They split the crowd wide open again, this time from the outside. In the middle of it was one of the little white tables, a dead man in a chair, an ambulance doctor, a pair of stretcher-bearers, and the automat manager.

"He gone?" Nelson asked the interne.

"Yep. We got here too late." He came closer so the mob wouldn't overhear. "Better send him down to the morgue and have him looked at. I think he did the Dutch.[1] There's a white streak on his chin, and a half-eaten sandwich under his face spiked with some more of it, whatever it is. That's why I got in touch with you fellows. Good night," he wound up pleasantly and elbowed his way out of the crowd, the two stretcher-bearers tagging after him. The ambulance clanged dolorously outside, swept its fiery headlights around the corner, and whined off.

Nelson said to the cop: "Go over to the door and keep everyone in here, until we get the three others that were sitting at this table with him."

The manager said: "There's a little balcony upstairs. Couldn't he be taken up there, instead of being left down here in full sight like this?"

"Yeah, pretty soon," Nelson agreed, "but not just yet."

He looked down at the table. There were four servings of food on it, one on each side. Two had barely been touched. One had been finished and only the soiled plates remained. One was hidden by the prone figure sprawled across it, one arm out, the other hanging limply down toward the floor.

"Who was sitting here?" said Nelson, pointing to one of the unconsumed por-

[1]*Committed suicide.*

The Automat was an inexpensive place to dine and, for Cornell Woolrich, the setting of a murder (courtesy Marianne Hardart).

tions. "Kindly step forward and identify yourself." No one made a move. "No one," said Nelson, raising his voice, "gets out of here until we have a chance to question the three people that were at this table with him when it happened."

Someone started to back out of the crowd from behind. The woman who had wanted to go home so badly a minute ago, pointed accusingly. "*He* was — that man there! I remember him distinctly. He bumped into me with his tray just before he sat down."

Sarecky went over, took him by the arm, and brought him forward again. "No one's going to hurt you," Nelson said, at sight of his pale face. "Only don't make it any tougher for yourself than you have to."

"I never even saw the guy before," wailed the man, as if he had already been accused of murder, "I just happened to park my stuff at the first vacant chair I —" Misery liking company, he broke off short and pointed in turn. "*He* was at the table, too. Why doncha hold him, if you're gonna hold me?"

"That's just what we're going to do," said Nelson dryly. "Over here, you," he ordered the new witness. "Now, who was eating spaghetti on the right here? As soon as we find that out, the rest of you can go home."

The crowd looked around indignantly in search of the recalcitrant witness that was the cause of detaining them all. But this time no one was definitely able to single him out. A white-uniformed busman finally edged forward and said to Nelson: "I think he musta got out of the place right after it happened. I looked over at this table a minute before it happened, and he was already through eating, picking his teeth and just holding down the chair."

"Well, he's not as smart as he thinks he is," said Nelson. "We'll catch up with him, whether he got out or didn't. The rest of you clear out of here now. And don't give fake names and addresses to the cop at the door, or you'll be making trouble for yourselves."

The place emptied itself like magic, self-preservation being stronger than curiosity in most people. The two table-mates of the dead man, the manager, the staff, and the two dicks remained inside.

An assistant medical examiner arrived, followed by two men with the usual basket, and made a brief preliminary investigation. While this was going on, Nelson was questioning the two witnesses, the busman, and the manager. He got an illuminating composite picture.

The man was well known to the staff by sight, and was considered an eccentric. He always came in at the same time each night, just before closing time, and always helped himself to the same snack—coffee and a bologna sandwich. It hadn't varied for six months now. The remnants that the busman removed from where the man sat each time were always the same. The manager was able to corroborate this. He, the dead man, had raised a kick one night about a week ago, because the bologna-sandwich slots had all been emptied before he came in. The manager had had to remind him that it's first come, first served, at an automat, and you can't reserve your food ahead of time. The man at the change-booth, questioned by Nelson, added to the old fellow's reputation for eccentricity. Other, well-dressed people came in and changed a half-dollar, or at the most a dollar bill. He, in his battered hat and derelict's overcoat, never failed to produce a ten and sometimes even a twenty.

"One of these misers, eh?" said Nelson. "They always end up behind the eight-ball, one way or another."

The old fellow was removed, also the partly consumed sandwich. The assistant examiner let Nelson know: "I think you've got something here, brother. I may be wrong, but that sandwich was loaded with cyanide."

Sarecky, who had gone through the man's clothes, said: "The name was Leo Avram, and here's the address. Incidentally, he had seven hundred dollars, in C's, in his right shoe and three hundred in his left. Want me to go over there and nose around?"

"Suppose I go," Nelson said. "You stay here and clean up."

"My pal," murmured the other dick dryly.

The waxed paper from the sandwich had been left lying under the chair. Nelson picked it up, wrapped it in a paper-napkin, and put it in his pocket. It was only a short walk from the automat to where Avram lived, an outmoded, walk-up building, falling to pieces with neglect.

Nelson went into the hall and there was no such name listed. He thought at first Sarecky had made a mistake, or at least been misled by whatever memorandum it was he had found that purported to give the old fellow's address. He rang the bell marked *Superintendent*, and went down to the basement-entrance to make sure. A stout blond woman in an old sweater and carpet-slippers came out.

"Is there anyone named Avram living in this building?"

"That's my husband — he's the superintendent. He's out right now, I expect him back any minute."

Nelson couldn't understand, himself, why he didn't break it to her then and there. He wanted to get a line, perhaps, on the old man's surroundings while they still remained normal. "Can I come in and wait a minute?" he said.

"Why not?" she said indifferently.

She led him down a barren, unlit basement-way, stacked with empty ashcans, into a room green-yellow with a tiny bud of gaslight. Old as the building upstairs was, it had been wired for electricity, Nelson had noted. For that matter, so was this basement down here. There was a cord hanging from the ceiling ending in an empty socket. It had been looped up out of reach. "The old bird sure was a miser," thought Nelson. "Walking around on one grand and living like this!" He couldn't help feeling a little sorry for the woman.

He noted to his further surprise that a pot of coffee was boiling on a one-burner gas stove over in the corner. He wondered if she knew that he treated himself away from home each night. "Any idea where he went?" he asked, sitting down in a creaking rocker.

"He goes two blocks down to the automat for a bite to eat every night at this time," she said.

"How is it," he asked curiously, "he'll go out and spend money like that, when he could have coffee right here where he lives with you?"

A spark of resentment showed in her face, but a defeated resentment that had long turned to resignation. She shrugged. "For himself, nothing's too good. He goes there because the light's better, he says. But for me and the kids, he begrudges every penny."

"You've got kids, have you?"

"They're mine, not his," she said dully.

Nelson had already caught sight of a half-grown girl and a little boy peeping shyly out at him from another room. "Well," he said, getting up, "I'm sorry to have to tell you this, but your husband had an accident a little while ago at the automat, Mrs. Avram. He's gone."

The weary stolidity on her face changed very slowly. But it did change — to fright. "Cyanide — what's that?" she breathed, when he'd told her.

"Did he have any enemies?"

She said with utter simplicity, "Nobody loved him. Nobody hated him that much, either."

"Do you know of any reason he'd have to take his own life?"

"Him? Never! He held on tight to life, just like he did to his money."

There was some truth in that, the dick had to admit. Misers seldom commit suicide.

The little girl edged into the room fearfully, holding her hands behind her. "Is — is he dead, Mom?"

The woman just nodded, dry-eyed.

"Then, can we use this now?" She was holding a fly-blown electric bulb in her hands.

Nelson felt touched; hard-boiled dick though he was. "Come down to headquarters tomorrow, Mrs. Avram. There's some money there you can claim. G'night." He went outside and clanged the basement-gate shut after him. The windows alongside him suddenly bloomed feebly with electricity, and the silhouette of a woman standing up on a chair was outlined against them.

"It's a funny world," thought the dick with a shake of his head, as he trudged up to sidewalk-level.

It was now two in the morning. The automat was dark when Nelson returned there, so he went down to headquarters. They were questioning the branch-manager and the unseen counterman who prepared the sandwiches and filled the slots from the inside.

Nelson's captain said: "They've already telephoned from the chem lab that the sandwich is loaded with cyanide crystals. On the other hand, they give the remainder of the loaf that was used, the leftover bologna from which the sandwich was prepared, the breadknife, the cutting-board, and the scraps in the garbage-receptacle — all of which we sent over there — a clean bill of health. There was clearly no slip-up or carelessness in the automat pantry. Which means that cyanide got into that sandwich on the consumer's side of the apparatus. He committed suicide or was deliberately murdered by one of the other customers."

"I was just up there," Nelson said. "It wasn't suicide. People don't worry about keeping their light bills down when they're going to take their own lives."

"Good psychology," the captain nodded. "My experience is that miserliness is simply a perverted form of self-preservation, an exaggerated clinging to life. The choice of method wouldn't be in character, either. Cyanide's expensive, and it wouldn't be sold to a man of Avram's type, just for the asking. It's murder, then. I think it's highly important you men bring in whoever the fourth man at that table was tonight. Do it with the least possible loss of time."

A composite description of him, pieced together from the few scraps that could be obtained from the busman and the other two at the table, was available. He was a heavy-set dark-complected man, wearing a light-tan suit. He had been the first of the four at the table, and already through eating, but had lingered on. Mannerisms — had kept looking back over his shoulder, from time to time, and picking his teeth. He had had a small black satchel, or sample-case, parked at his feet under the table. Both survivors were positive on this point. Both had stubbed their toes against it in sitting down, and both had glanced to the floor to see what it was.

Had he reached down toward it at any time, after their arrival, as if to open it or take anything out of it?

To the best of their united recollections — no.

Had Avram, *after* bringing the sandwich to the table, gotten up again and left it unguarded for a moment?

Again, no. In fact the whole thing had been over with in a flash. He had noisily unwrapped it, taken a huge bite, swallowed without chewing, heaved convulsively once or twice, and fallen prone across the tabletop.

"Then it must have happened right outside the slot — I mean the inserting of the stuff— and not at the table, at all," Sarecky told Nelson privately. "Guess he laid it down for a minute while he was drawing his coffee."

"Absolutely not!" Nelson contradicted. "You're forgetting it was all wrapped up in wax-paper. How could anyone have opened, then closed it again, without attracting his attention? And if we're going to suspect the guy with the satchel — and the cap seems to want us to — he was already *at* the table and all through eating when Avram came over. How could he know ahead of time which table the old guy was going to select?"

"Then how did the stuff get on it? Where did it come from?" the other dick asked helplessly.

"It's little things like that we're paid to find out," Nelson reminded him dryly.

"Pretty large order, isn't it?"

"You talk like a layman. You've been on the squad long enough by now to know how damnably unescapable little habits are, how impossible it is to shake them off, once formed. The public at large thinks detective work is something miraculous like pulling rabbits out of a silk hat. They don't realize that no adult is a free agent — that they're tied hand and foot by tiny, harmless little habits, and held helpless. This man has a habit of taking a snack to eat at midnight in a public place. He has a habit of picking his teeth after he's through, of lingering on at the table, of looking back over his shoulder aimlessly from time to time. Combine that with a stocky build, a dark complexion, and you have him! What more d'ya want — a spotlight trained on him?"

It was Sarecky, himself, in spite of his misgivings, who picked him up forty-eight hours later in another automat, sample-case and all, at nearly the same hour as the first time, and brought him in for questioning! The busman from the former place, and the two customers, called in, identified him unhesitatingly, even if he was now wearing a gray suit.

His name, he said, was Alexander Hill, and he lived at 215 Such-and-such a street.

"What business are you in?" rapped out the captain.

The man's face got livid. His Adam's apple went up and down like an elevator. He could barely articulate the words. "I'm — I'm a salesman for a wholesale drug concern," he gasped terrifiedly.

"Ah!" said two of his three questioners expressively. The sample-case, opened, was found to contain only tooth-powders, aspirins, and headache remedies.

"But Nelson, rummaging through it, thought: "Oh, nuts, it's too pat. And he's too scared, too defenseless, to have really done it. Came in here just now without a bit of mental build-up prepared ahead of time. The real culprit would have been all primed, all rehearsed, for just this. Watch him go all to pieces. The innocent ones always do."

The captain's voice rose to a roar. "How is it everyone else stayed in the place that night, but you got out in such a hurry?"

"I — I don't know. It happened so close to me, I guess I — I got nervous."

That wasn't necessarily a sign of guilt; Nelson was thinking. It was his duty to take part in the questioning, so he shot out at him: "You got nervous, eh? What reason d'you have for getting nervous? How'd *you* know it wasn't just a heart attack or malnutrition — unless you were the cause of it?"

He stumbled badly over that one. "No! No! I don't handle that stuff! I don't carry anything like that — "

"So you know what it was? How'd you know? We didn't tell you," Sarecky jumped on him.

"I — I read it in the papers next morning," he wailed.

Well, it had been in all of them, Nelson had to admit.

"You didn't reach out in front of you — toward him — for anything that night? You kept your hands to yourself?" Then, before he could get a word out, "*What about sugar?*"

The suspect went from bad to worse: "I don't use any!" he whimpered.

Sarecky had been just waiting for that. "Don't lie to us!" he yelled, and swung at him. "I watched you for ten full minutes tonight before I went over and tapped your shoulder. You emptied half the container into your cup!" His fist hit him a glancing blow on the side of the jaw, knocked him and the chair he was sitting on both off-balance. Fright was making the guy sew himself up twice as badly as before.

"Aw, we're just barking up the wrong tree," Nelson kept saying to himself. "It's just one of those fluke coincidences. A drug salesman happens to be sitting at the same table where a guy drops from cyanide poisoning!" Still, he knew that more than one guy had been strapped into the chair just on the strength of such a coincidence and nothing more. You couldn't expect a jury not to pounce on it for all it was worth.

The captain took Nelson out of it at this point, somewhat to his relief, took him aside and murmured: "Go over there and give his place a good cleaning while we're holding him here. If you can turn up any of that stuff hidden around there, that's all we need. He'll break down like a stack of cards." He glanced over at the cowering figure in the chair. "We'll have him before morning," he promised.

"That's what I'm afraid of," thought Nelson, easing out. "And then what'll we have? Exactly nothing." He wasn't the kind of a dick that would have rather had a wrong guy than no guy at all, like some of them. He wanted the right guy — or none at all. The last he saw of the captain, he was stripping off his coat for action, more as a moral threat than a physical one, and the unfortunate victim of circumstances was wailing, "I didn't do it, I didn't do it," like a record with a flaw in it.

Hill was bachelor and lived in a small, one-room flat on the upper West Side. Nelson let himself in with the man's own key, put on the lights, and went to work. In half an hour, he had investigated the place upside-down. There was not a grain of cyanide to be found, nor anything beyond what had already been revealed in the sample-case. This did not mean, of course, that he couldn't have obtained some either through the firm he worked for, or some of the retail druggists whom he canvassed. Nelson found a list of the latter and took it with him to check over the following day.

Instead of returning directly to headquarters, he detoured on an impulse past the Avram house, and, seeing a light shining in the basement windows, went over and rang the bell.

The little girl came out, her brother behind her. "Mom's not in," she announced.

"She's out with Uncle Nick," the boy supplied.

His sister whirled on him. "She told us not to tell anybody that, didn't she!"

Nelson could hear the instructions as clearly as if he'd been in the room at the time, "If that man comes around again, don't you tell him I've gone out with Uncle Nick, now!"

Children are after all very transparent. They told him most of what he wanted to know without realizing they were doing it. "He's not really your uncle, is he?"

A gasp of surprise. "How'd you know that?"

"Your ma gonna marry him?"

They both nodded approvingly. "He's gonna be our new Pop."

"What was the name of your real Pop — the one before the last?"

"Edwards," they chorused proudly.

"What happened to him?"

"He died."

"In Dee-troit," added the little boy.

He only asked them one more question. "Can you tell me his full name?"

"Albert J. Edwards," they recited.

He gave them a friendly push. "All right, kids, go back to bed."

He went back to headquarters, sent a wire to the Bureau of Vital Statistics in Detroit, on his own hook. They were still questioning Hill down to the bone, meanwhile, but he hadn't caved in yet. "Nothing," Nelson reported. "Only this account-sheet of where he places his orders."

"I'm going to try framing him with a handful of bicarb of soda, or something—pretend we got the goods on him. I'll see if that'll open him up," the captain promised wrathfully. "He's not the push-over I expected. You start in at seven this morning and work your way through this list of retail druggists. Find out if he ever tried to contract them for any of that stuff."

Meanwhile, he had Hill smuggled out the back way to an outlying precinct, to evade the statue governing the length of time a prisoner can be held before arraignment. They didn't have enough of a case against him to arraign him, but they weren't going to let him go.

Nelson was even more surprised than the prisoner at what he caught himself doing. As they stood Hill up next to him in the corridor, for a minute, waiting for the Black Maria, he breathed over his shoulder, "Hang on tight, or you're sunk!"

The man acted too far gone even to understand what he was driving at.

Nelson was present the next morning when Mrs. Avram showed up to claim the money, and watched her expression curiously. She had the same air of weary resignation as the night he had broken the news to her. She accepted the money from the captain, signed for it, turned apathetically away, holding it in her hand. The captain, by prearrangement, had pulled another of his little tricks—purposely withheld one of the hundred-dollar bills to see what her reaction would be.

Halfway to the door, she turned in alarm, came hurrying back. "Gentlemen, there must be a mistake! There's—there's a hundred-dollar bill here on top!" She shuffled through the roll hastily. "They're all hundred-dollar bills!" she cried out aghast. "I knew he had a little money in his shoes—he slept with them under his pillow at nights—but I thought maybe, fifty, seventy dollars—"

"There was a thousand in his shoes," said the captain, "and another thousand stitched all along the seams of his overcoat."

She let the money go, caught the edge of the desk he was sitting behind with both hands, and slumped draggingly down it to the floor in a dead faint. They had to hustle in with a pitcher of water to revive her.

Nelson impatiently wondered what the heck was the matter with him, what more he needed to be convinced she hadn't known what she was coming into? And yet, he said to himself, how are you going to tell a real faint from a fake one! They close their eyes and they flop, and which is it?

He slept three hours, and then he went down and checked at the wholesale-drug concern Hill worked for. The firm did not handle cyanide or any other poisonous substance, and the man had a very good record there. He spent the morning working his way down the list of retail druggists who had placed their orders through Hill, and again got nowhere. At noon he quit and went back to the automat where it had happened — not to eat but to talk to the manager. He was really working on two cases simultaneously — an official one for his captain and a private one of his own. The captain would have had a fit if he'd known it.

"Will you lemme have that busman of yours, the one we had down at headquarters the other night? I want to take him out of here with me for about half an hour."

"You're the Police Department," the manager smiled acquiescently.

Nelson took him with him in his streetclothes. "You did a pretty good job of identifying Hill, the fourth man at that table," he told him. "Naturally, I don't expect you to remember every face that was in there that night. Especially with the quick turnover there is in an automat. However, here's what you do. Go down this street here to Number One-twenty-one — you can see it from here. Ring the superintendent's bell. You're looking for an apartment, see? But while you're at it, you take a good look at the woman you'll see, and then come back and tell me if you remember seeing her face in the automat that night or any other night. Don't stare now — just size her up."

It took him a little longer than Nelson had counted on. When he finally rejoined the dick around the corner, where the latter was waiting, he said: "Nope, I've never seen her in our place, that night or any other, to my knowledge. But don't forget — I'm not on the floor every minute of the time. She could have been in and out often without my spotting her."

"But not," thought Nelson, "without Avram seeing her, if she went anywhere near him at all." She hadn't been there, then. That was practically certain. "What took you so long?" he asked him.

"Funny thing. There was a guy there in the place with her that used to work for us. He remembered me right away."

"Oh, yeah?" The dick drew up short. "Was *he* in there that night?"

"Naw, he quit six months ago. I haven't seen him since."

"What was he, sandwich-maker?"

"No, busman like me. He cleaned up the tables."

Just another coincidence, then. But, Nelson reminded himself, if one coincidence was strong enough to put Hill in jeopardy, why should the other be passed over as harmless? Both cases — his and the captain's — now had their coincidences. It remained to be seen which was just that — a coincidence and nothing more — and which was the McCoy.

He went back to headquarters. No wire had yet come from Detroit in answer to his, but he hadn't expected any this soon — it took time. The captain, bulldog-like, wouldn't let Hill go. They had spirited him away to still a third place, were holding him on some technicality or other that had nothing to do with the Avram case. The bicarbonate of soda trick hadn't worked, the captain told Nelson ruefully.

"Why?" the dick wanted to know. "Because he caught on just by looking at it that it wasn't cyanide — is that it? I think that's an important point, right there."

"No, he thought it was the stuff all right. But he hollered blue murder it hadn't come out of his room."

"Then if he doesn't know the difference between cyanide and bicarb of soda at sight, doesn't that prove he didn't put any on that sandwich?"

The captain gave him a look. "Are you for us or against us?" he wanted to know acidly. "You go ahead checking that list of retail druggists until you find out where he got it. And if we can't dig up any other motive, unhealthy scientific curiosity will satisfy me. He wanted to study the effects at first hand, and picked the first stranger who came along."

"Sure, in an automat — the most conspicuous, crowded public eating-place there is. The one place where human handling of the food is reduced to a minimum."

He deliberately disobeyed orders, a thing he had never done before — or rather, postponed carrying them out. He went back and commenced a one-man watch over the basement-entrance of the Avram house.

In about an hour, a squat, foreign-looking man came up the steps and walked down the street. This was undoubtedly "Uncle Nick," Mrs. Avram's husband-to-be, and former employee of the automat. Nelson tailed him effortlessly on the opposite side, boarded the same bus he did a block below, and got off at the same stop. "Uncle Nick" went into a bank, and Nelson into a cigar-store across the way that had transparent telephone booths commanding the street through the glass front.

When he came out again, Nelson didn't bother following him any more. Instead, he went into the bank himself. "What'd that guy do — open an account just now? Lemme see the deposit-slip."

He had deposited a thousand dollars cash under the name of Nicholas Krassin, half of the sum Mrs. Avram had claimed at headquarters only the day before. Nelson didn't have to be told that this by no means indicated Krassin and she had had anything to do with the old man's death. The money was rightfully hers as his widow, and, if she wanted to divide it with her groom-to-be, that was no criminal offense. Still, wasn't there a stronger motive here than the "unhealthy scientific curiosity" the captain had pinned on Hill? The fact remained that she wouldn't have had possession of the money had Avram still been alive. It would have still been in his shoes and coat-seams where she couldn't get at it.

Nelson checked Krassin at the address he had given at the bank, and, somewhat to his surprise, found it to be on the level, not fictitious. Either the two of them weren't very bright, or they were innocent. He went back to headquarters at six, and the answer to his telegram to Detroit had finally come. "Exhumation order obtained as per request stop Albert J. Edwards deceased January 1936 stop death certificate gives cause fall from steel girder while at work building under construction stop — autopsy —"

Nelson read it to the end, folded it, put it in his pocket without changing his expression.

"Well, did you find out anything?" the captain wanted to know.

"No, but I'm on the way to," Nelson assured him, but he may have been thinking of that other case of his own, and not the one they were all steamed up over. He went out again without saying where.

He got to Mrs. Avram's at quarter to seven, and rang the bell. The little girl came out to the basement-entrance. At sight of him, she called our shrilly, but without humorous intent, "Ma, that man's here again."

Nelson smiled a little and walked back to the living-quarters. A sudden hush had fallen thick enough to cut with a knife. Krassin was there again, in his shirt-sleeves, having supper with Mrs. Avram and the two kids. They not only had electricity now but a midget radio as well, he noticed. You can't arrest people for buying a midget radio. It was silent as a tomb, but he let the back of his hand brush it, surreptitiously, and the front of the dial was still warm from recent use.

"I'm not butting in, am I?" greeted them cheerfully.

"N — no, sit down," said Mrs. Avram nervously. "This is Mr. Krassin, a friend of the family. I don't know your name —"

"Nelson."

Krassin just looked at him watchfully.

The dick said: "Sorry to trouble you. I just wanted to ask you a couple questions about your husband. About what time was it he had the accident?"

"You know better than I," she objected. "You were the one came here and told me."

"I don't mean Avram, I mean Edwards, in Detroit — the riveter that fell off the girder."

Her face went a little gray, as if the memory were painful. Krassin's face didn't change color, but only showed considerable surprise.

"About what time of day?" he repeated.

"Noon," she said almost inaudibly.

"Lunch-time," said the dick softly, as to himself. "Most workmen carry their lunch from home in a pail —" He looked at her thoughtfully. Then he changed the subject, wrinkled up his nose appreciatively. "That coffee smells good," he remarked.

She gave him a peculiar, strained smile. "Have a cup, Mr. Detective," she offered. He saw her eyes meet Krassin's briefly.

"Thanks, don't mind if I do," drawled Nelson.

She got up. Then, on her way to the stove, she suddenly flared out at the two kids for no apparent reason: "What are you hanging around here for? Go to bed. Get out of here now, I say!" She banged the door shut on them, stood before it with her back to the room for a minute. Nelson's sharp ears caught the faint but unmistakable click of key.

She turned back again, purred to Krassin: "Nick, go outside and take a look at the furnace, will you, while I'm pouring Mr. Nelson's coffee? If the heat dies down, they'll all start complaining from upstairs right away. Give it a good shaking up."

The hairs at the back of Nelson's neck stood up a little as he watched the man get up and sidle out. But he'd asked for the cup of coffee, himself.

He couldn't see her pouring it — her back was turned toward him again as she stood over the stove. But he could hear the splash of the hot liquid, see her elbow-motions, hear the clink of the pot as she replaced it. She stayed that way a moment longer, after it had been poured, with her back to him — less than a moment, barely thirty seconds. One elbow moved slightly. Nelson's eyes were narrow slits. It was thirty seconds too long, one elbow-motion too many.

She turned, came back, set the cup down before him. "I'll let you put your own sugar in, yes?" she said almost playfully. "Some like a lot, some like a little." There was a disappearing ring of froth in the middle of the black steaming liquid.

Outside somewhere, he could hear Krassin raking up the furnace.

"Drink it while it's still hot," she urged.

He lifted it slowly to his lips. As the cup went up, her eyelids went down. Not all the way, not enough to completely shut out sight, though.

He blew the steam away. "Too hot — burn my mouth. Gotta give it a minute to cool," he said. "How about you — ain't you having any? I couldn't drink alone. Ain't polite."

"I had mine," she breathed heavily, opening her eyes again. "I don't think there's any left."

"Then I'll give you half of this."

Her hospitable alarm was almost overdone. She all but jumped back in protest. "No, no! Wait, I'll look. Yes, there's more, there's plenty!"

He could have had an accident with it while her back was turned a second time, upset it over the floor. Instead, he took a kitchen-match out of his pocket, broke the head off short with his thumbnail. He threw the head, not the stick, over on top of the warm stove in front of which she was standing. It fell to one side of her, without making any noise, and she didn't notice it. If he'd thrown stick and all, it would have clicked as it dropped and attracted her attention.

She came back and sat down opposite him. Krassin's footsteps could be heard shuffling back toward them along the cement corridor outside.

"Go ahead. Don't be bashful — drink up," she encouraged. There was something ghastly about her smile, like a death's-head grinning across the table from him.

The match-head on the stove, heated to the point of combustion, suddenly flared up with a little spitting sound and a momentary gleam. She jumped a little, and her head turned nervously to see what it was. When she looked back again, he already had his cup to his lips. She raised hers, too, watching him over the rim of it. Krassin's footfalls had stopped somewhere just outside the room door, and there wasn't another sound from him, as if he were standing there, waiting.

At the table, the cat-and-mouse play went on a moment longer. Nelson started swallowing with a dry constriction of the throat. The woman's eyes, watching him above her cup, were greedy half-moons of delight. Suddenly, her head and shoulders went down across the table with a bang, like her husband's had at the automat that other night, and the crash of the crushed cup sounded from underneath her.

Nelson jumped up watchfully, throwing his chair over. The door shot open, and Krassin came in, with an ax in one hand and an empty burlap-bag in the other.

"I'm not quite ready for cremation yet," the dick gritted, and threw himself at him.

Krassin dropped the superfluous burlap-bag, the ax flashed up overhead. Nelson dipped his knees, down in under it before it could fall. He caught the shaft with one hand, midway between the blade and Krassin's grip, and held the weapon teetering in mid-air. With his other fist he started imitating a hydraulic drill against his assailant's teeth. Then he lowered his barrage suddenly to solar-plexus level, sent in two bodyblows that caved his opponent in — and that about finished it.

Out in the wilds of Corona, an hour later, in a sub-basement locker-room, Alexander Hill — or at least what was left of him — was saying: "And you'll lemme sleep if I do? And you'll get it over real quick, send me up and put me out of my misery?"

"Yeah, yeah!" said the haggard captain, flicking ink out of a fountain pen and jabbing it at him. "Why dincha do this days ago, make it easier for us all?"

"Never saw such a guy," complained Sarecky, rinsing his mouth with water over in a corner.

"What's that man signing?" exploded Nelson's voice from the stairs.

"Whaddye think he's signing?" snarled the captain. "And where you been all night, incidentally?"

"Getting poisoned by the same party that croaked Avram!" He came the rest of the way down, and Krassin walked down alongside at the end of a short steel link.

"Who's this guy?" they both wanted to know.

Nelson looked at the first prisoner, in the chair. "Take him out of here a few minutes, can't you?" he requested. "He don't have to know all our business."

"Just like in the story-books," muttered Sarecky jealously. "One-Man Nelson walks in at the last minute and cops all the glory."

A cop led Hill upstairs. Another cop brought down a small brown-paper parcel at Nelson's request. Opened, it revealed a small tin that had once contained cocoa. Nelson turned it upside down and a few threads of whitish substance spilled lethargically out, filling the close air of the room with a faint odor of bitter almonds.

"There's your cyanide," he said. "It came off the shelf above Mrs. Avram's kitchen-stove. Her kids, who are being taken care of at headquarters until I can get back there, will tell you it's roach-powder and they were warned never to go near it. She probably got it in Detroit, way back last year."

"She did it?" said the captain. "How could she? It was on the automat-sandwich, not anything he ate at home. *She* wasn't at the automat that night, she was home, you told us that yourself."

"Yeah, she was at home, but she poisoned him at the automat just the same. Look, it goes like this." He unlocked his manacle, refastened his prisoner temporarily to a plumbing-pipe in the corner. He took a paper-napkin out of his pocket, and, from within that, the carefully preserved waxpaper wrapper the death-sandwich had been done in.

Nelson said: "This has been folded over twice, once on one side, once on the other. You can see that, yourself. Every crease in it is double-barreled. Meaning what? The sandwich was taken out, doctored, and rewrapped. Only, in her hurry, Mrs. Avram slipped up and put the paper back the other way around.

"As I told Sarecky already, there's death in little habits. Avram was a miser. Bologna is the cheapest sandwich that automat sells. For six months straight, he never bought any other kind. This guy here used to work there. He knew at what time the slots were refilled for the last time. He knew that that was just when Avram always showed up. And, incidentally, the old man was no fool. He didn't go there because the light was better — he went there to keep from getting poisoned at home. Ate all his meals out.

"All right, so what did they do? They got him, anyway — like this. Krassin, here, went in, bought a bologna sandwich, and took it home to her. She spiked it, rewrapped it, and, at eleven-thirty, he took it back there in his pocket. The sandwich-slots had just been refilled for the last time. They wouldn't put any more in till next morning. There are three bologna-slots. He emptied all three, to make sure the victim wouldn't get any but the lethal sandwich. After they're taken out, the glass slides remain ajar. You can lift them and reach in without inserting a coin. He put his death-sandwich in, stayed by it so no one else would get it. The old man came in. Maybe he's near sighted and didn't recognize Krassin. Maybe he didn't know him at all — I haven't cleared that point up yet. Krassin eased out of the place. The old man is a miser. He sees he can get a sandwich for nothing, thinks something went wrong with the mechanism, maybe. He grabs it up twice as quick as anyone else would have. There you are.

"What was in his shoes is the guy's motive. As for her, that was only partly her motive. She was a congenital killer, anyway, outside of that. He would have married her, and it would have happened to him in his turn some day. She got rid of her first husband, Edwards, in Detroit that way. She got a wonderful break. He ate the poisoned lunch she'd given him way up on the crossbeams of a building under construction, and it looked like he'd lost his balance and toppled to his death. They exhumed the body and performed an autopsy at my request. This telegram says they found traces of cyanide poisoning even after all this time.

"I paid out rope to her tonight, let her know I was onto her. I told her her coffee smelled good. Then I switched cups on her. She's up there now, dead. I can't say that I wanted it that way, but it was me or her. You never would have gotten her to the chair, anyway. She was unbalanced of course, but not the kind that's easily recognizable. She'd have spent a year in an institution, been released, and gone out and done it all over again. It grows on 'em, gives 'em a feeling of power over their fellow human beings.

"This louse, however, is *not* insane. He did it for exactly one thousand dollars and no cents — and he knew what he was doing from first to last. So I think he's entitled to a chicken-and-ice-cream-dinner in the death-house, at the state's expense."

"The Sphinx," growled Sarecky under his breath, shrugging into his coat. "Sees all, knows all, keeps all to himself."

"Who stinks?" corrected the captain, misunderstanding. "If anyone does, it's you and me. He brought home the bacon!"

Race and Detection

Pauline Elizabeth Hopkins (1859–1930)

Although Pauline Hopkins has been the subject of two recent biographies, surprisingly little is known about large stretches in the life of this pioneering playwright, performer, orator, novelist, journalist, short story writer, biographer, editor, and public intellectual. Two early influences on her were Frederick Douglass, whom she heard speak in Boston, and William Wells Brown, who awarded her a prize for an essay entitled "The Evils of Intemperance." During the late 1870s and the early 1880s, she was billed as "Boston's favorite colored soprano" and wrote original pieces for and performed with family members in a troupe known as Hopkins Colored Troubadours. Literary historians regard *Slaves' Escape, or the Underground Railroad* (also known as *Peculiar Sam*) as the first dramatic work by an African American woman.

After stints as a public speaker and a stenographer in the 1880s and 1890s, she resurfaced at the turn to the twentieth century as a prolific writer and influential editor for the Boston-based *Colored American Magazine*, which has been described as the country's first black magazine; and her only novel published in book form during her lifetime, *Contending Forces* (1900), was brought out by the same company that published the periodical. She believed that fiction could educate her readers, mostly middle-class blacks who were often unacquainted with history or biography. Hopkins served as editor of the women's department, literary editor, and editor-in-chief of the journal before being fired in late 1904 for her outspoken political views after Booker T. Washington acquired the magazine. In 1916 she launched a new Boston-based journal, the *New Era Magazine*, but it folded after two issues.

Widely recognized as the earliest African American mystery story, Hopkins's "Talma Gordon," published in 1900, has rightly been discussed by scholars in connection with her use of popular genres to explore racial themes. This multi-layered tale not only owes a debt to Poe in its use of a locked-room mystery and reference to pirate treasure but also features both a racial mystery and a romantic (or marital) mystery. In addition, the story addresses the implications of United States imperialism for African Americans in the wake of the Spanish-American War and in the midst of the on-going, bloody subjugation of the Philippines.

Talma Gordon
by Pauline Hopkins

(1900)

The Canterbury Club of Boston was holding its regular monthly meeting at the palatial Beacon-street residence of Dr. William Thornton, expert medical practitioner and specialist. All the members were present, because some rare opinions were to be aired by men of profound thought on a question of vital importance to the life of the Republic, and because the club celebrated its anniversary in a home usually closed to society. The Doctor's winters, since his marriage, were passed at his summer home near his celebrated sanatorium. This winter found him in town with his wife and two boys. We had heard much of the beauty of the former, who was entirely unknown to social life, and about whose life and marriage we felt sure a romantic interest attached. The Doctor himself was too bright a luminary of the professional world to remain long hidden without creating comment. We had accepted the invitation to dine with alacrity, knowing that we should be welcomed to a banquet that would feast both eye and palate; but we had not been favored by even a glimpse of the hostess. The subject for discussion was: "Expansion; Its Effect upon the Future Development of the Anglo-Saxon throughout the World."

Dinner was over, but we still sat about the social board discussing the question of the hour. The Hon. Herbert Clapp, eminent jurist and politician, had painted in glowing colors the advantages to be gained by the increase of wealth and the exalted position which expansion would give the United States in the councils of the great governments of the world. In smoothly flowing sentences marshaled in rhetorical order, with compact ideas, and incisive argument, he drew an effective picture with all the persuasive eloquence of the trained orator.

Joseph Whitman, the theologian of worldwide fame, accepted the arguments of Mr. Clapp, but subordinated all to the great opportunity which expansion would give to the religious enthusiast. None could doubt the sincerity of this man, who looked once into the idealized face on which heaven had set the seal of consecration.

Various opinions were advanced by the twenty-five men present, but the host said nothing; he glanced from one to another with a look of amusement in his shrewd gray-blue eyes. "Wonderful eyes," said his patients who came under their magic spell. "A wonderful man and a wonderful mind," agreed his contemporaries, as they heard in amazement of some great cure of chronic or malignant disease which approached the supernatural.

"What do you think of this question, Doctor?" finally asked the president, turning to the silent host.

"Your arguments are good; they would convince almost anyone."

"But not Doctor Thornton," laughed the theologian.

"I acquiesce whichever way the result turns. Still, I like to view both sides of a question. We have considered but one tonight. Did you ever think that in spite of our prejudices against amalgamation,[1] some of our descendants, indeed many of them, will inevitably intermarry among those far-off tribes of dark-skinned peoples, if they become a part of this great Union?"

"Among the lower classes that may occur, but not to any great extent," remarked a college president.

"My experience teaches me that it will occur among all classes, and to an appalling extent," replied the Doctor.

"You don't believe in intermarriage with other races?"

"Yes, most emphatically, when they possess decent moral development and physical perfection, for then we develop a superior being in the progeny born of the intermarriage. But if we are not ready to receive and assimilate the new material which will be brought to mingle with our pure Anglo-Saxon stream, we should call a halt in our expansion policy."

"I must confess, Doctor, that in the idea of amalgamation you present a new thought to my mind. Will you not favor us with a few of your main points?" asked the president of the club, breaking the silence which followed the Doctor's remarks.

One of the three Boston locations of the *Colored American Magazine*, for which Pauline Hopkins worked from 1900 to 1904 and the periodical in which "Talma Gordon" appeared in 1900 (*Colored American Magazine*, 1902).

[1]*The mixing, in marriage and/or sexual union, of persons of different races.*

"Yes, Doctor, give us your theories on the subject. We may not agree with you, but we are all open to conviction."

The Doctor removed the half-consumed cigar from his lips, drank what remained in his glass of the choice Burgundy, and leaning back in his chair contemplated the earnest faces before him.

We may make laws, but laws are but straws in the hands of Omnipotence.

> "There's a divinity that shapes our ends,
> Rough-hew them how we will."[2]

And no man may combat fate. Given a man, propinquity, opportunity, fascinating femininity, and there you are. Black, white, green, yellow—nothing will prevent intermarriage. Position, wealth, family, friends—all sink into insignificance before the God-implanted instinct that made Adam, awakening from a deep sleep and finding the woman beside him, accept Eve as bone of his bone; he cared not nor questioned whence she came. So it is with the sons of Adam ever since, through the law of heredity which makes us all one common family. And so it will be with us in our reformation of this old Republic. Perhaps I can make my meaning clearer by illustration, and with your permission I will tell you a story which came under my observation as a practitioner.

Doubtless all of you heard of the terrible tragedy which occurred at Gordonville, Mass., some years ago, when Capt. Jonathan Gordon, his wife, and little son were murdered. I suppose that I am the only man on this side of the Atlantic, outside of the police, who can tell you the true story of that crime.

I knew Captain Gordon well; it was through his persuasions that I bought a place in Gordonville and settled down to spending my summers in that charming rural neighborhood. I had rendered the Captain what he was pleased to call valuable medical help, and I became his family physician. Captain Gordon was a retired sea captain, formerly engaged in the East India trade. All his ancestors had been such; but when the bottom fell out of that business he established the Gordonville Mills with his first wife's money, and settled down as a money-making manufacturer of cotton cloth. The Gordons were old New England Puritans who had come over in the "Mayflower"; they had owned Gordon Hall for more than a hundred years. It was a baronial-like pile of granite with towers, standing on a hill which commanded a superb view of Massachusetts Bay and the surrounding country. I imagine the Gordon star was under a cloud about the time Captain Jonathan married his first wife, Miss Isabel Franklin of Boston, who brought to him the money which mended the broken fortunes of the Gordon house, and restored this old Puritan stock to its rightful position. In the person of Captain Gordon the austerity of manner and indomitable willpower that he had inherited were combined with a temper that brooked no contradiction.

[2]Hamlet *(5.2.10–11).*

The first wife died at the birth of her third child, leaving him two daughters, Jeannette and Talma. Very soon after her death the Captain married again. I have heard it rumored that the Gordon girls did not get on very well with their stepmother. She was a woman with no fortune of her own, and envied the large portion left by the first Mrs. Gordon to her daughters.

Jeannette was tall, dark, and stern like her father; Talma was like her dead mother, and possessed of great talent, so great that her father sent her to the American Academy at Rome, to develop the gift. It was the hottest of July days when her friends were bidden to an afternoon party on the lawn and a dance in the evening, to welcome Talma Gordon among them again. I watched her as she moved about among her guests, a fairylike blonde in floating white draperies, her face a study in delicate changing tints, like the heart of a flower, sparkling in smiles about the mouth to end in merry laughter in the clear blue eyes. There were all the subtle allurements of birth, wealth, and culture about the exquisite creature:

> "Smiling, frowning evermore,
> Thou art perfect in love-lore,
> Ever varying Madeline,"[3]

quoted a celebrated writer as he stood apart with me, gazing upon the scene before us. He sighed as he looked at the girl.

"Doctor, there is genius and passion in her face. Sometime our little friend will do wonderful things. But is it desirable to be singled out for special blessings by the gods? Genius always carries with it intense capacity for suffering: 'Whom the gods love die young.'"

"Ah," I replied, "do not name death and Talma Gordon together. Cease your dismal croakings; such talk is rank heresy."

The dazzling daylight dropped slowly into summer twilight. The merriment continued; more guests arrived; the great dancing pagoda built for the occasion was lighted by myriads of Japanese lanterns. The strains from the band grew sweeter and sweeter, and "all went merry as a marriage bell."[4] It was a rare treat to have this party at Gordon Hall, for Captain Jonathan was not given to hospitality. We broke up shortly before midnight, with expressions of delight from all the guests.

I was a bachelor then, without ties. Captain Gordon insisted upon my having a bed at the Hall. I did not fall asleep readily; there seemed to be something in the air that forbade it. I was still awake when a distant clock struck the second hour of the morning. Suddenly the heavens were lighted by a sheet of ghastly light; a terrific midsummer thunderstorm was breaking over the sleeping town. A lurid flash lit up all the landscape, painting the trees in grotesque shapes against the murky sky, and defining clearly the sullen blackness of the waters of the bay breaking in grandeur

[3]*From "Madeline" by Alfred Tennyson.*
[4]*From* Childe Harold *by Lord Byron.*

against the rocky coast. I had arisen and put back the draperies from the windows, to have an unobstructed view of the grand scene. A low muttering coming nearer and nearer, a terrific roar, and then a tremendous downpour. The storm had burst.

Now the uncanny howling of a dog mingled with the rattling volleys of thunder. I heard the opening and closing of doors; the servants were about looking after things. It was impossible to sleep. The lightning was more vivid. There was a blinding flash of a greenish-white tinge mingled with the crash of falling timbers. Then before my startled gaze arose columns of red flames reflected against the sky. "Heaven help us!" I cried; "it is the left tower; it has been struck and is on fire!"

I hurried on my clothes and stepped into the corridor; the girls were there before me. Jeannette came up to me instantly with anxious face. "Oh, Doctor Thornton, what shall we do? Papa and Mamma and little Johnny are in the old left tower. It is on fire. I have knocked and knocked, but get no answer."

"Don't be alarmed," said I soothingly. "Jenkins, ring the alarm bell," I continued, turning to the butler who was standing near; "the rest follow me. We will force the entrance to the Captain's room."

Instantly, it seemed to me, the bell boomed out upon the now silent air, for the storm had died down as quickly as it arose; and as our little procession paused before the entrance to the old left tower, we could distinguish the sound of the fire engines already on their way from the village.

The door resisted all our efforts; there seemed to be a barrier against it which nothing could move. The flames were gaining headway. Still the same deathly silence within the rooms.

"Oh, will they never get here?" cried Talma, ringing her hands in terror. Jeannette said nothing, but her face was ashen. The servants were huddled together in a panic-stricken group. I can never tell you what a relief it was when we heard the first sound of the firemen's voices, saw their quick movements, and heard the ringing of the axes with which they cut away every obstacle to our entrance to the rooms. The neighbors who had just enjoyed the hospitality of the house were now gathered around offering all the assistance in their power. In less than fifteen minutes the fire was out, and the men began to bear the unconscious inmates from the ruins. They carried them to the pagoda so lately the scene of mirth and pleasure, and I took up my station there, ready to assume my professional duties. The Captain was nearest me; and as I stooped to make the necessary examination I reeled away from the ghastly sight which confronted me—*gentlemen, across the Captain's throat was a deep gash that severed the jugular vein!*

The Doctor paused, and the hand with which he refilled his glass trembled violently.

"What is it, Doctor?" cried the men, gathering about me.

"Take the women away; this is murder!"

"Murder!" cried Jeannette, as she fell against the side of the pagoda.

"Murder!" screamed Talma, staring at me as if unable to grasp my meaning.

I continued my examination of the bodies, and found that the same thing had happened to Mrs. Gordon and to little Johnny.

The police were notified; and when the sun rose over the dripping town he found them in charge of Gordon Hall, the servants standing in excited knots talking over the crime, the friends of the family confounded, and the two girls trying to comfort each other and realize the terrible misfortune that had overtaken them.

Nothing in the rooms of the left tower seemed to have been disturbed. The door of communication between the rooms of the husband and wife was open, as they had arranged it for the night. Little Johnny's crib was placed beside his mother's bed. In it he was found as though never awakened by the storm. It was quite evident that the assassin was no common ruffian. The chief gave strict orders for a watch to be kept on all strangers or suspicious characters who were seen in the neighborhood. He made inquiries among the servants, seeing each one separately, but there was nothing gained from them. No one had heard anything suspicious; all had been awakened by the storm. The chief was puzzled. Here was a triple crime for which no motive could be assigned.

"What do you think of it?" I asked him, as we stood together on the lawn.

"It is my opinion that the deed was committed by one of the higher classes, which makes the mystery more difficult to solve. I tell you, Doctor, there are mysteries that never come to light, and this, I think, is one of them."

While we were talking Jenkins, the butler, an old and trusted servant, came up to the chief and saluted respectfully. "Want to speak with me, Jenkins?" he asked. The man nodded, and they walked away together.

The story of the inquest was short, but appalling. It was shown that Talma had been allowed to go abroad to study because she and Mrs. Gordon did not get on well together. From the testimony of Jenkins it seemed that Talma and her father had quarreled bitterly about her lover, a young artist whom she had met at Rome, who was unknown to fame, and very poor. There had been terrible things said by each, and threats even had passed, all of which now rose up in judgment against the unhappy girl. The examination of the family solicitor revealed the fact that Captain Gordon intended to leave his daughters only a small annuity, the bulk of the fortune going to his son Jonathan, junior. This was a monstrous injustice, as everyone felt. In vain Talma protested her innocence. Someone must have done it. No one would be benefited so much by these deaths as she and her sister. Moreover, the will, together with other papers, was nowhere to be found. Not the slightest clue bearing upon the disturbing elements in this family, if any there were, was to be found. As the only surviving relatives, Jeannette and Talma became joint heirs to an immense fortune, which only for the bloody tragedy just enacted would, in all probability, have passed them by. Here was the motive. The case was very black against Talma. The foreman stood up.

The silence was intense: We "find that Captain Jonathan Gordon, Mary E. Gordon, and Jonathan Gordon, junior, all deceased, came to their deaths by means of a knife or other sharp instrument in the hands of Talma Gordon." The girl was like one stricken with death. The flowerlike mouth was drawn and pinched; the great sapphire-blue eyes were black with passionate anguish, terror, and despair. She was placed in jail to await her trial at the fall session of the criminal court. The excitement in the hitherto quiet town rose to fever heat. Many points in the evidence seemed incomplete to thinking men. The weapon could not be found, nor could it be divined what had become of it. No reason could be given for the murder except the quarrel between Talma and her father and the ill will which existed between the girl and her stepmother.

When the trial was called Jeannette sat beside Talma in the prisoner's dock; both were arrayed in deepest mourning. Talma was pale and careworn, but seemed uplifted, spiritualized, as it were. Upon Jeannette the full realization of her sister's peril seemed to weigh heavily. She had changed much too: hollow cheeks, tottering steps, eyes blazing with fever, all suggestive of rapid and premature decay. From far-off Italy Edward Turner, growing famous in the art world, came to stand beside his girl-love in this hour of anguish.

The trial was a memorable one. No additional evidence had been collected to strengthen the prosecution; when the attorney-general rose to open the case against Talma he knew, as everyone else did, that he could not convict solely on the evidence adduced. What was given did not always bear upon the case, and brought out strange stories of Captain Jonathan's methods. Tales were told of sailors who had sworn to take his life, in revenge for injuries inflicted upon them by his hand. One or two clues were followed, but without avail. The judge summed up the evidence impartially, giving the prisoner the benefit of the doubt. The points in hand furnished valuable collateral evidence, but were not direct proof. Although the moral presumption was against the prisoner, legal evidence was lacking to actually convict. The jury found the prisoner "Not Guilty," owing to the fact that the evidence was entirely circumstantial. The verdict was received in painful silence; then a murmur of discontent ran through the great crowd.

"She must have done it," said one; "who else has been benefited by the horrible deed?"

"A poor woman would not have fared so well at the hands of the jury, nor a homely one either, for that matter," said another.

The great Gordon trial was ended; innocent or guilty, Talma Gordon could not be tried again. She was free; but her liberty, with blasted prospects and fair fame gone forever, was valueless to her. She seemed to have but one object in her mind: to find the murderer or murderers of her parents and half brother. By her direction the shrewdest of detectives were employed and money flowed like water, but to no purpose; the Gordon tragedy remained a mystery. I had consented to act as one of the trustees of the immense Gordon estates and business interests, and by my advice the Misses Gordon went abroad. A year later I received a letter from Edward Turner, saying that Jeannette Gordon had died suddenly at Rome, and that Talma, after refusing all his entreaties for an early marriage, had disappeared, leaving no clue as to her whereabouts. I could give the poor fellow no comfort, although I had been duly notified of the death of Jeannette by Talma, in a letter telling me where to forward her remittances, and at the same time requesting me to keep her present residence secret, especially from Edward.

I had established a sanitarium for the cure of chronic diseases at Gordonville, and absorbed in the cares of my profession I gave little thought to the Gordons. I seemed fated to be involved in mysteries.

A man claiming to be an Englishman, and fresh from the California gold fields, engaged board and professional service at my retreat. I found him suffering in the grasp of the tubercle-fiend — the last stages. He called himself Simon Cameron. Seldom have I seen so fascinating and wicked a face. The lines of the mouth were cruel, the eyes cold and sharp, the smile mocking and evil. He had money in plenty but seemed to have no friends, for he had received no letters and had had no visitors in the time he had been with us. He was an enigma to me; and his nationality puzzled me, for of course I did not believe his story of being English. The peaceful influence of the house seemed to soothe him in a measure, and make his last steps to the mysterious valley as easy as possible. For a time he improved, and would sit or walk about the grounds and sing sweet songs for the pleasure of the other inmates. Strange to say, his malady only affected his voice at times. He sang quaint songs in a silvery tenor of great purity and sweetness that was delicious to the listening ear:

"A wet sheet and a flowing sea,
   A wind that follows fast,
And fills the white and rustling sail
   And bends the gallant mast;
And bends the gallant mast, my boys;
   While like the eagle free,
Away the good ship flies, and leaves
   Old England on the lea."

There are few singers on the lyric stage who could surpass Simon Cameron.

One night, a few weeks after Cameron's arrival, I sat in my office making up my accounts when the door opened and closed; I glanced up, expecting to see a servant. A lady advanced toward me. She threw back her veil, and then I saw that Talma Gordon, or her ghost, stood before me. After the first excitement of our meeting was over, she told me she had come direct from Paris, to place herself in my care. I had studied her attentively during the first moments of our meeting, and I felt that she was right; unless something unforeseen happened to arouse her from the stupor into which she seemed to have fallen, the last Gordon was doomed to an early death. The next day I told her I had cabled Edward Turner to come to her.

"It will do no good; I cannot marry him," was her only comment.

"Have you no feeling of pity for that faithful fellow?" I asked her sternly, provoked by her seeming indifference. I shall never forget the varied emotions depicted on her speaking face. Fully revealed to my gaze was the sight of a human soul tortured beyond the point of endurance; suffering all things, enduring all things, in the silent agony of despair.

In a few days Edward arrived, and Talma consented to see him and explain her refusal to keep her promise to him. "You must be present, Doctor; it is due your long, tried friendship to know that I have not been fickle, but have acted from the best and strongest motives."

I shall never forget that day. It was directly after lunch that we met in the library. I was greatly excited, expecting I knew not what. Edward was agitated, too. Talma was the only calm one. She handed me what seemed to be a letter, with the request that I would read it. Even now I think I can repeat every word of the document, so indelibly are the words engraved upon my mind:

> MY DARLING SISTER TALMA: When you read these lines I shall be no more, for I shall not live to see your life blasted by the same knowledge that has blighted mine.
>
> One evening, about a year before your expected return from Rome, I climbed into a hammock in one corner of the veranda outside the breakfast-room windows, intending to spend the twilight hours in lazy comfort, for it was very hot, enervating August weather. I fell asleep. I was awakened by voices. Because of the heat the rooms had been left in semidarkness. As I lay there, lazily enjoying the beauty of the perfect summer night, my wandering thoughts were arrested by words spoken by our father to Mrs. Gordon, for they were the occupants of the breakfast room.
>
> "Never fear, Mary; Johnny shall have it all — money, houses, land, and business."
>
> "But if you do go first, Jonathan, what will happen if the girls contest the will? People will think that they ought to have the money as it appears to be theirs by law. I never could survive the terrible disgrace of the story."
>
> "Don't borrow trouble; all you would need to do would be to show them papers I have drawn up, and they would be glad to take their annuity and say nothing. After all, I do not think it is so bad. Jeannette can teach; Talma can paint; six hundred dollars a year is quite enough for them."
>
> I had been somewhat mystified by the conversation until now. This last remark solved the riddle. What could he mean? Teach, paint, six hundred a year! With my usual impetuosity I sprang from my resting place, and in a moment stood in the room confronting my father, and asking what he meant. I could see plainly that both were disconcerted by my unexpected appearance.
>
> "Ah, wretched girl! you have been listening. But what could I expect of your mother's daughter?"
>
> At these words I felt the indignant blood rush to my head in a torrent. So it had been all my life. Before you could remember, Talma, I had felt my little heart swell

with anger at the disparaging hints and slurs concerning our mother. Now was my time. I determined that tonight I would know why she was looked upon as an outcast, and her children subjected to every humiliation. So I replied to my father in bitter anger:

"I was not listening; I fell asleep in the hammock. What do you mean by a paltry six hundred a year each to Talma and to me? 'My mother's daughter' demands an explanation from you, sir, of the meaning of the monstrous injustice that you have always practiced toward my sister and me."

"Speak more respectfully to your father, Jeannette," broke in Mrs. Gordon.

"How is it, madam, that you look for respect from one whom you have delighted to torment ever since you came into this most unhappy family?"

"Hush, both of you," said Captain Gordon, who seemed to have recovered from the dismay into which my sudden appearance and passionate words had plunged him. "I think I may as well tell you as to wait. Since you know so much, you may as well know the whole miserable story." He motioned me to a seat. I could see that he was deeply agitated. I seated myself in a chair he pointed out, in wonder and expectation — expectation of I knew not what. I trembled. This was a supreme moment in my life; I felt it. The air was heavy with the intense stillness that had settled over us as the common sounds of day gave place to the early quiet of the rural evening. I could see Mrs. Gordon's face as she sat within the radius of the lighted hallway. There was a smile of triumph upon it. I clinched my hands and bit my lips until the blood came, in the effort to keep from screaming. What was I about to hear? At last he spoke:

"I was disappointed at your birth, and also at the birth of Talma. I wanted a male heir. When I knew that I should again be a father I was torn by hope and fear, but I comforted myself with the thought that luck would be with me in the birth of the third child. When the doctor brought me word that a son was born to the house of Gordon, I was wild with delight, and did not notice his disturbed countenance. In the midst of my joy he said to me:

"'Captain Gordon, there is something strange about this birth. I want you to see this child.'

"Quelling my exultation I followed him to the nursery, and there, lying in the cradle, I saw a child dark as a mulatto, with the characteristic features of the Negro! I was stunned. Gradually it dawned upon me that there was something radically wrong. I turned to the doctor for an explanation.

"'There is but one explanation, Captain Gordon; there is Negro blood in this child.'

"'There is no Negro blood in my veins,' I said proudly. Then I paused — *the mother!* — I glanced at the doctor. He was watching me intently. The same thought was in his mind. I must have lived a thousand years in that cursed five seconds that I stood there confronting the physician and trying to think. 'Come,' said I to him, 'let us end this suspense.' Without thinking of consequences, I hurried away to your mother and accused her of infidelity to her marriage vows. I raved like a madman. Your mother fell into convulsions; her life was despaired of. I sent for Mr. and Mrs. Franklin, and then I learned the truth. They were childless. One year while on a Southern tour, they befriended an octoroon[5] girl who had been abandoned by her white lover. Her child was a beautiful girl baby. They, being Northern born, thought

[5]*Person who is one-eighth black.*

> little of caste distinction because the child showed no trace of Negro blood. They determined to adopt it. They went abroad, secretly sending back word to their friends at a proper time of the birth of a little daughter. No one doubted the truth of the statement. They made Isabel their heiress, and all went well until the birth of your brother. Your mother and the unfortunate babe died. This is the story which, if known, would bring dire disgrace upon the Gordon family.
>
> "To appease my righteous wrath, Mr. Franklin left a codicil to his will by which all the property is left at my disposal save a small annuity to you and your sister."
>
> I sat there after he had finished the story, stunned by what I had heard. I understood, now, Mrs. Gordon's half contemptuous toleration and lack of consideration for us both. As I rose from my seat to leave the room I said to Captain Gordon:
>
> "Still, in spite of it all, sir, I am a Gordon, legally born. I will not tamely give up my birthright."
>
> I left that room a broken-hearted girl, filled with a desire for revenge upon this man, my father, who by his manner disowned us without a regret. Not once in that remarkable interview did he speak of our mother as his wife; he quietly repudiated her and us with all the cold cruelty of relentless caste prejudice. I heard the treatment of your lover's proposal; I knew why Captain Gordon's consent to your marriage was withheld.
>
> The night of the reception and dance was the chance for which I had waited, planned, and watched. I crept from my window into the ivy-vines, and so down, down, until I stood upon the windowsill of Captain Gordon's room in the old left tower. How did I do it, you ask? I do not know. The house was silent after the revel; the darkness of the gathering storm favored me, too. The lawyer was there that day. The will was signed and put safely away among my father's papers. I was determined to have the will and the other documents bearing upon the case, and I would have revenge, too, for the cruelties we had suffered. With the old East Indian dagger firmly grasped I entered the room and found—that my revenge had been forestalled! The horror of the discovery I made that night restored me to reason and a realization of the crime I meditated. Scarce knowing what I did, I sought and found the papers, and crept back to my room as I had come. Do you wonder that my disease is past medical aid?

I looked at Edward as I finished. He sat, his face covered with his hands. Finally he looked up with a glance of haggard despair: "God! Doctor, but this is too much. I could stand the stigma of murder, but add to that the pollution of Negro blood! No man is brave enough to face such a situation."

"It is as I thought it would be," said Talma sadly, while the tears poured over her white face. "I do not blame you, Edward."

He rose from his chair, wrung my hand in a convulsive clasp, turned to Talma and bowed profoundly, with his eyes fixed upon the floor, hesitated, turned, paused, bowed again, and abruptly left the room. So those two who had been lovers parted. I turned to Talma, expecting her to give way. She smiled a pitiful smile, and said: "You see, Doctor, I knew best."

From that on she failed rapidly. I was restless. If only I could rouse her to an interest in life, she might live to old age. So rich, so young, so beautiful, so talented, so pure; I grew savage thinking of the injustice of the world. I had not reckoned on the power that never sleeps. Something was about to happen.

On visiting Cameron next morning I found him approaching the end. He had been sinking for a week very rapidly. As I sat by the bedside holding his emaciated hand, he fixed his bright, wicked eyes on me, and asked: "How long have I got to live?"

"Candidly, but a few hours."

"Thank you; well, I want death; I am not afraid to die. Doctor, Cameron is not my name."

"I never supposed it was."

"No? You are sharper than I thought. I heard all your talk yesterday with Talma Gordon. Curse the whole race!"

He clasped his bony fingers around my arm and gasped: "*I murdered the Gordons!*"

Had I the pen of a Dumas[6] I could not paint Cameron as he told his story. It is a question with me whether this wheeling planet, home of the suffering, doubting, dying, may not hold worse agonies on its smiling surface than those of the conventional hell. I sent for Talma and a lawyer. We gave him stimulants, and then with broken intervals of coughing and prostration we got the story of the Gordon murder. I give it to you in a few words:

"I am an East Indian, but my name does not matter, Cameron is as good as any. There is many a soul crying in heaven and hell for vengeance on Jonathan Gordon. Gold was his idol; and many a good man walked the plank, and many a gallant ship was stripped of her treasure, to satisfy his lust for gold. His blackest crime was the murder of my father, who was his friend, and had sailed with him for many a year as mate. One night these two went ashore together to bury their treasure. My father never returned from that expedition. His body was afterward found with a bullet through the heart on the shore where the vessel stopped that night. It was the custom then among pirates for the captain to kill the men who helped bury their treasure. Captain Gordon was no better than a pirate. An East Indian never forgets, and I swore by my mother's deathbed to hunt Captain Gordon down until I had avenged my father's murder. I had the plans of the Gordon estate, and fixed on the night of the reception in honor of Talma as the time for my vengeance. There is a secret entrance from the shore to the chambers where Captain Gordon slept; no one knew of it save the Captain and trusted members of his crew. My mother gave me the plans, and entrance and escape were easy."

So the great mystery was solved. In a few hours Cameron was no more. We placed the confession in the hands of the police, and there the matter ended.

[6]*Nineteenth-century French writer of African descent.*

"But what became of Talma Gordon?" questioned the president. "Did she die?"

"Gentlemen," said the Doctor, rising to his feet and sweeping the faces of the company with his eagle gaze, "gentlemen, if you will follow me to the drawing room, I shall have much pleasure in introducing you to my wife — née Talma Gordon."

Chester Himes (1909–1984)

During his early years, Chester Bomar Himes's family moved frequently before settling in Cleveland, Ohio. After failing to complete his first year at Ohio State University, Himes was convicted of armed robbery in 1928 and served seven and a half years in one of the country's toughest prisons, surviving not only the pervasive violence of the "stir" but also a fire that claimed over three hundred of his fellow inmates in 1930. While in prison, he read *Black Mask* and taught himself the craft of writing, composing fiction on a typewriter in his jail cell and publishing stories, initially in black newspapers and magazines. His breakthrough came in 1934 when he sold the first of several stories to *Esquire* magazine. Himes credited his status as a published author with protecting him "against both the convicts and the screws. The black convicts had both an instinctive respect for and fear of a person who could sit down at a typewriter and write, and whose name appeared in newspapers and magazines outside. The screws would never really kill a convict who was a public figure, or else convicts like Malcolm X and Eldridge Cleaver would never have gotten out of prison alive."

Himes published five novels, beginning with *If He Hollers Let Him Go*, between 1945 and 1955, and in the 1950s, Himes left the United States for France. Eight novels featuring the black Harlem police detectives Grave Digger Jones and Coffin Ed Johnson appeared between 1957 and 1969, the first of which was *For Love of Imabelle*. During the 1970s, Himes published two autobiographical volumes, *The Quality of Hurt* and *My Life of Absurdity*. Featuring two black policemen, "He Knew," his first detective story, anticipates not only the Coffin Ed and Grave Digger novels but also more recent African American detection about black males by writers such as Gar Anthony Haywood, Walter Mosley, and Gary Phillips. Unaccountably left out of Himes's *Collected Stories*, the story is reprinted here for the first time.

He Knew
by Chester Himes

(1933)

Detectives John Jones and Henry Walls tramped their dreary beat, heads pulled down into the upturned collars of their overcoats like the heads of startled turtles, hats slanted forward against the cold December drizzle. Dismal warehouses and squalid tenements flanked the narrow, cobblestone street. [Mi]sty streams of water swirled down the incline of the street toward the levee. The river made sluggish sounds against the wharves. Here and there the semi gloom was relieved by a sputtering arc lamp. It was the zero hour, quiet with the sinister quietness of a prison yard on a mid-winter night. The regular squish-squish of the detectives' thick-soled shoes on the wet pavement was the only salient sound in the sinister quietness.

Walls bent his tall stoop-shouldered frame into the rain and twisted his splotched, yellow, mulish features into a grimace of extreme distaste. "A hellava night to be chasing burglars," he grumbled.

Jones grunted without looking about. If he minded the nasty weather, his harsh black face gave no sign of it. He trudged steadily ahead, his short, solid body swinging slightly with his unvarying stride. His hard, black eyes were fixed straight ahead.

"I don't know what the devil the 'Cap' was thinking about, anyway," Walls complained, talking half to himself as if to drive away the eerie ghosts which seemed to lurk in the edges of the shadows about them. "If these muggs what's been robbing these dumps had a job in mind, they could spot us a mile away and lay off. Now, if I had half the sense of an ordinary truck horse I'd duck into some warm speaky and sneeze for the rest of the night."

Jones didn't answer. He was thinking of the precinct captain's orders himself. There had been a number of warehouse robberies down in the river front district of late and the captain had called the bureau and asked for a couple of detectives to patrol the district at nights.

The captain had told them when he gave them their orders: "This business has gone too far — murder. Old Smith, the night watchman for Greenbaum Importers was the second to be murdered during the past two months. I'm putting you two men on this job because it's a Negro neighborhood and I believe that it's Negroes who are pulling these jobs. You fellows are plodders and it's plodders what we need. Just stick around the river front. Sooner or later these young wiseacres are going to come back and pull some more jobs. They're not smart; if they were they'd shoot down these old night guards in cold blood. You'll get 'em if you stick there. And when you get 'em, bring 'em in." The captain's mouth had been a grim line when he had said this.

And Jones' mouth was a grim line now as he thought about it. God, the pity of this new crop of youths who were turning to crime, he reflected. Mere boys whose motto seemed to "money or the morgue." And what did they do with the money? Bought shiny tin automobiles to ride about in, and spent a lot of sucker money on painted come-on molls in foul gyp joints, or tried to beat down the house percentage in some trim gambling joint. God, the pity of it, he repeated in his mind.

Walls pulled a large, gold-filled watch from his vest pocket and paused for a moment in the circle of radiance from an overhead arc light to see what time it was.

"Three-twenty-two," he muttered. "Two hours and 38 more minutes of this slush in this ghost-ridden rat hole and then me for a good long swig of mule and a dry bed." He accelerated his pace to catch up with Jones, who had walked ahead.

"John, you're a lucky man," he said abruptly. "You got a wife and some kids and a home to go to after a nasty night's work like this. Now me, I just got a room in a stuffy boarding house where —"

"Sure, come around to dinner sometime, Henry," Jones broke in. His voice was hoarse as the river boat fog-horns and startlingly unemotional.

"Nope, you got me wrong, John," Wall protested. "I wasn't fishing for an invitation. I was just thinking about those youngsters of yours that you were telling me about the other day, and that fine wife of yours. You know, John, a man doesn't realize how much he misses a wife and some tots until he gets to my age. I was 52 yesterday and there wasn't a soul in the whole world who give a damn whether I was living or dead. Now take my kind of life for instance...."

But Jones wasn't listening. He was thinking of his wife and those youngsters of his and he was wondering if he was so lucky as Walls seemed to think he was. For the tough dick that he was, his eyes had become singularly wistful when he thought of his family.

There was Rose, she was 15 now and sharp as a needle, but she seemed a little too wise for a girl of her age. And there were Johnny Jr. and Bobby, his 19-year-old twins. What wouldn't he do for those youngsters, but still they weren't satisfied. He tried to give them everything they needed and some spending money besides, but they wanted more. They had to have expensive clothes and money and more money. He couldn't see what they did with all the money they said they had to have, unless they were gambling, and he hated to think that a son of his was gambling.

His eyes clouded with worry as he thought of them. He had noticed a certain furtiveness in their actions of late; and the other day when Johnny dropped a roll of bills from his pocket and he had asked him where he got so much money, Johnny had become ugly and said something about having a dad who wouldn't give him any money and that he had to get it the best way he could.

And he didn't like that gang of young hoodlums his sons were running around with, either. There wasn't a single thing about them which he could just put his finger on and say he didn't like; they said they attended the East high school where his boys were seniors this year, and they all belonged to the same little Athletic club, so they said; but he just didn't like the way they were shaped up, the way they talked in slangy whispers out of the corners of their mouths. He'd seen so many crooks in the making during his years on the force that....

His thoughts were interrupted by the staccato sound of gun shots that ripped the silence of the night. He and Walls broke into a run, cut obliquely across the glistening cobblestone street. Their shoe soles slipped on the wet surface of the cobblestones and once Jones slipped to his knees.

A cry for help came from the direction of the silk warehouse, down near the end of the block.

They leaped to the sidewalk and sprinted in the direction of the warehouse, hugging the dark shadows next to the walls to keep from being observed. At the entrance to the warehouse they separated, Jones slipping in through the unlocked front door while Walls went around to the alley entrance at the side.

Their approach had been scarcely audible but the sounds of scuffling bodies from within had ceased at their appearance. Jones felt his way cautiously through the opaque darkness of the large receiving room in front. He heard Walls call to him from behind a partition at the rear of the front room. And suddenly, startlingly, the stygian gloom of the interior was lit up with a cluster of bright, orange flashes followed by the sharp barks of small automatics.

There was something unnerving about the sudden barrage of shots. Jones felt that he would never get his gun from his holster, and when he did, he fired several times in the direction from which the flashes had come with unreasoning panic.

Walls bellowed: "Hold 'em, John, I'm coming!"

A voice from the darkness said, "Jeeze, that's —." But the rest of the sentence was drowned by the roar of Walls' gun as he began firing at random from the rear of the room.

Jones ducked behind a convenient crate and tried to pierce the darkness with his gaze. He could hear his breath whistling through his nostrils and the thumping of his heart in the silence which followed the shooting, then he heard Walls stumble against something in the darkness.

Another cluster of flashes punctured the gloom, and then a voice was heard saying: "Hold it, you damn fool! That might be —"

Jones and Walls fired simultaneously in the direction from which the flashes had come.

Some one screamed. A voice said: "Oh, God!" very softly. An instant later there was a very slight scraping sound followed by a soft thud such as a body might make slipping to the floor.

Then a very weak voice cried: "Stop, for God's sake stop! I'm riddled!" There was a bubbly sound about the voice as if the speaker's mouth was full of food — or blood.

A light, what he'd give for a light, Jones thought. He experienced a sudden distaste for his job — shooting men down in the darkness, like rats, rats! For an instant he felt that he was going crazy. A cold, slimy film of sweat had collected on his forehead. A wound in his side which he didn't know that he had was beginning to pain him. Was there something familiar about that voice there in the darkness? His thoughts whirled chaotically.

Walls snapped on his pocket flash and found the electric switch. He flooded the room with light.

Jones struggled from his crouching position. He glanced at the blue clad body of a middle-aged man sprawled on the floor and recognized it as that of the murdered watchman. He felt a sudden murderous hate for the burglars who had murdered that man.

Walls stood immobile, as one in a daze. He wasn't looking at the watchman, he was looking at the bodies of the dead burglars. "Gosh, nothing but boys," he croaked. Then he noticed that Jones was shot.

He started toward Jones but Jones waved him away. "Get headquarters and tell them to send an ambulance right away," Jones directed.

The sound of running feet came from outside and the figure of a policeman showed in the lighted doorway. Walls brushed past the policeman as he hurried out to a telephone. "It's all over now," Walls called back over his shoulder.

Jones looked about at the policeman and nodded. Then he looked at the bodies of the three flashily dressed youths lying face downward beside the body of the watchman. He gave a violent start. He stared at the bodies with a horrified fascination. He knelt down beside one of the bodies and turned its smooth, brown face up to the light.

For a long moment Jones didn't move, he knelt there holding the body of the youth in his arms. His face turned a sickly gray, his eyes were dull enamel tinged with bitter agony.

The policeman moved over to him and looked down at the body of the youth. "Seems like an intelligent young lad," he remarked. And then as if struck by a sudden thought he said: "Gosh, I wonder how it would feel to have a son like that."

Jones wanted to tell him how it felt. He wanted to tell the whole world how it felt, he wanted to cry it aloud. He would always know, forever and ever. He would never forget. He had two of his own, Johnny Junior and Bobby, lying there on the floor — dead.

Ralph Ellison (1914–1994)

Although his fame rests primarily on the remarkable *Invisible Man*, winner of the National Book Award in 1953 and widely regarded as one of the twentieth century's greatest novels, Ralph Waldo Ellison was an accomplished essayist and short story writer. The grandson of a slave, he was named after Ralph Waldo Emerson and grew up in Oklahoma. Provided with a scholarship to attend Tuskegee Institute in 1933, Ellison studied music and sculpture and experienced the racial intolerance of the Jim Crow South at the Alabama school. While there he also discovered T. S. Eliot's *The Waste Land* and began developing ideas about the links between literature and music, especially jazz. In 1936 he left Tuskegee for New York City, living initially, like the unnamed protagonist of his famous novel, at the Harlem YMCA. He soon met Langston Hughes and Arna Bontemps and through them Richard Wright, who encouraged him to become a writer.

Between 1937 and 1944, Ellison published more than fifty-five articles and reviews and began to write short fiction. He gathered folk materials for the Federal Writers Project from 1938 to 1942 and served in the Merchant Marine from 1943 to 1945. Ellison began work on the book that would become *Invisible Man* in 1945, originally conceiving of it as a war novel. While his wife Fanny went to work, Ellison undertook what he called his "desperate gamble" to be a novelist, writing most of the book in Harlem "where it drew much of its substance from the voices, idioms, folklore, traditions, and political concerns of those whose racial and cultural concerns I share." Ellison published two influential collections of nonfiction, *Shadow and Act* in 1964 and *Going into the Territory* in 1986. Although he labored long and hard on a second novel, he was never able to complete it.

In 1999, five years after the writer's death, Ellison's literary executor John Callahan published *Juneteenth* from the extant fragments. Three years earlier Callahan edited a collection of Ellison's short fiction entitled *Flying Home and Other Stories*. Ellison's brief but powerful "The Birthmark," bearing the same title as Nathaniel Hawthorne's tale published a century earlier, was not included in that book. Arnold Rampersad speculates that the story was likely inspired by the harrowing experiences of James McMillen, whom Ellison met at the National Negro Congress in Washington, D.C. It is one of several texts by or about African Americans (including *The Confessions of Nat Turner,* Frances Harper's *Iola Leroy*, Sutton Griggs's *Unfettered*, Pauline Hopkins's *Of One Blood*, and Toni Morrison's *Sula*) in which birthmarks figure prominently. "The Birthmark" is reprinted here for the first time.

The Birthmark
by Ralph Ellison

(1940)

The summer heat struck them in a wave as they stepped from the car into the highway. Matt and Clara stood quietly, watching the highway patrolman pull his huge body from beneath the steering wheel. Matt turned and saw the other white man, the coroner, looking out across the green stretch of field fringed with pine trees, where two large birds circled slowly, black shapes against the still, blue air.

"Them damned buzzards," the white man said.

"Well, let's git going," the patrolman said.

Clara sighed, her broken face torn with anguish. "Oh God," she said softly. The white man looked on, silently.

When the white men turned to go, Matt tried to pull her aside. But she stood firm. The patrolman looked impatient. Matt gripped her arm. She shook her head.

"Then try to be brave, Clara," he whispered.

They stared behind the men, across the heat-simmering concrete to the bushes which lined the highway. They had walked a few steps when the small white man turned and faced them.

"You better send your woman back to the car," he said. "It ain't going to be so nice."

"Yes suh," Matt said.

He looked at Clara; maybe now she would go back, this was nothing for a woman to see.

"Yeah Clara, you better go on back. If it's Willie I'll tell you," he said.

He watched her face set resolutely as she wiped sweat from her forehead. Sun gleamed on her straightened hair. Matt knew she would refuse before she spoke.

"I got to know for myself, Matt," she said, "I'll be all right."

The white men exchanged glances as Matt tried gently to push her away. She stood her ground.

"Ain't no use trying to make me go, Matt. I got to know, I got to know for myself."

Matt swallowed hard and dropped his arm from her shoulders. It was no use, nothing could make Clara leave.

"Well let's git going," the coroner said. "I got to go back to town."

The patrolman hitched his brass-studded gun belt and grunted as he led the way. They went down an embankment into the bushes. As he went through, Matt caught a glimpse of the body. Drawing closer, he saw it was covered with newspapers. It lay in a clearing beneath the trees, upon the pine needle covered ground. "Lord, don't let it be Willie, Lord," Matt thought. He helped Clara along, his arm firmly around her shoulders. When they reached the body, the white men hesitated, as though they expected him to say something. He looked at the newspaper-covered mound and was seized with a feeling like fear. The very thought that it might be Willie under those colored comic sheets was almost more than he could bear. He looked at Clara standing tense beside him and longed to carry her back to the car and go home and wait for Willie to come in laughing and teasing them for thinking it could have been him. How could Willie let a *car* hit him?

Someone stirred; the white men were waiting. He looked at the body, seeing where blood had oozed from beneath the papers and was drying upon the ground. An insect droned. The pungent odor of pine hung in the heat.

Suddenly he felt Clara sag against him. For a moment he thought she was about to go faint. "Oh God," she whispered.

"You better go back, Clara. Go on back to the car."

"Naw, Matt. Please, I'm all right."

"But maybe it's a mistake...."

"Matt, I got to see," she said.

The coroner stood with is hands in pockets, waiting. The patrolman traced a line near the body with the toe of his boot, making a small furrow in the earth. Matt turned and looked pleadingly at Clara. He begged her with his eyes to leave, to go back to the car. He did not want these white folks to see her in sorrow. Then without a word the patrolman bent and swept the newspapers from the body, leaving only its middle covered. Matt closed his eyes as the man drew erect. It seemed hours before he could force himself to look. The body was hunched on one side, lying there upon straw-colored pine needles, the long legs bare. He saw the jaw hanging limply against the shoulder, the mouth gaping. Goddam, was this Willie?

A blood-creased cut started under the ear and disappeared beneath the chin.

Matt felt as though he would empty himself. He struggled, tying to make his mind reject the impressions it insisted upon recording. It can't be Willie, he told himself. The flesh was hacked and pounded as though it had been beaten with hammers. Worse than a stuck hog, he thought. He wanted to turn away, but knew he had to look. He *had* to.

Suddenly he became aware of Clara....

"That him?" a voice said.

He looked up. It was the coroner. Yes, that was it, he thought. Is it Willie? He was silent, looking. Where is the birthmark—but it ain't him, it *cain't* be him, he thought. Lord! The mark had been just below Willie's navel. Funny he'd remember that now, he hadn't seen it for years, not since Willie had been a kid. But nothing to do but look. He stepped in front of Clara to keep her from seeing as he steeled himself and bent to lift the last sheet of paper. Suddenly there was a swift movement. Clara screamed. A blow landed on his shoulder. He stumbled backward and pulled quickly erect, his face blank with surprise. Pain knifed into his collar bone. He saw the patrolman get set to strike again. He stepped backward and threw up his arm. This man gone crazy?

"What you do that to him for, man?" Clara asked.

Matt groped for her to keep her quiet as he studied the white man's face.

"We didn't tell you to do that, nigger," the man said.

"Aw leave him alone, Turp. It don't make no difference," the coroner said. "Let him look."

Matt was dazed. He did not know what to do next and the patrolman's fingers played near his gun butt.

"I was looking for his birthmark, suh," he said finally.

"It don't make no difference, Turp," the coroner said. "Let the boy look."

"Okay, but I don't like it," the patrolman said. Matt looked at the coroner and saw the white man bow his head.

"It all right suh?"

"Sure, go on. You can look."

"Thank you suh."

When Matt lowered his eyes he noticed that the ribs had been caved in. The flesh was bruised and torn. It was just below his navel, he thought. Then he gave a start: where it should have been was only a bloody mound of torn flesh and hair. Matt went weak. He felt as though he had been castrated himself. He thought he would fall when Clara stepped up beside him. Swiftly, he tried to push her back thinking to keep her from seeing. Then Clara was screaming.

"Leave me go, leave me go!"

He felt himself reel as she pushed against him. Her voice shrilled in his ears. He watched her face, fascinated.

"I want to see," she screamed. "I want to see so I'll remember, Matt. These here white folks told us Willie was hit by a car, but didn't no car do that to him. They lynched Willie, Matt. They done lynched our brother...[1]

Matt was in a panic. He grabbed at Clara to clamp his hand over her mouth. He would have to get her away, quick.

"Naw, Matt. I know what I'm saying. I ain't gonna be the same after this, Matt, and I want to see it all so's I'll never forget why..."

"Shut up, Clara, hush..."

"They asked us last month to sign a piece of paper saying we wanted things like

[1]*Lynching is the practice whereby a mob takes the law into its own hands, maiming or killing a person accused of wrongdoing. African Americans in particular suffered under lynch law, especially in the South in the late nineteenth and early twentieth centuries. In addition to being hanged, it was not uncommon for the victim to be decapitated, mutilated, castrated, and/or burned beyond recognition.*

this to stop and you was afraid. Now look at my brother, he's lying there looking like something ain't even human. And these white folks talking 'bout a car hit him. He was lynched. Lynched! I'm gonna tell everybody, HE WAS LYNCHED!"

Matt felt a tremor shake her body and she swayed against him. As he tried to support her, he felt himself being snatched roughly around. The patrolman's red face was six inches from his own, glaring.

"Nigger, we told you that boy was hit by a car, understand?"

"But mister, don't no car do nothing like that—"

Matt tried to dodge as he saw the gun barrel flash in the sun. The blow glanced off the side of his skull, leaving a trail of pain. He tried to see the coroner but the colors stabbed his eyes. He sank to his knees.

"*Goddammit, I said a car hit him!*" the white man snapped. *"We don't have no lynching in this state no more!"*

"You lynched him, you know you lynched him," Clara shrilled.

"Shut up you black bitch!"

"You lynched him, yes you lynched him!"

He heard Clara's screams and tried to rise and the white man was cursing and someone was pulling his arm.

"Git up from there, nigger, and shut this bitch up!"

He stumbled to his feet, his head slowly clearing.

"You did it, you know you did it, lynched my baby brother. And now you trying to kill Matt. Aaaw Lord..."

Clara's voice died away to a moan as Matt steadied himself. He pulled her head against his shoulder, muffling her voice as he watched the white men. The coroner looked uncomfortable.

"He's telling you right, boy," the coroner said, "he was hit by a car. Feller saw him laying longside the road and called us."

"And you better remember that, nigger," the patrolman said. "And your sister better remember that, too. 'Cause a car might hit *you*. Understand what I mean?

Matt was silent, he did not understand. The whole side of his head ached. *If he only didn't have that gun....*

"Nigger, I said, do you understand?"

"I understand, suh," he said.

"Now git on back to town and send someone after the body."

"Yes suh."

Matt pushed Clara to go, feeling hot breath against the hand he held over her mouth. "Come on, Clara."

"Just remember that a car hit 'im, and you'll be all right," the patrolman said. "We don't allow no lynching round here no more."

Matt felt Clara's fingers digging into his arm as his eyes flashed swiftly over the face of the towering patrolman, over the badge against his blue shirt, the fingers crooked in the belt above the gun butt. He swallowed hard and pulled Clara tightly to him, catching sight of Willie between the white men's legs.

"I'll remember," he said bitterly, "he was hit by a car."

Suggested Reading

On Detection

Barzun, Jacques. *A Catalogue of Crime: Being a Reader's Guide to the Literature of Mystery, Detection, and Related Genres*. 2d ed. New York: Harper, 1989.

Cawelti, John G. *Adventure, Mystery, and Romance: Formula Stories as Art and Popular Culture*. Chicago: University of Chicago Press, 1976.

Eco, Umberto, and Thomas A. Sebeok, ed. *The Sign of Three: Dupin, Holmes, Pierce*. Bloomington: Indiana University Press, 1983.

Gosselin, Adrienne Johnson. *Multicultural Detective Fiction: Murder from the "Other" Side*. New York: Garland, 1999.

Haycraft, Howard. *Murder for Pleasure: The Life and Times of the Detective Story*. New York: Biblo, 1968.

Horsley, Lee. *The Noir Thriller*. 2d ed. New York: Palgrave, 2009.

Horsley, Lee, and Charles J. Rzepka, ed. *A Companion to Crime Fiction*. New York: Wiley, 2010.

Irwin, John T. *The Mystery to a Solution: Poe, Borges, and the Analytic Detective Story*. Baltimore: Johns Hopkins University Press, 1994.

Klein, Kathleen Gregory. *The Woman Detective: Gender and Genre*. 2d ed. Urbana: University of Illinois Press, 1995.

Nickerson, Catherine R. *Web of Iniquity: Early Detective Fiction by American Women*. Durham, NC: Duke University Press, 1998.

Nolan, William. *The Black Mask Boys: Masters in the Hard-Boiled School of Detective Fiction*. New York: Morrow, 1985.

Rzepka, Charles J. *Detective Fiction*. Malden, MA: Polity, 2005.

Soitos, Stephen F. *The Blues Detective: A Study of African American Detective Fiction*. Amherst: University of Massachusetts Press, 1996.

Symons, Julian. *Bloody Murder: From the Detective Story to the Crime Novel*. 3d ed. New York: Mysterious, 1993.

Winks, Robin, ed. *Detective Fiction: A Collection of Critical Essays*. Rev. ed. Woodstock, VT: Countryman, 1988.

On Poe

Ackroyd, Peter. *Poe: A Life Cut Short*. New York: Doubleday, 2009.

Armstrong, Liahna. "The Shadow's Shadow: The Motif of the Double in Edgar Allan Poe's 'The Purloined Letter.'" *The Selected Writings of Edgar Allan Poe*. Ed. G.R. Thompson. New York: Norton, 2004. 863–73.

Gruesser, John. "Never Bet the Detective (or His Creator) Your Head: Character Rivalry, Authorial Sleight of Hand, and Generic Fluidity in Detective Fiction." *Edgar Allan Poe Review* 9.1 (Spring 2008): 5–23.

Kopley, Richard. *Edgar Allan Poe and the Dupin Mysteries*. New York: Palgrave, 2008.

Muller, John P. and William J. Richardson, ed. *The Purloined Poe: Lacan, Derrida, and Psychoanalytic Reading*. Baltimore, MD: Johns Hopkins University Press, 1988.

Peeples, Scott. *Edgar Allan Poe Revisited*. New York: Twayne, 1998.

Pollin, Burton R. "Poe's 'Murders in the Rue Morgue': The Ingenious Web Unravelled." *Studies in the American Renaissance* 1 (1977): 235–59.

Silverman, Kenneth. *Edgar A. Poe: Mournful and Never-ending Remembrance*. New York: Harper, 1991.

Thoms, Peter. "Poe's Dupin and the Power of Detection." *The Cambridge Companion to Edgar Allan Poe*. Ed. Kevin J. Hayes. Cambridge: Cambridge University Press, 2002. 133–47.

Whalen, Terence. *Edgar Allan Poe and the Masses: The Political Economy of Literature in Antebellum America*. Princeton, NJ: Princeton University Press, 1999.

On Collins

Ashley, Robert P. *Wilkie Collins and the Detective Story*. Berkeley: University of California Press, 1951.

Law, Graham, and Andrew Maunder. *Wilkie Collins: A Literary Life*. New York: Palgrave, 2008.

Nayder, Lillian. *Wilkie Collins*. New York: Twayne, 1997.

Peters, Catherine. *The King of Inventors: A Life of Wilkie Collins*. Princeton, NJ: Princeton University Press, 1993.

Taylor, Jenny Bourne, ed. *The Cambridge Companion to Wilkie Collins*. New York: Cambridge University Press, 2006.

On Twain

Baetzhold, Howard G. "Of Detectives and Their Derring-Do: The Genesis of Mark Twain's 'The Stolen White Elephant.'" *Studies in American Humor* 2 (January 1976): 183–95.

Fishkin, Shelley Fisher, ed. *The Stolen White Elephant and Other Detective Stories*. By Mark Twain. New York: Oxford University Press, 1996.

Gribben, Alan. "'That Pair of Spiritual Derelicts': The Poe-Twain Relationship." *Poe Studies* 18.2 (December 1985): 17–21.

Gruesser, John C. "The Purloined Critter: Twain's Parodic Homage to the Originator of Modern Detective Fiction in 'The Stolen White Elephant.'" *Poe Writing/Writing Poe*. Ed. Richard Kopley and Jana Argersinger. New York: AMS, 2010.

Hale, Virginia. "Mark Twain, Detective." *Connecticut Review* 14.1 (Spring 1992): 79–84.

Kaplan, Justin. *Mr. Clemens and Mark Twain*. New York: Touchstone, 1983.

Messent, Peter. *Mark Twain*. New York: St. Martin's, 1997.

Powers, Ron. *Mark Twain: A Life*. New York: Random, 2005.

Rogers, Franklin R. Introduction. *Simon Wheeler, Detective*. By Mark Twain. New York: New York Public Library, 1963. xi–xxxviii.

On Chesterton

Coren, Michael. *Gilbert, The Man Who Was G. K. Chesterton*. New York: Paragon, 1990.

Knight, Mark. *Chesterton and Evil*. New York: Fordham University Press, 2004.

Murphy, Bruce F. Introduction. *The Innocence and Wisdom of Father Brown*. New York: Barnes, 2005. vii–xiv.

Oddie, William. *Chesterton and the Romance of Orthodoxy: The Making of GKC, 1874–1908*. New York: Oxford University Press, 2009.

Wills, Garry. *Chesterton*. Rev. ed. New York: Image, 2004.

On Conan Doyle

Freeman, Kyle, ed. *The Complete Sherlock Holmes*. By Arthur Conan Doyle. 2 vols. New York: Barnes, 2003.

Hardwick, Michael. *The Complete Guide to Sherlock Holmes*. New York: St. Martin's, 1986.

Hodgson, John A., ed. *Sherlock Holmes: The Major Stories with Contemporary Critical Essays*. New York: Bedford, 1994.

Hoehling, Mary. *The Real Sherlock Holmes: Arthur Conan Doyle*. New York: Messner, 1965.

Jaffe, Jacqueline. *Arthur Conan Doyle*. Boston: Twayne, 1987.

Starrett, Vincent. *The Private Life of Sherlock Holmes*. Engelwood Cliffs, NJ: Prentice, 1993.

Stashower, Daniel. *Teller of Tales: The Life of Arthur Conan Doyle*. New York: Holt, 1999.

On Harte

Duckett, Margaret. *Mark Twain and Bret Harte*. Norman: University of Oklahoma Press, 1964.

Merwin, Henry Childs. *The Life of Bret Harte, with Some Account of the California Pioneers*. Boston: Houghton, 1911.

O'Connor, Richard. *Bret Harte: A Biography*. Boston: Little, 1966.

Scharnhorst, Gary. *Bret Harte: Opening the Literary West*. Norman: University of Oklahoma Press, 2000.

_____. Introduction. *The Luck of Roaring Camp and Other Writings*. By Bret Harte. New York: Penguin, 2001. vii–xxiv.

On Freeman

Faderman, Lillian. *Surpassing the Love of Men: Romantic Friendship and Love Between Women*

from the Renaissance to the Present. New York: Morrow, 1981.
Foster, Edward. *Mary E. Wilkins Freeman.* New York: Hendricks, 1956.
Glasser, Leah Blatt. *In a Closet Hidden: The Life and Work of Mary E. Wilkins Freeman.* Amherst: University of Massachusetts Press, 1996.
Reichardt, Mary R. *A Web of Relationship: Women in the Short Stories of Mary Wilkins Freeman.* Jackson: University of Mississippi Press, 1991.
Westbrook, Perry D. *Mary Wilkins Freeman.* Rev. ed. Boston: Twayne, 1988.

On Orczy

Mallory, Michael. "Baroness Orczy: The Mother of English Mystery." *Mystery Scene* 107 (2008): 14–16.
Marcus, Laura, and Chris Willis, ed. *Women Detective Stories.* New York: Oxford University Press, 1997.
Staples, Katherine. "Baroness Emmuska Orczy." *British Mystery Writers, 1860–1919.* Ed. Bernard Benstock and Thomas F. Staley. *Dictionary of Literary Biography.* Vol. 70. Detroit: Gale, 1988. 229–34.

On Green

Hayne, Barrie. "Anna Katharine Green." *10 Women of Mystery.* Ed. Earl F. Bargainnier. Bowling Green, OH: Bowling Green University Popular Press, 1981. 152–78.
Maida, Patricia D. *Mother of Detective Fiction: The Life and Work of Anna Katharine Green.* Bowling Green, OH: Bowling Green University Popular Press, 1989.
Ross-Wagaman, Cheri Louise. "Anna Katharine Green's Experiment with Feminism in the Detective Novel." *The Mid-Atlantic Almanack* 3 (1994): 41–54.
Sims, Michael. Introduction. *The Leavenworth Case.* Anna Katharine Green, New York: Penguin, 2010. ix–xxi.
Welter, Barbara. "Murder Most Genteel: The Mystery Novels of Anna Katharine Green." *Dimity Convictions: The American Woman in the Nineteenth Century.* Athens: Ohio University Press, 1976. 130–44.

On Glaspell

Angel, Marina. "Susan Glaspell's *Trifles* and *A Jury of Her Peers*: Woman Abuse in Literary and Legal Context." *Buffalo Law Review* 45 (1997): 779–844.
Ben-Zvi, Linda. *Susan Glaspell: Her Life and Times.* New York: Oxford University Press, 2005.
_____, ed. *Susan Glaspell: Essays on Her Theater and Fiction.* Ann Arbor: University of Michigan Press, 1995.
Bryan, Patricia L. "Stories in Fiction and in Fact: Susan Glaspell's *A Jury of Her Peers* and the 1901 Murder Trial of Margaret Hossack." *Stanford Law Review* 49.5 (1997): 1293–1363.
Gainor, J. Ellen. *Susan Glaspell in Context: American Theater, Culture, and Politics, 1915–48.* Ann Arbor: University of Michigan Press, 2004.
Glaspell, Susan. "The Hossack Murder." *True Crime: An American Anthology.* Ed. Harold Schechter. New York: Library of America, 2008. 179–95.
Mustazza, Leonard. "Generic Translation and Thematic Shift in Susan Glaspell's 'Trifles' and 'A Jury of Her Peers.'" *Studies in Short Fiction* 26 (1989): 489–96.

On Daly

Etheridge, Chuck. "Carroll John Daly." *American Hard-Boiled Crime Writers.* Ed. George Parker Anderson and Julie B. Anderson. *Dictionary of Literary Biography Vol. 226.* Detroit: Gale, 2000. 100–05.
Mertz, Stephen. "In Defense of Carroll John Daly." *The Mystery Fancier* 2.3 (May 1978).
Ross, Dale H. "Carroll John Daly." *Critical Survey of Mystery and Detective Fiction.* Ed. Carl E. Rollyson. Pasadena, CA: Salem, 2008.
Ruhm, Herbert. Introduction. *The Hard-Boiled Detective: Stories from* Black Mask *Magazine (1920–1951).* Ed. Herbert Ruhm. New York: Vintage, 1977. viii–xviii.
Server, Lee. "Daly, Carroll John." *Encyclopedia of Pulp Fiction Writers.* New York: Facts on File, 2002.

On Hammett

Hammett, Dashiell. "From the Memoirs of a Private Detective." *Detective Stories.* By Hammett. Claremont: Coyote, 2009. 3–9.

_____. *Lost Stories*. Ed. Vince Emery. San Francisco: Vince Emery, 2005.

Johnson, Diane. *Dashiell Hammett: A Life*. New York: Random, 1983.

Mellen, Joan. *Hellman and Hammett: The Legendary Passion of Lillian Hellman and Dashiell Hammett*. New York: HarperCollins, 1996.

Panek, Leroy Lad. *Reading Early Hammett: A Critical Study of the Fiction Prior to the* Maltese Falcon. Jefferson, NC: McFarland, 2004.

On Woolrich

Bassett, Mark T. *Blues of a Lifetime: The Autobiography of Cornell Woolrich*. Bowling Green, OH: Bowling Green State University Popular Press, 1991.

Corliss, Richard. "That Old Feeling: Woolrich's World." *Time* 8 December 2003.

Nevins, Francis M. *Cornell Woolrich: First You Dream, Then You Die*. New York: Mysterious, 1988.

Renzi, Thomas C. *Cornell Woolrich: From Pulp Noir to Film Noir*. Jefferson, NC: McFarland, 2006.

On Hopkins

Ammons, Elizabeth. Introduction. *Short Fiction by Black Women, 1900–1920*. Ed. Elizabeth Ammons. New York: Oxford University Press, 1991. 3–20.

Brown, Lois. *Pauline Elizabeth Hopkins: Black Daughter of the Revolution*. Chapel Hill: University of North Carolina Press, 2008.

Cordell, Sigrid Anderson. "'The Case Was Very Black Against' Her: Pauline Hopkins and the Politics of Racial Ambiguity at the *Colored American Magazine*." *American Periodicals* 26.1 (2006): 52–73.

Gruesser, John Cullen, ed. *The Unruly Voice: Rediscovering Pauline Elizabeth Hopkins*. Urbana: University of Illinois Press, 1996.

Wallinger, Hanna. *Pauline Elizabeth Hopkins: A Literary Biography*. Athens: University of Georgia Press, 2005.

On Himes

Bryant, Jerry H. *"Born in a Mighty Bad Land": The Violent Man in African American Folklore and Fiction*. Bloomington: Indiana University Press, 2003.

Gruesser, John. "Chester Himes, 'He Knew,' and the History of African American Detective Fiction." Chester Himes Special Issue, *Clues* 28.1 (2010): 15–21.

Margolies, Edward, and Michel Fabre. *The Several Lives of Chester Himes*. Jackson: University Press of Mississippi, 1997.

Milliken, Stephen F. *Chester Himes: A Critical Appraisal*. Columbia: University of Missouri Press, 1976.

Sallis, James. *Chester Himes: A Life*. New York: Walker, 2002.

Skinner, Robert. *Two Guns from Harlem: The Detective Fiction of Chester Himes*. Bowling Green, OH: Bowling Green State University Popular Press, 1989.

On Ellison

Callahan, John. Introduction. *Flying Home and Other Stories*. By Ralph Ellison. New York: Random, 1996. ix–xxxviii.

Ellison, Ralph. Introduction. *Invisible Man*. By Ellison. New York: Random, 1995. vii–xxiii.

Gruesser, John Cullen. *Confluences: Postcolonialism, African American Literary Studies, and the Black Atlantic*. Athens: University of Georgia Press, 2005.

Jackson, Lawrence. *Ralph Ellison: Emergence of Genius*. Athens: University of Georgia Press, 2007.

Rampersad, Arnold. *Ralph Ellison: A Biography*. New York: Knopf, 2007.

Reckley, Ralph, Sr. "Ellison, Ralph." *The Oxford Companion to African American Literature*. Ed. William L. Andrews, Frances Smith Foster, and Trudier Harris. New York: Oxford University Press, 1997. 252–54.

Wiegman, Robyn. "The Anatomy of Lynching." *Journal of the History of Sexuality* 3.3 (1993): 445–67.